A LIVING NIGHTMARE

Larry went cold when he heard the growling. He peered up into the night. All thoughts of caution deserted him when he saw what hung there.

It was a monster. That's all he could think of to describe it. A huge, hairy, muscular, drooling *monster*. It hung from the wall of tires, only its front claws holding it to the roof of the Pit. Its oval body, like a gray egg, swayed above the dilapidated Pontiac. Its tail, as thick as a man's arm, flailed every which way for balance.

Then, in one swift motion, the creature released its grip on the roof, pushed off from the wall with its back feet, and lunged at Larry with a rumbling roar.

Larry screamed. He started running for the front gate before the creature even hit the ground.

Still roaring, the monster scurried after its prey with mounting speed and a deadly determination. True, the boy had a head start — but the creature was a hell of a lot faster.

And it knew it.

JUNKYARD

BARRY PORTER

ZEBRA BOOKS
KENSINGTON PUBLISHING CORP.

ZEBRA BOOKS

are published by

Kensington Publishing Corp.
475 Park Avenue South
New York, NY 10016

First printing: November 1989

Printed in the United States of America

Monday

The lazy, gibbous eye in the night sky looked down on the frightened man. The man did not return the stare, but he was grateful for its sickly light. He stumbled, regained his balance, and his right hand went instinctively to the bottle in his coat pocket, to make sure it was all right. He considered taking a swig from it, but he didn't want to stop. He had to keep moving. The moon was watching him. He wrapped his ragged coat tighter around his lithe frame and moved on, his eyes lowered to the gutter.

The street was deserted. Midnight was three hours gone. The bitter cold that must hide during the day came out now and pushed into Harry's clothes, making his breath catch. God, he could use that drink now, just to warm him up.

Can't stop, he convinced himself, turning a corner. *Gotta keep moving, keep going, find . . . find . . .* What? He'd forgotten. He tried to concentrate on what was happening, what he was doing. He was a long way from the railroad yard, of that he was certain. A long way from the warm fires and lukewarm bodies of his compatriots. He was looking for, for — no, not looking *for* something, but running away. Escaping. He had to get away, keep away from the stink. Oil stink from the trains, human stink, body stink, the stink of alcohol and hurried sex and failure. Far away.

The wind was weaker on this street, but the cold had settled everywhere and it bit hard. He cursed the coat he wore, a coat he'd bought five years ago when he'd had money and a job and family. He wasn't aware it had been five years, though; it was last week to him, clear and sharp in his memory. He had so few events in his life now to measure the time by.

He came to another intersection and paused to determine which way was best. *One's as good as another,* he thought, but then he corrected himself. One way might take him back to the railroad yard. He couldn't go back there. Not tonight, maybe not ever. Of course, he'd felt this way before—and he'd always ended up going back. There was safety in numbers; he recognized that whenever his bottle was empty. But it was still a quarter full tonight, and he had a long way to go to . . .

Where the hell am I going, again?

The lights on the street were bright, but they had a rough time cutting through the early morning fog. The bleak gray mist didn't roll, even when Harry moved through it. It just sort of slid around him—barely sucking at his arms and legs, trying to hold him back. He thought it similar to swimming through a thick oil spill atop calm waters. Or crawling through mud on a dry day. He felt like he could burrow into it, maybe dig himself a little hole like some vermin, and find himself some warmth. Except on this night, only the density of the earth could provide the real warmth he needed.

Which way? The thought came clearly as he stood in the middle of the intersection, He turned in circles. All paths led to darkness and cold. If he moved on, he'd probably get lost. He'd have to wait until things cleared up a bit. His knees seemed to understand the logic, for they weakened, bent, and plopped him on his butt on the hard macadam. His numb fingers grasped for the bottle they could not feel. Eventually he maneuvered it into the open, uncorked it. He brought it up to take a swig—then stopped. He felt a tiny prickling all across his back. He knew the feeling; though it routinely occurred on a street just like this, it always happened during the day.

Someone was watching him.

He looked around. No one. Who in their right mind would be out on a night like this? Soon his eyes rose. Through the salt tears, through the blanket of mist, he greeted the moon's attention. He raised his drink, called "Salute!" and gulped a mouthful.

Now what? Again that certainty that he couldn't go anywhere until the night was banished. All he could really do in the meantime was find somewhere to sleep, preferably somewhere warm, though he wasn't picky. He grinned at the development. His plans seemed rational, even clear-headed. He was getting better.

It took him ten minutes to stand on his feet again, and another five to catch his breath leaning against a corner building. When he was ready, he stepped into the gutter and turned around to look up at the wall there. A hardware store. A sign in the window listing the opening hours. Obviously still in business, which meant the door was locked tight. Probably an alarm system, too. Shit.

He turned—slowly, so that his feet would not get con-fused—and examined the other three corners. One was a building just like the one behind him. Another was just a brick wall hiding God-knew-what; he was sure he wouldn't be able to climb it. The final corner . . .

Well, it was lost in the mist. He stepped out into the street again, crossed the intersection diagonally. Strangely, the closer he got, the darker the area seemed to become. There was something there, though, something tall that guarded faint alien shadows and gray silhouettes. Harry searched his memory, but he couldn't come up with any-thing in his wide-ranging experiences that would explain this place.

When he stood just outside the iron-barred gate and his eyes focused and rose to the peeling letters on the sign that arched the entrance, he nearly laughed out loud.

WINSOME JUNK

"Winsome Junk. Winsome Junk." He slipped it over his useless tongue a few more times, until whatever was funny about it disappeared. *Winsome,* he thought. *That's the town I'm in. Saw it in the train yard.* He looked beyond the gate again, to the sharp twists and curls and solid fists of junk that were piled high into alien landscapes and ancient towers. A junkyard. Just a junkyard.

He stood before the gate for a long time, studying it, too drunk to wonder why he didn't just enter and find a warm place to sleep.

7

Eventually the icy mist bit him into activity again. He moved to the gate and tried it. It took a little effort, for the metal hinges had rusted after so many cold, damp nights, but they soon gave with a squeal of pain and pulled Harry forward into their shadows.

Harry stood just inside the yard and examined it as best he could. He didn't see the small shack off to his right, but he couldn't miss the large, featureless concrete structure to his left. It looked like the perfect spot for a night's sleep; unfortunately, it was also the perfect place for a night guard to while away the hours. Best not to risk it until he'd exhausted all the possibilities in the yard. He moved on, careful not to disturb the night.

Past the concrete structure, across a small open area, Harry could make out a tunnel of some sort, like a corridor without a roof. Another clear thought broke through his haze: *Lots of stuff in there. Have all the privacy I want. Maybe crawl under something, find some blankets or old tires . . .*

And an overriding need: *Warmth.*

As he moved farther into the darkness, another thought, almost a song, drifted through his head. Words, spoken to him in jest and warning by the people he wanted to leave behind: *Don't go near the junkyards, Harry. They'll eat you alive.*

But with warmth and sleep so close at hand, and most of a bottle of liquor swirling in his brain, he took up the words in song, humming them to himself between fits of laughter. They meant little to him now—just comforting noise.

He moved through the maze of junk for some time. The piles of half-familiar objects rose to great heights on all sides, threatening to topple and crush him. He dared not touch the walls. Occasionally the path would split; the junk had been collected for a long time, piled here and there till their foundations would take no more—a labyrinth, to which there was no solution because there was no objective.

But there were a few clearings, places where only flat dirt lay, and he came to one of these. A wall of junk surrounded the area. He could stand in the center of it, get his bearings, and eye a place to spend the night.

The answer came quickly. Against an irregular mound of tires rested a car. It was an old car—he didn't know the

8

model or year, didn't give a damn—black in the mist, with surprisingly little rust. As he got closer, he saw that somehow the mound of tires, at least twelve feet high, had grown over the car, so that only the driver's half was exposed to the outside. Weird. Like the tires were slowly digesting the car. It reminded him of some of the fungus he'd seen on some of his friends.

Harry peeked in the driver's window. The moon provided light enough to illuminate the inside. The seats looked like cheap vinyl, though they weren't torn too badly. Plenty of room in the back seat for a tired man. After some time, his own breath would warm the place up.

It suited him. But he knew instinctively that the God of this Earth was a cruel God, and he struggled not to raise his hopes as he reached for the door handle. *Probably locked*, he thought.

There were very few things in the universe that could have stopped him from trying to open that door—but just then, one of those things happened.

Something clattered somewhere near. It was loud, and the sound of scurrying steps followed it. Harry froze. He twisted his head around. He gasped when he saw, near a pillar of metal ten yards to his right, the mist actually swirling. Whatever had disturbed it must have been big—or fast.

An old fear rose. A bum has few possessions, even fewer responsibilities other than surviving, but there are times when both of those are threatened. Being rolled is a traumatic experience. That's why he had joined with other transients—so he would not be alone and vulnerable, as he was now. But who would follow him all the way out here? Someone from the train yard? Kids looking for someone to beat up for fun?

Harry knew that if he crawled into the car, even with the doors locked, he'd be a sitting duck. They—or maybe there was just one—would draw their plans against him and strike. Who would find his body in a deserted junkyard?

His mind cleared as much as possible. He blinked several times to wipe the diffraction. His first thought was to search around the car for a weapon. He found one. Sometimes God was kind; He gave you the tools you needed to succeed. The iron pipe felt powerful in his fist. Kids or bums, they'd probably rush off if they saw him running at them with this. Probably.

There was another sound—his ears were acutely sensitive now, though they rang just a little—and he followed it cautiously. As he stepped back into the labyrinth, he pushed his coat back so that the pocket holding his bottle would be safely behind his body, protected. He raised his weapon, ready for an instant assault.

Shadows slipped over him. His body was numb now. He knew he was scared, he just couldn't feel it. The cool air felt good rippling through his lungs. It kept him moving forward.

Teach those goddamn kids . . .

Something, a shadow, skittered across his path about twenty feet ahead. It kept low to the ground, almost crawling. Were they scared? Were they trying to sneak up on him? He stopped and listened, his eyes searching the darkness. The moon's light helped some, but it also made the shadows denser.

There! Another sound. Harry stood still, tried not to react to it. Yes, it was trying to get behind him. He listened further. Only one. Thank God, there was only one. He could certainly take care of one stupid little brat.

He moved—and lost his balance, crashing into a structure of metal and wood beams. He flailed outward. A rusty nail punctured the palm of his left hand; he withdrew it before the nail went deep, but the pain was severe. He hissed and backed into the shadows, sucking at the wound. *Infected, now. Fucking infected.* But he cleared his eyes of tears and was grateful it was his strong right hand that held the iron pipe. He could worry about the injury later.

A tin can plinked hollowly to his left. Harry gritted his teeth so as not to cry out. He moved toward the sound, fighting the panic that pushed back. Anger, irritated by the pain in his hand, flared; he was going to knock this goddamn kid's head off and hide *him* in the junkyard. He might even make a couple of bucks out of it.

He stopped and leaned into the shadows when he heard a strange clicking sound, like fingernail clippers, just around the next bend. Someone was there. He could hear the labored breathing now; the intruder was probably as frightened as he was. Well, he'd teach the nosey brat what *real* fear was.

A shadow loomed. Harry gripped his weapon tighter and prepared to pounce. The figure kept coming, solid and humped, still low to the ground. It moved lazily, as if it had nothing to worry about. Harry heard his own rasp, held his breath. He couldn't do anything about the loud drum of his heart. The pipe rose. The hand holding it shook, but there was enough power in it to kill.

The next instant, all of his anger, all of his pain, all of his intent for violence and death disappeared. The creature turned the bend and stared up at Harry. At first all he could make out was a disgusting outline of greasy hair, messed and matted. Then horrible details were drawn in. The thing was on all fours, as big as a German shepherd. Its eyes shimmered yellow, following Harry's outline — then glowed like embers upon meeting his glare.

Harry backed away. He thought the alcohol must be magnifying the creature's size. It couldn't *possibly* be that big. As he watched, the monster's snout pulled back, nose twitching uncontrollably, and Harry's attention spiraled to the crowded row of long, sharp teeth that glistened with the moon's eerie white. Those teeth were clamped about some dead thing that hung limp on either side of the snout. A powerful stench hit him in the face — and he suddenly realized the cause of those clicking sounds he'd heard. While Harry had waited around the corner, the creature must have been gnawing at the cat's bones. He gaped as the fat tabby's remains fell from the beast's mouth with a dull plop.

Its jaws now free, the creature let loose with the worst sound Harry had ever heard in his miserable life, and it alighted every nerve in the man's body. He turned and ran, ran like a man on fire. When his scream ended and he was forced to inhale before everything went black, he heard the pounding feet behind him. Getting louder. *Chasing* him.

Oh, Jesus, oh, Jesus —

Some unconscious memory took him through the maze again, back to the clearing. He erupted into the yard and aimed for the car. *It can't get in the car, it won't be able to get me there, dear Jesus, don't let it get me—*

Then he was choking, gasping for breath as an invisible hand clamped around his throat. Even in his drunkenness he knew he had caught his coat on some finger of metal sticking from a junk pile. He ripped it away. The tearing was loud and deep, morbidly reminding him of flesh parting under the insistence of sharp claws—

The creature was coming, coming fast. He saw its dark outline splitting the mist in the labyrinth's corridor. God, it was *huge.* Gorge rose in Harry's throat. He turned to squint across the thick fog of the yard. He couldn't see the car. It had to be ahead somewhere, just *had* to be. He ran forward, but his feet refused to cooperate and he stumbled.

The creature, not far behind, screamed with a primal hunger.

Sweet Jesus, where—

There! The long, sleek shape blotted the mist. The car was dead ahead. His stride lengthened, even while his knees threatened to collapse. Thunder raged around him as the monster descended. It sounded like a cavalry of horses.

Please, oh, please let the door be unlocked, please—

Numb fingers grasped the door handle, struggled, struggled, then:

Click.

The door opened. Harry shook with triumph, swung the old metal wide, and dived in head first. He had to reach back to shut the door, to seal that wall between himself and hell—but his arm fell to his side again as something jerked him backward.

Then everything was still. He didn't want to look. For a long while he just lay there across the front seat on his stomach and breathed deeply. He waited, tense, for something to break the calm. But there was nothing. No sound, no movement, no pain. It was as if he'd imagined it all.

Had he? Was it all just a hallucination?

His hand caressed the bottle in his pocket, searching for something familiar.

Maybe it's all right. Please let it be all right.

He contracted the muscles that would pull his legs into the car. They strained, but didn't budge. He was stuck.

Maybe it's frostbite. My whole body's numb.

Only one way to find out. He twisted in the seat; he didn't want to catch anything's attention with sudden movement. His eyes slowly focused down the length of his body, down his thigh . . . and saw the beast's snout resting over the shin of his right leg, its teeth impaled deeply in the flesh and, below that, the bone. His entire right foot was in its mouth.

The pain hit him just as the monster's claws dug into the earth and strained. Harry slid across the front seat, almost pulled completely from the car. He scrambled for something to hold onto. His body jerked again. The alcohol in his system dulled the agony somewhat, but not enough to keep Harry from feeling those teeth scrape against his bone. Flesh wilted in its wake. He screamed, over and over, the fog from his breath filling the car. A small battle ensued, a tug of war with Harry's body as the rope.

It was only a matter of time before Harry lost.

His screams were blocked by blood in his throat, and he began to welcome death. As his nerves exploded and numbed and a muggy darkness began to engulf him, he was left with a kaleidoscope of senses: that of being dragged from the car, across the yard, and deep into the graveyard of relics long abandoned. There, hairy shadows loomed. He managed a grin as the warmth of his own blood smothered him.

Ray Holscomb looked up from where he bent to pick up his books, and confronted the best pair of legs he'd ever seen in his long fifteen years. He knew instantly who they belonged to, and the impression that she stood there waiting for him to stop staring made him blush. When he stood, the prickly heat around his neck was still with him.

"Hi," she said brightly, as if she didn't notice his embarrassment.

"Hi, Pauline," he mumbled.

Pauline Martinez, dark eyes, dark hair, smooth brown skin that had been left undisturbed by acne, took up Ray's pace as he continued across the quad. Ray felt distinctly conspicuous passing the other students; the school day was over, the area crowded, and he was painfully aware how ridiculous he must look with Pauline at his side. They just didn't belong.

He wasn't exactly a geek; he didn't wear glasses or excel in mathematics or laugh like a donkey. But he was freckled to the point where his face looked like a rash, slightly obese . . . and short. Brother, was he short. A regular midget.

And Pauline was tall. And beautiful. And wonderful. Ray desperately hoped she would not see the smiles and giggles this disparity would cause.

When he glanced at his companion, however, she didn't seem affected at all. In fact, she smiled.

"Guess what," she said.

"Huh?"

"Guess what I need from you."

Ray nearly tripped. He stopped to look at her. "What?"

"I *really* need some help on my algebra. Could you meet me sometime this week?"

Ray let out the breath he was holding and set off across the quad again, saying over his shoulder, "Sure."

She stayed beside him. "Great! I should have asked you at the beginning of the semester. It would've saved a lot of trouble with my mom and dad."

"I'll warn you, I'm not too hot at it myself."

"What'd you get on the last test?"

"B."

"I got a D. You'll help a lot."

"Okay." He made it to the corner. Beyond the building was the school exit and the street. He looked at his watch and was surprised he still had fifteen minutes to get to the meeting.

Pauline tapped him on the shoulder and looked puzzled when he faced her. "Is something wrong?"

"No, no. I just have to be somewhere in a while."

"Well, I was hoping I could talk to you about something. We could talk whenever you help me on the math, but . . . well, do you have a little time now?"

Ray looked around. The school was emptying fast. Maybe now he could loosen up a bit. Though, under Pauline's lovely gaze, that just might be impossible.

He looked at her and smiled. "You mean math isn't all I'm good for?"

14

She stamped a foot and lowered her head in that way that left her eyes large and glistening and Ray's heart pounding. She laughed. "We've been friends since sixth grade. Since when have I *ever* asked you for help on math?"

"Ah, but who asked me for help in writing that history paper?"

"A *year* ago!" she snapped with mock anger. When her laugh bloomed again, Ray found himself joining her. He did feel more at ease now that they were alone. Words seemed to spring to his mouth easier. It was a nice change. He had never considered himself really shy, but he was considered such by his peers because he had very little to say. Naturally, he was avoided so as to elude awkwardness — the bane of all teenagers. Here, though, was someone who never made excuses to avoid him.

He just wished his feelings weren't so strong.

"I need to ask you something," she said. Her voice was nearly a whisper now, as if she were the one suddenly embarrassed. Ray wondered if he should back up a few steps so as to make her more comfortable, but she made the first move — stepping closer to him.

"It's Nick," she said, and his heart sank. "You've been his friend for a long time, right?"

"Yeah. Since we were kids."

"Well, he and I have been dating for almost six months now, you know, and we've sort of . . . started getting serious."

Ray felt his internal organs slowly freeze. "Serious?" he asked.

"Talking serious. You know?" She gave him that look again, but there was no smile behind it this time. Only cautious study, as if she were reading his tiniest reaction.

"You mean, like, getting married?"

She smiled now. "No, not *that* serious. I mean . . ." She paused for a moment, then sighed. "Ray, you're Nick's friend, but you're my friend too. I'm trusting you not to tell him what we're talking about, or that we talked at all, okay?"

"Why not?"

"It would embarrass me," she said plainly. "It's just, I figured since you're probably his oldest friend, that you'd

15

know what he's really like."

"If you want to know something about him, why don't you ask him?"

"Because I want to know if he's a good guy. I mean, really. Some of my other boyfriends—"

Ray winced. He didn't want to hear this, didn't want to know that she had been in love with others . . .

"—my other boyfriends *seemed* to be really nice guys, and I would have bet my life that they were. But . . . you know . . ." She sort of shrugged and tried to hide her troubled expression by brushing her long hair back around one ear. She met his eyes again and whispered, "Sometimes a guy *pretends* to be a good guy until he gets what he wants, and then he loses interest."

Ray swallowed hard. He nearly lost his breath. All these years he'd known sweet Pauline as an innocent waiting for some Prince Charming, maybe some *short* Prince Charming, to sweep her away with pure love and devotion. It all blew up in his face, ripping away a part of his insides that left his knees weak.

"I'm sorry if this embarrasses you," she said, staring at him intently. "I've never done this before. I mean ask a guy's friends. I just thought, since we're friends too, that we could talk . . ." She took a breath. "I didn't mean—"

"No. It's okay. I just didn't . . . well." He lost all train of thought then, and waited for her to supply something.

"So," she said, "honestly, what do you really think of Nick? How does he usually treat his girlfriends?"

Hell if I know. But he couldn't tell her that. He knew his words would be important to her, and stuttering and mumbling inanities might expose him to her in a way that would kill him. So he thought furiously. What did he know about Nick's love life?

"Well," he finally said, "I think he's a nice guy. I mean, he never talks about girls the way the other guys do, like Larry and Mark do. He's always kind of quiet about it." She blinked a few times, waiting for more. "He hasn't dated a whole lot because his dad wouldn't let him. You know about his dad?" She nodded. "Well, Nick's always made it clear that he doesn't want to be like that. He makes an effort to treat people nice. For the most part." He tried hard not to

16

shrug as his words trailed off.

Pauline waited for something else. When nothing more came, she said, "So you think he'd treat me right?"

He nodded. "Yeah, sure. I know he cares for you, or he wouldn't waste his time." She frowned slightly at this; did he say something wrong? Hurriedly he added: "He's a nice guy, Pauline. My best friend." *Maybe not the closest these days,* he thought uncomfortably. "He's responsible and takes care of things," he ended lamely.

Pauline's eyes flickered and stared over his shoulder dreamily. An uncomfortable silence passed between them before her attention came back and she smiled. "Okay. Thanks." Ray nodded and grinned back, though he could feel he hadn't satisfied her. He wished they could start this again tomorrow, so as to give him time to think.

She began to leave when he called, "See you later, then?"

She turned to him and changed. Her face lit up, glowed as if they'd never talked about Nick and she'd never had any past boyfriends and she'd always been just the kind of woman he thought she was. It made him feel strong again.

"We have a date. I really need help on my algebra."

"All right. How about Wednesday?"

"That's fine. Thanks a lot, Ray." She bit her lip. "Remember, please don't say anything."

Ray placed his hand over his heart theatrically. "Never!"

The glossy lips rose coyly. "Bye!"

"Bye."

He moved to the side of the building and ducked down into the shadows so that he could watch her walk away unobserved. Her figure blurred as he watched, and by the time he blinked the tears away, she had turned the corner, gone.

Ray hurried to the car where Harry had been murdered that morning. He was ten minutes late for the meeting.

As he slowed to catch his breath, he looked around and wondered if their clubhouse had ever been found out. Surely none of their parents knew, or Ray and his friends would be dead or grounded for life by now. Parents were not wild about deserted junkyards. But from the beginning

17

the place had seemed perfect for four boys who were bored out of their minds. He stopped to study it, tried to be objective—but that was impossible. It was just a dark mound silhouetted against the red sky; nevertheless, it still sent a familiar chill of mystery and adventure and something forbidden through his boyish heart.

The Pit.

They'd called it that because it sounded so creepy. Actually the clubhouse was created four years ago completely *above* ground. A gale had toppled a tall pile of tires, and they covered what was left of an old sewage drainpipe—a ceiling section of the rounded concrete sewers that slithered beneath Winsome, a place that the gang had spent many hours exploring—and a '64 Pontiac that had come to rest against it. That had only been the impetus, however; it had taken the work of four boys—and the absence of a guard and dogs—to work the raw materials into a worthwhile sanctuary of secrecy and leisure. The bisectional concrete sturdiness of the sewage pipe was a natural for one wall: fifteen feet in length and hardly any cracks in its surface. The car pulled double duty as another wall and the exclusive entrance to the Pit, via the driver's door, across the front seat, and through the passenger's door. The boys stacked the tires around these objects, completing the third wall of the triangular room within, and piled them high atop the car and tank to make a high ceiling. The finishing touch, the roof, was constructed out of various wooden boards nailed together, laid atop the twelve-foot walls, and then covered with tires to give the outside a uniform look. The inside was of little concern to the boys; the rougher the better. Decorations beyond the tires on the roof were never even considered.

Four years ago, and for the following two, it had been their meeting place every day. They would play war games in the junkyard, the Pit their bunker, or draw wishful—and rarely executed—plans against their enemies, or watch the old color TV they'd discovered in the yard and was fixed up by Nick.

But the last two years brought a lot of changes. The Pit's meaning for four little boys was now modified to fit the views of four teenagers. For the first time, Ray realized how much things had changed. The Pit still looked like the same old hideout, but he knew very well that Larry and Mark now used it as a weekend haunt, where they guzzled beer stored in a small cooler and pushed porno videos into a VCR hooked up to the TV that once played cartoons. Nick, he knew, considered the place uncool and stopped using it altogether.

Ray himself just avoided it. He realized that it had become a dirty place to him, not because of the beer and blue movies, but because it was a place that tempted him to hide away, to slip further into an antisocial trance and waste his life away in a warm hole that smelled of old rubber. Not that he ever hoped to enjoy great popularity. In fact, it would be easy to just roll up inside that familiar, comforting room and completely forget about the world outside — and that was why the temptation of the Pit was so scary.

He tried the handle of the Pontiac. It was unlocked — naturally, since the other three must have been waiting here for a while. He stepped in, slid across the front seat, and entered the Pit through the other door. The relief he felt when he entered the room frightened him.

Larry Santino and Mark Kishbaugh — inseparable as always — were seated together in front of the cheap TV in the middle of the room. Wires from the old VCR sprouted from the set like the snakes of Medusa's hair. The machine was turned off, though, and Larry and Mark were watching a game show. No doubt Nick had nixed their dig into their porno collection.

"Hey!" Larry called when he saw Ray. "The shrimp is here!"

"Stuff it, Larry," Ray said with a smile.

"Stuff what, big boy," Larry lisped.

Mark hit him in the stomach and complained, "Great! I couldn't hear the answer to that one." He pointed at the game show. Larry just laughed and shook his head.

Ray looked around for Nick. He found the other boy sitting calmly in a corner, a cloud of blue cigarette smoke disappearing into the shafts of light that broke through the tires. Nick stood and approached Ray with a calmness he had nurtured for years.

"How you doing, Ray?"

Tall, muscular, his face hard-edged and brutally hand-some, Nick was everything the other three guys wished they could be. He was the "lucky bastard," as Larry put it, the one who got all the girls and won all the fights. Even his voice had taken only a day to change, and was now forever low and even.

Ray felt like he was in the presence of an adult. Nick even shook his hand in greeting—what kind of friends did that except really elderly friends? He could see why Nick had outgrown the Pit; the clubhouse and Nick Jurgen once went together like boys and dirt, but now it was just kind of silly and childish, much too uncool for a guy who wore leather jackets in the summer.

It was a mystery, then, why Nick had asked his three old buddies to meet him here. Worse, as the older boy greeted him, Ray wondered how he'd explain his tardiness. He'd promised Pauline not to tell, but he hadn't thought up a convincing story.

Larry and Mark nodded at Ray, Mark's attention mostly tuned to the TV. They lay back on a mattress that had seen plumper days, each with a beer in hand. Nick himself had a beer which he now picked up off the top of the cooler. No one offered Ray one since they knew he'd never acquired the taste for it.

They all horsed around a bit, joking and insulting until they were comfortable with each other again, before Nick got down to business.

"All right, guys," he said sitting on the cooler, "this is it."

"The news at last," Larry said without excitement. Mark elbowed him in the ribs, shushing him; his attention remained glued to the TV where Wink Wilson and some fabulous babe handed over a car to some guy who couldn't even afford a decent suit for the broadcast.

"I need to ask you all something," Nick said. "It's important, so don't screw around, all right?"

"We won' screw wit' youse, mas'er," Larry burbled. Mark elbowed him again—and received an answering elbow back. Mark doubled up, groaning loud around a laugh.

"Teach you to—" Larry began.

"*Hey!*" All eyes returned to Nick, who looked back menacingly. "This is important, I told you. So listen."

"Come on, guys," Ray pleaded. He wanted to get out of the Pit and home to dinner. He hadn't actually told his parents about this meeting, and he'd probably get a talking to from them about "calling first."

"Go ahead, Nicky, we're listening." Mark was intent on Nick now rather than the fabulous babe's cleavage.

"Okay." Nick lowered his head and seemed to think for a moment. Ray thought that if he'd been standing, he would have paced. Finally, Nick took a swig of beer and let it slip down his throat and settle before announcing: "I need to use the Pit Friday night. Alone."

Ray looked at Larry and Mark. The two boys looked at each other. Their mouths hung open like they weren't quite getting Nick's meaning. Larry was the first to speak again.

"What . . . this Friday? Like, Friday night?"

Nick nodded, looking a bit uncertain himself. "Yeah. All night. I can't have any interruptions. You guys can go somewhere else that night, can't you?"

"But, Nick, that's our Beer and Beaver night," Mark piped up. "It has been every weekend. You know that."

Ray couldn't help grimacing. Two guys with nothing better to do than spend hours guzzling farmboy alcohol and staring at a progression of sexual positions between strangers. Another reason Ray feared the Pit: more than once he'd been invited, and tempted, to join them. His Friday nights were no laugh riots either.

Nick stared at the two friends on the mattress. Ray never was very good at reading the emotions behind that bony face, but he thought he saw a flash of anger. Nick didn't like to beg.

"Guys, you can let me have it for one night. One lousy night isn't going to kill you."

"Yeah," Larry said, "but it's kind of a tradition, you know. I mean . . ." He looked at Mark. Mark finished the sentence with, ". . . what else we gonna do?"

"Go see a movie."

"We don't have that kind of money—"

"You got money enough to buy this shit!" Nick threw his empty beer can at them. They dodged it, then returned to their previous positions as if nothing had happened. Nick stood and walked into a corner, his back to the three of them.

"It costs a lot to go to a movie these days, Nick," Mark said. His voice was gentle, trying to keep things calm in this small room. "We can't get in for kids' prices anymore, like we used to."

"And there's nothing else to do in this lousy town," Larry added. He kept glancing at Mark for confirmation. "We don't even have a car so's we could go to Wilmington."

"Don't even have our licenses yet," said Mark. "I've flunked twice now . . ."

Nick was about to burst, Ray could see that. Before it could happen, Ray bent down and put a hand on Larry's shoulder. "Look, guys, it's only one night. You could come over to my house and watch TV. We could rent something—"

"Not a—" Mark began.

"—a monster movie or something," Ray interjected. "Make it a gross horror flick. There's lots of those. We could make popcorn or something. Have a good time." If Mom will let us, he thought. "Come on, it's only for one night."

"One fucking night," Nick spat from his corner. His boots were stamping now, his fists bunched at his hips. "I ask you guys for *one* goddamn favor—"

"All right. God." Larry took a breath. Ray nearly laughed at how funny he looked. It must have just hit him how serious this Friday was to Nick. Larry just wasn't very quick at picking up moods. "What're you going to use it for anyway?" he asked, sounding like a child who saw no way out of a parent's order.

Nick returned to the cooler, opened it, hunted for another beer in the ice. He didn't say a word. Didn't even look at them.

"Well?" Larry insisted—purposely pushing, now.

"None of your damn business," Nick answered.

Mark whined, "Hey, Nick, if you're going to kick us out on our traditional night, at least you could tell us what—"

Nick was glaring at them. "It's a *girl*, all right!"

That shut them all up. The implication settled around them. Mark was honestly shocked that one of their group, even Nick-who-got-all-the-girls, might be close to getting lucky. Larry felt a smile pull at his thin lips, which were

22

already in a perpetual smirk. Ray was distinctly sick to his stomach. He knew the next question from the other two, and he knew he didn't want to hear the answer. He rose to leave—wasn't quick enough.

"Who is it, Nick?" Mark asked. His eyes were still wide with amazement, "Is it . . . you know, the girl you've been dating? Pauline?"

Ray was sure Mark knew exactly who she was. They'd had classes together. He'd probably had a crush on her, just like every other guy in school. *Don't act so dumb just for Nick's sake*, he thought bitterly.

Nick bit his lip at the name. He must have decided there was no way to keep the news from them, because he nodded and grunted, "Yeah."

Jesus. Ray felt the ice water pour into him. *Jesus, did I have to hear about all of this in one lousy day? Couldn't it have been staggered a bit, like over a few years?*

"All right, Nicky baby!" Larry hooted. He slammed his elbow into Mark again. "The first one to get lucky!"

Nick didn't look at all proud. He suddenly stuck his finger in Larry's face and ordered, "Hold on! Just wait one second! I *know* you guys. I've known you for years. I didn't want to tell you because I knew how you'd react. But I want to make something perfectly clear to *all* of you." He included Mark and, sheepishly, Ray in his demanding gaze. "If *any* of you show up or sneak around here Friday night" —he paused to think— "or Saturday morning, I'll kill you. I swear it." He visibly balked at how loutish this sounded— but he met their doubt with determination. "Seriously, guys, if you show up . . . it'll be the end of our friendship."

The words filled the room, forcing a lengthy silence when he finished. Then Larry said, "Cool out, guy. We're your friends. You should have told us things were getting this serious between you and Pauline. Then it wouldn't be such a surprise. Heck, Mark and I could have spruced this place up a bit."

Nick looked around. "It's going to need it anyway. I'd appreciate your help in getting rid of the beer smell in here."

"No problem," Mark said before Larry could back out.

"I'm . . . I'm sorry about the surprise," Nick added quietly. He rubbed the back of his neck with an open palm.

"It's just . . . well, we haven't really seen much of each other lately what with school and all. And this is the only private place I have access to."

Haven't really seen much of each other lately what with school and all. Ray mulled the words over in his head. They had been busy with school four years ago, too, and it hadn't made any difference to their friendships. It was the "all" that was the problem. The different likes and interests. The new friends — particularly *girl*friends. Larry and Mark were lucky since they both seemed to have similar ideas of what made a "great" weekend. Ray and Nick used to go to a movie every Friday night . . . until Nick started dating regularly. And then that day Ray himself had introduced him to Pauline. Since then, he'd been dying little deaths. Fridays became quiet evenings that would lead off even quieter weekends. He wasn't really surprised; like any guy, he had always known that women would eventually enter each of their lives, and that it would probably be wonderful. The problem was that it never happened at the same time for each friend. Mark and Larry had a few dates between them, but Ray seemed resigned to duplicate his older brother's fate: forced to remain dateless until sometime in his mid-twenties. Curse of the Holscombs.

"Ray?"

The deep voice drew him back to the Pit that held them. He blinked a few times and focused on Nick.

"Ray's off in Neverland again," Larry snickered, "Must be nice."

"It smells better than this place," Ray said.

Before Larry could retort, Nick asked, "What do you say? Does it bother you?" His question covered more than just Ray staying away from the Pit Friday night; Ray could see that clearly in the other boy's manner. *He knows,* Ray realized. *He's always known. Maybe that's why he's been avoiding me.* But that was nonsense. Nick never avoided him. He just spent his free time with someone closer to him. His girlfriend. Pauline. It was only natural.

So why do I feel slighted?

Ray realized he was in Neverland again. Nick was still staring at him, waiting for some answer that would wipe away his guilt. Ray's discomfort grew. How could Nick ask

24

him such a delicate question in front of these guys? He couldn't possibly answer honestly with them gawking at him . . .

"No, Nick," he said, his voice flat. "I don't mind." He prayed his eyes would give a different answer, but Nick wasn't looking at him anymore.

"Good. So it's settled." He nodded to Larry and Mark. "And I really could use your help to air this place out."

"Least we can do," Mark said, "since we're the ones who had the fun stinking it up." He guzzled his own beer while landing a sharp elbow in Larry's ribs. Larry doubled up and groaned, spilling beer on Mark's crotch. Mark jumped up, cursed, and wiped at his pants. The stain only spread.

Larry laughed hysterically. "Nice move, Super Shit!"

"Goddamn slob!" Mark screamed.

"Oh, stop getting so worked up. You'll wet yourself again."

"Stupid smelly motherfucking faggot!"

They were good friends. Larry held his belly and howled at the crowning insult.

Nick glanced at Ray and shrugged.

Ray felt helpless. There was no way he could talk to Nick now. At least Larry and Mark's clowning made it easy for him to make a quick exit. "Gotta get back home," he explained, "before my dad wakes up to kill me." The others called their good-nights, and as Ray stepped through the Pontiac, he heard Nick calm the other two and describe his plan to build a vent in the Pit.

Ray closed the car door firmly behind him and ran out of the junkyard.

A block away from Winsome Junk, Ray slowed to breathe deeply of the evening air. It stung his nose with its cool freshness — an advantage of living in a small town far away from the industrialized cities. Of course, it was this same small town that made his Friday nights so dull. Two movie houses, a skating rink that preteens frequented, and that was about it unless you had a car and an extra hour or two to drive north or south on the highway.

Jesus! Stop thinking about it!

25

He did. His eyes focused on the neighborhood around him. There wasn't much of a border between the business section and the residential areas. Winsome Junk lay between the two. Ray noticed that someone, the owner perhaps, had made an attempt to blend the atmospheres: iron gate bookended by brick walls out front, a chain link fence on the sides, and a tall, white picket fence protecting the chain link in the back. Unfortunately, it was all in such disrepair that the junkyard was a black smudge in both tracts. Funny that no one did anything about it. He'd seen the disdain in his mother whenever they would ride by it in the car: a glance, a half-concealed sneer, a shake of the head, followed by a quiet hiss.

As he left the dark wound behind and skittered closer to home, another smudge grabbed his attention—something unnatural on this street of trimmed grass, white and brown houses, and quiet people. A long tattered poster had been hurriedly attached to a light post. The tape along the bottom of the paper had dried and peeled away from the steel, leaving the message obscured as it twisted in the wind.

Ray passed it, stopped. He bit his lip, knew he was already late, that his parents were probably worried, but he couldn't pass the mystery without a cursory investigation. He returned to the post and pulled the poster straight, squinting to read the faded mimeographed words.

He recognized the name immediately. Mary Hawthorne, a girl in the neighborhood, several grades lower than him. Her puppy—a beagle she had received last Christmas, he remembered—was lost, and her parents were offering a reward. No amount of money was mentioned. Still, Ray searched his memory; maybe he'd seen the dog somewhere. He could always use a couple extra bucks.

But what would you spend the money on, Ray?

He knew what his dad would say: save it for college. Mom, of course, would back him up. And his older brother would just laugh, as he'd already been through all that.

Well, it didn't matter, anyway. He couldn't remember seeing any dog, beagle or otherwise, roaming the streets. He let the poster roll back up and continued home,

A minute passed, and the underlying message of the

26

poster reached him. He felt a distinct chill slip beneath his jacket. For the past two years there had been missing dogs, missing cats—and eventually missing children. Teenagers and younger. His parents had sat him down after the third disappearance, several months ago, and given him an impossible list of safety rules. He remembered some of it now, and cursed. One rule was: "If you're going to be late, give us a call."

He was really in for it. For the next ten minutes, he tried to think up a worthy defense. Nothing came. He was never good at that sort of thing, and usually just told the truth and accepted the punishment. He would never mention the junkyard, though. The meeting with his pals was always at an unnamed or made-up location.

The more he thought about it, though, the more he was convinced he could avoid any excuse tonight. He could just simply state a different truth: that there hadn't been a disappearance for weeks and weeks, that the kidnapper or murderer or whatever must have moved on.

Except . . . Mary Hawthorne's dog was missing.

When he entered his house and ran for the stairs, he was still uncertain as to what he would say to his parents. So he wasn't at all prepared to hear: "Ray! Go upstairs and wash up for dinner." He blinked a few times, waited for more. When none came he continued his ascent, put his jacket away, and did as he was told. He then hurried downstairs again, into the dining room—and ran into a wall of attention as everyone around the table froze and eyed him. He paused, suspended on his toes as if he were about to fall over a cliff. When he regained his balance, he kept his head lowered and moved quietly to his seat.

Time began again. His mother choreographed the food around the table; his brother, Don, continued the cycle while in the midst of some complaint; and his father, planted at the end of the table, centered his attention solely on the paper folded next to his plate, a spoon held lengthwise to keep his place. Ray did his part to keep the food moving, but more and more he stopped to watch the dishes pile up around his dad. The man was oblivious to it; he leisurely forked potatoes onto his plate, the slowness of the action proportional to the interest of the article.

Ray would have laughed had it not been for death in the air. Apparently his father was equally unconscious of the blue smoke billowing around his head. Ray zeroed in on the cigarette stub held securely between the man's lips. Its tip alternating from an ash black to a warm orange glow that made Ray sick to his stomach. He let it go for nearly a minute before finally breaking in on Don's recital with: "Dad!"

Don shut up and looked to the end of the table. Ray's mom paused between bites. His father's head never moved; only the eyes peeked out from under heavy brows, those flat brown irises demanding: *Who would dare?*

"The Rule," Ray said simply.

The Rule being "Thou shalt not smoke at the dinner table when food is present." Ray recognized the brief flash of anger in his dad's face, the one that made apparent his own Rule: "I own the goddamn dining room, the goddamn table, *and* the goddamn food." But Ray did not blanch, and the cigarette was snuffed out before Mom had a chance to start in.

Ray somehow knew that his thrust would not go unchallenged. Barely a minute passed before his father asked, "And where have you been since school got out, Raymond?"

Raymond. Ray gulped. He opened his mouth, but his mother jumped in first.

"You know we've talked about this, Ray. You had me worried sick."

"Sorry," Ray mumbled.

"Was it a girl, Ray?" Don asked. He let loose with his best shit-eating grin.

"Shut up," Ray shot.

"Where were you, Ray?" His father's voice always sounded so patient and reasonable right before there was big trouble.

"With Nick and the guys."

"Nick?" his mom said around a carrot. "You haven't seen him for quite a while, have you? You two used to go out all the time."

"Nick's got a girl, Mom," Don provided. "Saw him with her once when I was driving." He drove a delivery van for one of the local shops—the best he could get with a business

28

degree — and was always telling them who he'd seen with whom and what they were probably up to. Mom usually frowned at this gossip, but Don and Ray both knew she was enticed by it.

"Ray," she said, "why didn't you tell me? That's wonderful news."

Wonderful for them, but . . . But Ray just shrugged and managed a smile. "He wanted to talk to Larry and Mark and me today," he said. "Just wanted to see us altogether and shoot the shi — uh, shoot the breeze."

"He's that one that always wears the leather stuff, isn't he?" his dad asked. His face was full of disapproval.

"He's a good guy, Dad," Ray insisted. "He used to help me out a lot in shop class. I wouldn't have gotten a B in it without him."

His dad shrugged, went back to his paper. His mom asked Don about his new, and first, girlfriend, and Ray was grateful the attention was back on his brother. He pushed his fork under the hamburger patty slicked with ketchup and pushed it in his mouth. No use; he'd lost his appetite. It was even a chore just to chew. His jaws turned lazy, and the meat went stringy and foreign in his mouth.

Nick and Pauline.

Pauline and Nick.

Pauline . . .

Aw, Jesus, he was getting tired of all this crap. He wished *some*thing would happen in this nowhere town to take his mind off it. Anything.

Less than a mile away, in the very heart of this nowhere town where the social and physical decay of Winsome had just taken root, Edward Robert Kelton sat in his reading chair with mounting horror. He was reading an article in the *Winsome Daily*, buried on page 10 where he might have missed it had he not been such a methodical man. The article told the story of a group of bums, once men and women, who had strayed from the train yard and other town fringes where the police usually tolerated them; strayed because they were searching for a missing friend. No one knew the missing man as more than "Harry," but they were certain he existed, that he had wandered away early this morning, and that they were worried about him. They explained that he was unstable. This nearly pulled a laugh from Ed, as it pulled a laugh from many Winsome folk who had caught the report that night while sitting in their comfortable chairs—except that Ed knew something that none of those other Winsome folk knew, something that haunted his life and often dragged him into dark, horrible nightmares, and that knowledge stopped the laugh dead.

He believed he knew what had happened to poor, unstable Harry. He believed he knew why the half-assed search party organized by the bums—and eventually broken up by the police when the call of Harry's name began to disturb the respectable residents of Winsome—was hopeless. He even believed that the bums were better off now that they and their kin had been escorted out of town.

Harry the bum had last been spotted on Oak Street, heading west. Oak Street passed only a block away from the junkyard. One unfortunate turn . . .

Memories came flooding back before he could stop them. Images flashed: the moon high in the night sky, lighting the yard with an ethereal glow; his dogs, Death, Terror, and Beau pawing at the door, barking at the windows; following the Dobermans to the shed, cold sweat making his shotgun slippery; then the yellow eyes and cries of hunger . . . the claws . . . the blood . . . and finally the silence.

All three dogs gone. Ed helpless. It had broken him; the final straw that had sent him running away from his business, his junkyard, and all his responsibilities—and right into a warm, comfortable bottle.

He had locked the gates and let Winsome Junk go. Just forgot about it—though now he realized he'd been fooling himself, that he could never forget. The disappearance of all those animals, then the kids, and now this bum. How could he have fooled himself for so long?

He stood and walked to the mirror over his stove. He looked past the fog his breath made on its surface, deep into the face that stared back and those eyes that judged. Not the prettiest picture, but it was an act he could not have accomplished two months ago. Before the long crawl from the safety of the bottle.

He sucked in air. It felt good to fill his lungs with odors absent of alcohol. His head was clear. His body strong again. Now it was time to clean his conscience. Now it was time to do something about that goddamn junkyard once and for all.

Even if it killed him.

Tuesday

Mark Kishbaugh awoke feeling distinctly guilty.

It didn't take him long to figure out why. The conversation with Larry the day before was still fresh in his mind. *How could I have done it? Idiot!*

He had stayed in the Pit after the meeting with Nick. Nick had offered to walk home with Larry, but the latter had relented, making some excuse to stick around the clubhouse. What he didn't say was that he knew, though no words or even a look had passed between them, that Mark wanted to talk to him. Nick said his goodbyes without suspicion; after all, the Pit was more Larry and Mark's now than anyone else's. They probably wanted to view some of the pornos Nick had denied them. He understood, though he stepped out shaking his head and grinning crookedly; they were all friends, so what the hell.

But with Nick gone, the two friends had the opportunity to draw their plans against him.

They didn't speak at first, just lay on the mattress and watched the start of another game show. They could lie like that for hours on end, and feel completely comfortable. They had been this way with each other ever since they could remember. It was true they were inseparable; they made up two sides of a rusty coin, each possessing attributes for the deficiencies in the other. Even their births were close: both were 16, Larry born exactly a week before Mark. They lived on the same street, grew up playing the same games, fought the same enemies and achieved mediocrity in the same classes.

Yet they had moments of brilliance — together, of course.

It was their idea to build the Pit, and they had master-minded its construction. Now they would claim their rights as creators.

As they lay on the mattress and thought furiously behind glazed expressions, Larry's eyes narrowed with mischief and he turned to his companion.

"I know what you're thinking," he began. He usually had to start the ball rolling by yanking the ideas from his friend's brain.

"I don't mind giving up the Pit for one Friday night," Mark said carefully. "It just . . ."

"Yes?" Larry grinned.

Mark licked his lips, unable to stop the thought. "It just seems a shame to give up our Beer and Beaver festival completely, you know?"

"I know," Larry answered. "I know, I know." The words said: *Come on, Mark buddy, come on!*

"Just seems a shame," was all Mark would allow. Something had stopped him from sharing the complete thought, but Larry gratefully supplied it:

"Especially when we could see the real thing, eh, Marky?"

The plan expanded from a glimmer, and soon they were discussing it outright, without the hidden meanings and sidelong searches for acceptance.

Nick had suggested they help build a vent, so as to make the Pit less stuffy — "Especially with all that heavy breathing that'll be going on," Larry cracked — and pull the beer smell out. Larry had suggested cutting a hole in the ceiling boards; Mark had added a small door with a hinge to the idea, so that the vent could be opened or closed. Nick had agreed to it all.

What Nick did not count on was that such a hole would be perfect for spying. Larry and Mark could reposition the mattress under the hole before Friday night. They could have their beer party on the roof, without anyone the wiser.

"Marky," Larry said with a trace of admiration, "you're pretty damned smart for a guy with a last name like Kishbaugh."

"Shut up," came the laughed reply.

But now, the morning after the plan's conception, with the sharp light breaking through his curtains and exposing

33

him like a prisoner against the inner wall, Mark began to have his doubts. Not that the plan wouldn't work, but whether it was worth doing. Nick had made it pretty clear that a lot was at stake.

Why the hell did I tell Larry? If I'd just left . . .

It wasn't the first time he'd given his friend the tools for building a disastrous master plan, though, to be fair, Larry had always taken the blame and the punishment with him. Unfortunately, Mark's guilt and better sense never caught up with him in time to shut his trap. Now it would be too late. It was always too late once Larry had hold of it.

Larry was counting on him. They were friends, they had created a plan together that would provide a little excitement in their lives, maybe something they could brag about years from now — there was just no way Mark could back out without disappointing, perhaps even disillusioning, his friend. Larry would never take his ideas seriously again . . . and Mark could not live without that attention.

Besides, he had tried to back out once before. It would be the same old story. Larry would point out — rightly — that the whole thing was Mark's idea from the beginning, that Larry was just going along with *him* because he was his friend. Guilt would be slung from that corner, too, and that load would be heavier than what he carried now.

So he was stuck. He had to go through with it. What was the worst that could happen?

They could get caught, and that would be the end of their friendship with Nick. Mark lay in bed with his eyes closed and gave that ultimatum a good look. It disturbed him more than he thought it would, even more than Nick's half-serious threat on their lives. It was not an idle threat. Nick would not put up with some good-natured ribbing on this. Larry considered it just another in a long line of pranks — and so did Mark, to a certain extent. But to Nick it was much more, and that fact bothered Mark no end. He wondered what happened to the good old days, when they could just about kill each other one week and forget about it the next.

When his dad knocked on the door for him to get ready for school, Mark had come to a tepid solution: between Larry and Nick, the best he could do was make sure they didn't get caught Friday night. He took some comfort that Larry would agree to this wholeheartedly.

He forced himself up, showered, dressed, and hurried out to the kitchen. There was no time for breakfast, but his dad made him eat anyway. Mark took it in stride; Mom was off to work early again and his father — going overboard as usual — was trying to be Super Dad. Once finished with the checklist he used to convince himself Mark was happy, healthy, and learning something in the classes he would now be late for, his father sent him rushing out the back door with a sloppy kiss on the forehead. Mark couldn't stand sloppy kisses on the forehead — but he smiled just the same.

All thoughts of Dad and Larry fell away once he was out on the street. Fog shrouded the neighborhood and seemed to grow thicker the farther he traveled. Slivers of fear prickled his body, making him itch beneath the heavy coat. He would have to stop reading those horror books Larry kept lending him, the ones where dead, rotting creatures sneaked up on you in the dead of night, or in fog like this—

His fear climaxed when he recognized the dilapidated fence ahead of him, gray in the mist — pale fingers reaching out for him. The mountains of bulk beyond, hazy black in the fog, paralyzed his body and thoughts. It was like some leviathan staring up at him from the ocean depths. Waiting. Hungry.

For eleven school years he had passed the junkyard. In sunshine and fog. Even at night. So why was he scared of it *now?*

He couldn't put words to it, couldn't even reason it out logically so that his scattered mind would be satisfied. The raw fear was too demanding. Some instinctive part of his brain, a white center of survival hidden in the suffocating cold of reason, begged his legs to run in the opposite direction. His heart agreed, already pumping madly for the extra energy he'd need.

But he didn't move. Couldn't move — except forward, to school.

This is silly . . . just plain dumb . . . The thoughts didn't help. He wanted to walk fast — hell, *run* — past this place. But his legs would not cooperate. They took on weight, a ton around each foot, and his progress became uncontrolla-

35

bly stilted. He thought he must be moving like a scrawny Frankenstein monster in this gloom.

The chain link fence helped decide him. When the wooden barrier gave way to the thin metal lattice, thin as a veil, his primal fears took shape. He knew then that if he continued forward, something would reach through the chain link and grab him. He could cross the street — but he knew immediately that that would be worse: the creature would just break through the fence and he would suffer the agonizing tension of *waiting* for the nightmare to crash toward him, hot breath cutting a path through the mist, throat releasing a horrid cry as the claws descended —

No, it was better to stay near the fence and get it over quickly. Better for it not to happen at all, but there seemed no escape.

Unless . . .

Unless he ran like hell to the end of the street.

He'd be at a corner, then; the corner of a business district. Plenty of people, even at this time of the morning. At least someone would hear his screams. However, if he was attacked *before* he reached the corner, the fog would swallow his cries and muffle the sounds of the monster feeding . . .

He peered ahead, through the mist. No corner in sight. In fact, he could barely see fifty yards in front of him. The junkyard went farther than that. Much farther. Perhaps, in this swirling world, forever.

"This is stupid," he murmured, surprised to find his voice reassured him. "This is really stupid. There's no monster. Never has been for as long as I've passed this place." Buoyed by the words, he stepped forward. The first step relieved him. He was in Winsome, on a street he'd traveled a million times. The nightmare world slept soundly beyond the chain link on his left.

The second step brought terror crashing down on him.

As his foot hit the concrete, a sound like metal on metal broke the quiet. Adrenaline surged through his veins, and he was off with a scream filling his throat. He ripped into the sheets of mist, his fingers tearing at the cold, his legs pumping, pumping —

He didn't feel any of it. All he knew was fear and panic.

All he knew was to get away before . . .

But his mind wouldn't allow the horrible ending. He had to concentrate on splitting the heavy air. His eyes searched. Implored. There was only the fog in front of him—and somewhere, somewhere soon, please, God, that street corner.

His legs burned with the energy, trying desperately to keep up with the fear pulling him along, always just enough behind that his death was assured. *Where is that goddamn corner?* It wasn't coming; it was nowhere in sight. He was smack in the middle of the nightmare world, where the junkyard would never end, and his race with death would go on and on until the claws—

If he had hoped for the corner to suddenly appear then, he was sadly mistaken. He was only halfway past the junkyard, still an eternity to go. But he couldn't go on. The panic had taken only seconds to eat away all his energy, leaving him with shaky limbs. He slowed his pace. His veins filled with tired blood again, the adrenaline spent. He sucked in great lungfuls of gray air. His eyes closed as he prepared to die.

But behind the panic and the terror, there had always been a foundation of reason. How could there be something waiting for him in the junkyard? It was ridiculous. All he'd heard was a cat knocking over some piece of junk. It was only his imagination and the creepy surroundings that sent him racing pell-mell like some baby . . .

Except that he now heard a rustling from beyond the chain link fence, some *huge* bulk rushing toward him. The dull thud of feet against dirt, of *claws,* grew louder. Metal and wood rattled and cracked as the monster pulled itself from the nightmare world and into Winsome.

Something hit the fence just behind him.

He managed a breathy cry and tried to run again. But he knew it was too late. He had let reason slow him and now the unreasonable would pull him into the maw of death.

A cold wind pressed against his lower leg, followed by a sudden jerk. His foot was swiped from beneath him, and he heard a sickening *crack* as he fell. The concrete was hard and cold and slapped his nose enough to make it bleed. Mark felt wheezy, just on the edge of blacking out, but the white center of his brain forced his hands forward. His fingers wrapped around the curb and pulled him into the gutter. The pain came then, demanding his attention, but he did not stop. Once over the curb, he rolled away, over and over, into the street. When he hit the opposite curb, he lay still on his back, breathing deeply, limbs stiff and eyes wide as if in death. Every nerve waited for the final blow that would carry him to darkness.

It never came.

He lifted himself on his elbows. He was lost in the fog, only a curb to go by. He held his breath and listened. Nothing. He squinted his eyes and made out something lying across the street. Too small to be a monster. He realized they must be his school books.

The rest of the street was empty. Nothing moved.

What happened?

Did anything happen?

Was there something there or was it just his imagination?

He went back over it. He had definitely heard something (*cats, just cats*) and felt something (*your ankle giving out, that's all*). But there was sure no sign of any monster lurking about now.

He touched his ankle. It wasn't too bad. Only a slight twinge of pain. Maybe a sprain, but nothing major. And no evidence of claw marks.

Though his heart demanded rest, he stood and found he could walk on the ankle without a limp. Looking down at his leg, he noticed a small stain on his shirt. Blood. He touched his nose and winced at the raw skin. He sniffed the blood up and wiped it with his hand. Good enough until he got to school.

Embarrassment touched him now. He thanked God he was alone. This had never happened to him before, and he'd passed the junkyard countless times on worse days than this. Maybe this thing with Larry was really getting to him. Maybe the monster was his guilt.

Then again, maybe that was all, as his dad would put it, psychological bullshit.

At least no one had seen him rolling around like a fool. He could hide the hurt nose and ankle. It would be his secret, something to laugh at when he was less jittery. He

38

looked at his watch. He'd be late for school, but *that* certainly wasn't anything new. He should hurry, though.

His books lay spread out on the sidewalk, close to the junkyard's fence. Mark stepped across the street, each step careful and measured—he still didn't have complete control of his limbs yet. Strangely, against his will, as he approached the opposite curb he felt the old fear returning. The muscles in his legs bunched, threatening to cramp, and prepared to carry him down the street in a hurry if he should just trip the panic wire again.

He stopped and took a breath. *Get hold of yourself!* He tried to force his body to relax. It helped a little; when he moved forward again, he was more in control. Still, his eyes avoided the dark forms beyond the fence.

In a minute he had all but one of his books—one which had fallen in a small hole beneath the fence.

"Shit."

He could not keep his attention from the junkyard now. He peered deep into the swirling fog—*swirling*, as if some creature had made a hasty escape . . . or had hid to attack again. Mark listened, heard only the hollow wind against the dark forms beyond the fence. And he sure couldn't *see* very far into that place. He also couldn't stand here waiting for the sun to scatter the nightmare. He would have to leave now, with or without the book.

He stood on tiptoe so as to read the book's title. Algebra. He had a test in algebra this week.

"Shit again."

His face went through several expressions before resting on determination. This was no way for a sixteen-year-old to act. What was his was his, monster or not. So he held his other books in front of him as a shield, counted to three, and stepped forward, reaching, reaching . . .

A great black shape rushed him, four legs pushing it hard, teeth glinting even in this fog, and it was *outside* the fence where it could easily grab him and hold him down and—

Mark fell back, stumbled, hit his back so hard it cut his scream short.

The creature, a small brown beagle with large brown eyes and a white spot around one ear, stopped and tilted its head to stare at him quizzically.

Mark stared back. His anger grew. When he got his breath back, he cursed a blue streak, every demeaning word and phrase he could think of aimed at the puppy. The beagle just watched him uncomprehendingly. Mark was so consumed with embarrassment that he grabbed up his algebra book without a second thought. He aimed a false kick at the dog — the beagle ignoring it — and then, his anger at a fever pitch, took off running down the street.

His pants were dry by the time he reached school. He tried to put the morning out of his mind, and eventually those fearful moments became as insubstantial as the morning fog. But he would always remember the shame of having pissed his pants over a damned puppy.

The beagle watched the boy run away. He had hoped the boy would have some scrap to toss him. He hadn't eaten in quite a while and his stomach growled now to remind him.

The dog's name was Pups. He was four months old and already famous in Winsome, for his picture had been plastered all over town. He once belonged to a girl named Mary Hawthorne, whose parents now offered a reward for his safe return. However, no one had shown any interest in him since his escape from the Hawthorne back yard. He had been on his own ever since.

Pups didn't like being alone. It was cold and there were no regular meals. He sniffed the cool morning air, hoping to pick up something flavorful. The boy's scent was gone, but he detected something else. Something lurid, but promising. Something inside the junkyard.

It was another animal, definitely, though Pups could not determine if it was dead or not. Pups didn't fear it. In his life's experiences, there were two kinds of animals: those you played with and those you ate. From the smell, this hinted familiarly at the latter.

Still, Pups was cautious. He was not in his element. He stepped slowly to the wire fence, nose twitching, pulling in the flavors and images. Friend or food? Pups' stomach growled again. His tiny brain determined that there wasn't much choice; he had to get in there.

He set his paws to digging. It began to hurt after a while; he wasn't used to such hard earth, though the dew on the ground helped assuage his toes when he paused. He kept up the routine until he had cleared a hole beneath the chain link fence — one large enough for him to crawl under.

One more sniff for courage, and then he was in. He squirmed and thrust, and accidentally managed to get his collar stuck on a wire at the fence's bottom. He struggled a bit, until the struggle turned to panic and he backed up. When he stood on the sidewalk again, he was free of the collar. He shook his head, bristling the fur on his body. It felt good. Almost as good as when he'd first broken out of the back yard, though he still wished he were back there again.

Pups was not one to give up. He dug the hole deeper, maneuvering around his collar still caught on the wire. Finally he was through and standing on the other side of the fence. In the junkyard.

Adventure awaited. The smell was stronger here. Pups had it pegged as some sort of food now, though there was another odor just beneath it, something more pungent and rancid. Perhaps something alive.

Pups looked back out to the street. The fog had lifted a little, but the area was still deserted. Nothing out there except more hunger pangs. He drew his eyes to the spirals of junk behind him. There was food in there somewhere. That was certain. The disturbing smell beneath it was smaller, perhaps a cat. Pups was afraid of cats, but if he didn't bark at this one it might share the food. The attempt would be better than going hungry.

So Pups moved deeper into the yard.

He followed the scent with the speed of an expert. Somehow he felt it would be best to move in and out of this place as quickly as possible. The smell grew stronger, pulling him forward, begging him to steal it away and conceal it in his belly. He was eager to comply; his nose tingled with the thought.

Then he stopped. A horrible odor in the wind. One instantly recognizable. He could make out the shapes a few feet ahead of him, beneath a jungle gym of iron bars. He approached the black lumps carefully, circling like a buzzard. He managed cautious sniffs until he was sure what they were and stored the offenses in his brain.

They were three thin piles, each around six inches in length. Droppings. Still warm, still strong in the wind.

Pups curled his nose in disgust — but he did not walk away from the area. He was bothered. He knew what droppings meant. He knew what their warmth meant. Freshness. The animal — or animals — had been by recently. The length told him they were not just cats. They weren't anything he had encountered before, and now he had to make a serious decision on whether he should stay or get the hell out.

If he had been another rung up the evolutionary ladder, he might have made a run for it. But he was still an animal driven by instinct and need. His stomach demanded a meal, and there was no hope of one in the near future unless he discovered the source of that beautiful smell that now even masked the droppings.

He turned his tail on the offending piles and followed his nose.

He wound his way through the labyrinth of junk and came upon a stack of wooden crates, the letters painted on their sides long faded. Pups paused for a moment, listening, nose sucking in the hints. The meat was very strong now. Definitely behind this one large crate up front.

His mouth watered; the tiny lolling tongue had a hard time controlling it. He clamped his jaws shut, allowing the saliva to wet his chin, then stepped around the large crate slower than any puppy had ever moved.

He stopped near the corner and pressed hard against the wood; he barely felt the prick of slivers. He listened again, but did not allow himself the advantage of taking in the smells because of the sound his sniffing would make. Silence greeted him. That scared him more. He stifled the start of a whimper. He had never felt so bad about anything, not even messing the floor back home, but he still couldn't retreat; the attraction of food, of a full belly for the first time in two days, was too much. If necessary, he would have to fight for that lovely piece of meat.

He waited a long time before pushing his little eyes around the corner of the crate. He was slightly surprised by the sight that greeted him — then unnerved.

The ground, still hard dirt with little gravel, wound down into a vertical hole. Various wooden crates, some yellow with age, walled in the trail, and several crates had been stacked just above the hole, as if to mark the pit with a warning.

Pups examined the area for a long while. The trail seemed normal at first: about three feet wide, two yards long, falling at a slight angle, and a hole of equal width waiting below. The hole might have gone deep underground or just a few inches — it was impossible to be sure, for beyond the crusty border there was flat black. Not even Pups' animal eyes could break past that darkness.

However, after some time he began to discern evidence that another animal or animals had passed this way: finger-like prints in the dirt; small clumps of hair hidden in the shadows of the crates; an occasional clawed swipe across the face of those same crates; and that ever-present *living* odor just below that of the meat.

Pups whimpered. The food was close, very close. Maybe just a few inches inside that hole. Only his uncertainty at what *else* waited in that hole kept him tortured with indecision.

Then something made his mind up for him.

Splat.

A piece of meat — the piece of meat — was thrown from the hole. A luscious meal spit from the darkness. Pups couldn't keep his nose from pulling in its flavor. His stomach growled, acid stabbing his insides. He curled a bit in pain.

The meat waited for him, just five feet away. It was warm, he could see that. His nose told him more, like how it would taste, how easily it would tear in his mouth and slide down his throat and take care of the scraping inside his belly. Another sniff. He couldn't place the meat — it didn't unlock any image inside his young mind — but it was red, fresh, thick, with juice already melting into the gravel.

It was better than home.

It was paradise.

Still, there was that black hole looming behind it, ready to jump out and swallow him should he wander too close.

43

He paced back and forth at the mouth of the trail, whining uncontrollably. What could he do? Why wasn't the girl here to help him?

He stopped and stared at the meat again. His tongue, sorely dry, scraped his muzzle, desperate to taste the odors that excited his nose. Then something deep inside him clicked. A decision came smoothly, almost naturally. There was no going back now.

Pups looked beyond the meat for the last time. The hole. Just a hole in the ground, like the holes he once dug in his yard back home. Not very deep. The darkness was only shadows that would roll back as he approached. Nothing to worry about.

Unless something moved.

He lowered his head and peered carefully into that harmless hole. No movement. No sound. The overpowering odor of the meat covered any disturbing smells from the darkness. It would be okay, if he hurried.

Hurry — Hurry —

But his instincts forced caution. He began with a single step toward the treat. The hole remained unmoving. Another step. Another. A whimper of tension escaped him, but he kept on. That meat looked so damned good, the *best*, better than the girl would ever feed him. Why weren't there a crowd of animals around this catch? There might be soon. Better hurry, *hurry* . . .

And he hurried, skittering, head kept low, his muscles suddenly taut and powerful and ready to fight or carry him away in an instant. He was ready for any challenge as long as he could get his teeth around that juicy morsel.

He closed on it, nearer, almost on top of it, and still nothing had stopped him. The hole was just a hole, without movement, filled with nothing but frightened shadows that would only hide at his approach. The meat was beneath his nose now — *God*, the smell! — and he paused just a tiny moment to savor the conquest. Its raw freshness hit him full in the face. Saliva fell from Pups' mouth and mixed with the crimson juices. He still couldn't identify what kind of meat it was, but to a starving dog, meat was meat was meat —

He couldn't stand it any longer; the tension of getting his mouth around that flesh and getting *away* was tremendous.

He bowed down now and slipped his jaw beneath the meat—so sweet!—and set his legs to digging into the hard ground, pushing his tiny body and burden back up the trail. The delicious juices left a slime trail like a snail as it slithered over the gravel.

Pups was making good progress. Relief began to sprinkle around him—and then his world blurred in panic as a giant, dark bulk exploded from the hole. Pups froze and stared helplessly at the creature hurtling at him. There was little time for study, only seconds, but the stench of the beast brought all the images to him in a flash: misformed snout stuffed with teeth, molten eyes, and the dark, stringy hair heavy with grease and blood, like the juices on the meat.

It triggered a single response in Pups' mind: *Death*.

A deafening sound, in a range that drove dogs wild, split the air, and Pups should have fallen down dead right then. Yet a part of him had been prepared for this, some inner sanctum of his instincts that kicked in and forced immediate action. As the monster bore down, Pups dropped the meat, skittered backward a few feet before whirling around, and ran like hell back up the trail, to the real world, to people, to safety—

—right into the savage teeth of another monster that had crept up behind him. Pups had time for one last yelp. His final thought—strong enough to break through the blur of dark fur and red eyes around him—was of the girl who had once rubbed his tummy and laughed at his playing and sniping.

He screamed for her, but the cry only lifted bubbles through the slit in his throat.

Larry caught Mark that afternoon in the hallway, just as Mark's class was getting out. He didn't want Mark to think he'd been waiting just around the corner for the last half-hour—he had—so he started walking casually down the corridor when he spied Mark exiting his classroom. He didn't call out until Mark was close, as if they just happened to be passing each other, their meeting just a coincidence.

Mark was not surprised to see him—and not particularly

pleased either. They saw each other most of the day anyway since they shared three of their five classes.

He was taken aback, however, when Larry said suddenly, "By the way, I talked to Nick a little while ago, and he wants to meet us at the Pit at three-thirty. Okay?"

What with all the students passing around and between them and the noise and the way Larry acted as if he were in a hurry, it just wasn't the time or place for Mark to go into his uncertainty about their secret plans. Not that he could have ever expressed these doubts to Larry. But his face spoke volumes, twitching and looking away, and some of it did transmit between the two friends.

Larry took hold of Mark's arm, as if to get control of him. "Hey. Remember now, what we have to do. We have to keep up our influence on the place. Right?"

"Right," Mark answered half-heartedly. Larry's grip tightened, not painfully, but Mark could not have moved away.

"We have to protect the place we built, you and me," Larry continued. He looked worried, so Mark nodded reassuringly. "We have to protect our beer in the icebox and our VCR and TV and movies. It's *our* place. Remember that. He hasn't used it in years, yet he's been bossing us around. Nick's our friend, and we're letting him use it 'cause he's our friend, but that doesn't mean he can kick us out completely, right?"

"Right, right." Mark couldn't look at him. He watched the passing students.

"So today," Larry said, "when we see him, we gotta make sure Nick loves the idea of cutting a vent in the ceiling. We can't let him back out of it. He has to be with it."

Mark clearly heard the intent in those words, since they had applied to him so many times. Let Nick think *he* was the one who had suggested the vent, that it was all *his* idea, so that if they get caught or Nick starts feeling awkward about the potential spy hole, Larry can come right back at him with: "It was all *your* idea, man. You were all for it *then*." Mark wondered if Nick would fall for it as he himself had so many times. Was Nick that gullible? Could be worth a try just to find out—

He was pulled back to the crowded hallway when Larry shook his arm good-naturedly. "Don't worry, Marky," he

46

said, smiling. He leaned in closer and dropped his voice to a whisper. "Just keep thinking of that Friday night, with a cold brew in hand and a hot show starring Pauline Martinez." His face was beaming with that crafty pride again—that old look that Mark now realized looked like the killing zeal of an insane general. The whisper was gone as he continued. "I'll take care of it, Marky. Just let me do all the talking. You just follow along, like always. We'll do it. We'll do it."

"Right," Mark said. He tried to smile, to give his friend the old I'm-behind-you bit he'd been giving for years without thinking, but Larry's expression told him that it had come out a withering leer, something painful applied to his lips. To cover, he patted Larry once on the shoulder and called, "See you at three, then!" as he melted into the ocean of students.

He heard Larry behind him yell: "Three-*thirty!*" Mark waved over his shoulder and hurried on.

As he swam upstream against the nameless bodies, he realized that he was burning up. That last thing Larry had said, about Pauline, made it all suddenly real to him. It seemed all done with now, that Friday night pushed to the past, and he could make out clearly how wrong it was.

He *liked* Pauline. He'd known her for eighteen months, since their student government days, before she'd ever met Nick. He'd even had a crush on her, though he knew that she was not the kind of girl who would ever go out with him. But that was okay; there were other girls, less demanding, whom he liked, and still did like to this day. Besides, when the initial crush on Pauline had passed, he'd recognized her abilities. She was smart, outspoken, sometimes brash, and managed to get things done efficiently. Not really his type of woman after all, now that he thought about it. But he liked her, and she would always say hi to him if they passed in the hallway.

So why do this to her?

Larry would argue that they weren't doing anything to her, not if she didn't find out. She and Nick would have their fun and would never be the wiser. Mark once would have gone along with that—and it disturbed him that things weren't that easy nowadays. Now he *thought* about it, suffered over it, even put himself in Nick and Pauline's place. Why couldn't he just push it out of his head and follow Larry, the natural leader?

Because I'm a sop, he thought. *Dad has ulcers because he's always worried about things. Guess I'm going to inherit that.* As if in answer, his stomach hissed like static on a radio.

When his last class finally came to an end, he automatically checked his watch. Ten after. He had hoped to forget about the meeting and just go home, but the time reminded him. *Just go home anyway,* he told himself. The idea died quickly; he knew with a certainty that in twenty minutes he'd be in the Pit listening to his best friend manipulate Friday night into a guilty pleasure.

It took ten minutes to kick through the dirt field on the corner, cross at the light on Midway, dart around the corner of Maclean's Grocery, and make his way up the length of Oak to finally stand before the faded sign that whispered Winsome Junk. He blinked a few times, still slightly cautious of the place since this morning. The embarrassment was gone, but he didn't hesitate to call himself a fool. Monsters, huh? Right. In this place, this *homey* place, where he and his friends once met every day for years on end? Pretty damn slow monsters if they hadn't caught up with the gang by now.

Yet he didn't move immediately to enter. There was no rolling fog now to activate his imagination—or any stray puppies to sneak up behind him and shout boo—but there was an impalpable dread that covered the junkyard. It was like the smell of death without a visible corpse: a place to be avoided.

He was expected. Larry would give him hell if he went home now. He *had* to enter. So, pausing long enough to offer a curse to the cloudy sky, he stepped under the sign and through the dark maze.

Inside the Pit, he found Nick and Larry already moving the TV and VCR to a corner of the room—apparently Nick and Pauline weren't planning to watch television Friday night. They greeted Mark—Larry's slyly relieved grin evident on his face—and Nick instructed them on where to move the icebox, tool chest, and dirty blankets and clothes.

He picked up one large blanket and said, "I should get

48

this one cleaned up. It doesn't look too bad."

Mark glanced at Larry. Larry's eyes bobbed wide as the implication hit him: they won't be able to see anything if Nick and Pauline are covered up. An instant passed where Mark thought his problems were solved — and then Larry announced, "Uh, it's supposed to be warm this Friday, Nick. Probably won't need it." Nick looked at him, unconvinced. Larry saved the situation with a leer and added, "Besides, you two will be generating your own heat."

Nick threw the blanket at him while Mark tried to laugh naturally. No more was said about the subject.

Mark watched with morbid interest as his best friend grew into a good-natured stiff. He kidded Nick a little bit more, just to test the limits, but for the most part remained a helpful servant.

Mark admired Nick for not giving in and joking about his night with Pauline. He came close to a laugh now and then; most of the time, though, he just rolled his eyes at Larry's comments and kept his thoughts to himself.

When everything had been moved and it looked like Larry was about to push the vent idea, Nick hit them with another surprise.

"All right, guys. Help me pull this mattress next to the wall here." He gestured to the concave concrete of the sewage drain, then grabbed hold of one corner of the mattress and waited for the other two to follow suit.

Larry hurried forward, without so much as a glance at Mark. "Hey, uh, I don't know, Nick. You might want a lot of room to move around in —"

"Come on," Nick growled, rolling his eyes again. "Put it up against the wall."

"But, Nick . . ." Mark nearly gasped. Larry's voice was actually faltering in the midst of a con. Nick waited for them patiently; could he tell what was going on? It seemed obvious to Mark — though, of course, he was aware from the beginning of the secret betrayal that was planned, something Nick, in his blind trust, probably would not expect from his friends. In fact, he *shouldn't* expect it, if they were *really* his friends.

The guilt gnawed at Mark's mind just as Larry turned to him for help.

49

"What's wrong?" Nick asked. He stood straight again, letting the mattress corner fall back. "What's the matter?"

What's the matter, Mark thought, *is that Larry couldn't think up a convincing argument for this—and now it's up to me.* Larry kept his back to Nick, so that his panicky eyes could meet Mark's fully. He bit his lip as the silence stretched on.

Finally, not really aware of what he was doing, the words sprang from Mark's mouth as natural as could be. "Actually, Nick, it's not going to be that warm out. We just didn't want you to ruin the blanket by washing it. Spit keeps it together—and probably some of Larry's sweat from when he watches those porno movies." Larry's mouth gaped at this; Nick laughed a little. "The thing is, we once had the mattress against that wall, but because the concrete curves down like that, any cold air swishing in through the ceiling and the tire cracks comes right to the bottom of it. Really, Nick, if you put the mattress there, you're going to freeze your ass off."

Mark clamped his mouth shut. *What the hell did I do?* But he could see what he'd done just by looking at Larry's face. He'd saved his friend's great idea, put the plan back in action when the expert couldn't. He was Larry's hero of the hour, according to that lopsided, controlled grin, and when Nick left he would probably get a pat on the back—along with a ton of extra anguish.

But did it really convince Nick? He studied the older boy's face and saw that, yes, the magic had worked there, too. Old, wise Nick was buying it. He nodded and said, "Yeah, you're right, Mark. Let's keep it in the center of the room. Maybe I'll try to get a heater in here too," and Mark couldn't help noticing that Larry nearly bounced up and cheered. When Nick turned his back to them and moved to a corner for something, Larry gave a thumbs-up to Mark and did a silent little jig. He returned to normal when Nick turned back. Mark blushed; he felt sicker than ever.

"We still got a smell problem, guys," Nick said, standing between them. "I like that idea of a vent you had."

"Well, you mentioned it first, I think," Larry said judiciously. "The place could use some airing out. Mark and I just got used to the beer smell, is all, and never did anything about it." He grinned his fox grin. "Just like I'm

50

sure Mark's used to his come smell in here whenever he's alone."

"Shut up, freak!" Mark growled. Here he'd just saved his friend's ass, and now he was being insulted. He knew what Larry would say later: "Just gotta keep up normal appearances Marky." And Mark would end up nodding in agreement.

"It's okay," Larry said, "as long as you clean up after yourself."

"Goddamn . . ." But Mark gritted his teeth and let it go before it got worse.

Nick took up the slack. "Chill out, guys. Jesus, sometimes it's hard to believe you guys are best friends. You're always at each other's throats."

"He started it," Mark complained—and felt stupid for saying it.

Larry began "Poor—" but Nick interrupted.

"Come on! We still got some work to do. I like the vent idea. So let's get one started today. I want this place smelling okay by Friday." He looked at the other two with some exasperation. "Okay?"

They nodded. To show his good faith, Larry punched Mark in the arm and muttered, "Just joking." Mark didn't say anything, just nodded and smiled.

"Where, then?" Nick asked. He stepped into the center of the Pit and spun around slowly, his attention tilted to the ceiling. "I don't want a place too close to the mattress"— Mark gulped—"in case it rains."

"Right!" Larry moved to Nick's side with agility, ready to take control once more. "I thought I saw a place over here— yeah, right there." He pointed to an area just a few feet horizontal from the mattress. It looked different from the rest of the ceiling: dark and pocked with rot, the wood's grain hidden beneath the stain. Again, Mark marvelled at Larry's prescience; he *must* have had this part planned, and it made Mark wonder if the stain in the ceiling was really natural, or prepared.

Larry continued to convince. His skill to make it sound impromptu was probably also well practiced, down to the slight hesitation before the right words, and the uncertain, yet sincere, tone.

"Looks like it's pretty well rotted here. See? The rain over the years must have slipped through the tires up top and soaked into the wood just at this point. Mark saw it a couple of weeks ago, when we had that storm through here, and he kept screaming it was going to drip through and fill the place up with water. Of course, he never did anything about it."

Mark winced at the withering glare from Nick.

"We could kill two birds with one stone," Larry continued. "We could cut a hole here and get rid of the bad part of the ceiling. At the same time we could make a vent to clean the place out." Larry stopped; even Mark knew it was enough. Larry kept his eyes trained on the stain, as if he were figuring out some complicated engineering detail that would produce the desired result.

But Nick didn't grab the bait—not immediately. He stood beneath the rotted oval in the ceiling and jumped up on Larry so that his hand could test it. It was twelve feet up, so there wasn't too much weight behind the fingers that brushed the wood. Nonetheless, they could all see how easily the rotted portion cracked and flexed. It could conceivably give way the next time a storm pounded it.

But Mark noticed an additional strange thing—something that made him wonder just who was playing who here. As Nick jumped up at the ceiling, his eyes would flick downward, over Mark's head, toward the mattress a few feet away. He did it a couple times, as if gauging the angle from that height to see if the mattress could be seen by anyone looking through the vent from outside.

Apparently he was satisfied it could not, at least not without some maneuvering that would alert someone in the Pit. He announced, "All right, then. We'll build it here. Just a small one, though. I don't want to change your place here too much."

Mark held a giggle behind his locked lips. He wondered who would wink at him first, Larry or Nick?

Next, Nick grabbed a hacksaw from the tool chest and they moved outside. He instructed them to find a small piece of wood, about a hand's length in size, that they could use for the vent's door. Mark found one about that shape, but Larry made him put it back. "Find something bigger," he murmured, and moved on with his eyes searching the ground. Mark did as asked.

Eventually Larry found a thick piece of plywood, nine inches square.

"Isn't it kind of big?" Nick asked when he saw it. "A lot of rain could get in the hole."

"So we close the vent when it rains," Larry said. "Anyway, if you want the smell that's in there now to be cleared by Friday, you're going to need a hole at *least* this big."

Nick agreed, and they climbed the steeple of tires to the top of the Pit. Mark hadn't been to the top for at least four years, when they'd first built the place. The word "Pit" made the clubhouse sound subterranean, but it had applied only so far as to describe the *illusion* of the interior. Despite that, he was still amazed by the height the Pit actually did reach. The view was startling: the entire junkyard, from front to back, was visible. Mountains of junk, objects common and bizarre, stood before him, rising like alien rocks pushed from the planet's core — unmoving, though their sharp edges were always threatening. Many of the piles were at least as tall as the Pit, as if they had been carefully stacked together to form towerlike structures. Shadows sucked most of their color away. Foreboding.

Mark was glad it was still day. The rubbish looked naked in the gray sunlight, exposed somehow. Now he could see their dark intentions plainly. They waited for the prey that would crawl through their labyrinth. They would watch the prey's every move, wait with heavy patience to lock it in and close off any escape.

Mark grinned at the thought. Such subtle stalkers were the towers, yet here was a boy, of mid-height and mid-intelligence, a boy who had long ago manipulated their bodies into his own creation, studying those puny spires and harmless heaps with a certain margin of contempt.

Of course, it would be different when darkness came. Especially if he were forced to skitter through their dark maze alone. But for now, he felt as if he were observing the relics of a forgotten kingdom — an empire left to decay. Would anyone want to be ruler of such a place?

He knew Larry would.

They stepped carefully now from the mountain of tires

stacked above the sewer pipe to a thinner layer, only about two high, laid across the boards that acted as the Pit's ceiling.

"How we gonna find the right spot without moving all these tires?" Mark asked.

"It's over here, dummy," Larry replied. He walked with determination, a loping gait that had his feet swishing from one tire hole to the next. It reminded Mark of those army obstacle courses he had seen on TV. Except Larry's moved slower, more methodically. Mark and Nick found themselves following without comment.

As Larry crossed the length of the roof, his pace became less sure. His head zipped back and forth, like a bird's, long hair lightly slapping his features while those black slits searched out the stain that would mark the spot.

Mark and Nick halted, watching. Mark felt edgy. The view's impact had diminished, and now the sharp winter wind was finding its way into his jacket. He shivered, wishing he were home.

"Hey, guys," he began, "maybe we should—"

"Back this way, I think," Nick called to Larry.

"No, no," Larry answered back, "it's over—"

And then he found it. His right foot stepped through a ring of tar-black tires—and kept going. A *crack* sounded back to the other two boys. They hurried forward as best they could. It wasn't long before Mark got his foot caught in a tire ring and fell flat on his face. Fortunately, only rubber waited to catch him.

Larry was cursing as Nick reached him. His one leg was buried inside the two stacked tires, his crotch lying painfully against the top one; his other leg was twisted into an odd angle, causing him to wince with pain. Nick set his hand-saw to the side, grabbed Larry under the arms, and pulled him up. Since his back was turned, Larry wasn't ready for the help. He found himself rushing to save his dignity; when he was standing again he pushed away from Nick, breathing hard, crouching, as if prepared to continue some fight with an invisible enemy. Unfortunately, the sudden movement made him trip over another pile of tires, this time to land full on his back.

Mark had caught up to them by then. He held his hand

out to Larry, but the other boy just lay there across the tires, staring up at the sky, lips set firmly into a scowl.

"You okay?" Mark asked.

"Goddammit," Larry muttered.

Mark figured that meant he was okay, but he knew enough not to offer his hand again; it would just get it slapped away. Instead, he turned to Nick, who was staring down at the hole Larry had made.

"Jesus, Larry," Nick called, "I think you cracked the whole ceiling."

Larry sat up abruptly. "Bullshit. There should be just a hole there about the thickness of my leg. We can use that to put the saw through and start cutting."

"Is it the right spot?" Mark asked.

"Of course it is!" Larry demanded. He jumped up, apparently unharmed, and moved past Mark with shadowed eyes. "I wouldn't have fallen through if the wood wasn't rotten."

"He's right," Nick confirmed. "It's the right spot. You can still see some of the stain. But, hell, I tell you, this crack looks like it—"

"Doesn't matter," Larry interrupted. He looked down at his handiwork. "If the crack's too bad, we'll cover it with tar."

"*You'*ll cover it with tar," Nick said.

Larry looked at him and smiled. "Mark and I will cover it with tar."

Mark called, "Hey!" but the other two were already grunting with the effort of moving the tires away from the hole. Mark hurried forward to help. In minutes they had the immediate area cleared; smelly and rotten black tires surrounded them, stacked five high.

Nick had been right. Larry's fall had cleared away a pretty good-sized hole, and from one corner of this hole a crack took off across the roof, petering out after about a yard run. It didn't look bad enough to need some tar, but Mark was sure Nick would insist on it, in case it rained Friday.

"All right, guys, give me the vent door." Nick took the piece of wood and set it over the hole. Mark handed him a pen and he drew the outline of the wooden block onto the roof. When he handed it back, they could see that he wouldn't have much left to cut—Larry's fall had made a hole about five inches in diameter, close to the nine inches square needed.

Nick set himself firmly on his knees and started sawing. He cut it in four sections, and the thin strips of wood fell through the hole, into the Pit. *More shit to shovel,* Mark thought.

Nearly done, Nick paused to look up at them. He said, "I need one of you guys to go down into the Pit. Find a long strip of wood somewhere and nail it underneath the hole here. That'll keep the vent door from falling in when I check to see if it fits."

Larry glanced at Mark and jerked his head once, then returned his attention to Nick's work. Mark didn't feel put upon; he just went.

By the time he entered the Pit with a long stick that he'd found outside, Nick was done with the hole above. It looked pretty good from where Mark stood. Something else disturbed him, though: the ceiling bowed slightly where Larry and Nick rested. The obvious bulge made him shiver, and a plot played itself out in his mind . . . He and Larry would get up on the roof Friday night. The bulge would give them away to the lovers. Nick would yell up at them, maybe even rush out to kill them. It was all clear. The bulge would be the fuse that would explode the tenuous ties that now held them to Nick.

Mark felt a hot wave prickle his skin. He shook it off and hurried over to the tool chest, where he knew he'd find a handful of nails. *Best thing to do is not to think about it.*

A face tipped through the hole in the ceiling and looked down at Mark. "Hey, Marky," Larry said. The way his long, stringy hair fell down and swung around the top of his head like a wispy beard nearly made Mark crack up.

Instead he just smiled and said, "Yeah?"

"How you going to get up here to nail that board? I can hold the board in place for you from here, but how you gonna do the nailing?"

"Uh," Mark said. *Plop.* Another burden, as if he should have had all this figured out hours ago. He looked around for something to stand on. The TV might do, but if he fell through it Larry would be madder than hell.

56

So he looked up and said, "Hell if I know."

"Great." His head disappeared, and Mark heard him discussing the problem with Nick. A couple of minutes passed. Mark wondered if they'd forgotten about him; he was incredibly bored anyway, and wanted to go home. But then he heard the car door of the Pontiac open and close, followed by the passenger's door, to reveal good ol' Larry to save the day.

"The plan's simple," Larry began, hitting Mark with his best shit-eating grin. "You lift me up on your shoulders, and I hammer the board into place."

"Why am I on the bottom?"

" 'Cause you're the heaviest. Can't have the heaviest on top. It's against physics."

Mark knew that his friend didn't know a dip about physics, but it sounded reasonable anyway. It wasn't that Larry was trying to get the less painful job; it was just bad luck that Mark was heavier and should naturally be at the bottom. So he let it go at that.

They handed the stick up to Nick through the hole. He would hold it in place when they were ready. Then, by Larry's instructions, Mark fell to one knee to allow his friend to climb onto his shoulders. The ceiling was twelve feet high, so Larry found it necessary to *stand* on Mark's shoulders instead of sit. Mark felt the difference as Larry's shoes dug in painfully around his neck. They both leaned against the curved cement wall to steady themselves.

"Come on!" Nick hollered from the hole.

They were a comic nightmare as they moved clumsily to their place beneath the hole. "Hurry!" Mark begged. "Do it!" While Nick held the piece of wood in place, Larry hammered the nails into it. The ceiling around them bounced with the pounding; fortunately, the weight of the tires above kept it together.

Mark's upper torso was screaming to him now. He could take the strain in his legs, but his shoulders—"Goddammit, Larry, hurry it up!"

There was a pause to the banging above, followed by a curse. "Hold it steady!" Larry called. "I smashed my thumb!"

"Sorry."

There was more cursing and pleading for speed—at one point Larry shifted his feet to regain his balance, and Mark nearly broke into tears due to the pain—but their perseverance proved successful. By the time Mark's stamina gave out and he doubled over to let Larry fall, the plank of wood was nailed securely across the middle length of the hole: big enough to keep the vent door from falling through, thin enough to keep the vent functional.

"Ta da!" Larry called upward. He had landed on his feet, of course. He moved behind Mark and rubbed his sore shoulders. The rub was too strong and clumsy, and caused more discomfort than relief. Mark managed to shrug him off. Larry looked up at the hole again. "Look okay up there, guy?"

Nick's head came through the hole. Mark was faintly amazed that his hair stayed in place, even upside down. "Okay," Nick said, "but hand the hammer up here. The nail ends are poking through the roof."

Larry tossed it up and there was some more banging from above. Then Nick called a warning and dropped the hammer and saw through.

"Okay, Nick," Larry called. "Give her a try."

"Shit!" The word wafted down from the top, without much power behind it.

Larry and Mark both asked, "What?"

Nick's head appeared again. "I meant to buy some hinges for this thing today, but I forgot. You don't happen to have any hidden away somewhere down there, do you?"

Larry answered, "Nope. We're going to need something to prop the vent open with, too. You won't want it all the way open Friday night. Just enough to keep it from getting stuffy."

And enough for us to see into, Mark thought.

"I can get some hinges from home," he said.

"Naw, that's okay," Nick said. "I'll·get some tomorrow. Thanks." His head went back up. Mark and Larry stood together, staring up at the hole. Nick placed the vent door over the space and it clicked into place. The single rod they had nailed across the hole kept the door in place.

"It works," Nick's muffled voice called down.

"Yup," Larry called back. Then he looked at Mark and

lowered his voice. "It works perfect, huh?"

Mark waited for the wink, but it never came. There seemed to be a moment when uncertainty crossed his friend's face, though he couldn't be sure: it was ripped away as Larry stared back up at the hole. Nick had removed the vent door and stuck his head through again.

"The door fits perfect," he said to them, "but it's a bitch trying to get it back out of the hole again. We should put a handle on its back."

"Just tie a string around one end so that you can pull it up," Larry offered.

Nick seemed satisfied with this, and told them he'd do it tomorrow when he connected the hinges. "Coming down now," he concluded, then closed the vent for the night.

Mark was still rubbing his shoulders. "I'm going home now, Lare. I'll see you guys later."

"Wait a minute." Larry hurriedly took his arm and spoke in a conspiratorial way. "I mean, you could stick around. We can make sure the vent works out. We may have to move the mattress around, find the perfect place, you know?"

"Won't Nick know if you move the mattress?"

"Naw. We probably won't have to move it that much. If he says anything, we can put a little water down where he wants it and say there's a leak there. He'll have to go along with the move then."

Jesus, Mark thought with a hint of admiration, *he's got every angle covered*. He could see, too, the excitement that had been concealed in Larry's face all afternoon because of Nick's proximity. This was making his week, maybe his month. *We're going to pull one over on cool Nick*. What could be better?

"Um, I don't think so," Mark said. He spoke carefully, to give the impression that he was upset about leaving. "I really have to get home to dinner. It's getting late."

"It's only five," Larry said.

"We eat at five. Sorry." He shrugged. "We have the rest of the week, Lare."

Larry stared at him for a long time. His eyes were narrowed and black in the waning light. Mark nearly lost his balance, as if the gaze were a wind pushing at him. He knew those eyes were summing him up, peering straight into his soul. He tried to control the shivers coming over him. The moment was broken as Nick entered the Pit. He walked toward them, then stopped, frowned, and sighed with paternal exhaustion as he retrieved the hacksaw and hammer from the ground and put them away.

Mark approached him. "Uh, Nick, I have to go now. It's getting late."

Nick didn't turn from the tool chest. "Okay. Thanks, guy. I appreciate the help."

"No problem. See you guys tomorrow."

Larry said he'd stick around. They were discussing using a broom handle to open the vent from inside the Pit when Mark closed the car's metal door behind him.

The junkyard awaited. It would have bothered him if his mind had been set on the images he'd conjured earlier from the Pit's roof. But he was involved in other things, things like trust and betrayal and how it felt to be the guy in the middle of a tug of war. The icy wind hit him full in the face as he stepped beyond the dark junkyard gates. Down the street, around the corner, hands dug deep into his jacket pockets. He already felt his cheeks and forehead being rubbed raw. Even the gray sky seemed to grumble with the invasion of another premature winter night.

The streets were deserted. Brown leaves cartwheeled past him, along with errant pieces of garbage. He shivered. He had the distinctly chilling feeling that he was the last person on Earth. He had felt that way before on lonely walks home, but it disturbed him a great deal now; it reminded him of this morning, with the fog and that damned beagle.

And then, as if by the flick of a switch, his heart stumbled. It pumped harder so as to catch up. It demanded he move faster, while his bones grew heavy and forced him to slow. The conflict sent him into a cold sweat.

Oh, God, not again. How could he lead a normal life if this was going to happen every time he was outside alone? Why now? *Is this the kind of nervous breakdown Mom keeps threatening to have?*

The tension was growing. He began to run. He hoped to outdistance the cold, maybe keep the crawling panic behind him. His breath came heavy after only a few yards; the evening's gray deadness weighed him down, like the fog this morning.

No, it's not like the fog this morning, he thought. *Don't think that. It's a clear evening. Still some light behind the clouds. Not black, just gray. Thar be no monsters here—*

And then he heard the click just ahead. Around the corner. A click, and then a soft thumping sound, like something had just sensed him and stopped.

Mark stopped, too. He pressed himself against the fence. *I'm not near the junkyard,* he reminded himself. *I'm almost home. This is not like this morning. Nothing like this morning.*

But the fear stayed with him. He couldn't help that, couldn't even fight it.

Another sound, like a step taken. There was definitely something around the corner—and it was coming closer. Mark looked behind him. Long way to the next corner. But a big, strong brick wall along the way. Nothing would be able to grab him if he ran for it.

But when he faced forward again, those hopes died. The creature was too close. He wouldn't get very far before it turned the bend and smelled his panic. Then it would be over.

Dammit! Twice in one day is too much! The pressure in his bladder was immense. *If I piss over a dog again—*

But whatever was around the corner, he was sure it was larger than a dog. Much larger. He could *hear* that much. And just what runs around Winsome on a day like this that's bigger than a dog? He didn't have an answer, and his terror doubled uncontrollably. He couldn't move, so he held his breath and listened with an intensity rarely found in a teenager.

Apparently the creature could hear him too, for as Mark froze, the noise around the corner ended. Now there was only the wind between them.

Mark wondered if he should call for help. Stupid idea. Who would hear him except the creature? Another glance behind him. Larry and Nick might be done, and Larry often came this way. Maybe if he waited long enough . . .

The sound of something—*nails?*—scraped against the wall. Whatever it was, it was saddled up against the bricks around the corner like Mark—and it was pushing closer. He didn't have long.

The sound stopped inches from the end of the corner.

The time for planning was over; there was only one path left open to him, the only one that his panic allowed. On the count of three, he would run like hell all the way home, no matter what followed. He bent his knees in readiness. They cracked loudly, and he nearly lost his nerve right there — along with a few ounces of urine.

One . . .

The scraping noise remained silent. Was the creature crouching around the corner, like him, ready to make a run for it — or to pounce when he raced past?

. . . *two* . . .

He braced himself. This was it. The Last Run of Mark Kishbaugh. Tears clouded his vision as his leg muscles tensed.

He never hit three. As the number passed through his mind and adrenaline electrified his legs, a dark figure jumped from around the corner and confronted him. He screamed and collapsed, his legs completely dead now, all power of control gone. He rolled into a ball, prepared for the tearing strikes of the beast.

But all that came were two high-pitched screams. Then silence.

A minute passed until he dared look out from under his arms. He stared up at a girl, about fourteen, with two scrawny legs supporting a thick, heavy coat, long, brown hair, and eyes as wide as his own. Her hands pressed against her mouth, as if she had just screamed a foul word in front of her grandparents.

"Are you all right?" she asked, her voice wavering with emotion.

He tried to speak, but nothing came out. He waited until his throat unclenched then tried again. "Yeah," he said. "Who are you?"

"Mary Hawthorne. I live on Mantinger Street."

"Oh. Oh, yeah." He didn't make any move to get up since he was sure his legs wouldn't hold him yet. His arms quivered under even the slightest force.

Eventually he managed to move his back against the brick wall. He sat there as though it were the most natural thing in the world, though he was unable to look up at the girl when she spoke to him.

"I, I heard something around the corner," she explained. "I didn't know what it was. I was kind of scared, you know, with those kids disappearing a couple of months ago . . ."

He nodded. All he could think of was, *Thank God I didn't piss myself.* He lifted his eyes from his crotch before the girl caught him at it.

"Well, will you be okay out here?" she asked.

"Yeah."

"Okay, well . . ." She had nothing more to say. They both felt foolish and wanted to forget the entire incident.

She made a farewell sound and started to walk away — until Mark, suddenly hot with anger, demanded, "What are you doing out here?"

She faced him. "I'm looking for my dog. A little beagle named Pups. Have you seen him?"

Hell. All this for a dog? He sneered and said, "No, I haven't seen any goddamn dog." She was younger than him, and he knew what a natural pain kids could be, but he wanted her to feel guilty for what she had done. "Why don't you look for him during the afternoon, like any normal person?"

She planted her hands on her hips and stepped toward him with such an expression of outrage that he pulled his legs closer to his body for fear of getting stomped on.

"I've been looking for my dog for days now!" she told him. "I've looked for him *every day* after school! I was heading home when you started playing games around the corner! What are *you* doing out here if *you're* such a normal person?"

His anger was suddenly gone, replaced by embarrassment. Her accusation that he was "playing games" around the corner made this whole situation sound dirty and somehow his fault. He explained, "I was coming home from a friend's house. I didn't mean to scare you."

She backed off, her feelings also changed. "Well . . . I guess we both should have said something. You'll be okay?"

In answer, he rose to his feet, brushed off his pants and smiled. "Okay. And good luck." He wondered if he looked as dashing as her return smile made him feel.

"Thanks," she said. "Bye."

"Bye."

She turned and moved off across the street, looking so calm that Mark wondered how frightened she really could have been. He shrugged. Maybe her mind was elsewhere. Girls were like that, flitting from one thing to another with perfect ease. Probably more worried for her damned dog than herself—

It came to him then. Before he could try to forget it and just head home, he called out to Mary. She doubled back a few steps and they spoke across the deserted street between them.

"Your dog," he said. "You said it was a beagle? A puppy beagle?"

Her eyes lit up. Her fingers curled as if to grab at something. "Yes! You've seen him?"

"Um, yeah. I saw him this morning. He was over near the junkyard."

Some of her excitement seemed to wane at mention of the place. She took a breath for courage, and said, "Winsome Junk? Which side?"

"King Street. He stopped there for a while. I don't know if he's still there, but—"

"You didn't see my posters?" she demanded abruptly. When he admitted he hadn't, she glared at him as if he'd broken a law. "Well, if you see him again, please hold on to him and call me. My number's on the posters I hung up all over town." She emphasized the last few words for the blind man she faced.

"Uh, okay," he answered, and watched her back as she walked away. *Stupid little brat. I pity any boyfriends she'll have.* The silent insult somehow made him feel better, less a fool for his own actions. He took one last look at his crotch — dry, thank God — and hurried home, humming loudly to fill the disturbing quiet in his mind.

Mary was in a fit. She knew she must look silly moving so fast and with such long strides, but she felt the need to hurry. The only reason she didn't run to the junkyard was because she knew she'd be exhausted by the time she got

64

there—and something told her she didn't want to be too tired to run away once she arrived.

Why? What's to fear—except Pups not being there—

Don't think that! She hadn't been this close to finding him before. She was old enough to know that the larger the expectation, the greater the pain of disappointment. So when she arrived, she would search carefully, but maintain a forced calm. It would be no big deal. Maybe he was there, maybe not . . .

Oh, hurry! Hurry!

She did hurry, and reached the junkyard just as the clouds above began to ripple with darkness. It was getting late, already past dinnertime. Mary's mom would be worried sick by now, but she couldn't turn back, not with Pups so near.

As she turned the corner onto King, she stopped to watch two older boys cross the street up ahead. They looked familiar, though she couldn't see much detail in this light. They were talking about something, the smaller boy occasionally raising his voice and erupting with a silly laugh. At the corner down the block, they parted company.

The street was deserted again. Mary was alone.

She stood there until she saw the street lights go on. They brightened her route markedly, though she could see it wouldn't last long with the fog descending. She was on the street that the boy had said he'd seen Pups on, but she would still have to hurry if she wanted to spend any time searching the area.

The wooden fence on her left petered out; the junkyard was then exposed through the chain link fence. She gave the trash a cursory look. Her hand clapped against the wire as she walked the length of it. She examined the ground near the fence closely, checking for any holes that a small dog might slip beneath or get caught in—

There! Dirt made a line across the sidewalk, pointing to a hole beneath the fence. Recently dug. And something shiny beneath the fence . . .

She struggled a bit before the collar came free in her hand. She turned it over and over in her hand like some ancient jewel. Here was the proof she needed to stay on. Pups had dug here, lost his collar here. But where was he now?

Her attention focused beyond the wire fence. The fog was heavier now; it transformed the sharp-edged heaps of junk into hazy black figures, some bent, some straight, like some mammoth, disfigured animals looking out at her from their cage. A Dr. Seuss nightmare.

She considered heading home at this point. It was late and getting darker. The street lights would be faint glows soon, unable to even reach the street. Walking home would be bad enough, but roaming around inside the junk-yard . . .

However, as she turned away, a single image rose up in her mind: Pups, helpless, slowly starving; crying for his owner; lost; terrified; and probably somewhere inside that ghastly yard.

Mary couldn't stand that. She knew her mother would be fuming by now, and she would get a long lecture on Following Rules—rules she usually embraced religiously. But these were special circumstances. An innocent child (well, he is only a puppy) was in danger. She could no more leave Pups to this place at night than Mary's mother could leave Mary. Surely, if she explained it in this manner to her mother, she would understand. Her father might even congratulate her on her "gutsiness," as he often did with Mary's brother.

So it was decided, in that brief second it took to turn away and turn back. Her concern swallowed any fear. Her conviction formulated a logical plan.

She began by calling out the dog's name.

She had thought the fog would swallow most of her voice, but it actually seemed to accentuate it. The echo bounced around for so long that it distorted her second call. It didn't matter. Pups did not come and he did not answer. Perhaps he wasn't even in there at all.

But that suspicion was immediately abandoned; her instincts told her differently, and in this case she felt it right to follow her emotions rather than her reason. Pups was in there, lost somewhere in that dim maze of garbage. He *had* to be. He wouldn't answer her calls, but maybe he was sleeping—or *injured*.

She must hurry. The night and the fog and the fear were

working against her — and they were growing stronger. She must find him *now*.

Mary lost all hesitation. She hurried down King Street, in search of the dark kingdom's entrance.

A black nose, the nostrils scarred with red flesh, quivered in the night.

The smell was strong, almost overpowering. The creature looked out from beneath a stack of TV shells and irreparable stereos. Deep black eyes, the size of a man's fists, penetrated the darkness. It could see nothing, not a hint of movement.

But the *smell* was there.

The creature stirred quietly, careful not to attract attention. Prey was scarce; it would not pay to scare this one away. It stepped from beneath its resting place and, once out, paused to draw its tail in beneath its body. It froze then, like a hunting dog pointing out a dead fowl for its master. The nostrils vibrated, pulling in the flavors at an incredible rate.

Yes. The smell was still strong. The prey was not moving away. That was good.

Primitive pictures passed through the creature's mind. Pictures of food, of raw, red meat. A growl crawled up the back of its throat. It had enough presence of mind to squelch the sound seconds after it was formed.

It waited a short while longer, to get its bearings in the darkness, then lifted its nose again. Still there. It shivered with anticipation, but there was no time to savor the feeling. It had to hurry.

It moved fast, though with heavy deliberateness. The scent led it unerringly through the twisted corridors of the yard. Instinct assured it that it couldn't go wrong as long as it followed the scent — the same primal instinct, wedded with ingenuity and strength, that had kept it alive for so long.

She had no preternatural feeling that she was being stalked, or even that she was being watched. She was alone, and was in the midst of the tingling uncertainty that accompanies a lonely soul in the gloom. Her paced quickened as she discerned the corner ahead. Around it and a few feet more, she came to her first aim. Tall, black iron gates reached high into the mist. A sign, unreadable, arced across the entrance; for a moment she pictured that sign as the blade of a guillotine, waiting for her to step beneath it.

Stop this! Stop it right now! she implored herself. Her arms wrapped around her shoulders, hoping to spark some warmth. It didn't work.

Her eyes inevitably fell from the gate to rest intently on the junkyard beyond. *He's in there somewhere. Afraid. I can feel it. If I leave now, he'll think I've deserted him.* Worse, *she* would think so too—and she could never live with that guilt.

She stood at the threshold for a long time, in the silence and the suffocating fog, afraid that any movement would stir the creatures hidden in the world beyond. It *was* a new world; right now, she couldn't even be sure she was in the same universe. The only things she could see were the gate and the outlines of the land inside. Nothing else. No stores, no buildings, no changing lights or passing cars. No people. It was only Mary Hawthorne and this junkyard.

And, somewhere, Pups.

The uselessness of standing there came to affect her, and she made her decision. Her hand touched the cold metal. The gate gave easily. Not even a squeak. Oddly, the lack of protest convinced her that there was no harm in entering this place. With that belief to guide her, she pushed the gate further and stepped beneath the guillotine, into the yard, with her shoulders squared and her eyes nailed forward.

Come what may, she would stay until she found her puppy.

The smell was maddening now. Still, the creature would not allow the hunger to consume it. It remained in the dark niches of its kingdom, slithering from heap to heap, careful to remain silent in the night. It sensed movement now, up ahead, near the border. There was little wind, so at times the scent would be lost. But it would always return soon enough with a renewed strength.

Along with its power, the smell now also provided information. It flowed into the creature's brain, where it was sifted and detailed. Possibilities were eliminated or validated. In seconds, the information manifested itself into an image: the promise of hot flesh, fresh, soft enough to tear, thin bones to get a good hold on—and all of it vibrating with the throb of a warm pulse. This was more than just food; it was *life*, existing only to grow larger, to reach a peak, so that it could be brought down and digested.

The creature's stomach squeezed a sound out. Saliva rose to cover its mouth. The scent disappeared for a moment—a moment that shoved a cold tongue up the bristles of the creature's back. But it returned, of course. Even more distinct.

Here was easy prey, it said.

The beast scurried forward—as always, silent as the mist.

"Pups?"

She let the name echo, until it finished exploring every contour of the junk that stood before her. There was no reply, from animal or otherwise, but she knew that her voice could not have reached *every* place in the yard. The area was too large for that. She would have to move toward its center.

Instead, she called again. Something kept her back. As her voice bounced around, she studied her surroundings, attempting to make out some details through the mist.

She was between two buildings, that was clear. Neither was very large though the one on her left was certainly more secure, as it was made of concrete; the other was built with plywood and covered with flecks of yellow that reminded her of chafed skin, probably a shed.

Unconsciously she moved closer to the concrete structure. It appeared to be locked up tight, but she thought she could force her way into a window if she needed to. The rectangular concrete box looked amenable to housing a person for a few hours. It bothered her, now that she thought of it, that a place like this wouldn't have some sort of guard. At least some dogs. Yet as far as she could tell, there hadn't been anyone here for months.

Then why'd the gate open so easily?

She shivered, called out again.

Then she started.

Was that a cry? Was Pups trying to answer? Why didn't he come forward and greet her? She peered at the hazy columns in the mist that looked incredibly like the legs of giants. A lot of garbage out there. It was likely that Pups was lost in the corridors the junkpiles formed. But why wouldn't he continue to whine so that she could get a bearing on him?

She called again, twice, and the syllables mixed into unintelligible sounds. It didn't matter. He *must* recognize her voice.

—And there it was again! Another cry. Or was it a squeak? Maybe just a piece of metal scratching against another, disturbed by the wind or a cat. But it sounded like it had come from a living creature. There was something warm and urgent about it, a sound that could only be produced in the throat of an animal.

She took a step.

Stopped.

A glance behind her told her she was still close to the front gate, still visible from the street. It would take only a few steps to change that—just four feet forward and she would be visible only to those in the junkyard's arena, completely cut off from the real world.

Another squeak. Just a hint, as if the sound baited her to come closer.

Still she wavered.

The creature was going mad. Bloodthirst coursed through its veins, forcing eruptions of adrenaline and saliva and pangs of hunger. It couldn't bother being quiet now. Every rugged exhale brought a growl. It fidgeted back and forth, each period bringing it closer to exposure from under a tower of metal.

It could see the meat, near the shelters that marked the entrance. And that meant the prey would be able to see *it* if it wasn't careful. What could it do? The piles of junk halted here; the creature could move to the left or right, to the very borders of the yard, but it wouldn't be any closer to

70

her. All that lay between them was a flat expanse of gravel. It was becoming clearer to its primitive mind that the only option was to rush the young female. She would scream, but its own roar would drown that out. The prey might then freeze or run.

The last was a risk. Maybe a good risk. The creature knew it was faster.

It dug its claws into the dirt—a steady grip would be important for its initial pounce.

It hit her hard,

Mary couldn't move. It wasn't the cold or the guilt at keeping her mother worrying. Something else. Something that made it hard to breathe and made her every limb as heavy as concrete. She was afraid to move; it would draw attention to herself.

But whose attention?

She didn't know—but she was sure that she was being watched. That was the creepy feeling crawling over her body. She knew something ghastly, something like a pervert, was watching her and *drooling.*

The thought dragged shivers through her body.

God, please God, I've got to get out of here . . .

The need to find Pups was gone now. With the creeping fear came the awareness that her dog was no longer here, that she was truly alone in this dark world. Alone with whatever was watching her.

Just turn and run. That easy. Just turn . . . and . . .

But her body would not cooperate. She was stuck there, awaiting the slightest movement from the land before her that would release this cold grasp of fear. Whoever was watching her could plot all he wanted; she would remain as still as stone until he appeared.

She was easy prey.

The creature smelled the fear. It saw the wide, seeking eyes. It sensed she was going to bolt soon. It sensed that she was aware of its presence. Yet she stood there, unmoving, while the creature vibrated with indecision.

71

All right. If she ran, she ran. It would have to attack anyway. Resolution came. Its body responded with a primal instinct. Haunches bent, muscles bulging, it allowed the blood lust to consume it. Jaws opened wide; the tongue quivered with the anticipation of warm chunks of meat.

Ready . . . ready . . .

Screeeeeeeeee

Mary screamed and turned toward the horrible sound.

Cold relief washed over her when she saw the revolving blue and red light atop the outline of a car in the street. It still rocked back and forth from the sudden, skidding stop.

Mary rushed toward the police car with as much dignity as she could gather. It didn't help that her already shaky body was now slick with sweat. She thought she must look like she'd just spent a couple hours in the sewers.

The deputy who leaned across the passenger seat to talk to her didn't seem to notice her condition. He asked simply, "You Mary Hawthorne?"

She nodded, unable to trust her voice right now. Warm air came from inside the car, pushing back the black gates and shadows lurking behind her.

The deputy was saying something; it seeped through her haze slowly.

". . . mother yelling all sorts of things at the sheriff. You better get in with me and I'll get you home, okay?"

She nodded again. There was a moment of awkwardness when the door popped and Mary found herself unable to step away from the car to let the door open wide. But the warm ghosts from the car's heater and the familiar crackle of unknown voices on the police radio drew her back into the real world—a world where it was very dark and her parents were waiting for her. It became imperative that she get out of the fog. She stepped to the side and let the door swing forward. Then she was in. Breathing again. Safe next to a man in uniform with a gun.

She wasn't sure how long she sat there with her eyes closed and lungs working overtime, but the deputy didn't say anything for quite some time. He just stared at her, no emotion on his face.

Finally a soft voice, warm and strong: "You okay, Mary?"

"Yes," she said. Her voice sounded fine.

"What were you doing in there?"

"Looking for my dog." She looked at him. "He's gone, though. Gone forever." She was too exhausted to accompany the pain with tears. They would come later, when she was back in her bed at home. They would go on for days, until the pain became a numbing ache that she could learn to ignore.

The deputy reached across her and shut the door. "I'm sure he was a good pup," he said. "Your parents will find you another good one."

She nodded, her throat too tight again to speak. She stared distantly out the window, into that world of mist. The fog barely curled as they pulled away from the curb.

From the bog of junk left behind, echoing after them, came an unsatisfied growl.

Sheriff Martin K. Peltzer breathed a little easier when Deputy Jenkins reported he'd picked up the girl. It wasn't just that it would make the girl's mother stop calling him up every five minutes to shriek about his incompetence, but . . . well, dammit, this town had seen too many missing kids the last few years. Way too many.

And he wasn't above admitting that securing the safety of Mary Hawthorne made him feel less like an incompetent and more like the protector of the people, that highly regarded, and goddamned difficult, duty he had been elected to.

He turned from the radio and stared at the map on the wall behind his desk, as he had every day for the past two years. The same tiny red flags still hung there in their respective locations—locations in Winsome where the children had last been sighted. Five children, ranging from twelve to seventeen years old. Disappeared completely. Sheriff Peltzer found that if he stared at the map long enough, the flags would blur into drops of blood. His town was bleeding, and he couldn't do anything to stop it.

Again, for the countless time, he went over the chronology. Maybe there was a clue there that he'd missed the

73

million times before; maybe some connection that only now his tired mind would allow to pass into his consciousness.

Shellie Johnson . . . the first . . . twelve years old . . . last seen leaving her house for a friend's place . . . gone . . .

He remembered that first call from a hysterical mother. The pleading, the reassurances . . . eventually the threats made by both parents when it was clear the sheriff was getting nowhere. But there had been nothing to go on. Little Shellie had just passed down the block, turned a corner—and disappeared. Had it really been two years ago? Nearly that: twenty months.

Mario Sintral . . . fifteen years old . . . a runaway . . . last seen by Hal Maclean when the boy stole some fruit from his grocery store . . . gone . . .

A sad case, he remembered, because there was no pleading or threats from the parents. The mother was dead, the father an alcoholic. There were quite a few families like that in Winsome, and it bothered Peltzer no end. He remembered the sickness in his belly, like some cold gruel pushed down his throat, as the father just blinked and shrugged at his questions. The drunk never even asked if Peltzer would keep him informed. Peltzer had never received a phone call from him either, and it had happened seventeen months ago. The kid probably wouldn't have gone missing if the school hadn't called. Mario had been a pretty good student. Peltzer could have wished the kid had gotten to another town and started a better life . . . could have if he didn't have one of the kid's shoes in the evidence room. Found a block from the grocer's—where a little red flag now poked out of the sheriff's map.

Ron Ramirez . . . fourteen years old . . . class brain . . . last seen running from a bunch of boys who had just beat him up outside the school . . . gone . . .

The boys who had beaten him said they didn't really have a reason. Maybe it was the way he looked, so tall and lanky without a pound of muscle; maybe it was because he always screwed up the grade curves in his classes; maybe it was because they knew he would get out of Winsome some day and be something important, while the rest of them . . .

Well, whichever, they'd given him a moderate beating, enough to bloody his nose. He had escaped them and run

74

like hell back home—except he never reached home. He never reached anywhere. As far as anyone was concerned, he just disappeared.

Ten months ago, Ron's parents had been new to Winsome, part of the new district that covered the north edge of town. They were nice people, very polite, even after he'd given them the news. The father, a strong, stiff man, stood, shook his hand, and thanked him for coming. Peltzer had wanted to tell him that he really felt for the family, that when he was a kid he had been beaten regularly for the same reasons Ron was—but all he could do was tell them he would do his best to find their boy.

A month later, Mrs. Ramirez came by the station to drop off their change of address. They were moving away from Winsome. Far away. And right then, looking into that poor woman's eyes, Peltzer had wished he could have gone away, too.

William Granton . . . sixteen years old . . . high school football guard . . . last seen by his friends when they split up to walk home after some tag football in the park . . . gone . . .

The pattern had emerged. A wicked voice deep inside the sheriff had begun whispering: *"Serial killer, serial killer . . ."* In a large city it was frightening, but in a small town like Winsome it was a devastating horror. The odds put every child in danger. Neighbors were watched by other neighbors for any eccentricities. Small town friendliness became a thing of the past. And the pressure on the police department became a daily burden.

The Granton family was destroyed. Just passing their house, as Peltzer sometimes did on his way home, a stranger could see that there was something wrong in there, something dead and reeking. A family once active in the town was now locked behind peeling paint and crumbling concrete. Friends who once visited them and offered support dried up. Only six months ago. All of that in six months,

No clues came in. William's friends were no help. The boy was stout, strong, the football team's first string. What could possibly rip him from the world without a trace?

Julia Gomez . . . please God, the last . . . seventeen years old . . . last seen walking home from her boyfriend's house . . . gone . . .

Mrs. Gomez, thank God, was strong. She kept her husband and two sons together. They were okay. The disappearance was reported two months ago—an eternity to that family—but they were still okay. Julia's boyfriend, he heard, wasn't so great. He had loved the girl. When Sheriff Peltzer had talked to him, he swore over and over that he would have driven her home if he hadn't been sick with the flu. She volunteered to walk home. She was a thoughtful girl. The more Peltzer questioned him, the more the boyfriend shook his head, dreamily, like he was trying to blur the reality around him. Peltzer thought it best to leave him be for a few weeks.

More friends were questioned. Julia had been a parent's dream: a good job at the grocery store, no drugs, no promiscuity, good grades—a woman headed for college and a bright future. Now it was all gone.

Disappeared.

Sheriff Peltzer let his eyes refocus on the red flags in his map. There were six, though he tried not to think of the last one. It ruined what little pattern there was. That last flag belonged to Harry the Bum: a full-grown male, not from Winsome, someone that the sheriff avoided now as people once avoided Harry when he was alive.

But the red flag was there nonetheless, to remind him that the killer was still around. Peltzer wondered what the map would look like if he included the calls he'd gotten about missing animals. How many cats and dogs had disappeared into thin air? Too many to keep track of. So what the hell was going on?

Animals and children . . . Some sort of Satanic ritual in Winsome? Sick as it made him, it was worth considering—except that every sacrificial cult he'd heard of always left the bodies, or at least the blood, to be found. And that was the worst aspect of this case, both for the sheriff and the families: not knowing whether the children were dead or alive. Not a single body had been found. Not even a drop of blood. How could it be?

Peltzer clenched his thin, wiry fingers into a fist of frustration.

A pattern. He needed a pattern. With this last victim, he

had thought he'd found one. Mario Sintral: last seen at Maclean's Grocery. Julia Gomez: a good job at Maclean's Grocery. And when he studied the map, he found that Harry the Bum's disappearance was within two blocks of the store.

Harve Maclean? A murderer? Sixty-year-old widower with a reputable and lucrative business. He'd lived in Winsome for forty years. His wife dead for ten. Why would he do this all of a sudden? It didn't make sense. What's more, Peltzer's instincts told him that it just wasn't the answer.

He had conducted an investigation into past and present employees of the grocery store, but still there was nothing tantalizing. The whole idea seemed wrong to Peltzer, anyway. What would a grocery store have to do with the disappearance of five children? Filling sausages up with some special meat, are we? A sick thought for a sick world. It was a well-worn plot device used in a lot of horror movies, but in real life he knew it couldn't be pulled off. Not for long, anyway. Not for two horrible years.

Besides, most of the disappearances had occurred between early evening and early morning—around the midnight hours. Without bodies, they couldn't pinpoint the times any closer. But those were the times when the grocery store was closed. No employees or owner hanging around; at least, there shouldn't be.

So it was something else. Someone else. Someone who spent a lot of time around Harve's store late at night. Extra patrols in that area would have to continue, though they hadn't discovered anything so far. Beyond that, he couldn't think of anything else. Not until they had something more to go on. Not until the next one.

Two months since Julia, he thought, ignoring Harry the Bum again. *Please, God, let her be the last. Let the horror move on.*

But it wouldn't move on. The horror was very happy with his surroundings. In fact, the horror had every intention of staying for a long, long time.

It took very little effort for a similar horror to slither its way into Ed Kelton's dreams. It no longer had a swamp of alcohol to crawl through; it made its way through the dark

77

passages with the ease of long practice, as if it had been visiting Ed for years instead of just a few months.

Just a few months . . .

It was that horrible night in early September, when he had felt the disturbance. Ed had learned to sense unwelcome visitors to his junkyard. It was a natural ability, one that a man alone easily believes in. And relies on.

He'd owned the place since his late twenties — back when the junkyard was the *least* of his enterprises, and he had a big house, and a pretty wife to egg him on — but it had remained pretty much uninhabited until he came to live his days there. Once he was planted, and certain he would never again work his way anywhere else, it didn't take long for the junkyard to become a natural extension of himself, as any last chance is wont to do.

Though he felt like staying hidden away until he died, he forced himself to leave his nearby, small — small*er* — home each morning to arrive at the yard by six. There, he would spruce the place up, make some calls to scrap houses — and, most important, learn to *sense* trespassers. He prided himself on knowing when anyone or anything, man or beast, evil or good, entered his property. He knew it as well as a dog senses the tickle of a flea. Fortunately, he was smart enough to realize that a trespasser wasn't likely to be as harmless as a flea. That, coupled with the ugly specter that whispered he wasn't nearly the man he used to be, led him to believe he should not meet the invasion alone.

So he would release his children.

Death, Terror, and Beau: the Dobermans he had raised since pups, only a year ago. His children. There followed countless, otherwise lonely hours together, and inevitably a silent symbiosis had formed between master and servants. They watched over each other. Ed wondered how he had ever gotten along without them. God knew he could have used them years ago; the damned front gate and chain link fence didn't do squat. The dogs were the missing ingredient. They were perfect for junkyard duty: months of demanding, loving training had created hot-blooded killers — vicious protectors of their master's last estate.

So he was not wholly unprepared when that summer night brought the itch of a unique and bloody invasion.

Beau, the most restless of the children, was sniffing at the door and whining. Ed had been about to go home about then, and would have if Beau hadn't been acting up. He waited, though, and after a while the presence pressed against him. He shivered with the cold, slimy certainty.

His eyes shot to his children.

Beau was still whining, and was now pacing in front of the door. Perhaps in empathy of their master and brother, Terror and Death also fell into an agitated state.

Soon they were all certain of it. Something had entered their yard.

"Jesus," Ed muttered. His knees trembled beneath him, but he made it to the door and opened it.

The children were let loose. Ed was right behind them. He held his shotgun securely. It was a routine they followed without thinking: Death, Terror, and Beau would track until the trespasser was found — usually just a bum or some town brat. Then Ed would fire a shot into the air just to get the invader moving, and that would be that. The dogs might chase after their victim, but Ed had trained them not to bite hard. It wasn't that he was afraid of being sued for inflicting dog bites on a transient, but there was still a core of human decency within Ed that prevented him from inflicting any unnecessary pain, even on those who violated his rights.

This time was different, though. There was a disturbing edge to his emotions tonight. His finger pressed against the shotgun's trigger. He realized, with a distant shock, that he was prepared to blow away anything that made a move toward him, man or beast.

The dogs felt it, too. Ahead, they salivated, and Ed sensed he would not be able to call them off if they attacked. In fact, none of them felt any comforting restraint. Tonight, Ed and his children were out for blood.

The children stayed together. That bothered Ed; usually they fanned out. They must have hold of something big to be confident enough to bunch up like that. Ed could feel it too. This wasn't just some transient or town kid. This was something bigger. Something different. Something . . . *deadly*.

They covered the expanse of gravel in no time and

79

plunged into the labyrinth. The lights of civilization were left behind. Shadows twisted around them. Dark forms towered to unknown heights.

Jesus, I hate this, he thought. Everything was going too fast. He should call the children back, try to calm them down. *But I can't even calm myself down. No way. We gotta catch up with whatever's out here and be done with it.* The shotgun felt strong in his hands.

Darker and darker. Ed kept catching himself hunched over when there was nothing above him but the night sky.

Going too fast, damn it!

There were stars in the sky, but not a single piece of junk reflected it. The towers repelled the light, or maybe sucked it up like some black hole. And with every step, every moment deeper into the darkness, Ed grew more certain of a horrible belief: that the junk closing in around them was *alive*—that the yard was breathing.

Should have put lights up out here years ago.

"Goddammit," he snapped out loud. "You've been through this maze a thousand times on nights when you couldn't even see your hand in front of your face 'cause of the fog. What the hell's *wrong* with you?"

His children glanced at him. Beau whined. When they realized their master was just releasing some of the strain they themselves felt, they turned again and continued on.

Still too fast.

Ed was frightened. He was also confused and disoriented. But he knew the yard like he knew a good drink, and when that knowledge came back to him, he became aware that his children were leading him back toward the front gate: they had been going in circles.

He called them to a stop when they were still in the shadows of the junk towers. They could see the concrete shelter across the clearing. An orange and flickering white light fought for control of the room: the lamp and TV. A well-known sportscaster spoke over the distance, echoed faintly in the junk behind them.

Ed warmed to that familiar spot, but he didn't move toward it. Instead he looked down—and his mouth fell open.

The Dobermans pointed at the wooden shed far to the

left, where even the street lights didn't reach. They were motionless except for their noses, which twitched and spit steam into the air.

"What is it, boys? What've you got?" Only Beau looked back at him, and whined with uncertainty. Ed gave him a pat on the flanks to let him know everything would be okay.

His hand froze above the black fur when master and children heard a sound. Grating, unnatural. Something scraping slowly through the grain of the wooden shed.

Now all three Dobermans were whining. Ed stood erect again. The shotgun's barrel pointed in front of him, his trigger finger begging to pull. He felt three pairs of eyes turn to him, awaiting a decisive order.

He nearly called out—but something told him that it would not help, would probably scare off whatever was there. *But that's what I want, right? To get whatever that is off my property.*

Still, there was a powerful streak of curiosity in Ed Kelton; that same curiosity that long ago made him take chances on the stock market and real estate, just to see what would happen; that same curiosity that made him follow a pretty young woman around his junior college until he found out her name and dated her and married her; that very same curiosity that brought him to the edge of ruin, and made a man wonder just how much alcohol it took to wash the real world away. His curiosity, forever young, drove him forward with only his gun and children to protect him.

They weren't enough.

There was no other way to approach the shed than by crossing the clearing that separated the shelter from the junk. It was about twenty feet across, just a few seconds of breathing space before reaching the front gate. But to Ed and his children, with each careful footfall punctuated by the grating shriek of split wood, the expanse was an endless, desolate desert. They were exposed. Ed was sure he would die out here if he didn't hurry—yet, if he hurried, he might walk into something . . .

Beau growled, startling Ed into a faulty step. He slipped, recovered, but the break was enough to make him come to a full stop. The dogs backed up a bit to stay near him. They

remained between him and the shed. All three were growling—a sound so low that Ed felt it in his feet more than he
heard it.

The shed was silent for a long while. Ed began to believe
that whatever had been there was now gone. But then the
horrible *screeeeee* came back, running ants up Ed's spine, and
he knew then and there that the thing was waiting for them.
It *wanted* to be found.

"All right," Ed whispered to his children. They moved
forward again, faster this time, their eyes ever watchful.
The tearing sounds came closer together, darting from
around the left side of the shed, near the brick wall that
joined the iron gate. Ed steered his party in a wide arc, so
they wouldn't have to round the sharp corner of the shed to
meet their prey.

The dogs were excited, their whines long gone. Ed's own
breath was ragged with fear-laced determination. The shotgun's trigger was warm against his skin; it comforted him.

They stopped about five feet from the shed. The back was
revealed to them; though shrouded in darkness, Ed thought
he could make something out, a hunched figure about
waist-high. The dogs' growls grew to ferocious barks. Spittle
flew across the gap, into the shadows—but the dogs would
not move forward for the attack without their master's
order.

Ed raised his gun to his chest and aimed at the hunched
figure. "Come out now," he hollered, though he knew the
thing didn't understand him. "Come out or I'll kill you!"

The figure did exactly the opposite. It moved farther back
along the length of the shed, disappearing around the other
corner. It did not fall completely out of sight, however; its
shadow, elongated by the street light somewhere far behind
it, fell against the ground there, and went still. The creature
was waiting there, perhaps in the hope that Ed would follow
it.

Ed stopped. The shadow was disturbing: a black lump
with static hair springing out at uneven areas. Nothing
really could be made of it. It could be an animal or some
lunatic wild boy in a heavy coat. Anything.

Then it turned slowly, to its profile stretching across the
dark earth. A snout. Low brow. Sharp, short ears. And

teeth that dripped when the mouth opened.

"Jesus," Ed breathed. The dogs were going wild now. Every ferocious outburst shook them closer to the shed. A few more minutes and they wouldn't wait for their master's order.

"Hold!" he called. The dogs didn't even turn to look at him, just kept on barking. "Hold, dammit! Get back here! Beau!" Beau glanced at him, then joined his brothers again in their fury.

Ed grumbled. The scene had lost its intensity; now he was merely irritated that he couldn't control his usually well-behaved children. He'd have to get their attention the hard way. He raised a hand to swat Terror on the butt.

That's when real terror turned on him, and Ed's reign of his kingdom came to an end.

Black globs—that's all he saw—fell from the shed's roof. One large, bristly mass slammed onto Terror's back. Ed heard the dog's spine snap with teeth-jarring clarity. There wasn't even enough time for a painful cry to escape Terror's mouth. Two smaller creatures descended on Death. He managed to throw one and ground his teeth into the leg of the other. Mixed screams filled the night: low rumbles, ghostly howls, and long, prolonged squeaks that drove Ed to cover his ears. Death and the creature on his back danced in circles. The dog's forepaws came up intermittently to push away the other creature that had recovered. All the while he shook his head violently, trying to rip the dark creature's leg from its body, to throw it, to rip it into pieces. He might have done it, might even have escaped, if the large black creature that had broken Terror's back hadn't come into the picture. It rushed Death like a crazed animal. A heartbeat later its teeth were into Death's throat, tearing chunks away until there was nothing but thin red strings covering the bone. Death fell over and disappeared beneath the creatures who suckled his wounds.

It was over in seconds. Two of Ed's children wiped out before his very eyes, and he didn't even have time to raise his shotgun. Rage surged in him, combating with fear for control of his body. His eyes burned; he hadn't blinked in ages. A scream deep inside of him soared to the surface:

What the fuck is going on?

83

He raised the shotgun and aimed at the larger of the creatures. It raised its head. Ed winced at the tendons that hung from its mouth, taut, as the ends were still connected to the dog. Then Ed lost all conscious thought. He just aimed, took a breath to steady his hands, and pressed the trigger.

He pushed the gun up just in time. Beau — sweet, noble Beau, the best of his children — ran across his sights, into the midst of the feeding demons. He jumped the larger one and sank his teeth into its neck. His paws slipped against the creature's back, trying to find purchase. Its frenzied grasping pushed dark, greasy hair away, exposing the malformed bumps of the thing's spine that pressed up against its gray-splotched skin. Beau whined a bit at the sight of the muscles that bulged around those bumps. Yet he struggled on; his jaws were clamped so tight around the back of that beast's neck that not even a crowbar could have separated the two animals.

The creature whipped him around viciously. Beau bounced from one side to the other of his victim's back. The two smaller beasts tried to aid their brethren, but the dance was so wild that they couldn't get close enough for a good bite. It was like watching some rodeo clowns attempting to catch a rider on a wild bronco: the rider was still hanging on, but there was no denying he was in trouble.

Ed brought the muzzle of his shotgun down again. If he couldn't get a good shot at the big one, he'd take out the two smaller ones. Then he and Beau would rip up the bronco together, rip him into a million goddamn pieces . . .

Except that Ed forgot that there were more than three of the creatures. The fourth, as large as the one Beau fought, the one that had drawn them in with its shadow, had continued around the shed during the commotion and made its way behind the man with the gun. It rushed at him now; it was lean from many hungry days but possessed a ferocious strength. Ed didn't hear its roar until the weight crashed into him from behind.

The gun went off. Clear miss. Ed rolled, kept rolling, to put distance between himself and the attacker. He hit the edge of the shed. Pain lanced up his side, but he ignored it. The terror was enough. His hands felt coldly empty — the shotgun was gone, twisting into the darkness. Ed's vision stopped spinning long enough to watch the huge creature — bigger than any of the Dobermans — roll off its side where it had landed, stirring up a windstorm of dust, and jump back on its feet.

Blood-red eyes narrowed on Ed. It charged. Ed's vision spiralled into an expanding black maw crowned by deadly teeth.

He screamed.

Through the pain and the tortured cries, there must have still been a sense in Beau that told him his master was in trouble. Without a thought of the consequences, Beau let loose of his quarry, scrambled for balance on the gravel, and bolted. He hammered into the thing rushing Ed and sent them both flying. They rolled around each other, a vicious dance that spit dust and howls into the air. Then they were up and facing each other. Their lips curled back into snarls. Saliva and blood pooled between them.

Ed took advantage of the respite. He was up and running as best he could. Pain exploded in his right leg. It was torn pretty bad; when he brought his hand up from it, his fingers were painted a glistening red. He wouldn't get far this way. Already he was stumbling about. Worse, the yard was spinning, his stomach too. If he passed out . . .

But protection was near. He was at the front of the shed, leaning against the door for support. Once inside he could push something up against the door and hope for the best.

But what if the damn thing is locked up? Was there anything in there worth locking up — besides me? In his delirium, he couldn't remember. Panic screamed in his head.

The door opened when he pushed, and he fell in with a sob of relief. The fall took the wind out of him, but he continued to move, afraid the darkness would overtake him before he was safely hidden. He had to get his legs pulled in, close the door, before the creatures came around that corner. Seconds, if that. He grunted, cried out, pushed and sweated until his body ached to rest. When he was in, his panic renewed: he couldn't find anything large enough to push against the door. His big, bony body would have to do the job.

He lay there with his eyes closed for a long time. Eventually, blood stopped pounding so noisily in his ear, and he could hear the dying screams of another. Through the uneven cracks of the wall to his left, he looked out on the battleground he'd barely escaped. He watched, helpless, as the beasts—two large ones and two about half the size—concentrated on the only prey in sight: Beau. Poor, sweet, brave Beau. Ed screamed his name over and over, until his voice was hoarse and the sobs clutched at his throat.

The creatures were merciless. Beau had been getting the best of the beast that had attacked Ed, but he was no match for the onslaught of the other three. Beau fought back valiantly; his teeth flashed and pulled black meat from the hairy mounds over and over. But then his attacks turned desperate, and soon after his roar rose into a painful, prolonged scream. Four black forms descended on him. Beau's agony soared above them as he disappeared from view. Scaled tails, like giant worms, whipped about as deformed muzzles buried themselves in the body.

In the end, the yard settled into a quiet wet chewing sound. Ed had turned away from the image. He kept up a light knocking against the shed wall with one bloody fist. That and his choked sobs kept the feeding sound from his ears.

Terror. Death. And finally Beau. All gone. In less than five minutes.

The junkyard had opened up into hell.

At the thought, the creatures looked up from their meal. Ed knew they sensed him nearby. He would be next. At this point, he would gladly go. He wanted desperately to escape the pain of his loss and his injuries.

But the beasts were no longer interested in him. Ed watched as one large creature grabbed Beau's open corpse and dragged him away, into the depths of what was now their kingdom. The other big one scurried over to the remains of Terror—still recognizable, though his broken spine twisted him into an unnatural shape—and likewise pulled the dog away. This one limped slightly, due to the injuries Beau had inflicted on the back of his neck.

Death's ravaged remains took several trips by the two smaller demons. When the last piece of meat was carried away, the two larger creatures returned. They looked out

86

over the bog of blood before them, their noses working fast. Then they began the careful process of kicking dirt onto the puddles. Minutes later, they surveyed the scene once more. There was still evidence of a deadly battle—tufts of black hair, dots of blood, even a dog tooth Ed could see from his vantage—but the beasts seemed satisfied. They lurched into the shadows, their tails slithering behind them like obedient white worms.

The night continued on in silence.

The shed that had never held anything worthwhile now sheltered a single human life. Ed lay there, planted with his back against the raw wood, and waited for death. He willed it. He prayed for it. But it never came. Whatever God there was in the universe, He would make sure that Ed Kelton remained among the living long enough to experience every facet of his only lifelong companion: loneliness.

He awoke the next morning, still weak. He managed to crawl from the shed and make his way to the concrete shelter. There, he ate and drank and rested the whole day. He didn't call anyone. He never went to the hospital. He knew he was not a respected man in this community, and if he even hinted at such a wild tale . . .

Not even Beau's tooth, which he'd recovered from the battleground, would convince anyone. Especially the goddamned worthless sheriff. He was as certain of this as he was of what made a good drink.

A good drink. His only comfort. It was natural that he fell into it with abandon. He never forgot that night he lost his children—they haunted his dreams every night, and brilliant, crimson scenes would flash before his eyes during the day, scenes that only a good drink could wash away—but the junkyard became less important to him. He learned to avoid it in life as he wished he could in memory.

He stayed home.

He talked to no one.

Six months passed before he lived again. He remembered that morning when he'd awakened dying for a drink, gone to his wallet, and found it empty. Out of money. He'd have to go to the bank. But he couldn't get himself dressed. It was more than clumsy, it was physically impossible.

So he lay there on his bed, unable to even move out of

the sunlight hammering through the open window . . . and slowly some coherent thoughts eased through the haze. There was some pain along with those thoughts, but not too bad.

He never went to the bank. He stayed in the house for weeks, eating whatever was left in the cupboards and refrigerator. He stumbled through some calisthenics in front of the TV until, a week and a half later, he began to notice some ease in them. Always, he managed to live without going to the bank; though he was improving, he knew that if he had some money in his hand, he would spend it on some shiny bottles of amnesia.

The pain returned, but he found different ways of handling it. Mostly exercise. Running, jumping, push-ups, sit-ups, until his heart was hammering the memories away.

Now, as he lay in bed and replayed the nightmare of that night again, his body barely stirred. Some part of his heart still ached for the loss, but it was redirected into anger and determination.

Soon. It would have to be soon. He wanted to return to the junkyard and the daylight. He wanted to be able to hold money in his hand again and walk past a liquor store without stopping. And there was only one way he could do that.

He would have to purge the demons from his property, as he'd purged them from his body. Six months ago he had thought he would be able to fend off the Devil himself with a twelve-gauge and his three children at his side.

He had been wrong. Horribly wrong.

But this time, he'd be ready.

This time, *they* would be destroyed.

Wednesday

Larry Santino woke that morning thinking of Rhonda Banes, the pretty brunette in his Health Science class. He'd been looking to each new school day as a chance to get to know the fifteen-year-old beauty better. They were at the talking-and-shy-flirting stage, and Larry figured that in a week or two he'd get a sign whether he should ask her out or not. It looked good. He wondered if maybe he wasn't going to get lucky this time out. All he could say to that was, It's about goddamn time!

The thought of getting lucky gave rise to other thoughts. Before long, in his half-sleep haze, he felt his erection press against the sheets. He resisted the temptation to touch it. It was kinda nice just to lie there with his eyes closed, imagining the things he'd give his left nut to do with Rhonda. Touching himself would make the dreams end too soon — not to mention the mess he'd have to clean up. Better to just lay there and *imagine* for a while . . .

The fantasies were reaching a climax when Larry's mother walked into his room. Fortunately his door was closed, so he heard it swing across the rug in time to flip over onto his belly and hide his dreams. He resisted the groan that came with the move; to lie flat on his stomach, he nearly broke his pecker off at the shaft. Even with his mother well in the room now, he took a moment to check himself out. It was still there, still throbbing, only bent to one side and growing more and more painful.

He covered his embarrassment with a long and angry: "Mom!"

His mother was short, dark-skinned, thanks to her South

89

American background, with clear green eyes that were always wide behind her thick glasses. She was in her early forties, but she appeared much older, with her gray hair, creased face, and plump frame. Larry still shrilled at those occasions when someone mistook her for his grandmother; fortunately she didn't leave the house much anymore. She usually traveled outside by moving inside: she was always in a trance, exploring some interesting place or event inside her head. Or maybe just wishing to forget everything around her.

She was in this trance when she walked into Larry's room, so didn't comment on what she hadn't seen. Still, Larry's embarrassment and anger at being interrupted without a knock forced him to continue.

"Mom!"

She stopped, snapped back to her house and her son's room. Green irises blinked at him through the glasses. Larry thought you could hang those eyes on a Christmas tree, they were so damned big.

"Mom," he said again, this time more whiny than angry.

"What?"

What, indeed, he thought. *Um . . .* "You . . . you woke me up!"

"Oh." She frowned — Larry recognized it as such only because the creases around her mouth deepened — and that was all. She then busied herself ripping the sheets from his bed.

"Hey!" he called. He didn't have to check to know he still wasn't calmed over Rhonda yet. He clutched at the sheets.

"I have to wash these, Larry," his mother scolded.

"I'm still in them."

"Get up. You'll be late for school."

"I still got time."

She pulled at the sheet until he let go. "Get up!"

Larry hopped out of bed, really steaming now, grabbed the pile of clean clothes he always set next to his bed the night before, held them close to hide his crotch, and stormed out of the room.

"You're supposed to knock before coming in!" he called over his shoulder.

His mom didn't answer. She was off on another trip

somewhere. He tried to think back; was she always like this, or was it a change after Dad was gone? He wasn't sure. He'd never paid attention to things like that before.

So why waste time with it now?

He hurried on.

In the shower, Rhonda was forced from his mind by other concerns. His best friend, his pal since day one, had been acting kind of weird lately. Well, not actually weird; it wasn't like Larry hadn't seen this sort of thing in Mark before. Mark always felt guilty about being caught for some less-than-honorable action. He didn't have the creative skills and brash balls it takes to make a plan come off. Larry did, and he knew that the *last* thing you'd better worry about is getting caught, or that's exactly what would happen. Larry believed in creating your own future, and accordingly he believed that if Mark didn't get his act together by Friday night, they might have some trouble.

Trouble with Mark was nothing new, either. They'd always had their fights. All friends do. The proof of their friendship was that they could muddle their way through it and still stand each other.

This year had been a little different though. Even Larry, in his headfirst rush through life, felt a change. Like Mark, the born follower, exerting himself just a little bit. Like Mark's guilt getting the better of him. Like Mark leaving his best friend hanging at the Pit last night. Larry could feel the approach of that time when Mark's guilt would overpower any argument Larry could think up to convince him. The good old days were dying.

It shook the hell out of him. He stood in the shower, eyes closed, the spray hitting his face with a calming pressure. For a moment he wondered if this was what his mother felt when she went travelling in her head.

Then, as he stood there, enclosed, sticky-warm, a cold thought slithered through.

I'm losing him.

They were drifting, he and Mark, drifting in different directions and unable to paddle closer together. Mark's rejection of him last night at the Pit was, to Larry, an indication of betrayal. Where could they go from there but apart? Jesus, it was just like Nick and Ray when Pauline

91

came into the picture. Not that he blamed Pauline. It could have been any prying woman. And he'd seen the change in Nick immediately — what Larry liked to call the "Yes, Dear" syndrome also known as being "whupped." Ray did his best to keep up the friendship; it was Nick who let it go, probably at that bitch Pauline's insistence. They were still friendly toward each other, Larry reminded himself . . . but that wasn't the same as being friends. Not anywhere close.

From then on, Larry swore he wouldn't let it happen between Mark and himself. Not that it was likely. There were too many years there, too many adventures and guilty secrets they shared. They *needed* each other. Not even a woman could come between that. So far it had proved out: they'd each had a couple of dates this year — well, semi-dates, nothing big — and Larry hadn't detected any change. Hell, friends were supposed to grow *closer* with stories and lies about their girlfriends. Nick must have just fucked it all up.

So why am I so worried now, when there's not even a woman involved?

He knew why. Because it involved him directly. Mark was upset about something he'd done. Somehow, he felt, Mark must believe that good ol' Larry had betrayed him.

So go talk to him, stupid. Work it out. Whatever it takes.

The thought's calming effect surprised him. Maybe he was just being paranoid. After all, there're a lot of problems to deal with when you're a teenager. Maybe that's all this was. Maybe Mark just needed someone to talk to. Maybe this Friday night stunt was putting too much burden on him when he had other problems to worry about. Certainly, if his best friend asked, Mark would spill the beans. Who else could he trust?

The scenario put a different spin on the day. Larry actually felt a degree of relief. Out of the shower, dressed, he managed to avoid his mom before leaving the house. He had neither a lunch nor lunch money. His mom always told him to fix it himself, there was plenty of stuff in the kitchen, but he didn't want to waste time with it. He was never hungry around noon, anyway. He preferred to spend lunch doing exercises in the school yard, trying to find the muscle hidden around his skin-and-bone frame. Rhonda Banes might appreciate an improved stature.

During the lunch period at noon, Pauline Martinez realized she had made a mistake. She'd made plans that morning to talk with her friend Monica Evans, They'd been friends since fifth grade, when Monica had spilled turpentine all over Pauline's watercolor painting, a work of art Pauline later admitted was wretched, and the latter girl had broken into tears. They'd had lunch together that day, and after Monica finished apologizing profusely, they began to find out they had a lot in common. In particular, they liked the same boys. There was never any competition between them, for they were truly friends, but there were times Pauline felt a little uncomfortable talking about her feelings for a certain boy when she knew Monica felt the same.

Fortunately, Monica had never shown any interest in Nick — a fact that hadn't bothered Pauline in the least, until today. Now there was a good chance she would find out *exactly* what Monica thought of Nick: she had arranged a meeting with Monica after school to tell, or at least hint, about the Friday night she suspected Nick had planned. Exactly what Monica would say to the idea was up in the air — and the fact that she wasn't certain what her friend would say made Pauline extremely nervous.

At noon, that worry gave way to guilt, for she suddenly remembered that she'd already made plans with Ray for after school. They were supposed to study algebra together. Dumb mistake. But what else could she expect with so many crazy things happening this week?

She admitted to herself now that her reason for studying with Ray had not been to better her math skills — she really could not care less about algebra since models and nurses, her chosen professions, never use stupid algebra. She had really wanted to pump some impressions of Nick.

This bothered her, too. If she didn't trust Nick, why was she going out with him? If she wasn't certain he was a nice guy, maybe the *right* guy, why was she even considering being intimate with him?

The answer was immediate and direct; Monica had stated the facts to her the weekend after Pauline's first disastrous indiscretion: *When it comes to sex, girl, the nicest guys in the world can become the biggest jerks in the world; they will lie, steal, and hurt even themselves to get in your pants*.

Words to live by. And Pauline *had* been living by them. Yet there had been those times when she'd thought she'd found that panacea called love that would transform even the worst scoundrel into a Prince Charming—until after she'd slept with him. There was no greater pain in her book than to see strangers leering at her in the hallway and knowing with certainty that her Prince Charming had gabbed. Always, this was followed by the dump, sometimes placed on her gently, other times thrown on her with a snarl.

Experience did not go ignored, even at the age of seventeen. It was much easier to play the waiting game. If a guy left her because she wouldn't consent to sex, to hell with him. He was a shit, then, anyway, no matter how cute. And, though it had resulted in quite a few lonely Saturday nights, at least she hadn't seen a leer in the hallway lately.

And yet the question remained: What about Nick? Why didn't she make it clear to him that this Friday night would just have to be another date? Why did she feel the need to pump Ray for more information? It wasn't right. The only excuse she had was that Nick was the nicest, gentlest, most gentlemanly guy she'd ever been out with. He didn't even try to kiss her on their first date.

And, somehow, all of this worried her.

She had to be careful. A talk with Monica now seemed a necessity. Things always looked clearer when she volleyed information with her friend.

And that, unfortunately, meant she would have to break her meeting with Ray.

She was sure he'd understand.

She found him sitting against a wall in the shade, munching on a sandwich. Ray liked to sit alone and watch the birds descend on those more daring souls who ate their lunches in the middle of the yard. When he saw how irritated his classmates became over those damn birds, it somehow made him feel loftier, height being so important to

94

one lacking it. So the intrusion on his much-needed entertainment was unwelcome and he tried to ignore it.

Until he recognized the legs.

He stood before Pauline could sit next to him. The hurried action dumped his lunch bag upside down and splayed its contents against the concrete. Ray ignored it, hoping it would stifle his embarrassment, but when he turned to face Pauline, she had disappeared, bent over to pick up his lunch.

He was so flustered by this that he didn't help her. When she had it all in hand and in the bag again, she straightened and gave it to him. Only her smile and easy tone managed to calm him somewhat.

"Hi, Ray. Sorry about that."

"That's okay."

"I wanted to talk to you about our meeting today—"

"Yeah," he said hurriedly, "I told my mom I might be a little late getting home—unless you wanted to go to my house . . ." He broke off when he saw the change in her expression.

"I'm sorry," she said. "I can't make it. I really do need help on my algebra, so maybe we can find another day soon."

"The test is next week."

"I know. Maybe early next week. I'm sure I could make it then." She paused. She found herself searching for words to fill the silence between them. "You could come over to my house, we could lay everything on the coffee table, have two big mugs of soda, and get to work. I really could use your help on it," she added lamely. Her fingers brushed his arm, as if willing some resolve.

Ray's lips, which had been moving for some time, finally formed words. "Is it something bad that you have to—"

"No."

"—something I could help you with, if you're in trouble—"

"No, nothing like that. I just have to talk to Monica about some stuff. It's important."

Monica. He knew Monica. He'd met her a couple times when she and Pauline were hanging out. He wanted to blame her for his disappointment, but he knew that would

95

be unfair. He could see by Pauline's expression that something important had come up. Some girl thing.

"Well, that's okay," he said, and smiled. "We can do it next week. No biggie."

Her face lit up, all burdens lifted. He felt dashing and duped at the same time.

"Great," Pauline said. "I'll talk to you about it Monday. We can make plans." She touched his arm again, gave it a reassuring squeeze.

He nodded, agreed. Pauline thanked him and turned to leave. It was then, when she turned her back to him and started moving away, something surged within him, some emotion he couldn't control. It called for some release, kept screaming to him, *She's going! She's going! Quick!* He stammered for words.

"Uh, Pauline . . ."

She stopped and faced him. Waiting.

Oh, shit, Ray, don't blow this for Nick. Still, a part of him . . .

"Um, you're going out with Nick this Friday, right?"

She nodded and stepped closer. Her arms folded gracefully over her breasts. A clear sign of concern lined her smooth face. Still waiting.

What? What are you going to say now, idiot? Tell her not to go with Nick anymore just because he wants to — oh, hell, Nick would kill you!

His mouth was very dry, so he swallowed a couple of times. His eyes wandered to the birds beyond Pauline's shoulder. They swooped and buzzed around in a blur. He had a tough time bringing his eyes back to her again.

He breathed once and said, "He's really a nice guy, Pauline. I would tell you if he wasn't. I wouldn't let him . . ." He couldn't think of anything more that wouldn't sound silly. He shrugged.

Her features softened. "I know, Ray. I know you would. Thanks." She met his eyes for a while longer, then smiled fully, said a quick "Bye," and walked away.

He didn't watch her go. He sat and burrowed into his lunch. His gaze traveled across the open field. The birds were very active today. Half the kids were already retreating to the cafeteria.

Hey, did you see that look she gave you? an errant thought whispered. *Maybe she likes you, Ray.*
Oh, shut up!

Larry met Mark in the hall between their third period classes, as they did each school day. Mark didn't avoid him, but he seemed distinctly uncomfortable—which was frustrating for Larry since he had spent the day convincing himself that everything would be all right between them.

"You're going to the Pit after school, right?" said Larry. "Nick wants us to help him out." He couldn't resist adding, "Maybe you weren't there when Nick mentioned that yesterday."

"I don't remember. I don't think I can, though . . ."

"Why not?" Larry shot. He was surprised to find he'd been expecting that answer, and that his reply had been poised since their greeting.

"I've got stuff to do at home."

"What stuff? You never have stuff to do at home. Your old man does everything for you."

"He does not. He's not even home when I get home."

"So what have you got to do?"

"Just, you know, clean up and stuff."

Larry wanted to go on badgering him—he knew Mark was lying and he wanted him to at least admit it—but there was too much working against him: the crowd, the haste of their pace, the warning bell for their next classes.

"Well, look," he said, "just . . . just call me or something. Maybe we can meet there later."

"Maybe tomorrow."

"Yeah, okay. Tomorrow. We can prepare for Friday."

"See you," Mark called, and disappeared into the crowd.

Larry felt a cold heaviness in his belly. Nothing felt right anymore. He stood in the middle of the corridor, ignoring the swarm of students around him. He tried to get his mind to think this out straight, but it was still all too jumbled. Mark hadn't actually blown him off, but . . . He was probably scared of getting caught Friday night, yet . . . A seed of chicken shit in his friend, that's all, though . . .

Maybe tomorrow.

Yeah, sure. Larry thought hard. What was it? As far as he could tell, Mark wasn't avoiding him. In fact, he was only avoiding the junkyard and any talk of the place. Therefore, he was afraid of the plan. That was all. He didn't want to go through with it. Chicken shit. Not all that surprising, especially considering that Nick's ultimatum on their friendship had been pretty harsh. Something like that was bound to get to Mark.

So, Larry figured, all he had to do was cancel the plan for Friday night. Nothing simpler. Except . . .

. . . except he couldn't do it. Dammit, it was a good plan. One of his best. A capper. The kind that he and Mark had enjoyed a million times in the past and should be enjoying now.

So what the hell's going on? Why does he suggest these great ideas, then make me feel guilty when I make them work?

Because he's a fucking psycho, that's why.

No, that was too pat, even for him. Not psycho. He considered it, and decided that Mark was just being immature. Mark would never take on the responsibility that Larry always grappled with. Mark always left him to supply the details and implement them. And then, when it was presented with the final touches, Mark would scowl and turn in shame. As if he could ever come up with something half as lavish—

Then it erupted in his mind:

Ah! Jealousy!

That brought him back to the real world and got his legs moving toward his next class. Jealousy. Of course. All those years of inspired but formless suggestions, and it always took good ol' Larry to make them concrete and perfect. Mark could never do it alone. There would always be that dependence . . .

The expansion of this theory into a realistic explanation demanded Larry's full attention. In his last class of the day, when the teacher called on him for an answer, he stared past her with a glazed expression for several seconds before realizing everyone was watching him. A few snickers sprang up. He reddened and said simply, "I don't know," even though he didn't know what the question was. He never did hear the answer, for his thoughts fell immediately back to formulating.

By the time the bell rang, announcing the end of school for that day, he had every answer he needed except the final, important one: How to get the old Mark back. Cancel the Friday night plan? Out of the question. Larry's dignity would be irreparably damaged. Besides, Mark would keep doing the same thing every time buddy Larry came up with the means of pulling off a great one. Pretty soon, Mark would think he could control him.

There was a hope left, though. Mark hadn't pulled out of the plan yet. He might still go through with it — and enjoy it. Then his confidence in his friend and himself would be returned.

But as he walked across the quad, Larry knew deep down that that was a false hope. It was obvious that Mark was uncomfortable with the whole thing. By Friday, he'd be dead set against it, and if Larry *made* him go through with it, he might ruin it on purpose just to spite him.

So, despite the revolutionary brain use Larry had put to the problem, not much had changed. He was still confused and frustrated, and it all bubbled up into an angry energy. He put his thoughts aside. It was imperative that he get rid of the energy soon or risk blowing up at the first passerby who looked at him wrong — a tragedy that happened occasionally, and usually led to an additional fight with his mother.

The anger surged, blotting his face with warm pricks, as he waited at the corner for the light to change. When it hit green, he let loose.

There was no pacing or steady breathing; he ran to let off steam, hoping that his emotions would tire themselves out pumping his heart and muscles. When his grunts became frustrated growls, and a scream began to rise within him, he ran harder, picked up speed. His breath became a wheezy pant, but he continued on at the same rate.

He quickly outdistanced any of the other kids walking home. He was alone on the sidewalk. The brittle wind scraped across his temples, to tear his long hair back. Larry knew that if he kept it up his face would be rubbed red raw, but the high he felt burning away all that energy and the liberating *speed* that carried him away from the school and the other kids and into this desolate world of his own—the combination was just too pure to give up.

Until he reached the junkyard.

He would have rushed right through the iron gates if he hadn't seen the police cruiser approaching. Instead, he gradually changed direction so that he was moving along the yard's side, on King Street. He wanted to look back to see if the police car would follow him around the corner, but the squeal of wheels from behind told the story. He slowed his run to a jog and tried to look casual—an impossible act when he was hot, sweaty, and clutching every lungful of air.

He knew the officer wouldn't just pass him. With his long hair and torn T-shirt and jeans, he was the kind of kid who might just as well carry a sign reading: TROUBLE. The car pulled up next to him, close to the curb, and slowed to match his speed. Larry cut to a lazy walk. The car shot ahead a little, then matched his pace again. Larry tried not to look at it.

The passenger window came down. A voice called.

"Hey."

Larry glanced at the lone officer in the car. He looked familiar, but that wasn't strange; Larry had been stopped by just about all the officers of Winsome. He nodded to the man, kept his eyes forward. The officer leaned over the passenger seat to get a better look.

"Where you headed?" the officer asked.

"Home." He was still breathing hard; even the single word was difficult to get out clearly.

"Home, huh? What're you running from?"

Not *What are you running for?*, but *from*. As in: "You've committed a crime and were caught running *from* it."

"I'm not . . . running *from* . . . anything," he said between breaths.

"You want a ride?"

This couldn't help but draw Larry's attention. When was the last time a police officer had offered him a ride? Never. They just hassled him a while, then left. So what was this guy up to? He stared into the car's shadows, but could only make out the outline of the guy. He thought of stopping and approaching the car, but the authority in that black and white vehicle repelled him.

In any case, the last thing he needed was to be brought home to his mom in a police car. Even if she didn't see, the neighbors would.

He said, "Naw, I'm almost home."

"Oh, come on," the officer said, sounding friendly. "I drive the same damn route hour after hour and I'm getting bored to death. Let me drive you home so I can see some different scenery."

Really pushing, Larry thought. It chilled him. *I wonder if it's a good idea to turn this guy down. An angry cop can be a real pain.* Still, just the idea of riding home in a police vehicle was against his nature.

"I'm okay. Thanks," He tried to sound sincere. He even offered a smile.

"You sure?" said the officer. The car pulled a little closer to the curb. Larry thought the wheels might jump it, so he moved closer to the chain link fence. "If you're almost home," added the officer, "it wouldn't be too much out of my way. You could listen to the police line, too."

Larry bristled, irritated. *What the hell? Is this guy some sort of pervert, or what? Picking up little kids for deviant reasons. That's it. Maybe all those kids gone missing around here went for a ride with this guy. Yeah, Larry, why don't you just tell the officer that. Go ahead.*

He almost did snap, "Leave me alone!" but he let the words pass as breath. He shook his head and looked forward again. "No thanks, *sir.* I'll be okay."

"You like to run, huh?"

He's not giving up, Larry, my friend. He's going to keep bugging you till he has you in his trunk—or he's in your trunk, if you know what I mean . . .

Larry just nodded, oddly disturbed by the amusing thoughts.

"Not running from anyone, are you? No one's chasing you?"

Ah. The man's a cop after all.

"No, sir. I just like to run."

"I see." And without a word of parting, the window rolled up and the cruiser pulled away. Larry's eyes didn't leave it until it disappeared around the corner. He stopped, surprised that he was still gasping for air. The run couldn't have taken *that* much out of him. Probably just a reaction to that creepy cop. Well, no matter. It was over.

He backtracked, paused at the corner in front of the junkyard to see if the police cruiser had come around the block — it hadn't — then slipped through the iron gate and into the labyrinth. His mind was so occupied that he nearly got turned around at one point, but he eventually found his way to the '64 Pontiac waiting beneath the fortress of black rubber.

In the Pit, he was further surprised to find Ray with Nick. There had been a time, he reflected, when the sight was anything but uncommon; Ray and Nick were once as inseparable as he and Mark. Times change. Still, it was good to see them together again, actually laughing.

Then it struck him that Mark was absent. The same confusion seemed to cross the faces of the other two boys when they saw him enter the Pit alone. Larry felt a pang of guilt and actual pain at that.

Nick was first to recover. "Hey, Lare," he offered in a cheerful voice, "how's it going?"

"Okay. Nearly got stopped by another cop."

"Again?" Ray said. "Jesus, they're always stopping you for nothing."

"I don't even have a car yet." He managed a smile. "Just think of the fun I'll have when I get one."

"You should get your hair cut," Nick offered. He let a grin slip out; his own hair was long in back — though cut around the front and sides — and styled better than Larry's. In fact, Larry's long-everywhere style could only kindly be called "natural."

"You sound like my mom," Larry cracked. "In fact, with your hair, you look a little like her."

Ray busted up. Nick just shook his head, but the grin remained.

Larry came closer. "What's that?"

Nick was fiddling with something. "Hinges," he said. "The final touch on the vent."

"Yeah?" That sly, devious feeling came back to Larry. He always enjoyed that sensation of seeing more of the picture than anyone else. Of course, half the fun was sharing the secret with a friend.

He looked over at Ray. "What're you doing here, small stuff?"

"I came over to help. I know I'm a day late, but I figured you guys wouldn't get everything done in one day."

"Didn't," Nick said. He looked up at them and held the hinges up. "Grab the nails and hammer and let's go."

Ray was just as awed by the view from the Pit's roof as Mark had been the day before. "I wished I'd known about this before," he told the other two. "We should put a lawn chair up here, nail it down somewhere."

"Yeah, couple of brews and watch the sun set," smarted Larry. "Sounds thrilling."

Nick was on his knees. They'd cleared the tires away from the vent again and removed the small door. Nick hammered the hinges into place while Larry steadied the piece of wood across his lap. After a few bent nails and corrected angles, the job was done. They tested it. The hinges squeaked a little — something Larry knew he could fix before Friday — but the vent moved effortlessly. They propped it open with a stick Ray found and stood back to study their creation.

"Looks good, guys," Nick said.

"Perfect," Larry whispered.

"Maybe now we'll get some fresh air in there," Ray remarked.

This last touched a nerve in Larry. He was just thinking that this vent added something nice to his and Mark's place: he always thought of the Pit as his and Mark's place since no one else bothered to use it anymore. Even Nick had to ask them to use it Friday — and Ray *never* used it. The both of them had become more visitors than owners, and it came to Larry that here was a visitor criticizing his host's home. Friend or not, *no one* had a right to insult anything so close to him.

So Larry glared at Ray and quipped, "Never complained about it for four years. Getting a little delicate in your advanced age, Ray?"

Ray demonstrated his "delicacy" with a very strong middle finger in the air. Larry felt himself go red. He forced a grin. "Demonstrating your dick size, Ray?" he said.

"Screw you," Ray answered, but it didn't come out very well. His voice had not changed yet — the only one of the four guys whose voice hadn't — so the words lacked any real power.

"Squeak!" Larry said, laughing. It was just too perfect to pass up. "Squeak! Squeak! We got ourselves a big, fat rat here, Nick."

"Shut up," Ray said gently. He turned away to examine the vent. Larry stayed right behind him.

"Hey, guys," Nick began. "We've still got some tarring to do on that crack."

"Or is it a delicate young vermin we have on our hands, hmmm?" Larry said to Ray's back. "Perhaps . . . a *fe*male! A lady! Have you fooled us all these years, Ray, only to be revealed at puberty? Just so you could get by that ancient 'No Girls' rule of the Pit?" He reached around to Ray's front, up under his shirt. "Is that fat or breasts, R—"

Ray whirled around and slammed Larry's arm away. "What're you doing? *Stop* it!"

"Larry!" Nick growled at the same time. But Nick was far behind them, at the other end of the Pit's roof. He wouldn't interfere in a little razzing. Larry was sure of that. Especially when the victim was so easily upset. It was just too perfect.

Besides, Larry couldn't stop. Everything was rushing by him in a blur, and he couldn't get his hands on any of it. Things were changing too fast. Ray and Nick, he and Mark, school, the corpse he had for a mom — all of it shifting into new shapes that none of his talking and cajoling could control. Now there were very few things he could count on to stay rock solid. Like the junkyard. And the Pit. The Pit wouldn't change unless *he* changed it. Even the vent was his idea, really. And now this little squib, this little baby, was complaining about something he shrugged off and ignored most of the time. Well, goddammit, God *damn* him —

"Say, Ray, that's right. You're not a lady. You're a lady's man! Jesus, how could I have been so stupid? Women crawl all over you, maybe that's why I got confused. Remind me, Ray. When was the last time you had a date?"

Ray nearly gasped. His eyes went wide and his mouth drooped and he might have looked completely frozen if his fingers weren't curling into fists.

Behind them, Nick watched them just as intensely, ready for whatever happened next.

"Or should I ask," Larry said in his trained silky voice, "when was the first time—"

Ray was on him before the last word was released. His small, chubby hands slapped across Larry's throat; they weren't large enough to completely encircle his neck, but they clutched at the two thick stalks on either side of his Adam's apple and *squeezed* with all their strength.

Larry was taken completely by surprise. He might have stood there and let his neck be torn away if Ray hadn't screamed, *"At least I have a fucking dad!"* That was enough to send Larry into blind action. He punched out and grabbed and gouged until he realized he had to get Ray's fingers away from his throat *now* or the Pit's new vent would be decorated in beautiful warm crimson. He brought his arms up and knocked Ray's grip outward and away. Then his own hands were around Ray's throat, pushing the smaller boy back onto a pile of tires.

God, it would be so easy to just squeeze, go on squeezing, watch him turn blue, stiffen out, just let his body relax in my hands and then bury him under the tires . . .

But he heard Nick behind him and knew he didn't have the time. Just seconds. He had to do something. With some effort, he let the memory of his dad's death roll off him and away, so that when he finally spoke, it was with a clear, controlled growl, one that punched right into Ray's soul with its power.

"You'll never see a woman look at you like she wants you, Ray. You'll never enter a room and see a woman's face light up just because you're there. You'll—"

And then it was over. Larry was lifted off his feet by the hand of some terrible god and dropped on his back two yards away, near the edge of the roof. A shadow descended on him. He did his best to control his scream, but a ghostly groan managed to get by. His body was beyond command, folding into an embryonic shell to protect itself.

When Larry looked up, he was eye-to-eye with the devil himself.

"And *you*," Nick hissed caustically, "won't live to see seventeen, you goddamn piece of *shit!*" Then he was up and pulling Larry with him. Larry flew again, pushed across the roof. He bounced off some tires and just saved himself from going over the edge — a fifteen foot drop to the sharp metal of the Pontiac.

"What the fuck's wrong with you?" Nick screamed at him. He took a step toward him, and Larry scrambled to a sitting position. Nick stopped. His hair blazed out in the wind, as if his head was consumed with a black flame. "What is it, Larry?" he called, "Are you drunk? Is that it?"

The rage drained from Larry's body. He sat calmly, exposed, still only a foot from the roof's edge. He couldn't meet Nick's eyes.

"What is it, Lare?" Nick called again.

"I'm just . . . just tired of his whining." He kicked a tire over the edge. "Just tired of it."

Ray's squeaky voice reached him against the rising wind. "I don't whine, you goddamn fatherless scarecrow!"

Larry looked up. "Jesus, Nick, listen to him! He can't even cuss right."

Nick's tone was even again, almost sad. The former rage had either been spent or contained. "I thought you were his friend, Larry."

Larry thought about that for a long time. Friends seemed to be becoming an endangered species lately. Finally he shrugged and said, "Guess so."

"Then what the hell's this all about?"

Larry knew that he'd reason it out till doomsday and he still wouldn't have an answer. So he shrugged again, folded his legs, and watched their reaction. He almost grinned. In a way, this whole scene was familiar: Nick standing up for little Ray. How long since they'd seen *that?*

Nick just stared back, expecting some sort of answer.

"Don't know," Larry supplied.

Nick watched him for a while longer. His expression was hard to read; Larry stopped trying. Ray stood beside Nick until the wind died, then turned and started down the gradual side of the Pit.

"Gotta go, Nick," he said over his shoulder. "I'll talk to you later."

"Tomorrow," Nick called. He still stared death at Larry. "Meet me here tomorrow, okay? We'll hang out. Maybe get

106

the tarring out of the way."

Larry perked up a little at this. He waited until only Ray's head was showing, then called out, "Sorry, Ray." He thought he heard a "Yeah" before Ray disappeared.

A minute passed. Nick approached the other boy, hands on his hips. Larry still sat. He played absently with his shoelaces, not really thinking of anything. Nick dropped to his knees and waited for the other's eyes to meet his.

"I don't understand any of this." Nick said.

"Me neither."

"It's getting cold up here."

Larry looked around. "You wanna hang out in the Pit for a while?"

Nick glanced at the sun, estimating how much daylight they had left. He said, "For a little while, I guess. You can help me put the stuff away."

"Right."

Inside, their tools put away in the chest, Larry sat on the mattress while Nick leaned against the rounded concrete wall.

"Really weird up there, man," Nick said.

Larry had hoped they wouldn't get into that. He changed the subject with: "You know, I think Ray's been upset lately."

"Oh, he has, has he?"

"Yeah. He likes Pauline a lot. He's known her for years."

It was enough to rouse Nick away from the wall. He stood up straight and folded his arms. "Yeah? So?"

"This isn't an attack on Ray or anything, all right? It's just . . . well, I'm not so sure he likes the idea of you and . . . well, you know. This Friday."

Nick took a long time to answer, though not a part of him moved during that time. "Well," he said stiffly, "that's tough. She's dating me, not him. He had a long time to ask her out before I even met her."

"I know. I'm just saying, he's your friend and all—"

"And you just got done trashing him. What are you defending him for, now?"

"I'm not. I mean, Mark likes her too—"

"Oh, Jesus." Nick slumped forward and went to the cooler for a beer. "Look, she and I get along really well. I like her, she likes me. I can't help it if my friends like her too. She can't either. I'm not being mean or anything." He looked to see if Larry wanted a beer. Larry shook his head. Nick closed the cooler and snapped his can open. He took a long pull, licked the froth from his lips. "I can't help how other people feel, Lare. It's not my fault."

"It's not their's either," said Larry.

"Nope. Not anyone's. But I'm not giving up Pauline just to—"

"Hey, no one's asking you to. I'm just telling you what's been going on. I mean, you don't really talk to Ray that much anymore, do you?"

Nick nodded almost imperceptibly. He muttered, "I've got a lot going on," before the beer came up to wash his mouth out.

"Yeah," was all Larry could add.

Nick finished off the can and tossed it into a big plastic trash bag in the corner. He paused to look inside it. "Geez, when's the last time you guys changed this? I'll take it with me when I leave. If you have a beer tonight, Lare, take the can with you."

"Yeah, sure."

"Okay. I'm gonna go now." He paused at the Pontiac's passenger door to look back. "Take care, all right?"

"You, too. See you."

Nick nodded and was gone.

Larry decided to hang around a little. His mom was used to him coming home late; in fact, she barely questioned him at all these days. He pushed the TV over to the mattress and flipped it on. Still early, before prime time. Nothing but game shows. Mark loved game shows; Larry usually let him watch them if there was nothing else on. Sometimes they were okay, if he could volley questions and funny answers with Mark. He sometimes thought they should have their own game show; they sure as hell came up with better answers than any of the TV stuff.

Watching TV alone, though, was a pain. He looked around for something else. Their collection of porno video hits sat nearby. That might be okay, if he cracked open a beer to go with it. But not as fun as joining Mark in hooting jokes at the screen.

Shit! What the hell do I do alone around here?

There was nothing, really. There was no reason to come down to the Pit unless Mark was here and they could joke around together. He might try something new. Maybe grab a beer, slump on the mattress, and wallow in his problems for a couple of hours. But that didn't appeal to him either; he'd never built up an addiction to self-pity.

Nevertheless, some thoughts must have occupied his mind, for when he shook himself out of his trance, the sun was just dipping behind the world and deep shadows were filling the Pit. He looked around. He still lay on the mattress, boxed in by the harsh light of the TV.

Kinda scary being here alone.

Unlike Mark, he could keep thoughts like that from developing into panic. As far as he was concerned, there wasn't a damn thing that existed in the night that didn't in the day; you just couldn't see them as well, was all.

But by the end of the night, he would be able to name at least one.

The pangs of hunger that hit the creature and its brother were like death knells. Still, they waited until the daylight was gone before they ventured out of the hole. In all of their experiences, they had learned at least that. Besides, even the light-gray that pushed through the clouds on stormy days hurt their eyes.

It was dark now, though, and they scurried to the feeding place near the front gate, to see if anything had been left for them. Occasionally it proved out; every few months someone would be kind enough to leave a large mess of raw meat laid out on the gravel. There was never any opposition when they dragged it away. It was like a gift from the gods. The meat would last for a couple of weeks, usually, and during that time they could hunt and build a stock for the future.

But tonight they remained hungry. Of course, the night was young yet. There might be something later.

Unfortunately, they were hungry *now*. They would have

to hunt. The imperative was communicated between them with only a glance and heavy sigh. They then stood back-to-back, these two males, and sniffed the air, slowly twisting their heads back and forth to capture any errant odor that might lead them to an alley cat or stray pet. They stirred, excited, when a powerful odor sprang on them suddenly— then settled when they realized it was only the stench of their sisters. The search continued.

There!

The larger male stiffened. An involuntary groan slipped through his mouth, alerting his brother. They didn't wait for their sisters. They moved. There was little hesitation in determining which path to take; the maze of junk was nothing to them when they had a scent to follow.

The smaller male stopped next to his brother's front haunches when the sound hit them—a caustic sound, slightly irritating to their sensitive ears. They'd heard it many times before and had stored the distinctive wavelength in their small brains. It meant "meat." In reality, the "meat" were two alley cats fighting, and their hissing and spitting had given them away.

The brothers separated, following an almost instinctive attack plan. The alley cats were so busy fighting each other that they were never aware of the greater danger approaching. Then it was too late. They were killed silently and quickly. There was never a chance to warn other cats in the neighborhood that might decide to visit the junkyard.

Some of the meat was devoured on the spot. A rapid *click, click* bounced along the curved walls: claws made for holding, like a chipmunk's hands, and gnawing teeth clattering against the exposed bones. The feeding went on until the initial madness of hunger was assuaged. Then the remains fell between powerful jaws and were carried back to the hole, so that they may feed the One inside.

When the males emerged again, they met with their two sisters, smaller versions of themselves, who had several rats hanging from their mouths. The sisters also disappeared into the hole while the brothers busied themselves cleaning each other. Ten minutes later the four were reunited, and they set out to continue the hunt.

As they journeyed deeper into the yard, their movements

became more swift and sure; their memories and instincts melded and their dark world grew familiar again. They now hesitated only long enough to bring the odors to their brains, or to listen for the dangling of bait.

But then something new greeted them: a discomfort that rose as they moved closer to the yard's center, until, one by one, they came to realize that this area had . . . changed. They usually avoided it. It wasn't anything they could reason with: perhaps the unfavorable stench that surrounded the place, or the sight of those tall black walls with their own stinging odor, or even the mysterious flicker of light from within the structure that hurt their eyes so much. They had never thought it strange they should be repulsed by the smell of beer and garbage. Neither had they bothered to test the place; the yard was large enough that they could ignore the area without diminishing the take of their hunt.

But tonight there was that change. The revulsion was missing. The stench was gone, as was the flickering light within. There was only a pale orange glow slipping between the slivers of the wall—a light that did not hurt them in the least. In fact, it was attractive: soft and warm, suggesting some living creature.

They approached carefully. The smell of the old tires still existed, still disgusted them—but it wasn't enough to hide the new odor that reached across the small clearing. It tickled the very base of their curiosity. It stood them on their hind feet and made their mouths water. It *excited* them.

There was meat in there.

By consenting regard, they separated to investigate. While the three scurried about in the shadows and tried to maintain some distance from the area, the eldest brother dared to approach the Pontiac that bordered the shelter. He paused to sniff the air again. Yes, definitely something in there. Definitely some sort of meat. But there was an undefined aspect that forced caution on the creature.

In the abstract way of his small brain, the brother considered what to do next. There seemed to be no easy entrance to the place—or easy escape. They would have to draw the prey outside, to their turf.

The creature lay his claw against the car, along its well-

111

worn side. He waited for the wind's howl to die down, then slowly scratched the metal. Vestiges of paint curled and fell away as the sharp nails furrowed the surface. The loud *screeeech* didn't bother the creature in the least. He knew, however, that the sound would alert whatever meat lay inside the shelter, and might send it rushing outside.

There was movement. The orange glow was blocked for a moment as some form approached the other side of the tire wall. A voice broke through the cracks: "Nick?"

The elder brother's stomach growled. He quivered with anticipation. The images in his brain fell into place. Yes, he recognized the odor now. It had fooled him before because he had rarely smelled this sort of meat while it was still alive.

But this one was very alive. He could sense the warm pulse even through the dark rubber wall. This excited the brother further. He and his kin would have a fight on their hands. A challenge. Their frenzied bloodlust would erupt and, in the end, be fulfilled — food enough for all. Was there a greater satisfaction?

He stepped carefully behind the Pontiac, his long, gray tail following to wrap around him. There, he waited, listening, motionless but for the twitch of his nose.

More words from inside: "Ray, is that you? Are you out there? The car door isn't locked, you can come right in."

The creature had no wish to understand the words; they were only sounds to him. They were proof of life, sounds that said only *warm, red, juicy meat,* and that was enough. His stomach contracted painfully. The attack would have to come soon, or they would risk an uncontrollable rage that could result in their feeding on each other.

The elder brother did not fear that fate. It had not happened before, and with their hunting skills it would never happen.

He waited for the wind to rise, then squeaked to alert his brother and sisters that their prey was coming.

Larry had turned off the TV so that he could leave — but when the white glow plunged the Pit into darkness, a claustrophobic fear seized him. He had never realized the

112

place could be so pitch black. It felt like the walls were closing in—and who knew what kind of bugs came out when the lights were off? He reached up for the single light bulb that hung from the ceiling, and spent a couple terrified seconds grasping air. Then he felt the light's chain against his palm, thanked God, and pulled it.

A warm orange light filled the Pit. No moving walls. No bugs. Just the same old place he'd always known.

"Idiot," he muttered.

There was a noticeable difference in the clubhouse, however, from when the place was illuminated by the TV light. The sharp shadows and flickering, strobe-light effect was gone, replaced by a homey glow that didn't so much bounce off the walls as caress them. Larry was surprised at the difference in his mood a single 100 watt bulb could effect. It was strange that he and Mark had never used it when they watched TV on Fridays. The TV flicker had always been too mesmerizing, the mattress too comfortable, to bother.

In fact, the light served to calm him. With all the things going on with Mark and Ray and the plan this Friday, he must have gotten all worked up without realizing it. He had never been scared of the dark, even as a kid—yet when that TV went out a minute ago, he was about ready to dump in his britches.

He shook his head. *Get a grip, guy. You gotta turn out this light if you're going to leave the place.* Just the thought sent a chill through him.

He still needed a couple of minutes breathing time, so he took his time pushing the TV back to the corner where Nick wanted it stored. He made sure the tool chest was closed tight, then gave the mattress a little kick to put it in the proper place, within view of the vent.

Still thinking of the Friday plan, eh? You bet. Chicken shit Mark isn't going to change that.

The defiance made him feel better. Turning out the light didn't seem so bad now. He looked at the Pontiac's door to get his bearings, then reached up to pull the chain—

And that's when he heard the noise.

It was a screech, a horrible whining sound that nearly brought him to his knees, like fingernails across a blackboard.

113

Jesus, who the hell is doing that?

He thought it must be a cat—but the sound went on much too long, much too steadily for a small animal. It was close by, too. Very close. In fact, he thought it might be coming from the other side of the Pontiac . . .

He stepped up to the column of tires close to the back of the car and peered through the cracks.

"Nick?"

No answer. But he heard some movement out there. Someone trying to hide. It must be a trick. Someone trying to scare him. A single culprit came to mind.

"Ray, is that you? Are you out there?" He felt some anger, then decided it was best just to let the little brat have his revenge and make amends. "The car door isn't locked," he called, "you can come right in."

But there was no movement toward the car door, no answering voice but that of the wind's. Whoever was out there didn't feel like giving up just yet.

If it is Ray, I'm going to beat his tail now.

Of course, it could still be some animal. A large animal. Maybe a dog. His collar could be brushing up against the car. And when he heard Larry call out, he probably stopped and listened. He'd seen dogs do that a million times. But would a dog be waiting this long? Larry still felt there was something out there in the shadows still watching the Pit. It hadn't moved off, whatever it was, or whoever.

He moved his lips over a curse. If he didn't go now, he would be so late getting home that even his mom would notice. Jesus, if he didn't leave soon, he may as well spend the night here. No one would know. No one knew he was here.

That last thought scared the hell out of him. What if something happened, if whoever out there wasn't very friendly?

Jesus! Gotta get out!

He was about to move away from the wall when he heard more scurrying outside, like kids scattering after they've rung a doorbell. Did Ray get some neighborhood brats together to play a joke on him? He tried to make out something through the cracks between the tires, but there was nothing out there but a calm field and the distant

114

towers. But he could *hear* something move.

After a few seconds, he was sure that there was more than one.

More than one what?

They were moving hurriedly, definitely together. He could almost follow their direction, but the cement curve behind him began to echo the sounds and confuse him. When the shuffling ended, he wasn't sure where they were.

Who's they? What's going on here?

His mind leaped from question to question, pushed on by a soaring panic. He twisted around, eyeing the walls that surrounded him. He had to get out of here. He was a sitting duck if he stayed.

"Screw the light," he said as he rushed to the Pontiac's door. He hopped into the car and locked both sides, then peered out the driver's window. Still nothing out there. It looked just the same as always.

But I heard something, dammit! I know I did!

He stayed still. He wasn't sure how long but it felt like hours. His mind went round and round, unable to reach any conclusions. Every time his hand reached for the door handle, a convulsion of dread came over him and pulled his hand back to his side.

Then a clear thought made it through his confusion, one that he couldn't fault in the least:

I need a weapon.

He returned to the Pit, to the tool chest. There, he picked up a hammer—the same they had used to put the hinges on the vent—and burrowed back into the Pontiac. The lock clicked down once more on the passenger's side. Then, from somewhere, he found the courage to quietly, oh so quietly, raise the lock on the driver's side.

As the mechanisms inside the door rattled, he brought the hammer up to his chest. He held the tool so tightly that he was losing feeling in his hand. His fingers looked pale and dead. Still, there was enough energy wrapped up in his arm that he was confident he could send it flying, maybe several times, headed by the hammer, into whatever might attack him.

The door opened an inch. That was all he allowed. Then he sat back across the front seat and kicked the door the rest of the way. He tensed, waiting for something to grab his exposed legs. Nothing did.

He took a few more breaths, eyes peeled for any movement in the yard, until he found the strength to step completely from the Pontiac. He debated whether to close the car door. There was a chance he would have to get back inside in a hurry; yet, if he escaped, he couldn't leave the door wide open for whatever was out here—especially not with all that beer inside.

So he closed it—and left it unlocked. Somehow he didn't feel that the lurking figure in the junkyard would be able to open the door on its own.

He turned from the car to make his way across the clearing, then turned back. He couldn't, just *couldn't*, walk away without first testing the door's handle. *Chunk-chunk.* It was in good working order; he could still make it inside in seconds.

"Okay," he whispered, and took a deep breath. Something wet tickled his nose. He slapped at it, nearly crying out, until he realized it was only a bead of sweat that had fallen from his brow.

He took another breath and faced the vast junkyard around him. His heart stopped; which way to the front gate? Then he remembered. He swore at himself not to let panic get the better of him—as though it was something he could control.

The clearing around the Pit, surrounded by different corridors of the maze, had always seemed so small to him. Mark had once remarked that it wasn't even large enough to play ball in. Nevertheless, it was a vast, cold desert now, stretched far, too far for an unobserved escape.

Run? Or walk slowly so as not to call attention to himself? If he ran, he might get lost in the twisting pathways. And getting lost in the dark with whatever stalked him with only a hammer for protection did not seem like a good idea, even in his panic to get out fast. So he took it slow, nice and slow. At least, he figured, he would see them coming.

He brought the hammer up to his face. For a moment, he felt silly. If this was just a bunch of kids . . . He kept the hammer, though, foolish or not. He would just return it tomorrow. It would be daylight then, and Nick and Ray would be there . . .

God, why can't tomorrow come now?

Slowly, then. A step. Another to follow. Just one after the other until he got to the maze, then he could move a little faster under the cover of the junk, just so long as he kept the route square in his head and didn't get lost, because if he got lost now—

Another sound. This one was more than just a rustling; it was a rumble, like a small engine starting.

Or a growl.

He turned and looked above, from where the sound came, just in time to see a large black form jumping at him. He didn't have time to scream. He froze for just a second, a second too long, and then jumped as far as he could. The form tagged him in the shoulder and sent him rolling across the hard gravel. He continued rolling; he wanted to put a lot of distance between himself and the creature. After a few feet, however, his panic demanded he get up and run like hell before his attacker recovered first.

He came to a stop and lifted himself up. He stumbled, still dizzy. The stab of icy fear that accompanied it made him raise the hammer, ready for a death blow.

From that position, he could just make out what had jumped on him.

It was a tire from the roof of the Pit. Just an old, torn, black rubber tire that now lay harmlessly on the ground ahead.

He nearly crumpled right there. In the brief time it had taken to be hit and get up again, his body was drenched in sweat, his heart played bass drums in his ears, and every muscle vibrated with tiny convulsions. All for a lousy tire.

But something told him not to relax. He risked lowering the hammer, but kept it securely in one hand as he approached the tire.

He stood over the tube. Gave it a kick. Strangely, now that the embarrassment was palpable, he felt some responsibility for the tire. He considered storing it in the Pit for the night, or maybe just leaving it where it was until tomorrow, when he would return it to the roof. And now that some semblance of reason had returned, he also worried how he

117

would explain the unlocked car and the missing hammer to the guys when—

A noise.

The low rumble again.

Very much like a growl.

Larry went cold. He arced his head back, conscious of any sudden moves on his part. He peered up into the night.

All thoughts of caution deserted him when he saw what hung above.

It was a monster. That's all he could think of to describe it: a huge, hairy, muscular, drooling *monster*. It hung from the wall of tires, only its front claws holding it to the roof. It must have carried an incredible weight; even from where he was standing, Larry could see the tires beneath its front paws nearly folded in half under the strain. Its oval body, like a gray egg, swayed above the Pontiac. Its tail, as thick as a man's arm, flailed every which way for balance.

As Larry watched in silent horror, the back claws knocked another tire away. It was scrambling against the wall, trying to find some purchase that would lift it back to the roof.

It would have been a comical sight had not Larry been so close—and if he'd not seen the three additional monsters waiting for their sibling on the roof. The hanging creature worked harder beneath their encouraging calls.

If it keeps this up, Larry thought, *it'll bring down the entire wall, the entire clubhouse. The Pit will be destroyed.*

The creature's scrambling came to a climax. Shreds of rubber floated to the ground around him. The wall swayed with the weight and activity. The monsters above tried to grasp their troubled creature's front paws, but their own hands were inadequate.

Finally, the creature must have decided it was hopeless. Its frustration pulled a heavy growl from its mouth. It turned its head over its shoulder—Larry could clearly see the thick muscles bunching in its neck—and rested its beady red eyes on him. They narrowed, and the gray shadow of a snout pulled back, nearly disappeared, to push the crowded layer of sharp teeth forward. A tongue slipped lazily from the mouth, dripping saliva that encouraged hunger.

Larry stared at the nightmare picture in awe. He should

118

have run, made his escape right then before it was too late, but the sudden horror of the image—like stepping out in the path of a truck—nailed him to one spot.

Then, in one swift motion, the creature released its grip on the roof, pushed off from the wall with its back feet, and lunged at Larry with a rumbling roar.

Larry screamed—screamed like a little girl, his voice was so out of control. Panic would have kept him standing there, just waiting for death, if the creature had been charging across the clearing, but the threat of a crushing weight from *above* forced him into action. He reached the end of the clearing, heading for the front gate, before the creature even hit the ground.

The creature landed on its feet, but its weight forced it to its belly. It skidded across the dirt and gravel, raising a choking cloud of dust. It didn't hesitate to recover. Its powerful hind feet dug in and pushed the monster forward. The brother and two sisters screamed their excitement from the roof. But the creature needed no encouragement now. A primal bloodlust coursed through its veins; it would go mad if it did not capture this meat.

Still roaring, the monster scurried after its prey with mounting speed and a deadly determination. True, Larry had a head start—but the creature was a hell of a lot faster.

And it knew it.

The maze was laid out in his mind as he raced around its corners. At one point his momentum nearly took him down the wrong corridor. He considered going on—there was no time to backtrack even a few feet—but some deep reason made him turn around and continue down the right path. Afterwards, he was thankful he had, for he wasn't at all sure where that other corridor would have led. Perhaps to a dead end. Literally.

He was on track to the gate now, though. If he could just keep up the speed . . .

A sharp corner appeared. He whipped around it, his velocity slamming him into a tall pile of television and stereo parts. Some of the jagged metal grabbed at him, ripped through his clothes and flesh. A single piece of wire acted like a hook and stretched his arm back painfully until he removed it from beneath the skin. His left side was cut up pretty bad, but he didn't stop. His legs kept pumping, numb to any exhaustion until they had him through the gate safely.

The creature behind him also knew the maze, and it flew through the passages without hesitation. Every step it took, the creature grunted with the effort and the frantic hunger tearing at its mind. Though Larry's heart was deafening in his ears, he heard every sound. He knew the thing was right behind him — gaining. And since they both knew the route, the race between them was now a matter of speed.

Larry let loose with all he had. He willed himself to hear the rumble fading into the distance behind him; even if it was only an illusion, perhaps it would divert his panic long enough to reach safety.

It didn't work. The thunder of the creature's claws gripping the earth only grew louder, sounding now like a platoon of men racing across a front. Larry pressed himself. His legs were giving out, but he kept pushing, pushing, to the gate. He could see the entrance, the black iron looming, just ten yards away, eight, the beast's stinking breath ruffling up his pants legs, five yards, the mouth opening wide, all it needed was a foot to bring him down and tear out his throat, two yards, *just two fucking yards, please God,* the monster surging faster, ready to strike, a roar growing, like his panic, bringing with it teeth that would easily bury themselves in his flesh and *tear —*

He pushed through the gate, nearly taking it from its hinges, and fell exhausted into the middle of the street.

Silence followed him.

He lay there for a long while, his whole body pulsating up and down as it took in air. His exposed flesh glistened under the street lamps. He waited with his eyes squeezed tight and his hands over his ears. The pain would be bad enough, but he didn't want to see his own blood or hear the tearing sounds . . . and, later, the wet chomping as he was eaten alive.

But none of it ever came. Not this night. After a horrible eternity passed, and the cold night air began to chill him, he rolled over and looked around.

The street was quiet and deserted. The junkyard itself looked calm, unaffected. Even the gate was closed again.

He was alone. There was not even the feeling that something was watching him. He stumbled to his feet and stood perfectly still for a moment, listening for the slightest noise. Still nothing. Only the wind.

He backed away from the yard. His eyes never left the front gate. He walked backward all the way to the corner, until the black iron melded with the darkness, and then he ran like hell toward home.

His legs really hurt now, aching with the unaccustomed stress. His left arm was still torn and bleeding; it felt on fire. He did his best to run evenly so as not to make it worse.

He made it down the length of Barker Avenue without incident. When he crossed the street at the corner, he heard a sharp noise. He started—then ran again. His legs didn't carry him very far before exhaustion and the blinding pain in his arm brought him down.

The noise was closer. A deep grumble. A growl.

As he lay there in the street, exposed and helpless, he silently offered a prayer for the first time in his life. While he spoke it, he kept his eyes open; this time he wouldn't remain blind to his fate. He had to meet what was coming with some shred of dignity, even if his lids fell shut in the end.

So he rolled over, the evocations still rolling from his mouth. His vision was blurry, but he could see some form at the corner. With some concentration he finally made out the source of the noise.

A car's engine.

A patrol car was just turning the corner and coming his way. In a few seconds, the car's lights would hit him. Then would come the spotlight on the car's side, and he'd be captured and coerced to go over everything that had happened. Then, maybe, something would be done about the monster. *If* the cop believed him.

Larry knew that the chances of that were slim, especially when he looked so torn up. They'd just figure he was drunk. The cop probably already smelled the beer on his breath from this distance. They were good at that. No, he'd

121

have to calm down and get a clear head before describing this night to *anyone*.

As quick as his injuries allowed, then, he rose to his feet and stumbled off down a side street. He didn't doubt the officer had seen him, but if the cop wanted to chase a kid home, that was his problem. Hell, at least he'd have a policeman protecting his rear.

The policeman had seen him, and thought of giving chase until he recognized Larry as the kid he had stopped earlier that day and offered a ride to. No use trying again. It looked like he was running for home anyway. If he saw him one more time, then he'd probably have to call it in. No use taking a chance so close to the residential area.

It was too bad, really. It had been a while since he'd picked up a lost child. The last time had been three weeks ago. Sweet little thing, really beautiful. She'd tried to duck away into an alley one night when he'd suddenly turned a corner and hit her with a spotlight. No use. The alley was a dead end. He just rode the patrol car up quiet-like to block the exit and walked right up to her. No problem, that one. Just another runaway. Not more than thirteen or fourteen. He shook his head. What the hell was the world coming to when you had so many kids running away from home?

Of course, now that he thought about it, he'd considered running away a couple of times when he was a kid. His mother was dead and his father sort of pressed it on him, you might say. The old man encouraged him to do it, though his words threatened otherwise. But that's what happens when a father loves his children too much. Maybe loves them in ways he shouldn't. And it was because he knew his dad really loved him that he didn't leave the old man until the day he killed him. Lucky he was an only child; he wasn't sure if he could have watched a brother or sister go through all that. Especially a sister. Certainly not someone as young as that runaway.

On the way back in the patrol car, the runaway had told him a similar story—only she was running from the violence, not the love. Her old man beat her, her mom just cowered. A story heard often, even in Winsome.

But she also mentioned that she was from out of town. From Harkford, a place about thirty miles south. She'd hitched her way up, and just came down from the highway to get some food. Something clicked in his mind when he heard the word "highway," and when she asked if he might have anything to eat, he was right there with his best smile.

He had food. He had a place for her to sleep. Shelter from the cold nights. He didn't have to work too hard to make it sound like paradise to this girl. He recognized the desperation in her eyes. And something else. Suspicion. It told him she was older than her years. Mature enough to think: *This is too good to be true*. A pity. Her childhood had ended long ago, though it should have had a few good years left. Sad, really. Still, she was desperate, and that had nothing to do with maturity. The promise of food and bed swayed her.

She was still uncertain when he got her to his home on the corner, the one built away from the neighbors. She followed him in, though. Maybe the uniform had convinced her it was safe. The suspicion died a little when he made her two sandwiches, stacked some chips on them, and let her wash it all down with a beer.

She was still nervous, he could tell, because she talked so much while feeding her starved stomach. She told him her name was Jamie. She told him how her folks would never look for her, how she told all her friends she'd be traveling east instead of north. And while he listened, his brain kept clicking, like embers crackling in a hearth, and the prickly heat started covering his skin.

By the end of her meal, he was certain. She needed him.

Those wide, green eyes, still so childish, looked at him with an almost embarrassed gratitude when he led her back to the bedroom. Of course that didn't last long when he secured the door behind them. He waited, still smiling. She was smart; in no time at all she realized why there were no windows in the room, why he had locked the door, and why there was no furniture except for a mattress and some handcuffs attached to rope.

She screamed, and went on screaming, only because she didn't know that the walls were soundproof. Or perhaps they were screams of ecstasy. It was obvious to him that she

123

enjoyed it. Just like all the others. All the begging and crying in the world couldn't hide the lust he saw in their eyes. And when they actually bled for him . . . then he knew it was love: a devotion that would last forever.

Just like his dad had loved him.

It was a love that went much deeper than the flesh — yet it was the flesh he had had a problem with, in the beginning. The memory made him nostalgic. How long since his first romantic liaison? About eighteen months, he'd guess. Shellie, her name was. Twelve years old and so very lovely. She had loved him so much.

Outside his patrol car, the hazy lights from neighborhood porches glided by, hypnotic, and he let his mind wander back . . .

The disposal of the flesh had been a real problem at first. His backyard was only so big, and he wasn't sure if there would be a smell or not. After scouting a few locations, the wide, bare fields on the outskirts of Winsome had seemed ideal. Just bury them in the middle of nowhere and nature would do the rest.

Except, after thirteen months, it turned out that all his loves had been from Winsome — he had not yet discovered the joyous anonymity of runaways — and Sheriff Peltzer, a man to be admired for his thoroughness, decided that the expanse of land outside of town might be just the place to start a manhunt for the bodies. He'd cursed himself the night of that announcement; he should have known that what was obvious to himself would be obvious to the sheriff. The sheriff was smart. He warned himself not to forget that.

The organized search started on schedule. He had thought of running then — but a morbid part of him made him stay to watch the progress. The search started far from where the bodies were, but they got closer and closer every day, eventually sniffing over the very graves several times. He had gotten close to outright madness when those dogs kept dancing over the same areas and the officers would keep digging and digging . . .

Yet, he didn't run then, either. Something kept him glued to Winsome. It was more than just a morbid interest in the search. He found that he actually liked the place, liked its people. He even liked working for the sheriff. This was his home. A *real* home, where he had friends who liked him and showed some kindness.

If he was to die, he wanted it to be here.

So it was a revelation when not a single body turned up and the manhunt was discontinued. It was a divine sign, one that stated clearly to him that this was his home now, that he could continue on here forever and remain safe. His loves would always stay secret.

Nevertheless, he knew it would not be wise to tempt fate again. He had to find a new burial spot. Where, he wasn't sure, but in the meantime he was curious as to what had happened out in the fields.

Why weren't the bodies found?

One night, six or seven months ago, when the police interest in the area had died, he'd driven out to the graves. Even after so much time away, he'd known right where they were.

They were empty.

The state police had dug in the right places. They'd hoped to find at least a shred of clothing or some dried blood. But someone had pulled the bodies away, had pulled everything away. What's more, they had covered their own tracks. All evidence was gone.

In short, whoever they were, they'd saved his ass.

It had disturbed him to think that someone or something else was in on his secret. Then he realized that this was exactly what he'd been looking for: a complete disposal of the flesh that would leave no trace.

He considered continuing his use of the fields, so that he would not have to search for a new gravesite, but the distance and time involved dissuaded him. It was too dangerous. If anyone saw him, particularly one of the other patrols, he'd be connected with the fields. And he knew that the sheriff was still convinced the bodies were out there somewhere. It would take only a small bridge to connect the two — and Sheriff Peltzer was smart enough to do it.

Therefore, it was necessary to find another site. And it would be advantageous if he could bring along his "disposal units" too.

He did some hard thinking, then went to work.

Some quick research at the library made him aware that there were sewers running from every part of Winsome to the fields. If he could draw these "helpers" down into the right tube and bring them up somewhere safe . . .

The next night on patrol, driving slowly through the darkened streets, brought the full potential of old Winsome Junk to light: unkempt, plenty of hidden areas, and apparently abandoned. He didn't know that that was to change shortly when a man named Ed Kelton and his three dogs would come home to roost. Excited as he was, he'd had a good laugh about it. He had passed the place a million times during his years of patrol. Mostly ignored it. Funny that it turned out to be his salvation.

It turned out to be much easier to find his next love: a young, strapping boy named William Granton who played football at Franklin High School. William was a handful, much tougher than the other loves, but he'd purposely picked a boy with some muscle this time, partly for the excitement but mostly so that he'd have plenty of meat to work with afterward.

He took extra care late that night to cut the boy up just right. They had to be neat chunks—and there had to be enough to span the distance between the fields and Winsome Junk.

It had been risky. He'd had some concerns over what might happen should the meat not draw the "helpers" into the sewer. Though he was aware the body parts would eventually float out to sea and no one there would know where they came from, it was still a hell of a chance. If the sheriff had orchestrated a manhunt into the sewer system that month, there's no question they would have found William Granton's remains. Then Sheriff Peltzer would have known what was going on with the bodies—no more mystery whether they were alive or dead. And that kind of lead surely would have spurred the sheriff on to further successes—and spelled the end for one of his most trusted deputies.

But luck was still with him. His secret loves stayed safe. The creatures had followed the parts, tied to various pipes and ladder rungs, all the way up to the manhole in front of the junkyard. From there, his plan had been more difficult.

He couldn't very well leave a trail of severed body parts from the manhole to the open front gate, even though he was the only one patrolling that area that night. He had to hope that the odor of the parts he'd left inside the yard would draw them in.

When he drove by the yard just fifteen minutes after three that morning and saw the manhole cover lying in the gutter, he'd known he had been successful. Another sign from a god who approved of his obsession.

More children disappeared. Mostly runaways from out of town, though there was that one Spanish girl he could not pass up. So lovely. Their eyes so wide and innocent, untouched by the real world. Their hearts still pure and strong. Their bodies so new to them—even the boys' skin was soft and smooth.

He could imagine what the cumulative effect would have been on the town and the sheriff if he had not discovered the advantages of runaways when he did. To him, it was just another sign that his gods were watching over him. It fit right into the pattern: first the creatures that disposed of the flesh, then the convenient location of the junkyard, and now the endless line of children who no one cared for or would even ask about.

It was perfect. There *had* to be someone protecting him from up high. Some gods who *approved* of him. As far as he was concerned, he had been handed a mandate—a mandate to love and be loved.

And as he drove through the dark streets of Winsome this Wednesday night, the car's heater blasting in his face, he was distinctly aware that it had been three weeks since he'd last loved.

Three whole weeks.

Deputy Kevin Gavel smiled inside the tight confines of his patrol car. Soon, very soon, his gods would give the nod, and he would love again.

Larry Santino burst into his house and stood in the light from the street coming through the open door. The house was dark except for a ghostly light from the living room. In his exhaustion, it took him a full minute to place it.

The chiming of the clock in the kitchen told him it was prime time. As he stepped carefully into the living room, he knew what he would find. There, in the center chair, her eyes glazed by the light of the black-and-white TV, sat his mother.

"Mom?" he said softly. He never bothered her during her shows at night; he wondered if it was safe.

There was no answer, just the droning of the laugh-track from the show she was watching. There wasn't a hint of a smile on her face.

"Mom? I'm home." Still no answer, but the need to *do* something forced him to continue. "I had an accident, Mom, I got attacked by . . . I don't know what . . . some kind of monster thing. . . ." He hurried on, glancing at her expression occasionally to see if there was any reaction. "I . . . I have to get cleaned up, start thinking straight, 'cause . . . 'cause I gotta talk to the police about this—"

He had moved to the kitchen entrance and picked up the phone on the wall. The next second, he was aware of movement behind him, some dark shape chasing him into the darkness, grabbing at him. He backed away, his imagination unleashed with a rush of adrenaline. He barely controlled a scream.

The kitchen light flicked on. His mother was inches away, suddenly alive. She stood with one hand on her hip, the other in a vice grip around the phone. Her eyes stared up at him, alight with fire. Larry was shocked by the shift of emotions on her face; the invisible hooks that once pulled her features into immobility had released their hold completely.

"*What* are you doing?" she demanded. "Are you *crazy?*"

"What?" he wheezed,

"*What?* You are not going to call *them!* I am *not* going to have the police tramping through my house asking questions about some wild story of yours!" She paused to breathe. In that moment Larry realized, with some dread, that the door behind which she imprisoned her emotions had suddenly exploded open. He was terrified where it might throw her.

"Mom—"

"*No!*"

"Mom," he hurried, voice rising, "I *have* to call them. These things that attacked me—"

"Monsters! There are no monsters! Only people are monsters! The police are monsters!"

"But they can help. They have to catch these things before they—"

"No, they—"

"Listen to me!"

Quiet filled the space between them. Both breathed hard, searched for the strength to reason this out.

Larry was the first to find the words. "Mom, please, just listen to what happened. I was . . . I was in the junkyard—"

"Larry—"

"I know, I know, you don't like me to be there. But I was, and I was alone . . ." He spoke quickly, afraid she would interrupt him before he told the entire story. She stood her ground, and searched his face for any glint of fabrication or exaggeration. When he was done, his last vestiges of strength left him and he slouched against the wall for support. "Well?"

She was much calmer now, though still far from the glazed separation he was used to. Her face grew pale as he told his story, but now the color was returning, burning her.

"It's crazy, Larry," she finally pronounced. "You can't call the police for that. They won't believe you. They'll say you're lying to bother them and they'll lock you up."

"They won't—"

"They will lock you up," she said loudly, pushing each word. "You were in the junkyard at night. You probably had something to drink—yes, I know you drink, you can't hide that—and you were alone. A shadow or a cat could become a monster if you're afraid—"

"I wasn't afraid, Mom, not until they showed up. And I got a good look at them. They weren't shadows and they weren't goddamn cats"—he pulled the phone from her grasp—"and I *am* calling the police!"

If he had expected her to slump into a chair and cry as he dialed, he was wrong. She exploded. Her hand jumped forward and slapped him in the face. Her other hand knocked the phone away from him, and then she pushed him backward, screaming into his face, *"The police killed your father! Is that what you want? Is that what you want them to do to you when they hear your crazy story? They know who you are! They'll take you away!"*

He wanted to turn and start running, just get away from this crazy woman and this dark house. He had wanted to get away for years, and he knew he could go through with it now if he just stepped out the kitchen door, just pushed his mother out of the way and kept on going . . .

But when he touched her, she sagged against him, and he found himself falling into the warmth, holding her, his eyes squeezed shut so that no one could see the pain or the tears. They clutched each other close. Her ragged sobs shook them both. His fingers touched her hair as he rubbed her back. The strands were so coarse they felt like wire. A picture popped into his head, of a time when his mother's skin was smooth and pink and her hair reminded him of shiny black cotton candy. He knew very well that the woman he held now was just different shades of gray. The color had drained from her since Larry's father's death; she had been left with a black-and-white world ever since.

"I know, Ma," he whispered. "I know."

"Please don't bring them here, Larry," she cried.

"Ma . . ." He lost his breath and had to pause to regain it. "Ma, I saw something in there, I swear I did . . ."

"Just dogs, Larry. They were just dogs."

He nodded. He remembered the time, for a few months, when his and Mark's Friday nights at the Pit were difficult to arrange because a guard and three Dobermans had popped up out of nowhere. They'd found another way in, but they had only found the nerve to do it once. Fortunately, there was a carnival in the fields by then, so they had other ways to spend their weekends. Then the guard and dogs had suddenly disappeared.

Or did they? Could these have been those same Dobermans he saw tonight—unbathed, unbrushed, and starving?

His mother's quivering voice reached him again. "They won't believe you, Larry. You know that." And he realized, then, that she was right—had been right from the beginning. The police wouldn't believe him. Not with his looks. And not with what happened to his father.

Larry released the breath he'd been holding, and felt

something comforting also slip from him. He shivered as he kissed his mother's forehead and assured her he would not call the police. He was going to bed. She hugged him tight. When she pulled away and started back to her TV, he saw the glaze return to her face—except now it looked more to him like a deep, paralyzing sadness.

He made his way back to his bedroom and shut the door. He lay on his bed, staring up at the shadows that hid the ceiling, and the question thrust its way between his calming nerves again.

Were those Dobermans I saw tonight?

The only question that mattered. And the answer was immediate—and disturbing.

Hell, no. They were . . . well, something like . . .

He twisted onto his side in frustration. He needed more time to think this all out. Things might be clearer in the morning, but he doubted it could be that easy. He had to tell someone about this. There was no way he could keep it to himself.

Mark . . .

Yes, Mark. He would talk to Mark tomorrow. Mark would listen to him if he was troubled. It would be another secret they could share, another bind.

In his exhaustion, his imagination took off with the idea. He and Mark would band together and inform the rest of the gang. Then the four of them would go forward, as close as they had been years ago, and rush into their greatest adventure. They would save Winsome—its children and parents and old people and very grateful, buxom teenage women—maybe save the *world* from these creatures from hell, these monsters . . .

These rats.

Thursday

Pauline had a lunch date with Nick that afternoon, as she did most afternoons, but today she wanted to wear something extra nice. Her talk with Monica the night before hadn't resolved too much — mostly because Monica didn't know Nick very well — but she had made it plain that if this was something Pauline felt deeply about, she should do it, and her friend would be there to help pick up the pieces again if the relationship went sour.

Pauline had spent the night, then, deciding whether to go through with whatever Nick had planned for Friday. Her good mood this morning — the way she examined her skin in the shower, her attention to the placement of every dark hair on her head, the time it took to pick the right outfit and the extra jewelry she applied — it all made her realize, as she was driven to school by her mother, that she had made up her mind, come what may.

At noon, Nick was already sitting in a grassy corner of the yard, away from the larger groups of kids, when Pauline arrived. He felt embarrassed that he couldn't tear his eyes away from her as she approached. She was a year older than him and about an inch or two shorter. In Nick's opinion — and the opinion of not a few guys in Winsome High School, including Ray and Mark — she was drop-dead beautiful: smooth, almond skin that glistened like swirling chocolate, brown eyes that sparkled even in darkness, and a body almost worthy of a Playboy center-fold.

All of which were the very reasons he had asked her out in the first place. It had been a shock when she had said yes, and actually seemed enthusiastic—and even more of a shock when he found that he enjoyed talking and listening to her almost as much as kissing her.

Almost.

He'd bought her lunch in the cafeteria and brought it out to the grass. He used to make his own lunch early each morning, before his dad would wake up from his nightly drinking bout, but somehow making a sack lunch for his girlfriend just didn't sound very romantic. Fortunately, he worked on weekends and always managed to save a little money for dates and lunches during the week—a fact he prayed his dad would never discover.

Normally, the tray lunches were supposed to stay inside the cafeteria, but he managed to sneak it by. As Pauline sat and dazzled him with a smile, he handed her her tray of meatloaf and soggy potatoes. A fly landed on the meat. He tried to swat it for her, but all he did was dip his thumb into the goo.

"Dammit!" he said. "Sorry."

She laughed. Something wonderful always washed over him when she laughed. It made him lightheaded and foolish. He couldn't stand feeling like a fool, but with her he decided it was worth it.

Jesus, he thought, *you're going bonkers over this one. What would your old man say? Maybe it's . . .*

Well, no, he wasn't sure that he actually loved her. He like her a lot and wanted to get into her pants desperately, but he wouldn't equate that with love. After all, he was young and still had a lot of time left ahead of him before he'd have to settle down. He still had years for, as his dad put it, "poking a stick in many a hole."

Pauline's knee touched his, and he banished the crude thought. Though he tried to manage some detachment when he looked at her—he hated the thought of looking like a lovesick puppy—it was impossible not to notice that Pauline looked exceptionally attractive today. She was wearing an outfit that was a little more revealing than her usual style; the extra necklace and wrist bands didn't help cover much of it. It struck him as a little garish at first, but since it was Pauline beneath it all, he was won over.

They briefly discussed their date for Friday night. Nick didn't want to go into too much detail because he wasn't at all sure if he'd go through with it or not—or if Pauline would let him go through with it. They'd both hinted at it, but there was nothing concrete.

Nick had once tried to push the issue through body language when they were in the backseat of her car, but she had made it clear that he was presuming too much. Nick took it in stride. He'd been dating since he was fifteen—young, but as long as he kept it from his dad, he could get away with quite a few things—and there were many times he'd tried to go "all the way." Every one of those girls had turned him down—even the ones he'd heard wouldn't. A few had seemed iffy on the subject, but he never forced it. No way was he going to be accused of rape. Besides, he wanted someone who wanted him just as badly.

So, in turn, he dropped each girl who turned him down and went on to the next. To be honest, he would have dumped them even if they *had* given in. After all, he was young. Why waste years on a relationship when he could be enjoying the fun of variety? It was just one more wonderful attitude picked up from good ol' Dad—one that seemed a little childish now that he sat next to Pauline.

Pauline was different from the others. He'd wanted to have sex with many of the girls he'd dated in the past, but now he wanted to share something better than just a quick pleasure with her. For the first time in his life, he made the distinction between sex and making love. He wanted to make love to Pauline in the worst way. It wasn't just her looks, but everything he knew about her.

And what was worse, once he realized she liked him, maybe even loved him, he was suddenly concerned with her feelings. He knew that if he dropped her, like he'd dropped the others, she would be hurt—and he could not imagine waking up each morning knowing he'd hurt her. It would kill him.

So he was screwed. What could he do? It was way too

complicated to figure out now, so he let it ride. Maybe wait until after they'd been together Friday night, when it would be, most assuredly, too late—then fate would decide for him.

". . . Friday."

Nick looked up to find Pauline staring back with amusement. "Huh?" he said.

"Your mind wandering, Nick?"

He poked at the meatloaf with his fork. "Just wondering what part of the cat this came from."

"Gross!"

He smiled, and she gave him one of her laughs. "So," he said "what about Friday?"

"I said that my mom almost had to use her car Friday night, and we wouldn't have been able to go anywhere." She tilted her head a bit. "Then you would have had to walk all the way over to my house."

"Your parents would have wondered who the hell I was."

"They wouldn't have been there. We would have been alone."

He watched for her smile, but she remained just on the verge of it. As if she were serious.

"Too bad," he said.

"Well, we have the car, so it's not all bad. We can go out for whatever you have planned."

"Who said I have anything planned?"

"You always do. Where we eat, what movie we see . . ."

"I always ask you, though. And then you just shrug and say, 'I don't care. It's up to you.'"

She laughed again at his imitation of her. "Well, I don't care. I'll follow you anywhere you want."

Nick couldn't breathe when he looked into her eyes. When she turned her attention back to her food, he was without a thing to say.

She filled the gap nicely. "What time do you want me to pick you up?"

"About six would be good. You don't have to dress as nice as you are today. I'm on a limited expense account, you know." He smiled to show he appreciated her efforts.

She nodded. "Okay. In that case"—she stood, brushing

grass from her clothes, and bent over to kiss him on the lips, making certain he caught just a glimpse of her cleavage—"I'll see you tomorrow."

He watched her walk away and wondered, as his father would, how a girl with such average breasts could make him feel so good.

Too much, Pauline thought worriedly as she walked to her next class. *Don't give him the world. He might expect too much Friday.*

But she could hear Monica's words now: *You're already planning on giving him too much.*

And maybe it was true. But she'd made up her mind now, and if she still felt this strongly about Nick Friday, she would go with him anywhere, come hell or high water.

Of course, she couldn't know that hell would be exactly what would come.

As Nick moved down the hallway to his next class, he was grabbed and pulled into a side corridor that was deserted.

He struggled until he realized it was Larry—a pale, shaky Larry.

"What the—"

"Nick, please, listen to me."

"I don't like to be handled like that."

"I know, I know. I'm sorry. Listen, there's something going on at the junkyard."

The impact of the emotion in Larry's voice made Nick pay attention. His brow knitted and he nodded for him to go on.

"I can't talk about it here," Larry said. "There isn't time, and I need time if you're going to believe me—I *swear* it's true. Just . . . we need time to talk. If you could—"

"Look, Larry, I can see you're upset, but I gotta get to class."

"Wait, Nick—"

"It can wait until after school. We can talk all you want

136

then. We'll meet at the Pit."

Larry's entire body winced. *"No!"* he demanded, immediately lowering his voice. "Not the Pit, Nick, I'm not going there."

Nick started to back away. There was something *really* wrong with this guy. He wasn't bent over or stumbling or drooling or any lunatic thing, but he was scared shitless over something.

"Lar," he said, hoping it sounded calm, "we can talk about this all you want after . . ."

"But not at the Pit, Nick, please—"

"Just—hey!" Larry was grabbing his arm again, trying to hold him still. Nick tried to jerk his arm away, but Larry had a surprisingly good hold—almost desperate. "Let go!" he demanded.

"Nick, please, Nick, we can't go to the Pit. Don't go there after class. There are . . . monsters in it." Nick blanched and tried to pull away again. *"Please!"* Larry insisted. "I swear I'm telling the truth, that's why I need time to talk to you—"

Nick thought he understood now. He stared at the other boy hard. "You're drunk."

"No . . ."

"I can smell it on your breath. Since when do you drink before coming to school?"

"I just . . . a little under my bed, I needed it to come here today after last night . . ."

"What happened last night? You mean the fight with Ray?"

"No, not the goddamn fight with Ray!" He jittered with frustration, took a breath. When he spoke again, his words were clear and controlled. "Look . . . please meet me at the dirt corner outside school after your last class, okay? I really need to talk to you, but it has to be there at the corner. *Not* at the Pit."

Nick still thought he was talking nonsense, but the desperation in Larry's face and gestures convinced him that there was something very wrong here.

"All right," he said, "I'll meet you after class. At the corner." He took a step closer, startling Larry. "But this better be damned good!"

Larry met his eyes. There was something dark and haunted there behind the alcohol-haze. "Believe me, Nick," he whispered. "It is."

A cold electric current ran through Nick's body, but he shrugged it off. Without another word, he jerked his arm from Larry's weakened grasp, nodded, and set off for class. He wasn't sure what the hell was going on. He'd never seen Larry drunk before, and he wasn't convinced he was drunk now. And if he wasn't acting this way because of alcohol . . .

Unconsciously, Nick's pace quickened. There was no way he was going to miss that meeting at the corner.

The rest of the school day passed in a whirl. The barely concealed panic in Larry's eyes kept coming back to him. What in the world could transform the unflappable Larry Santino into a quivering mound of jello? Nick thought it must be something with his mother, maybe having to do with his dead father.

But, of course, that didn't explain all that talk about monsters.

When he realized he wasn't thinking a whole lot about Pauline — especially after she went to all the trouble of dressing up today — his irritation rose even higher.

The corner Larry chose for the meeting was just a small dirt field that ended in a curb at the intersection of Oak and Midway. There had always been talk of planting grass there, but the regular army of kids going to and from school made that impossible. Nick joined the flux of high school kids going in that direction. He looked about him along the way, to see if Larry might be somewhere near.

When he reached the corner, he found Larry and Mark waiting for him. They both must have left their last class early, if they had gone at all. Beneath a gray sky, Larry looked a little less frail, though it was still obvious something powerful troubled him. Mark stood just a bit distant from him, looking slightly uncomfortable — probably for the same reasons Nick was.

When Larry hurried up to greet him, Nick grabbed his elbow and swung him around, walking them both around the corner. Mark followed without a word. There, Nick stopped and waited for Mark to take his place next to his friend. He then leaned his back against the wall, crossed his arms, and demanded, "Well?"

Larry glanced at them both. He seemed embarrassed, but from the beginning of his story his voice was calm and forceful. Mark and Nick listened to it all without a word or look between them.

When Larry was finished, his mouth clamped shut while he waited for the reaction. He knew he had made the entire incident sound reasonable, just like the old Larry. Nevertheless, the story was his most incredible to date, and relating it out loud, in the daylight, made even *him* scowl with disbelief.

Nick was the first to break the silence that had bunched up between them; Mark wouldn't even look at his friend. "Larry, this is . . ." He opened his hands, palms up, searching for the right expression. He settled for a smile and a shake of his head. "Dammit, Lare, this is nuts. You must know it sounds nuts."

"Yes," he said sadly. "I know it. But I swear it's the truth. And I wasn't drunk or imagining anything. Those creatures were *not* dogs or cats, and I didn't get *this* by running away from some little animal!" He unzipped one arm of his coat and lifted his shirt sleeve to reveal a thin scab running across his forearm. He didn't mention that it had been caused by a piece of junk while he was running away from the monster.

"Okay, okay," Nick said, looking at him a little strange again. "But *monsters?* Giant hairy things with tails longer than my leg and glowing red eyes and razor-sharp teeth? I mean, it's like something out of a cheap horror story."

"But it's what I saw. It was *real*. I know that sometimes I . . . exaggerate things to make a better story"—he glanced at Mark sheepishly—"but I haven't made up a single thing here. It happened, and I saw, *exactly* what I told you."

Mark still didn't say anything, but his sad eyes rested evenly on his friend.

"And you know just as well as me," Nick said, "that there's no such creatures on this planet. Hell, the way you describe it, it just sounds like a big rat — and rats do *not* get that size!"

Larry looked at him with that scary seriousness again. "But, Nick . . . what if they do?"

Their eyes didn't break for some time. A realization grew between them, a horrible reality that bounced back and forth against their foreheads, causing a throbbing pain, impossible to ignore.

When Nick finally broke away to seek Mark, he was gasping for breath.

"Do you believe this guy?" he asked.

Larry held his breath.

Mark's head was bowed toward the ground, perhaps so he would not have to participate in what they had been thinking, but his eyes lifted to Larry's when he said, quietly, "Yes. I think I do."

Then they were all staring at the sidewalk, descending to a deep silence initiated by the belief between them and the few students who walked by within earshot.

When the students were gone, Nick shrugged and asked, "Well, what should we do?"

"I say we go straight to the police," Mark said.

Larry was immediately on him. "No! We can't do that!" He took hold of himself, and added softly, "*I* can't do that."

"Why? Because of your dad?" Mark asked. "That doesn't mean any—"

"They won't believe me," Larry insisted. By his tone, he made it clear that there was no argument on this point.

Mark shrugged. "All right. What if *I* tell them? I'll say I was the one there last night, and that'll keep you out of it."

"A policeman saw me," Larry told them. "He might remember me and come around." His spirits were lifted, however; it was reassuring to hear how effortlessly Mark would make a sacrifice for him.

"Besides," said Nick, "if the police get into this and they believe you, they'll probably close the place up. My Friday would be ruined."

"*Jes*us, Nick!" Larry stammered. "Use the backseat of

her car!"

"Screw you," was all Nick offered. Pauline deserved better than the backseat of a car and he'd already gotten her hopes up of going somewhere nice. Well, at least more comfortable. He wanted to believe Larry's story for friendship's sake, but overall he knew, *knew,* that it was all just crazy talk. And there was no way in hell he was going to let crazy talk ruin his Friday night with Pauline.

"Besides," he added, hoping to further make his case, "*none* of us can go to the cops with such a nutty story. We'd have to find some sort of evidence to convince them, like footprints or hair or something."

"Well, I'm sure as hell not going back to the junkyard to find some," said Larry.

"Oh, don't be ridiculous. It's daylight still, you'd be there with Mark and me—" He stopped suddenly, shaken.

Mark touched his arm. "What's wrong?"

"Oh, Jesus," he said. It shouldn't have worried him, after what he'd just been saying to Larry, but the thought scared him just the same.

"I was supposed to meet Ray at the Pit after school," he told them. "He's there alone right now."

They ran hard, unwilling to pause for breath, all the way to the junkyard. Larry slowed as they approached the iron gate, but the camaraderie with his friends pulled him onward.

Once inside, Nick grabbed a steel pipe from a junk pile. He still didn't believe in these monsters Larry was talking about—well, not completely—but even if Larry's beast turned out to be a dog, it sounded dangerous enough to threaten Ray. Nick felt better with his hand wrapped around a solid weapon. Behind him, Mark did the same.

They exchanged glances, about to step into the labyrinth, when they noticed that Larry was not at their side. They turned and saw him standing just within the gate.

"Come on!" shouted Mark. The anger was apparent in his voice.

"I can't!" Larry shouted back. "Don't go in there. Those things can hide anywhere."

Mark's and Nick's eyes fell to the labyrinth. The wan light of day only managed to expose the peaks of the junk piles. Below, and getting darker as they moved closer to the ground, shadows—and perhaps something else—waited for them.

Larry was right. The towers of junk were perfect camouflage for anything that might want to surprise them. A hand could jump out from under a stack and pull them under before they could get a scream out. And they knew, from experience, that they would become even more vulnerable the deeper they traveled into that darkness.

"We gotta go," Mark insisted, but he didn't sound too convinced.

"We'll go fast," Nick said. "Step high and move fast."

Mark nodded. "Come on, Larry!" he called over his shoulder.

Larry paced back and forth in frustration. Mark and Nick wouldn't even look at him; they studied the shadows before them, trying to decide the best route, the *safest* route.

Larry thought they must be waiting for him. He was keeping them back. He, alone, might be endangering Ray with his hesitation. So, with a huffed curse, he stepped into the yard, moving past the concrete shelter—

And a sickening picture flashed behind his eyes:

Those bodies, pricked with black tufts that barely covered the gray-splotched skin, racing at him with terrifying speed, a speed he could never escape, their eyes, the size of half-dollars, burning with the fire of hunger, yellow teeth, solid, reminding him of ivory he'd once seen, perfect when combined with those claws for slicing into the skin, clamping deep, deep around his vital organs, and pulling back to *riiiiiiip*—

He froze, suddenly white and covered in a thick sweat.

"Christ, I can't," he said.

"Hurry up!" Mark demanded.

"No, no . . . I can't go."

Nick turned to him. "Ray's in there, Larry. Ray Hols-

142

comb, your friend. If you're right about these goddamn things, you'd sure as hell better . . ." His voice died as Larry moved to the small pile of pipes, hefted one larger than the other boys had, and moved quickly to stand at their side.

"Shit," was all he said, and he looked it. But he was there, with them, and ready to run into hell to save a friend.

"One," Nick said, his voice now so low that the other two could only hear him if they bent close. "Two . . ."

At three, they bolted into the dark maze, Nick in the lead, Larry next, followed by Mark. The shadows swallowed them, as they knew they would. They did not pause. It was forward, forward, with their weapons held high and their feet touching the ground as little as possible.

In moments, Larry and Mark were having trouble making out the guy in front of each. The shadows of the maze seemed thicker than usual, something like spilt ink that just keeps spreading and spreading, always growing darker, until the page is completely devoured.

Still they ran forward. Except for the rumble of their feet, they made as little noise as possible. They each would have liked to let loose with a warrior cry—not due to any boyish enthusiasm but in hope of scaring off any monsters that might be waiting for them in this chilling darkness—but did not.

It seemed to take hours before they reached the clearing that embraced the Pit. At the car, they stopped to regroup and catch their breaths. The run wasn't a long one from gate to clubhouse, but fear had taken most of their reserve.

Nick separated from them for a moment to look around. When Larry and Mark drew close again, he whirled on them.

"Larry, I thought you said one of those things threw a tire at you."

"I didn't say it threw one, I said it knocked one d—"

"So where is it?"

They looked around while Nick stared daggers at Larry.

There wasn't a tire anywhere near.

"I don't . . ."

"You said you didn't replace it," Nick said, gritting his teeth. "You didn't even touch it, and you said it didn't roll—those things are too old to roll, anyway. So, Lare, *where is it?*"

"I don't know. Maybe they took it—"

"Why would they take a tire? And where are the tracks? The tire would have left some marks. So would those things' feet." Nick opened his arms wide and moved toward the car. *"Where,* Larry? You said the largest one came jumping down at you. It must have disturbed some of the ground here when it landed. So where's the evidence?"

Larry searched the clearing in earnest. The fact was that there was no evidence: no footprints, no dragging tracks, no clumps of hair—nothing. The frustration made him want to grab Nick and beat his story into him until he believed.

"I *swear,* Nick—" he began.

Nick approached him, his feet stamping hard into the gravel with each step. His mouth was pulled back in a snarl. "What's going on here, Lare? Some sort of sympathy thing because of what you did to Ray yesterday?"

"No, no, I swear . . ." He backed away from the onslaught. His complete attention was on the pipe Nick still held tightly in his hands, the pipe that was now rising, higher—

"Hey!"

They both froze, Nick looking like some sort of well-dressed cave man, Larry struck dumb, unable to even cower. They slowly turned their heads to the one who had yelled at them.

Mark was still breathing hard as he spoke. "I can't pull you guys apart because I'm not strong enough and I'm not dumb enough, but if you don't stop *right now* I am going to leave here and I won't *ever* talk to you guys again."

Larry and Nick glanced at each other, then back at Mark. Mark stared back with a hard, level gaze that made them feel like freaks at a sideshow.

A moment passed, and Nick realized he was holding his pipe in the air. He lowered it and slumped into a casual stance.

"All right," he said. "Mark's right. We gotta think this through. Larry—"

"Larry," Mark interrupted, his jaw still set, "what do you think happened to the tire and tracks and stuff?"

"I don't know! They didn't catch me, so maybe they figured I would call the police or some exterminators or something. They had the whole night. They could have . . ." He ended with a shrug.

"What?" snapped Nick. "They could have what? They could have picked up the tire, scratched out all their tracks, got rid of every scrap of evidence? Did these things look intelligent to you?"

Larry pushed some errant hair back around his shoulders. The strands were gummy with sweat and some dirt. He hated it that way.

"Well?" Nick demanded.

Larry tried to keep his voice controlled—he would later be surprised that he tried to imitate Mark. "I don't have any answers for you, Nick. I can only tell you what went on here last night. You can beat me until I'm senseless, I'll tell you the same exact story—because it's true."

Nick glared at him, but he didn't seem to have anything additional to say.

Mark spoke, then. His tone was no longer calm; in fact, they could all here the fear behind it, and his words brought the fear home.

"Guys . . . if Ray's inside the Pit, why hasn't he heard us fighting out here and come out?"

Another frozen moment, one that truly brought a chill between them. They found themselves moving closer together again. Each held his length of pipe securely. All eyes were on the Pontiac door.

"We were pretty loud," whispered Larry.

"He should have come out, guys," Mark said.

"Maybe he was in there and went home early," Larry offered.

They all hung onto that suggestion for as long as

possible, but Nick finally had to answer it. "No. He'd wait for me. We were going to hang out today. He's in there."

"What else is in there?" Larry said, and felt Nick nudge him in the ribs.

"Come on."

Nick's soft command brought them all forward in silence. Nick tried the car door's handle, and it clicked: either Ray left it unlocked when he got here today or Larry didn't have the time or want to lock it last night, as he said. Nick opened it carefully; still, there was a shrill grind that put them all on edge.

Nick went in first. He moved across the front seat on his hands and knees. Larry was right behind him. Mark waited for room. At the passenger's window, Nick sat on his knees and peered into the Pit.

The TV was on. Its white glow was twisted away from them; if there was anyone in front of the set, they couldn't see him. The rest of the room was in darkness; the day outside wasn't bright enough to break through the spaces between the tires. Detail of anything was low; if the place was covered with blood, they wouldn't have seen it.

Larry wiggled up behind Nick and set his head on the other boy's shoulder. "I turned that TV off last night," he whispered.

"Are you sure?"

Larry paused. "Positive. I turned it off and put the light bulb on."

They looked at the room again. The shattered glass in the passenger window didn't help in their study, but they could at least tell that the TV, not the bulb, was on.

"So Ray was here," came a voice from behind them. It was Mark, squeezing into the front seat and pressing his head against the roof so he could see over them. "You know, he might not have heard us outside because he was listening to the TV."

"Doesn't work," Larry growled. "We would have heard the TV by now if it was that loud."

"So the TV's on without sound." Nick licked his lips. "Shit. I don't know what that means."

"We're gonna have to go inside," Mark said.

"That's easy for you to say, you fart," Larry whispered harshly, turning to him. "You're in back. If Nick and I get our heads bit off, you'll have a pretty good clue to run like hell —"

"Quiet!" Nick snapped. His hand reached for the door handle. "Get your pipes ready."

Larry and Mark pressed theirs against their chests. Their knuckles were already white and numb from holding them so tightly, but there was no way they were going to let up the pressure now.

The mechanism inside the door popped. Nick peered closely through the window. Nothing stirred inside. The TV light still flickered.

Nick redistributed his weight on his knees — the better to pounce forward or back if he needed — and pushed the car door open. He didn't have the strength or nerve to open it slowly, so its sharp, painful clicks filled the Pit. The curved concrete wall to the left twisted the sound around, making it hollow, as if the Pit were endless. For a moment Nick thought he was entering a sewer that led down to hell. The thought didn't help his nerves any.

At Larry's prodding, Nick stepped into the Pit. He stayed close to the door until Larry was standing with him. Mark made sure the driver's door was still open in case they had to make a quick escape, then he too moved to his friends' sides.

Even from this clearer vantage point, they could make out very little in the darkness. The TV's light seemed to have trouble penetrating the shadows; its glow didn't reach more than a few feet in front of it, to illuminate the edge of the mattress.

They couldn't talk now, not when they were so close to whatever they were after, but Nick gestured at the TV as if to say: *You see? Its sound is turned off.*

The other two nodded.

Nick took a step forward — and nearly swung his pipe around in panic when he felt the tug on his jacket. Larry was holding on to him, needing to stay close. Mark did the same with Larry. Nick swiped his hand away, giving them both a glare that made it clear they better be beside

147

him, not behind him.

In the midst of this silent argument, they heard the noise.

It came from in front of the TV, from somewhere on the mattress. A rustling noise. And then a wet sound, repeated quickly, like . . .

Chewing.

Gnawing.

They barely breathed. All three felt that any minute the Pit would be echoing the hammer of their hearts, deafening the eating noise as it deafened them now.

No one moved for the longest time. They just stared past the television, willing their eyes to part the darkness. Larry and Mark were all for retreating, but neither knew how to communicate this to Nick, even if their throats opened enough to allow them to talk.

Nick was just as frightened, but his curiosity and old sense of protecting Ray made him move ahead again. He made no notice that the other two bodies of his army were not following.

He stayed close to the wall, hoping the darkness would cover him too. Closer, closer, inches turning into feet. Unfortunately, the illumination from the TV did not grow proportionally: the thing in the darkness was still hidden.

The sounds were changing, though. He could make out the groans of the mattress as some great weight shifted on it, the gruff exhale of breath and the nasal inhale — and the quiet but unmistakeable lapping of some fluid.

And he knew, then, that he couldn't will himself to go any closer. This was it. He was halfway along the length of the Pit, several feet from Larry and Mark, the front door, maybe a couple feet from the TV and, hanging above it, the light bulb —

The light bulb!

He knew he could reach it. He knew he could pull the chain and step back quickly should anything charge. He knew Larry and Mark would be watching and would be ready to run. And he knew that once the light was on, it would expose whatever was on the mattress.

What he didn't know, what he couldn't know, was

148

whether the thing on the mattress was watching him right now and was waiting for him to lean closer. It would get him if it pounced right when he jumped toward the bulb. He might be pulled away before he could get the light on, and devoured in the darkness, leaving Mark and Larry to escape on their own with a half-seen story no one would believe.

He didn't have time to think all of this through, however. All he could do was rely on his instincts and his speed. If he was going to do it, it had to be *now*, or his nerve would leave him.

His heart hammered harder, so much that it drowned out the disgusting sounds from the mattress. He peered though the darkness, to that space above the TV, hoping that a little of the TV's glow would illuminate the bulb's chain, that he might get a good aim on it—

There!

He saw it: a dull silver filament that slivered through the darkness. He had to concentrate just to keep it in focus. It was higher than he thought, but he should be able to reach it without jumping up. The problem was whether he would be fast enough to escape any attack from the creature if it was watching him.

No time for that! Go!

And, with a final held breath, he went.

Larry and Mark nearly cried out when they saw Nick rushing toward the TV. They saw an arm raised, but it was empty; the other hand, the one at his side, held the pipe. He wasn't attacking, so what . . .

Nick grasped forward, above his head, fingers searching desperately in the dark. He couldn't see the chain anymore, not at this jerky pace, but he should have touched the damned thing by now. He'd better touch it in the next second, or his momentum would topple him over the TV and right into the lap of that form, that dark, hairy form he could just now make out atop the mattress—

His fingers touched something cold and sinuous, nearly so insubstantial that he thought it might be just a tickle of

149

wind. *This can't be it, can it?* But there was no time to continue searching. It had to be the chain, or he was a dead man. Wildly, his muscles contracted with panicky strength and pulled the chain right out of its hold.

The bulb burst with an orange glow, illuminating the room. Nick stumbled against the TV. He lowered himself, to catch his balance, while raising his pipe for protection. He could almost feel the wind of claws and teeth coming at him; the blurred rush of shadows and light due to the swinging bulb above made the images an abstract reality. Unable to control his fear any longer, Nick let loose with a cry of pure horror.

Behind him, Larry and Mark started at the sudden illumination — then screamed and charged forward with their weapons. Their eyes were glued to Nick, waiting for a hairy muzzle to slam into his middle.

And short, pudgy Ray Holscomb, sitting on the mattress with some cheese balls in one hand, a diet drink in the other, and the tiny headphones to his walkman radio snapped tight over his ears, screamed in surprise at the sudden light and three charging forms in the room. He bucked away until his back was against the wall and threw his can of soda at them, hitting Larry square in the forehead.

The shock passed in seconds, followed by a prickly relief. Nick and Mark busted up laughing, while Larry cursed at the can that had hit him and Ray cursed at everyone for nearly giving him a heart attack.

"What the *hell* are you guys *doing?*" Ray screamed, rising to his feet. His knees were still shaky, so that he looked slightly drunk as he approached them.

"Sorry," Nick said, still laughing. "Larry told us a hell of a story and we thought you might be a monster."

"What?" Ray squeaked. "What do you mean, a monster?"

"It wasn't a story," Larry said, still holding his forehead. A small trickle of blood squeezed between his fingers. "I know what I saw, and *you* believed it!"

He pointed at Nick; Nick looked away sheepishly.

Ray was calmer now, but his voice took on a wounded

tone as he said, "Come on, guys. You sneak in here and scare the shit out of me. What's this all about?" The last was directed at Larry with a touch of malice; he hadn't forgotten what went on the day before, and he wondered if this were some extension of it. Just a little game to scare the piss out of Ray.

But Larry's face was completely serious as he explained what he had encountered last night. It was the second time around for Mark and Nick, but the absolute conviction in Larry's voice made them shiver all over again.

When he was done, Nick added, "But we still haven't found any evidence, and no matter what went on here just now, I'm still not convinced."

"Ray," Mark said, "did you see a tire lying outside the Pit when you got here?"

"Nope. 'Course, I wasn't looking for one, but if it happened right out front like you said, Lare, it should have been obvious."

"No tracks or anything?" Mark pushed.

"I didn't notice. I wasn't looking for monster tracks when I got here."

"Was the Pontiac door unlocked when you got here?" Nick asked.

"Yeah, it was," Ray said. "I was going to talk to you about that. I figured either you or Larry left it undone last night."

"See," Larry said, stepping closer to Nick. "I told you. I ran out of here so damned fast that I didn't lock up. You *know* I wouldn't forget something like that, not with all our beer in here."

"He's right," Mark said grudgingly. "No way he'd put the brew in danger."

"Damn right!" Larry thrust his chin at Nick.

Nick stared at him levelly. "That only convinces me that you saw something last night that made you run away before locking up the place. That still doesn't prove that what you saw were monsters."

"Even if there were," Ray offered, "would they be smart enough to cover up their tracks?"

"Maybe it's instinctive," Larry said. "They don't want to

151

get caught. It's part of their survival. They know we hang out here, so they're protecting themselves."

"Yeah, but—"

"Maybe," Larry said, taking on a dreamy look, "maybe what made them so oversized outside changed a part of them *inside*, too. Maybe their brains are affected."

Ray looked at him, puzzled. "Oversized? What size are monsters supposed to be?"

Larry didn't answer. He lowered his head and licked his lips.

Nick grinned and explained, "Old Lare here thinks they may be some kind of rats."

"Rats? Jesus, Lar is this some kind of story or—"

"For the last time, it is not a story!" Larry stared hard at each boy, searching for the words that would convince them, that would put them over on his side. "I tried to call the police last night about these things. I was that sure. I was *positive*. And I still am. My mom kept me from calling because she said they wouldn't believe me." He felt his head filling with something, something that brought a strain to his throat, made it hard to swallow. "She cried in my arms last night. All over this monster thing. And even after all that, I'm positive of what I saw. Do you think I'd do that to my mom if I wasn't sure?"

None of the boys answered. They'd never met Larry's mom and he'd never spoken about her before, except to say that she wanted him home at a certain time. But the tears that Larry strained to keep back went a long way toward convincing them.

After a full minute, Mark spoke. "All right, then. What do we do?"

Nick shrugged and looked at Ray. Ray took a small handful of cheese balls and stuck them in his mouth while staring blankly at Larry's feet.

In the end, it seemed inevitable that the one who had planned their adventures in the past would plan this one too. Larry cleared his throat, blinked back his feelings, and announced, "We can't go to the police. We can't really go anywhere to get help without some proof. So we'll have to do this on our own. We'll search this place until we find the evidence we need."

When he finished, silence returned. Mark and Ray looked at each other and nodded. When they turned to Nick, he gritted his teeth and wobbled his head in uncertainty, muttering, "Well, I guess we have to . . ."

"You have a better plan?" Larry asked.

Nick paused, as if on the verge of saying something, but it ended with a shrug and, "Guess not."

"Good," Larry said, speaking with a renewed strength. "Then let's go find those bastards."

They searched in pairs, Ray with Nick and Mark with Larry. They looked for anything that might support Larry's story, or might at least look good to the police.

It took them an hour to find the first hole. It was the same hole that Mary Hawthorne's dog had approached so carefully, a pit at the end of a descending trail that separated stacked crates. The four could just barely squeeze between the crates; they kept their distance from the hole itself. It wasn't just the deep darkness beyond the edges that made them wary. From their vantage, it was clear that something dark and wet had soaked into the ground near the entrance; an attempt had been made to cover it up, but it still managed to rise to the surface, like some ugly birthmark on the Earth.

"This has got to be it," Larry said shakily. "Jesus, I wasn't dreaming. I knew I wasn't."

"Were you drinking?" Ray asked. It was obvious from his tone that he was only half-joking. Larry's cocky assurance about these monsters had disturbed him from the start . . . and he still hadn't forgotten yesterday. Having Larry in such a vulnerable position was almost a godsend.

Larry snarled, "Fuck you."

Ray stiffened with the instant surge of adrenaline. The raw emotions of yesterday were back again. He wouldn't let Larry get away with what he did, real friends weren't like that . . .

"It's a fair question," he said, "considering what you guys do Friday nights when *you* don't have dates, which is

153

most of the time."

Larry opened his mouth to snap back, but was shocked to silence by the voice behind him—Mark.

"Shut up, Ray. You're one to talk about not having dates."

"Goddamn fat fairy," Larry added under his breath. "I'd like to see what you would have done if you'd seen these things."

"I wouldn't have run!" Ray growled, embarrassed that his voice betrayed him again with a squeak. Larry and Mark laughed at the noise. "I wouldn't have run and screamed like a little girl!" Ray insisted.

For an unnerving moment, Larry wondered how the hell he knew that he'd screamed like a girl. Was Ray really behind this after all? He lashed out. "No, you would have pissed your pants like a little girl! You would have stood there and let those things gnaw your dick off! Well, at least I don't *act* like a little girl, Ray-dene. At least I *like* girls."

"The littler, the better, right?" Ray quipped. He'd spent most the previous night in bed trying to think of stuff he should have said to Larry when they'd fought at the Pit. Now the words seemed to roll from his lips without thought. Unfortunately, the jumpy mixture of anger and fear was still there, and already he was flinching away from any possible punch in the face.

But punches never got a chance to start flying. Nick was there, and he was sick to death of this fighting. He moved between Larry and Ray and stamped the ground hard with his boots, raising a small dust cloud.

"All *right*, already! Grow up! I'm tired of this."

Larry smacked his leg with one hand. "Super Nick to the rescue. Have to protect Miss Ray Lane, right Nick?"

Nick's hand flew out and grabbed Larry by the cuff. A second later, Mark's hand was over his.

"Come on, Nick," Mark said. "You know you always stand up for Ray. Ray's never fought his own fights in his life. Everyone at school knows that." He stared directly at Ray, not with hate, but with a more piercing look of pity. "Nick, you, and sometimes Lare and I, are the *only* reason

Ray's never been beat up by other kids. Maybe it's time to let him fight his own battles."

Nick glared back. "Get your hand off mine." Mark's hand came off. Nick pulled Larry closer, so that their noses almost touched. "We are not here to fight, right? We all came to help you. We've found your goddamn hole for your goddamn monsters, so what do you want to do about it?"

Larry looked away, his face red, and he didn't say a word until Nick let go of his jacket and backed away, holding his palms up to show that everything was calm again.

"A hole isn't enough," Larry finally announced.

"What?" the other three cried in unison.

"If we go to the police with my story and we tell them we found a hole in a junkyard, do you think that would convince them? It's just a lousy hole in a junkyard!" He paced, frustrated by this.

Ray scurried to the divide in the crates to point down at the hole. "Look there! That stain. They can analyze it. It might be blood."

"And it might not," said Nick before Larry could respond.

"Well, we have to do *some*thing. If these monsters have covered up—"

"Oh, *now* he believes in them again," Larry muttered. Mark snickered.

Ray ignored them and went on. "If these monsters have covered up their tracks, this hole is the *only* thing we have. If we can't go to the police with it, what *can* we do?"

No one could supply an answer. The silence was growing uncomfortably long again, so Nick found himself jumping in with something that had been troubling him from the beginning.

"There's still a question here. Why haven't these monsters attacked the Pit before last night?" He looked at Larry. "They could have gotten you and Mark any Friday night."

Larry shrugged. "Maybe they just got here recently."

"I don't buy that. From your story, it sounds like they

155

know this place well. The big one even followed you through the maze without getting lost once."

"It could smell me. It just followed the scent."

"Even then it could have taken a wrong turn. There's plenty of corridors that are real close to each other. With you halfway down one and out of sight, it couldn't have been sure which to follow—unless it knew you were headed for the gate and it knew the pathway."

Larry shook his head, still blind to the point. "So what if they've been here a while? Why's that matter?"

"They never actually went into the Pit, did they?"

"No."

"And they've never bugged us outside the place before, maybe because there's always been at least two of us around."

"So what's your point?" Ray asked.

"It's just that this seems like a one-time thing. I don't want any cops poking around here for nothing and closing the place up before Friday night—"

"*Christ*, Nick!" Larry exploded. "What's wrong with you? Do you want to put Pauline in that kind of danger?"

"I'm still not convinced there would be any danger. Look, we've found their hole. We can search the rest of the yard, every inch, for any other holes. If we cover them up, make sure they can't get out for a couple nights—"

"This is *nuts!*" Larry cried. "We can't just lock them away and hope they won't find another way out until Saturday so that you can have your little boff-o-rama—"

Nick's face went serious and red at the same time. He took a step toward Larry, his fists clenched. "Watch your mouth."

Ray leaned against the crates. He didn't want to hear any of this. It was just too . . . different from what it used to be.

Larry was wise enough not to tangle with Nick; he put his hands in front of him, as if to push Nick off, and said, "Hey, whoa. All right. I just meant that maybe you're not thinking clearly on this thing."

Nick's shoulders relaxed a bit, but there was still fire in his eyes. "Not thinking clearly?" he asked. "I seem to be the *only* one thinking clearly. You guys haven't come up with a single idea on what to do about these things. I say we push a mountain of junk over their holes and let them stew for a couple days. They'll starve and that'll be that. Then you can call some sort of health organization and complain about the smell."

"And you're sure that covering their holes will stop them?" Larry didn't make it a question; he could see that Nick was convinced.

"I'm risking my life on it—and I don't do that for anything. *Any*thing," he added, looking hard at Larry.

Ray usually found himself supporting Nick when there was a dispute, not because Nick always protected him but because Nick was usually the clearest thinker of the group. He could stand back and look at a problem and find the obvious solution that all of them had missed. This time, though, Ray felt an irritating prickle of doubt as he listened to his friend. If Larry was telling the truth—and, despite their disagreements, Ray felt he was—then it didn't sound to him like a good idea to just wait around for the things to starve.

"Um," he stammered. They turned to him, and he kept his tone under control as he told them, "I don't think we should do that. I think it might be best if we just call the sheriff."

Mark shook his head tiredly. "Ray, we've been over that. The police won't believe us. We don't have any proof."

"But we have this hole, and maybe more if we look for them. We can just say we saw something big go into them. Even if it was just a lost dog, don't you think the sheriff would send someone out—"

"No one from the police is going to help us," Larry said.

"But they *might*," Ray continued, but he knew he was losing them, losing their support and their camaraderie, and maybe losing them in worse ways if they didn't listen to him. "We should take the chance. I could tell my parents and they could come with us. The sheriff would listen to them—"

Larry was shaking his head just as wearily as Mark now, though Ray sensed a suppressed violence behind it.

"You're just not *getting* it, are you, Ray? You just don't *understand*." Larry slowly approached him. With every accented word, his hand chopped at the air. "No one's going to *believe* us because we don't have any *proof*. We're just a bunch of *kids* who they're going to throw in *jail* for being in this junkyard in the *fucking first place!*" The chopping hand turned to a fist that pressed against Ray's chest. Ray wanted to see if Nick would step in, but he couldn't make himself twist his gaze from Larry. He wanted him to see that he defied him, that he dared him to become just another bully.

Larry blinked at the silent accusation. Some of the fire left his eyes.

"All right, Larry," Nick's voice came.

Larry gave Ray a final little push with his fist, then whirled around, walked to a pile of sharp metal beams, and hefted two in his arms.

"All right, then," he said, looking back at the gang. "Let's get moving with this thing." He walked past them, down the little path between the crates, and pushed the beams halfway through the hole. Mark soon followed his lead, and right behind him was Nick.

Ray watched them in silence. When the hole was nearly plugged with the beams, he hazarded, "Hey, guys, couldn't we just—"

"Shut up, Ray!" Larry called.

"It's the only way!" Mark said, looking up at him.

Nick stood straight, hands on his hips. He grinned slightly. "Come on, Ray," he said softly. "Join us . . . or keep out of the way."

Ray ducked out of sight from them, and they heard his running footsteps grow softer with distance. Nick looked down at the other two. They wouldn't meet his eyes, but there was no look of triumph on their faces.

Their expressions changed when Ray appeared again with both arms filled with metal beams from the pile. "Let's get this done quick," he said, ignoring their smiles. "We have to find all the holes in this junkyard before night comes."

They were satisfied with their work in just half an hour. The beams had plugged the hole, and the entire pathway had been filled with any heavy junk they could find, including some fair-sized rocks. Then the crates were pushed over the whole thing. They didn't know what was in the crates, but it took the four of them just to lift one atop another. They were without doubt that the combination of junk would hold whatever was in that hole — at least for a couple days.

After a quick breather, they set out looking for more holes. They didn't find any, but they did discover what might have been smudged claw prints in the gravel beneath some of the towers, putrid droppings too large to have come from pets, and an old refrigerator lying on its side near the back fence with slash marks all over it — none of which was good enough to be used as proof for the police, but did further their own conviction that *something* was living beneath the junkyard.

Larry was a little more relieved every time another piece of evidence popped up to prove he wasn't crazy. By the end of the day, he was all smiles and happy mischief again, somewhat to the chagrin of the other three boys, who were now tired and afraid.

"Buck up, guys!" Larry called to them on their way back to the Pit. "We've got them covered. There isn't anything that can move that junk off the hole. Nick, you can even have your Friday night!" Ahead, where Larry couldn't read his expression, Nick nodded.

When they were inside the Pit, Nick found his voice again and was at once in control. "That's it, then, guys. Everything's set." He pushed the TV back away from the mattress. "The weather guy says it's not going to rain tomorrow, so we can put off tarring the crack in the roof until later." He didn't mention that he didn't have enough money to buy tar *and* take Pauline out Friday night, anyway. "I'm going home now. You guys can hang around if you want, but do *not* drink in here tonight, even with the vent open. And please don't show up tomorrow after school to mess the place up. All right?" He watched Mark

159

and Larry until they both nodded agreement.

"I'm going home, anyhow," Mark said He had no intention of sticking around in the dark after hearing Larry's story.

"Me, too," Ray and Larry said at the same time—then both frowned that they should agree on something.

"Good. Then let's get out of here." Nick clapped his hands and moved to turn the light out—and noticed that the chain was no longer hanging from the bulb. He'd pulled it out of the socket earlier, when they'd scared Ray. "Shit!" he said.

"Here . . ." Larry came forward and unscrewed the bulb. The Pit was plunged into darkness.

There was no time for fear to affect them. Almost immediately there was a sharp *bang*. "Damn it!" Nick spat. "It's darker than shit in here. Banged my shin."

The other boys laughed as they hurried to the Pontiac's door. "Won't be needing any lights tomorrow night," Larry cackled. Even Ray laughed at that.

And for those brief moments, as they stood there in the dark together, taking turns crawling across the Pontiac's front seat to the outside, they felt like giddy friends again, as if four years of change had never passed.

The setting sun set off a wind of bitter cold from the north swirling through the streets of Winsome. The boys were protected from the wind somewhat by the towers of junk that surrounded them, but the drop in temperature still seeped through and kept their feet stamping for warmth.

None of them would go off without the others, not tonight. They waited for each to move through the car, and then they would journey home as a group, like the old days.

Except it was taking a long time for Larry, the last one, to make it through the car. He had stayed back on purpose. His bond with Mark had been strengthened this day, despite the nightmare that was the catalyst, and that convinced him that their plans for Friday should move full steam ahead.

Alone in the Pit, he rushed over to where the mattress had been dragged and pushed the last two days, and positioned it near the vent again. He looked up at the trapdoor and reminded himself that it needed a string connected to the outside so that it could be lifted from its niche. Maybe he could get Nick to do it. He stood beneath the door and jumped, keeping his eyes on the mattress. Perfect view . . . as long as the mattress stayed in place. Chancy, but it couldn't be helped.

He heard his name called, rushed for the car door, pausing long enough to grab up a couple of porno tapes. When he emerged into the yard, he was met with commands to move his ass. He locked the car and hid the key the usual place behind the back left wheel.

"What took you?" Nick asked. "It's freezing out here and you're screwing around."

"Had to get these." He held up the tapes. "Figured if Mark and I couldn't watch them in the Pit tomorrow, maybe we could watch them somewhere else." He smiled, sure that his explanation would pacify them.

It did.

Nick said good night to Mark and Larry and walked with Ray as far as he could. Ray's mood had changed on the way home; Larry, in his good spirits, had teased Ray, which was about par, but the ribbing must have reminded Ray of the lashing he'd taken earlier in the junkyard.

"They don't really mean it," Nick said. "You know that." Ray only nodded and offered a lazy smile.

At the corner where their respective streets joined, Nick gave him a pat on the back and wished him a good night. Ray said, "See you later"; Nick noticed that his teeth were clamped tight, as if he were holding back some additional words.

It wasn't until Nick was climbing the porch steps to his house that he realized that the grimace might have been aimed at him. Or, rather, Pauline and him. He remembered now that everyone had wished him a "good night —

and a better tomorrow night," except Ray. He could understand why Ray wouldn't want him to have a great Friday night, but that was his problem. As he'd told Larry, Ray had had his chance and never used it. Pauline was his now, and he wasn't going to dampen his affection for her for anyone.

All thoughts, troubling or otherwise, concerning Pauline and Ray were wiped away, however, as he stepped through the front door of his home. All his attention went to moving stealthily. His old man's snore was rattling the roof, the drone of the TV backing it up, but he knew from experience that the slightest creak of a floorboard could wake him. Then the odds would be fifty-fifty whether the old man would go back to sleep or begin screaming and lashing out for blood.

In the past, after the violence had been spent, Nick always told himself and his little brother, Billy, that it was the alcohol that made their dad act that way. The truth was that their father was prone to outbursts even when he wasn't drinking—though he could be more reasonable then. Nick wished he'd gotten home earlier, before the evening bout had begun. It was impossible to ask his dad not to drink every night, but just tonight would have been fine. Then he could have asked for the car Friday night without a beating for his insolence; then he could have called Pauline and told her she wouldn't have to pick *him* up at the corner—an embarrassing procedure he had to go through every week.

But all that was in the crapper. The old man was well on his way to oblivion by now. If asked, he would insist that the car stay out front, gathering cobwebs, in case he should get a call to work somewhere—or, more likely, he should run out of beer.

So Pauline would have to pick him up, as they'd planned. All Nick could do now was make sure he didn't show up for their date with a black eye.

With that worthy goal in mind, Nick was extra careful in closing and locking the door, turning the hall light out, and snaking his way up the stairs. Midway, he stopped to give his mother's picture a kiss, as he did every night. The insurance money from her death kept this family under a roof, with food to eat, clothes to wear—yet also provided an excuse for the old man to avoid finding work: a double-edged sword if there ever was one. But Nick felt she was happier now than when she lived with the old man. He'd always been a drunk, so it was she who had kept up the payments on the house, all the appliances—and the life insurance. She knew. And Nick knew. The day that money ran out, Nick would take his brother Billy into one arm, take the picture of their mother in the other, and they'd walk out of this house forever, a family.

For now, though, they were stuck. *Perhaps*, Nick considered, reaching his bedroom, *it's best the old man is unconscious most of the time.*

Billy was sitting on his bed under the window, a weak lamp in the corner illuminating the homework scattered across his blankets. He looked up and smiled as his brother entered.

"Hey, Nick."

"Hey, Billy. What's up?" Nick made his way between their two beds—it wasn't a very large room—and hung his jacket up in the closet.

"Homework," Billy sneered. "Did you stop off at the Pit today?" Billy never grew up innocent, but his face lit up whenever Nick mentioned the clubhouse in the junkyard. It made Nick remember the excitement he used to feel for it.

"Yup," he said noncommittally.

"And?"

Nick glanced at him. "And what?"

Billy sat up on his bed, still grinning foolishly. "And is everything set for Friday? Are you going to get into Pauline's pants?"

Nick was never shocked by such questions from his brother. Billy was eleven years old, becoming more interested in girls, and Nick tried to instill in him that sex and love were not dirty or unnatural, as long as you took responsibility for them. He was always at odds with his father over this—though the struggle was secret—because of his father's insistence that their mother always consid-

163

ered sex to be a dirty, horrible thing. Nick knew that this couldn't be so, not that lovely woman on the stairway wall. But she might have thought that sex was a dirty, horrible thing when it involved the old man. *That,* Nick could believe.

Nevertheless, Billy's question was too personal, and Nick answered it with: "None of your damned business."

His slight smile gave him away, though. Billy burst with a "Ha!" that was so throaty that Nick thought he sounded like their father. "You'll get lucky," he added, curling back to his homework.

"Shut up."

Nick sat on his bed, waited for the noisy bounce of the springs to dampen, and then went about removing his boots. After all that had happened today, Billy's words brought him full circle, back to Pauline. For the millionth time, he imagined what tomorrow might be like, what might go wrong. Most of all, he prayed that he would not embarrass himself with her. The thought opened a whole new world of embarrassment for him. Fortunately he was certain she would never talk to anyone about it if he asked her not to. Even if he didn't ask her. She was that kind of girl. Special.

And because of her specialness, he knew, deep down, if she refused him tomorrow night, if she just said "No" once, he would not pressure her—and he'd stay with her the days, weeks, and months afterward, too. Just being with her was enough—and that scared him more than all the rest.

When the haze cleared, he looked up with the feeling that someone was watching him. Billy stared back, a toothy smile plastered across his face.

Nick managed to think, *He's going to be a heartbreaker someday,* before Billy started his needling song.

"Nicky's in lo-ove. Nicky's in lo-ove . . ."

Nick waited until the inevitable smacking sounds came to throw his pillow into his brother's kisser.

Across town, as the night grew darker, Ed Kelton

164

shifted down in his seat and prepared to wait and watch. The streetlights blinked on, but they weren't strong enough to make out his form behind the fog of the car windows. He was as cloaked in darkness as the world behind that iron gate across the street.

His mind wandered as he sat there, going back to all the research he'd conducted yesterday at the library. The trip outside had been a little unnerving—the Winsome Community Library was clear across town—but he'd driven slowly and was thankful that there weren't a whole lot of people inside the flat-box building.

The library's exterior hadn't been very impressive; there was some doubt as to whether they'd have *any* microfilm, least of all film of past newspapers. Luckily Winsome, though small, was up-to-date.

The librarian, a tall, lanky man with a crisp mustache, took a few minutes to show him how to use the viewing machine, and then Ed was off, lost in the past of Winsome and the surrounding areas.

Five hours later, he'd found what he wanted. It wasn't really a complete answer, but his head was clear enough to put the right pieces together and come up with a workable theory. The fact that he could connect anything was proof to him that he was returning to his old, crafty self, and that he might just get through all this after all.

But the theory he devised nearly dashed those hopes completely.

Two years ago, the state government convinced the locals that something could be done with the fields around Winsome other than feeding cows. They wanted to try to grow some crops there. The local government representative, James Thanimore—a name Ed Kelton had never heard before—was quoted as saying that the state government wouldn't listen to him when he told them that the soil and weather weren't right for growing the types of crops they requested. He said the state boys just smiled and said not to worry.

A few weeks later it was reported that the Department of Agriculture was involved. Mr. Thanimore tried to convince them; surely they knew that their crops wouldn't grow in Winsome. Thanimore came away from that meeting with a smile just as deceptive as the state boys'. He explained that the Department of Agriculture wanted to plant certain crops — now reported as tomatoes, lettuce, and various melons, a strange combination — that were not regularly receptive to areas like Winsome because they were testing new processes. A successful harvest could bode well for the entire country.

In other words, Ed thought, *the state boys told you that if you don't make waves, this little experiment might put Winsome on the map — and make your career.*

Not much more was heard from Thanimore or the state boys for some time. However, the mayor of Winsome was apparently briefed by Thanimore; during his speech for the 90th birthday of the town, he mentioned that the "steroid and potential crop development research instigated by our wonderful country could only find a home in one place: a place where the rivers run clear and the fields are fresh and . . ." — *Cut the crap, Mayor,* Ed thought. The bottom line was that there was some heavy duty government stuff going on in Winsome . . . and it had to do with the drug steroid.

Ed wasn't too disturbed by it. He'd heard of this sort of stuff going on all the time. People trying to grow bigger and better food, bigger and better beef, bigger and better everything. Irritation set in, however, when he couldn't find another word about it in the newspapers. Not one word.

He went back over the two years again, now searching more than just the local news sections. Still nothing. But he did find smaller pieces that fit around the big one. Things like Thanimore quitting his job and taking one somewhere in Washington, the offer and acceptance encompassing just two days. Then there was the small ad a week later, jumbled with the usual ads where anyone could buy or sell anything from Mickey Mouse telephones to old Buicks to ancient rocking chairs. This particular ad offered some prize real estate on the outskirts of Winsome — land, Ed guessed, that had served its country's purpose and had failed in some way, and was consequently returned to the common people.

After that, not a stirring or a hint about the Department of Agriculture's tests.

What sort of tests? Ed wondered. Bigger and better crops. By what method? He went back to what the mayor had said, something about steroids.

Steroids?

It sounded odd the first time he'd read it, and it still didn't read right. Athletes used steroids, not plants. Were they going to pump the soil full of the stuff so that Winsome would have crops that flexed muscles? Strange.

Fortunately he was in a library, so he simply looked up the first book on steroids he came across and flipped through the contents page. He stopped when he came to the chapter titled "History."

That's when everything began to click.

Ed learned that steroid was a drug originally used to treat dwarfism in infants. It increased the growth potential. Apparently that's what the Department of Agriculture, that benign organization, was trying to do with the crops they planted outside Winsome. Ed doubted they used the steroid drug itself, probably a variation of it. Or a mutation. After that . . . well, the experiment either failed or the funding was cut. Either way, the state boys left, along with Thanimore.

Without publicity.

Why no publicity? Not even a small paragraph in the back of the newspaper. This was supposed to be a big deal, though they'd apparently tried to keep a lid on it at the beginning; why pull out without any explanation? The embarrassment couldn't be that bad, even for the government.

Unless . . .

Ed could come up with only one explanation: wrong or right, it was what he came to believe. The experimental drug may have kept the crops the same size or increased their growth — the latter, more likely, since the state boys were all smiles at the beginning and must have done *some* testing before coming to Winsome — but the chemical, or some side effect, had left the plants completely inedible.

167

Perhaps even dangerous. So they'd cleaned up quietly and left. No need to tell the good folks of Winsome that they might have been in some danger, especially when they never got close to the chemical or the plants themselves, right?

Except they didn't get away clean. People never got to those plants, but *something* did. And the same thing that affected the plants might also affect the eaters. A young animal's growth could be completely screwed up. Different instincts. Different likes and dislikes.

Different *tastes*.

In that instant, the terror passed through him again: *huge eyes, huge bodies, huge teeth, huge—*

He had squeezed his eyes tight and gripped the table end until the cold sickness had passed. Now, slouched in his car, watching the front of the junkyard, he felt ill again. He was better at controlling it now, so this time it was gone in seconds. He shook his head clear. Tiny dots of sweat painted the dashboard.

All right. You know. You're sure. And, dammit, you're doing something about it.

He'd told himself that a thousand times since his visit to the library yesterday. It kept him calm. This horror would not go on. He would put a stop to it, or die in the attempt. His children's deaths would not go unanswered.

The decision had not been an easy one. All last night, he had tossed in bed, trying to devise the right plan. He eliminated outside help immediately. He couldn't contact the government or even the local authorities; they'd know instantly where these creatures had come from, and then they'd wonder about the rest of the town. Going public through newspapers was out, too; he knew what would happen. A town near an out-of-control biological experiment? A faulty test instigated by the United States government? Forget keeping it secret, though the state boys would try. And what if the surrounding towns, afraid for their own health, demanded that Winsome and its people be isolated and turned into permanent guinea pigs?

There was no way Ed was going to let that happen to his town.

So that left getting rid of the creatures himself. Quietly.

The next morning, many hours before the vigil he now kept outside the junkyard, he had contacted an old friend from Vietnam. He was surprised at how easily he could purchase just about any weapon in the world — and grateful that his friend would let them out on credit.

Ed was careful in his selections; he didn't want to take advantage, and besides, he knew that he couldn't very well take an arsenal with him into the monsters' lair. He already had a shotgun, so he looked for something different, something that could do the job at a distance, yet leave him without doubt that the victim was dead.

He decided on a flamethrower. There was a poetic justice in torching those hellish demons that was too tempting to let pass. His friend showed him the newer models, the ones that used various kinds of napalm, but the thought of that sticky chemical splashing about in what he presumed would be narrow confines made Ed lean toward an older model. He eventually chose an improved and modified version of the M2-2 flamethrower, first used at the end of World War II against the Japanese. The fuel tank, enlarged for this model, would hold regular gasoline, and his friend showed him how to adjust the nitrogen pressure tank so that the spray would reach only three yards. The original M2-2 had weighed about 70 pounds when the tanks were full, but his friend explained that the fuel and compression tanks were made of more modern, light-weight material. The strain would only be about 55 pounds. Ed smiled. No further questions were asked on either side of the transaction.

Ed had hurried home so that he could make his next appointment. He knew, from his days of working there, that no one passed by the junkyard in early afternoon. Kids were in school, and parents were either shopping downtown or having quiet affairs at home. So he entered the yard unseen, his trusty shotgun at his side.

It didn't take him long to find the hole behind the crates. He stalked the direction those beasts had dragged his children and then relied on his own instincts.

The hole wasn't very large — but large enough. He could squeeze through, as long as he wasn't encumbered with large belts or backpacks. That would alter his original plans, but he could make concessions. Beyond that, unless the walls opened wider inside, there wouldn't be any room to maneuver. But he wasn't going to retreat until he killed every creature inside there anyway, so that was not really a problem.

He spent the rest of the day at home, modifying the weapons he'd purchased. Some needed breaking down, so they'd fit inside the hole; others he created from scratch, like the metal shield that would precede him. By seven o'clock that night, he had most of the hard work done. Any details and fine-tuning could be done the next day.

So he had the knowledge and he had the hardware. All he had left to do was make sure he wouldn't be prevented from taking on the task. He was aware that, because of the disappearances in town, the police had stepped up their patrols around certain blocks — including the junkyard. Of course, just walking onto his own property would not be suspicious in itself — but if he walked in tomorrow night carrying his weapons just as a police cruiser rounded the bend . . .

Which was why he was now seated in his car outside the junkyard at night, freezing, waiting for the next patrol to pass. He figured it would come any minute now, if it kept up the routine of the past two hours.

And there it was. Headlights blinded him for a moment as the car made the turn around the corner. He sank lower in his seat. The patrol car drifted past without hesitating. There were several cars just like Ed's parked on this same street. Nothing suspicious about that. In seconds, the cruiser was gone.

Ed checked his watch. Nearly ten o'clock. He'd been here since seven forty-five. The police cruiser had kept up a schedule of about twenty minutes, give or take ten minutes. Plenty of time for him to park the car, get the gear out of the trunk, and make his way into the junkyard tomorrow night.

And two hours was *more* than enough time to be sitting

170

in a ice-cold car late at night. He started the engine and headed for home.

Quite a Friday night you've got planned, old buddy, he thought with a smile. *Maybe wilder than some of those Fridays you've spent hallucinating.*

Unfortunately, he couldn't know just how much wilder it would be.

On the far side of town, Deputy Kevin Gavel also filled his head with wild thoughts. He drove smoothly through the affluent streets of the west side. It was quite a way from the junkyard route, and one that Gavel didn't usually get. Things were too quiet here. One's mind started to wander. Every now and then, when Gavel broke through his haze to take a gander outside the window, he'd wonder where the hell he was. Then it would come back to him. The *new* neighborhood.

The houses, even the streets, around him had only been up for a year or two. New families filled them. This was the very edge of Winsome, far from the decay of the town's center. These were the privileged ones. It was quiet here, just like the advertisements for any small town. And boring. Gavel had hoped for *some* action to keep his mind off the loneliness.

Not that he loved the other posts. He didn't like the idea of spending all his time inside those ten blocks Sheriff Peltzer considered high-alert. There was always the chance that two patrol routes would cross. One of his brother officers might see him picking up a child that would go missing later. *That* he couldn't have, just couldn't. His word against a citizen was one thing; cop against cop was a hell of a cock fight.

In a way, this area was perfect for his appetites. His cruiser was the only one on this patrol. Behind the beautiful two-story houses was a wide expanse of land being readied for more homes some day: desolate, dark, spooky. Beyond that, a mile down the double-lane road, was the highway. A long way to go in the dark, but Gavel knew that runaways did it all the time. And, fortunately, that was part of his route, too.

He'd been out there countless times tonight, but that lonely road had been just that. Deserted. It was maddening. The loving itch had been coming on him strong all day, that familiar cold fork that stirred his guts and gurgled up prickly bubbles that floated out the pores of his skin.

He would have to do something soon. God, if he didn't —

But luck was with Kevin Gavel that night.

He turned the last corner of the residential area and sped out into the night along Benson Road. In the distance, the lights from the Interstate created a tiny sunrise on the horizon. The glow was pale, though, and fortunately did not reach very far.

Gavel slowed the car and peered carefully into the darkness on either side.

Ten minutes later, he picked up something. His heart surged as the outline became more distinct. Oh, yes, luck was with him tonight.

The form was male, actually just a boy if Gavel could go by his baby-smooth face. He was medium-height, dressed in a heavy brown coat, like ranchers would wear, jeans, and carrying a knapsack. Not anyone Gavel recognized. A runaway.

Another town? Gavel hoped and prayed. He giggled for a moment when he realized there was a drop of drool sliding off his chin. *Gosh, it has been a while . . .*

He pulled to the side of the road and shone his spotlight on the kid. For a moment, the boy looked like he might make a run for it — but then his frame deflated and he shuffled toward the cruiser, ready to accept his fate.

Gavel giggled again.

The boy stood near the passenger window, bent over, waiting for it to roll down so that he could speak. Gavel let him wait. When the moment was right, he surprised the kid by stepping out of the car and moving around the front to face him eye to eye.

No more than sixteen, Gavel figured. His brown hair was long and uncombed, and by the odor Gavel guessed

172

he hadn't been intimate with a shower in days.

The boy looked back at him and nodded uncertainly. "Sir," he said.

Gavel glanced down the road. Pure darkness. No one traveled this road this time of the night. Gavel pulled out his notepad and started doing the cop bullshit, asking a few key questions along with a lot he didn't need the answers to.

The kid was heading for L.A. To do what? He had no idea. Just to get away. He was from Sundale, a small town south of Winsome that lay beside the Bridgestone River, known throughout the state for its great fishing. The boy didn't like fish and he didn't like Sundale. His parents didn't care about him and his friends only hung on him if he would supply them with drugs.

Gavel looked up at this. "Got any on you now, son?"

"No, sir," The boy didn't flinch or make a grab for one of his pockets. Gavel believed him. Not that it mattered.

Gavel handcuffed the boy and shoved him into the backseat. As they drove back to town, Gavel tried to calm him by telling him that he was just doing his job, that he understood the kid didn't want to go back, that they'd straighten it all out at the station and everything would be all right.

The kid was visibly relieved by the chatter. Gavel figured he'd had enough of a taste of "freedom" to realize that maybe he had it pretty good back home. Oh, well. Too late now.

Gavel headed for home. The town was small enough that the sheriff usually let him park the cruiser in his garage if he was getting off late. He'd be able to drive it in, close the door, and get the kid in through the kitchen without anyone the wiser. Fortunately, nosey neighbors were not a problem. He was continually grateful for that.

The trip took about half an hour. During the drive, the kid asked twice whether Gavel shouldn't call in to the station to report he'd picked up a runaway. The first time, Gavel assured him that that wasn't necessary with runaways. The kid was unconvinced; apparently he'd been through this thing before. The second time, Gavel just smiled and said he wanted to stop off at home for something first, and that he could fix both of them a sandwich and something to drink. There was no hurry. The kid seemed to buy this. He even thanked Gavel.

Once inside the house, all of that changed. Gavel sat him down on a kitchen chair. The boy looked up at him and asked that he please remove the cuffs so he could eat easier.

Gavel considered this. He really should give the kid some food, get him washed up for the evening. But the cold gnawing inside him had been going on for too long. It seemed to come stronger recently, and with fewer days in between. He remembered when he could go months . . .

The heat was surging through him now. He didn't have to get to know his lover this time. The pounding heartbeat and the itchy fingers and the solid erection were already there, begging for some warmth, some love.

He looked down at the kid's face, watched the boyish features become more and more nervous, *God*, that fear did something to him.

"Fuck it," he laughed. He pushed the boy down the hall and into the soundproof room and latched the door behind them.

In his own cozy room, Ray Holscomb was in bed, but far from sleep. He put his hands behind his head and started to think. He had a lot to plan. Through the hours, his mind would wander, and when he'd break through the haze, he'd wonder *why* he was doing this. Then it would come back.

The pain and humiliation of the memories was sharp. He would *not* take the razzing from Larry and Mark anymore. He *couldn't* take it. Some of their words had cut too close to the bone; Nick *did* fight too many of his battles for him, and that embarrassing truth made him that much more determined to disprove it. Unfortunately, it was not likely he would ever grow taller than he was currently, and losing weight and gaining muscles would take too long. He had to devise a plan that would help him now.

He might have spent all night coming up with nothing if it hadn't been for just the right events having occurred at just the right time. It was perfect. And it was terrifying.

Somehow, someway, tomorrow night, while Nick was bucking away at Pauline to prove *his* manhood, Ray would remove the junk from the hole and kill those things that had scared Larry shitless. Once done, he would pull the bloody carcasses out of their lair, into the light of day, and there he would pose, maybe with one foot atop his capture, like a mighty African hunter gloating over his bagged lion. His picture would be in the newspapers. His friends would hail him. Hell, the whole town would hail him. Women would never overlook him again.

He'd be a real hero.

A star.

Best of all, he'd show that goddamned Larry who was the *real* man — and who was the mouse.

All he had to do now was come up with a plan that would get him through the adventure unscathed.

It was an involved job, but he knew he'd go through with it. There was no way he'd go back to the taunts of his friends, among others. He would shame them into respecting him, maybe even — it didn't seem so impossible in the comfy isolation of his room — convince them to admire him.

Still, he wasn't blind to the fact that he might fail. And if he did? If he never made it out of that hole?

Well, even death was better than being alone.

Some hours later, long after the boy had stopped fighting and started doing the things Gavel demanded, just minutes after Gavel finally killed him with his torture, Gavel looked up at the clock with eyes blurred by sweat, and groaned.

It'd taken longer than he'd estimated. He could understand that; the loneliness had been very strong this time, and his lover more willing than some of the others. He'd needed that extra loving, and the gods that watched over him complied.

But now it was much too late to take a drive out to the junkyard. By the time he was dressed and had his lover cut up, it would be light out.

No matter. He'd have to store the boy in a cold place, but he had the facilities down in his basement, right next to the chopping block. He'd have all day tomorrow to finish the job, wrap the pieces in, and cart them in his car. Then he could take them out to the junkyard just before his eleven p.m. shift.

Perfect.

Once more he was amazed and excited that everything should work out just right. Someone must surely approve of his loving, for they consistently protected him from exposure, even when he messed up a little. It had to be some primitive gods, for only they would possess such powers.

And he was sure their protection would continue as long as he didn't do anything wildly foolish — like keep a corpse in his house for more than a day.

Therefore, it was a *must* that he take the body away tomorrow. The angels in the junkyard would be expecting it. They would tell the gods. He could not disappoint.

Otherwise, he might not be allowed to love again.

And if that happened, he would surely die.

So: tomorrow, before his shift.

Friday night.

Perfect.

Friday

Friday.

The day was here, and its presence had a different effect on each of the four friends.

Mark, for one, spent the day in guilty silence. Like Larry, he too had felt good about the renewed bond between them. Things *felt* right when he was on his friend's side. But the activities planned for tonight continued to bother him. He actually flirted with the idea of calling it all off, but when he met Larry in the hallway between classes, he couldn't help sharing his friend's enthusiasm and laughing at the fun they would have tonight at Nick and Pauline's expense.

Then, in the middle of some jeer, Larry turned serious and asked, "What time?"

"Huh?"

"What time should we meet there?"

"I don't—"

"What time do you think *they'll* get there?"

"Well . . ." he stalled—then began calculating out loud, like Larry would. "They'll probably go to an early date, maybe around six or seven. They'll wait until it's good and dark to go into the junkyard."

Larry nodded along with him. "I think Nick told me they might see a movie."

"A movie. Probably a seven- or eight-o'clock showing. Figure they'd get out and drive to the junkyard about . . ."

"Nine. Nine o'clock. That's when we'll get there.

They'll be along sometime after that."

Mark felt funny when he heard the words. Suddenly all of this became real again, not just some game. They were actually going to do it. They even had the time down now.

Jesus.

Mark's mind worked again. "Hey, you know, Pauline might not want to go into the junkyard after dark. It might be too spooky for her. Nick might even lose his nerve after that sto—after what happened to you."

Larry shook his head, flashed his perfect teeth. "No way. Nick won't lose his nerve, and he never would have planned this unless he knew Pauline was gutsy enough to go with him. They'll go."

"But if they don't, we could be waiting on top of that damned roof for a long time."

"Yeah"—the devilish smile again—"but we'll have plenty of beer to keep us warm." He mirrored Mark's expression, then broke up laughing. "Geez, Marky, get hold of yourself. You're really jittered about this thing coming off, aren't you? Well, stop worrying. I'm the one that planned it, remember? Everything will come off—literally!" And he broke up again.

Mark tried to laugh; he had to force it, but it sounded natural. As the period bell rang, telling them they were late for class, they agreed to meet outside the junkyard at nine o'clock that night.

Larry then left his friend and moved down the hallway. As soon as he turned the corner, the smile slid off his face. Why had Mark been putting up such a false front? How could he still be so uncomfortable? He should be getting into it by now.

It's okay, he told himself. *He'll have so much fun tonight that old Marky will be plotting our next adventure by morning.*

He prayed that was true.

The fact that Mark was going along with everything—even helping him pick the right time to meet outside the junkyard—was a good sign. At least it meant he was interested; maybe he *was* getting into the swing of things. Once again, they had a secret between them, a shared

178

perversion. Larry grew more certain that, after a couple of brews and a little peep show, Mark would settle into his old personality.

So why can't I smile about all this?

The answer flashed before his eyes: those *things* in the junkyard. Their existence still left him unnerved. There was no doubt that that junk piled atop the hole would hold them; only a fairly strong person *outside* would be able to remove the objects one by one, someone with hands rather than claws.

Still . . .

He tried to wash it from his mind. He didn't want to be like Mark. He should be all smiles. This was Friday — *the* Friday! If he let this ruin the fun tonight, he'd be kicking himself for months. Worse, Mark might start in with the irritating refrain: *Told you so! Told you so!*

No. He'd just have to push those beasts from his mind. Let it go until Saturday. Then he and Mark could walk down to the sheriff together and tell their story.

Together.

The thought brought a smile back to him.

Nick was nervous all that day, but not about the creatures in the junkyard. Tonight, he would have a darn good chance of losing his virginity . . . and he would lose it to a girl whom he cared for. Wonderful fantasies slipped through his mind, but occasionally his daydreams would be interrupted by some serious questions: *Will my life change after this? Will my relationship with Pauline change?*

Pretty heady questions for a guy who used to drop girlfriends without any thought as to how they felt.

At lunch, Pauline was also nervous. They sat in their usual spot, in the school yard away from the other groups. Pauline was dressed a little less flashier than yesterday, but she still looked great. She always looked great. Nick wondered what she'd look like early in the morning before she showered or combed her hair or used mouthwash. Just as great, he decided.

The food on their trays was horrible, but neither felt

very hungry anyway. They picked at it, peeking at each other intermittently. They were both aware that they were acting like two shy kids on their first date. Embarrassing. Even childish. Still, neither had much to say until they reached *the* subject of the day.

"So what exactly do you have planned tonight?" she said. She smiled, but her expression looked warily expectant rather than joyful.

He thought the best reply might be a flip one, "Dinner. Movie. Romance. The usual fun." He shrugged and returned to his food.

"The usual?" She sounded a little disappointed.

"Well, yeah. You know, we could . . . take a walk later. Or do whatever. You know."

She nodded. Her expression looked like she was sitting on a sharp rock.

"You still want me to pick you up at six?" She knew about his father. Nick was grateful that she never showed any pity for him, just accepted the facts and planned around them. He liked that about her. It was hard to faze her. He wondered if it would stun her now if he blurted his *real* plans for tonight.

Don't take the chance.

"Uh, yeah," he said. "Six will be fine. At the corner." He had tried to catch the old man this morning before he began drinking, to ask about the car, but the man was still sleeping when he left for school. Under *no* circumstance would he waken the old man—even a fire in the house. Especially a fire in the house.

It was grating. He hated to be picked up at the street corner by his date. Pauline knew this, and she still didn't show any pity, but her hand reached across and held his for just a moment. When he looked up, one of those dazzling smiles was aimed at him. He smiled back.

Their date was not mentioned again until the bell rang and Pauline stood to leave. "Six o'clock, then," she said. She tilted her head, "Should I . . . bring anything special?"

Nick blinked a few times. *Bring anything?* he wondered. He saw the hint of a grin pulling at her lips, one she

180

wouldn't let go, but it meant nothing to him. He blinked again. *Is she making some sort of suggestion? Is she asking if I'm . . . kinky? No, not Pauline. But—what?*

He was taking too long to answer, so he stammered, "Uh, no, no. I've got plenty of money and all. You just bring yourself and the car. That should be enough."

She nodded once, satisfied with something. She let the smile go and waved. "See you then . . . lover."

He just sat there and stared after her like a lovesick idiot. That last word: just a term of affection . . . or consent?

He guessed he'd find out tonight.

Across the yard, Ray watched the most beautiful woman he'd ever known leave Nick and head for class. When she was gone, Nick was still sitting there. *What happened?* he thought. *Nick looks stunned. Did she call things off?* But Ray could see the smile on his friend's face even from where he sat. He watched, emotions tumbling over each other inside him, as the other boy stood and took the trays back to the cafeteria.

All right, so it's not off. Neither's my date for tonight.

He'd spent most of the day in a daze, psyching himself for the adventure this evening. One of his teachers had even called him forward after class, to ask why he was sleeping through the lecture. He couldn't tell her the real reason, so he just apologized and left.

The details of his plan occupied every moment now. Through each lecture, in the corridors between classes, even when a friend would bump up next to him and begin talking about some inane thing, his mind would be fixed on the adventure.

Adventure. Well, most of the time it seemed that way. But Ray had a realistic attitude, and he knew that through most of this "adventure" he would not be possessed by heroics or bravery—just the opposite, actually. At times, he seriously considered wearing some sort of padding inside his pants, should he accidentally wet himself.

181

It would be scary down there, no denying that. But with the right weapons and the determination he'd felt since yesterday, he was convinced he would win out.

Classes ended for the day and he burst out of the school, running home the entire way. The pounding of his heart and the aching strain on his muscles felt good. He had to be in shape for this thing tonight. This run, he thought, would loosen him up for the job ahead.

Maybe I should run to the junkyard tonight, too.

Once home, he called hello to Mom, put his books away, and made his way out to the garage. He locked the door behind him, just in case, then went through the junk stored there to find exactly what he needed. It didn't take long. His dad was a packrat just as much as Ray. Ray's mom only yelled at *him* because he chose his bedroom as his storage space.

He spent the rest of the day at the work table, building a weapon of his own devising. *This, too,* he thought as he built, *will be in the newspaper.* So it had to look good. Above all, though, it had to do the job—or the newspaper would feature only his gnawed bones.

Don't think that.

After an hour of reworking, he had it just right. All that was left was to test it.

The weapon was functional in many respects. It had to be large, but it would also be necessary to conceal it from his parents and curious passersby. He built around those constraints and came up with what appeared to be an extravagant canteen—exactly what he would call it should anyone ask. It was composed of a large, flexible plastic container, almost like a bubble, connected to a strap that would fit over Ray's left shoulder. The strap would then hold the container snugly beneath the opposite arm—similar to how a real canteen would be strapped on. He had tested the container for any leaks, then made his own hole near the top. He slipped a hose through the hole; its length stuck from the bubble not more than two feet, easy to handle.

He was sure it would be effective, but it still looked strange. Should anyone ask, he would explain that normal canteens were not enough for long hikes; therefore, after much thought, he'd devised a canteen-deluxe that allowed a person to simply squeeze water into their mouth, by way of the hose.

The explanation sounded convincing enough. With luck, the inquirer would merely smile and compliment him on his business sense. Of course, he would have to be sure not to pause and risk being asked to demonstrate it. *That* would be impossible, for this canteen was not destined to hold water.

Ray filled the bubble with gasoline and strapped the device on. With that, he attached a belt to his waist and a large gold trinket tied to a string that slipped comfortably around his neck. The side door opened. He peered around to make sure his mom wasn't near, then stood at the side of the house and aimed the bubble's hose at the brick fence.

He squeezed down on the bubble with his right arm. Gasoline was forced through the hose, onto the brick wall. Then, in one swift move, he reached around to the back of his belt and grabbed one of the firecrackers there—his dad always kept a collection of them after the Fourth of July while his right hand flicked open his dad's gold lighter hanging from his neck and lit the fuse. He threw the firecracker at the stain of gasoline against the fence.

WHOOOSH!

Ray expected the rush of fire and heat, but its intensity still surprised him. In seconds the burst was spent, leaving only a dark patch on the walls. Ray tossed his weapon and belt into the garage and stood at the door, waiting, his hand on the knob as though about to close it.

He heard the footsteps first, then the kitchen door opening. "Ray?" His mom. "I thought I heard something."

He struggled with the garage door for a second, then looked over his shoulder at her. "Sorry. I knocked over some of dad's junk trying to get this thing closed. I'll pick it up."

She frowned. "I have to talk to him about that. We can barely get the car in as it is." And then she was gone.

Ray breathed easier. His head bowed down in relief—and for a moment his panic returned. There, hanging from the string he'd attached to it, was his dad's gold lighter that he'd borrowed from the dresser upstairs. He'd forgotten about it in his rush to get rid of the larger weapons. Fortunately his back had been turned when his mom came out; she couldn't have seen it. He'd have to be more careful the rest of the day. He didn't want to get busted after coming this far.

He ignored the part of him that thought getting caught might be a pretty good idea. It was the reasonable part of him, the part that knew all of this was a crazy, dangerous idea. But that part had felt the humiliation of the past, too, and it did very little to convince Ray that he should forget his adventure.

Even if that adventure promised to get him killed.

Sheriff Peltzer wasn't expecting a call from Sundale, so he found himself asking the caller several times before he was convinced. The line sounded so clear.

It was a young deputy from that town asking about a runaway. He was calling all the neighboring towns himself, in addition to putting out the usual official requests, because the parents were making such a fuss and, Peltzer figured, because the deputy was bucking for either a raise or the job of sheriff.

Peltzer took down the information and said he'd keep an eye out and get back to the deputy. After hanging up, Peltzer shook off the initial cold scrape inside him. The words "missing child" always gave him that feeling these days. He reminded himself that most runaways were found.

With that in mind, he sat back in his chair, feet clomping atop the desk, and closed his eyes to think. If the boy went north through here, more than likely he was headed for the Interstate. The odds were also in favor of him picking up a ride between Sundale and here. If he didn't get a ride, then he was probably thumbing it. So if he was in this area, he was probably on Benson Road, the only road out of Winsome that passed the highway.

Peltzer scooted his chair to the radio and called up Jamison, the woman patrolling that area right now. He gave her the scoop, told her to keep an eye out, and thanked her. He always thanked his officers; he found that more things got done if he made orders sound like a request. Then he rolled over to his desk again and thought about who had had the same route yesterday and last night. There were only five officers under him, so it didn't take long to come up with the right names.

Connors answered his radio immediately and reported that he hadn't seen anyone fitting the boy's description yesterday. Connors had the day patrol. Peltzer tried Deputy Gavel at home, but there was no answer. The sheriff decided Gavel must still be sleeping; he had a late shift last night, and he knew the man liked a couple beers after work sometimes.

No hurry, he hoped. He'd call again later.

But Kevin Gavel was up, had been since noon. He was in his basement packaging his most recent lover. He'd found the axe work relaxing. The mess didn't disturb him. He could hose it all down later. For some reason, however, there remained an edge of uneasiness within him. He was nervous, fidgety. Like the loneliness, only without the cold.

He didn't understand it. Was it that he'd run out of plastic bags and had to use newspaper to cover the boy's parts? He'd done that before; it shouldn't affect him now. Was his queasiness due to some unconscious concern about tonight? Was he afraid that his gods would desert him and allow him to be seen? Well, really, what if he was? That was the purpose of the chop job. All anyone would be able to report would be that he brought several *small* packages into the yard. He could always say they

185

were just worthless pieces of junk and he was dropping them at the proper place. By the time anyone checked his story, the little packages would be gone. The angels would see to that.

So what was it? The answer eluded him. He didn't want to work himself up over it, so he occupied his mind with the wrapping. It had to be done just right, so that very little of the blood would drip through. That wouldn't look good and it wouldn't handle very well.

An embarrassing image flashed through his mind: walking across the street with his arms laden with gifts, meeting Sheriff Peltzer halfway across, and watching helplessly as the pieces, slick and red, *slipped* right out of his grasp. Hands and feet and white, hairy flesh everywhere. The head falling at the sheriff's feet and smiling up, to prove the boy's last emotion had been pleasure.

Gavel laughed out loud in his basement. His uneasiness was nearly gone now.

The day began to die, slipping behind the hills to the west. Scattered clouds caressed the stars. The wind that came was light, the air cold and crisp, almost invigorating.

To Nick, it seemed almost a perfect night for his date. Certainly better than he had hoped.

He was bouncing between his room and the bathroom, getting ready for Pauline. In half an hour, he had tried on four different shirts, combed his hair countless times, and found three pimples that he just *knew* would kill his chances tonight.

Billy stood by, watching with amusement, and even managed to interrupt his brother's hurried bustling once to point out that he was wearing boxer shorts.

"Huh?" Nick said, too harried to be irritated. He looked down at his pantless legs. Blue boxer shorts hung down around them.

"You're wearing boxer shorts," Billy explained. "You want her to see you in boxer shorts? Put on some of that tight underwear."

"I don't think I have any."

"You used to."

Nick looked. He did have some. He disappeared into the bathroom and came out again wearing a pair that provided only about two inches of material around his thighs. He didn't exactly look comfortable.

"They ride up on me," he said.

Billy shrugged. "Can't have looks and comfort all the time."

Nick realized who he was talking to and told his brother to shut up and mind his own business. Billy just smiled.

Fifteen minutes later, as he started down the stairs, he heard a whisper follow him, *"Good luck!"*

Nick returned to the door and looked down on his brother, frumped atop his bed, a comic book laid across his folded legs. Billy glanced up, expecting another tongue lashing for whispering so loud,

But Nick only smiled and whispered back, "Thanks."

It didn't take much to slip out of the house. By the way the old man was sacked across the couch, snoring a storm, some game show loud on the TV, it hadn't even been necessary for he and Billy to whisper. The door, *always* maintained by the boys, didn't squeak opening or closing. In seconds, he was down the street and heading for the appointed corner.

The wind was a little colder now, bringing bad winter news from the north, but Nick sucked it in. It would cool his blood. Cool everything. He needed to stay cool, or he'd be too worked up to do anything tonight.

He hit the corner, looked at his watch.

Two minutes to six.

He waited happily. Felt good. Not once did he look down the street to search; there was no doubt in his mind that she would show up.

And she did—a couple minutes late, but no matter. The lighting wasn't very good at the street, but Nick could still see the smile that lit her face as she drove up. He opened the door—and froze. Pauline was dressed in a beautiful blue outfit that he *knew* her parents didn't

187

approve. He approved, though. Oh God, he approved absolutely.

They drove off, barely able to take their eyes from each other, both flushed, nearly laughing at themselves for the way they were acting. Like some young, inexperienced kids on their first date. Embarrassing, should anyone see them.

But they wanted it to go on and on. It was exciting, in its way. They even enjoyed the uncertainty of where the night might lead.

Of course, neither could have dreamed where it would actually lead. No one could have, not even in their worst nightmares.

Sheriff Peltzer was worried. He'd tried again and again, but he just couldn't get an answer over at Kevin Gavel's place. Of course, where he was was his business, but it just seemed damned strange that one of his most reliable officers would seemingly disappear overnight. Besides, something inside Peltzer, one of those instinctive things that cops never question but just follow blindly, told him that there might be something wrong. And if there was something wrong with one of his people, he felt responsible.

It was six o'clock. He'd been at the office all day after doing his sporadic rounds. Connors came in to relieve him, and he honestly thought of going home and just planting himself in his favorite chair with some good fast-food junk and let the idiot box blur his troubles away.

When he was in his car, though, he caught himself in the rearview mirror. The uniform. The badge. He stared into those old, tired eyes, and knew that he wouldn't be around forever, that someone in this town, someone good and trusted, would have to protect these people someday. Kevin Gavel was high on his list. If something was going on in that young guy's life that he could help now, he figured he had the responsibility.

Responsibility. The monkey on every cop's back. Every *good* cop. And Sheriff Peltzer was a damned good cop.

188

He started the engine and pulled out onto Main Street. *What the hell?* his conscience argued. *Kevin's place is on the way, anyhow.*

He got there in less than fifteen minutes. One great thing about small towns was that everything was within a half-hour's drive. Especially friends. There was no place to park around Kevin's place, so Peltzer turned around and pulled up across the street. Again, some instinct made him pause in the car and just watch the place for a few minutes. Nothing happened. Only the trees, just beginning to bloom leaves on those thin branches again, made a move.

Kind of spooky, actually, that house all alone on the corner. Weird.

The thought disturbed him. But it came from his gut, so he listened. As he left the vehicle, he decided that some caution might be called for. Walk slow and quiet. Don't rush into anything.

Boy, this is getting weird . . .

But the strangeness of the house again impressed itself on him as he walked up the driveway, and caution no longer seemed unreasonable. It was a single story, just like all the other houses on the block, but it was built completely on the corner, facing diagonally, across the intersection. No other house on the block did that. It was as if it had turned its back on the neighborhood. The face of the house was painted plain white. Two big beams came up across the top of either side and joined in the middle to point at the sky, giving the house a large triangular front. Maybe that was the weird thing: with such a large front, it made Peltzer wonder what the hell was behind it.

There was a window on the left side of the front, probably looking into the living room. The curtains were drawn, but the lights were on inside. He could just make out the fuzzy outline of furniture. Peltzer wondered if he should risk a peek through the glass. If someone was inside looting the place or holding Gavel at gunpoint, it would be better if he had a look at the scene before he tried to bust in and break it up. Of course, if nothing was going on, and Gavel was on the couch there staring back, he'd look like a nosey fool.

The internal debate lasted just seconds. Peltzer always was a slave to the demands of his curiosity. *Better to be a fool than shot,* he figured. Words to live by.

So he surveyed the area to make sure none of the neighboring houses would have a good look at him, then casually sauntered over to the window. When he grew near, he pushed his body against the stucco wall, out of sight, until he was ready. It was dark. There was a streetlight off to the right, but it wouldn't be directly behind him, no need to worry about shadows. Everything seemed right.

In one swift move, then, he took a breath, stepped in front of the glass—

—and was met with a ferocious growl—a long, grinding thing that kept getting louder. Peltzer's nerves jumped away from him, pulled taut by the strong noise. He stumbled back, fell on the grass. The growl died—then came back, just as sudden and strong and vicious.

Peltzer, though unnerved again by the volume, managed to place it better this time. It wasn't coming from behind the window, but from the garage door to the right. Some slathering beast inside the garage . . .

And then he realized what it was. Prickly heat raced across his skin as he pushed himself to his feet. He was a goddamn fool after all. The growl was just somebody starting a car inside the garage—some old clunker due for a tune-up decades ago. That's all.

Except:

The garage door was down. Someone was starting a car—a car that obviously had some noxious congestion problems—with the garage door closed.

Peltzer knew of only one kind of person that would be stupid enough to do that. The word struck him like a lightning bolt.

Suicide.

All worries of thieves and neighbors were wiped from his mind. Peltzer thought only of Kevin Gavel's life. He rushed to the door and tried the knob. Locked. He began pounding as hard as he could. He saw the doorbell and pushed that, too. If someone didn't answer soon, he'd bust the damn door down, or maybe smash through the living room window.

Nothing was going to stop Sheriff Peltzer from finding out what was going on in there.

Gavel stored the pieces inside the trunk of his Chevrolet, closed the heavy door, and stood back against the garage wall to inspect the car. It was an old one, back when gas guzzlers were still popular. Wide, heavy, fading brown on the side with a black top. He'd used it a few times before to drop off lovers. It had proved perfect for the job—again, someone had been watching over him when he'd bought the vehicle fifteen years ago.

Despite its size, it was anything but conspicuous. No one ever stopped to give it a second glance. It looked perfectly natural parked outside the junkyard. In fact, it would have looked natural parked *inside* the junkyard. Gavel smiled at this. Disinterest was exactly what he wanted to generate tonight. It would be perfect.

Still, he maintained some concern. He'd used the police cruiser for the job the last few times, primarily because it was convenient for the speed he needed. No one paid much attention to a police car parked on a city street as long as its lights weren't going. And no one blinked an eye when they saw him scrubbing away at the car in front of his home the following day.

But tonight was different—and it worried him. He didn't feel like he could take any chances, couldn't make a single mistake. Maybe it was the extra patrols or the fact that he'd had this lover in his house longer than any other. Whatever, that familiar, sickly dread that he had only experienced in his dreams was pushing into his waking hours now—a clear warning he'd best take every possible precaution.

Which was fine. He'd used the Chevrolet before, and successfully. The problem was that he hadn't used it *recently*. He hadn't even turned the ignition on for a month.

So what if it doesn't turn over? Is that someone telling you to take the police car, against your instincts? Would the gods disagree with my own inner voice?

He shook with fright. With *fright!* He'd never done *that* before, not even when the sheriff had ordered that search of the fields.

Fright, he knew, could make you do stupid things. So he'd have to be extra careful. As long as he was extra careful, the night would come out right. Just make sure everything's planned to the second.

His eyes went to the Chevy. The only real uncertainty. *Test it.*

It wouldn't take long just to start the car and turn it off again. He wouldn't even have to open the garage—no use puzzling the neighbors. Besides, he wasn't exactly dressed for any unexpected company. They might get the wrong idea and call an ambulance.

Gavel giggled at the idea. The fear left him for a little while.

He pulled the keys from the trunk and stepped into the car. His hands caressed the wide, round steering wheel, almost willing the baby to gather its strength and ready itself for a successful start. When the time was right, he inserted the keys and twisted.

The car grumbled, shook the entire chassis. It felt like a rocket beneath him. His foot pressed the gas easy at first, then harder, finally kicking it as the car's roar began to die.

The engine stopped.

Gavel cursed and tried again. It went a little longer this time, growling like some demon, straining to keep awake and moving. Gavel glanced in the rearview mirror. Black smoke belched against the garage door, rising to float over his head like a dark rain cloud. He coughed a few times, along with the car. The stab of fear that came with the fumes and the night's first failure made his gas foot hesitate. The car died.

"Shit!" His rage rose unchecked. This *shouldn't* be happening. It felt *right* to take this car. He *had* to if he was going to be *careful*. So why, why, *why*—

192

In a single instant, he stopped breathing, he stopped cursing, he stopped beating the hell out of the car's dashboard, he just froze dead.

The doorbell was ringing.

It was accompanied by a loud banging against his front door.

Oh, God . . .

His nerves turned to ice. It seemed hours before he could animate himself. When he did, he moved *fast*.

Stumbled out of the car. Held the door open, bent, checked himself in the side mirror. A T-shirt, old jeans. Bare feet. Hair uncombed, face unshaved. Not too difficult to explain if his clothes hadn't been covered with the boy's blood.

The racket at the door continued, louder and more rapid now. Gavel heard his name called. It took a moment to place the voice. Once he had it, he leaned his weight against the car door and tried to blink away the flashing dots crowding his vision.

"Kevin? Kevin! You all right in there? It's me, Martin."

So there it was. Proof. The sheriff of Winsome, the man he admired, was here at just the *wrong* time. The gods were laughing their asses off now.

Gavel leaned against the door a moment that seemed frozen in time, motionless, unblinking, wishing he were far away and asleep so that he could control the mounting panic that had him by the throat. Then a voice broke through his confusion, a single voice that could have been the combined forces of his gods, here to save him.

It screamed: *MOVE!*

He moved.

His clothes were off, one, two, thrust behind the washer. He tore through the garage/kitchen door and hurried on to his bedroom to don a robe. On the way out, he stopped in front of a mirror. He'd scrubbed his face and arms and feet earlier, but it had only been a cursory cleansing. In the garage it had looked like his skin had been dyed pink, but he saw now that that had only been an illusion—perhaps some reflection from his

193

bloody clothing. Nevertheless, glimpses of crimson still smiled up at him: under his fingernails, between his toes, matting his hair. He nearly cried out at how obvious they seemed to him. His fingers, unbidden, rubbed coarsely at the tiny ruby lips that puckered his body, but he understood, he *knew*, that there was no time to get rid of it all.

The knocking and calling was much louder now. It was insistent. If Gavel didn't open the door soon, Peltzer would come right through it. And then any explanation would be too late.

Tired and haggard, he thought as he hurried to the door. His knees nearly gave out when he saw the door rattling in its frame. It was coming down. *Tired and haggard, I'm tired and haggard . . .*

It was pure inspiration that he hooked a bottle of alcohol on his way to the door. He popped the top and took a big swig, washing it around in his mouth before swallowing. Some of the liquor splashed on his chest. Perfect, Maybe the gods—

BAM BAM BAM

"Okay, okay, *okay!*" he called at the door. In the strain of fear, his voice sounded raw, tired. Again, perfect.

They're still with me.

He unbolted the door and opened it.

Martin Peltzer stood on the stoop, in full uniform, with anger convulsing his face. That initial emotion washed away when he got a good look—and whiff—of Gavel. His mouth dropped open. His nose curled.

Gavel was touched that the sheriff's first action was not to move away, but to place a compassionate hand on his deputy's shoulder.

"Christ, Kevin . . . are you okay?"

Gavel smiled. He had to play the part, though he was thinking clearly now. He knew he had to get out of the porch light, move farther back into the house's shadows so that the sheriff wouldn't get a good look at him. He tried a pained laugh, and it came out just right. He'd only had a single mouthful of alcohol, but at the moment it seemed very easy to play a drunk just entering the

194

world of the living again.

"Martin the sheriff." He slurred the words. "Come on in." He gestured into his house, splashing alcohol from the bottle onto the rug. Peltzer frowned again, but took a step in and closed the door behind them.

The sheriff gave the place the once-over. He didn't move very far, just a tight little circle in the center of the living room, as if he were just turning to face Gavel again—but the deputy recognized the sharp, squinting eyes that studied every little detail.

Gavel took the opportunity to look around himself. He was sure there wasn't any hint of his lover up here. He was always careful about keeping that tawdriness out of the front room. But it did look unkempt. To Gavel it was the natural, comfortable mess of a bachelor. To Peltzer, however, it would look like the disorder and neglect of an alcoholic.

When Peltzer's eyes rested on him again, Gavel knew that he had fooled the man.

"Kevin." The sheriff voice was unaccustomly soft, no doubt for the sake of Gavel's apparent condition. "What the hell's the matter, boy? What's wrong?"

"Nothing." Gavel spit a little on the sheriff's chest. Peltzer didn't even blink. "Nothing at all, I've just had a little binge, is all." He patted the sheriff's shoulder. "Don't worry, Martin, sir, I don't do it regular."

Peltzer nodded, but Gavel could tell his explanation was not convincing. When the sheriff turned away to continue his look around, panic coursed through him again. The voice came back, screaming: *Keep him here, Kev! Keep him here!* Gavel felt like collapsing. Inspired once more, he went with it, falling against Peltzer. Peltzer pushed back, steadied him. Gavel kept up the wobbling; it kept the sheriff close.

It wasn't long before he knew he'd underestimated the man, something he'd always warned himself not to do. He should have recognized nothing could block the determination in that big, lean body.

Peltzer took his deputy by the shoulders, steered him to a chair, and plopped him into it. "Now you just take

195

it easy," he told Gavel, and turned again to look around.

Gavel watched intently. The sheriff's eyes glistened with interest, examining every detail. Gavel felt that sick dread seize him every time the man looked at the garage door, or the basement door right next to it, as if Peltzer could see right through the wood and concrete and spy the blood. He shifted at the edge of his seat.

Peltzer spoke as he moved. It was his habit to maintain a conversation whenever he was examining a suspect's house. Gavel knew this. But he preferred to think that the sheriff kept him talking so as to calm the tension he felt in his deputy. That last *was* the reason, but Peltzer still used that infuriatingly calm tone that had driven many a criminal to confess.

"Kevin, I've been trying to call you all day. Is your phone working?"

"Uh, yes, it is." What else could he say? Peltzer was right next to the phone. He could pick it up and check. Gavel thought fast. "The ringing . . . it nearly burst my head open."

"So why not answer it?"

"It stopped ringing by the time I got to it."

"I called a couple of times. If the ringing bothered you, you should have taken it off the hook. Even a busy signal would have told me you were home and didn't want to be disturbed."

Gavel couldn't think of an answer, so he shrugged and looked despondent. "Sorry."

"Uh-huh." Peltzer moved across the room—toward the basement door.

Gavel was up, took a step. He checked his initial urge to grab the man and force him away from the door. Urgently, he said, "Sheriff—uh, what were you calling about?"

Peltzer stopped and faced him. "Got a call from Sundale. They had a report of a missing kid, they wondered if we might have seen him on Benson Road. You had the route last night. Did you see anyone?"

Gavel's throat was so tight that he couldn't force any words out of it. He shook his head to cover the silence.

"You're sure?"

"Yes," he managed. "Didn't see anyone. Usual desolation. He could have seen me coming, though. He could have hidden in some of the construction going on there."

Peltzer nodded. "Well, that's all I was checking on. I'll give Sundale the news when I get back."

He's leaving! Gavel thought. He moved forward to make sure Peltzer got to the front door—

—but Peltzer was twisting again, showing his back to Gavel, though the deputy could still see the big hand reaching for the basement's doorknob, the basement where all the cutting had gone on and he hadn't had time to clean up yet—

Gavel's arms went out to steady himself. His fingers found a heavy object, an award he'd won three years ago for rifle marksmanship, and they wrapped around it, held it tight. Every nerve in his body was alight, impatient for a burst of ferocious energy.

He forced himself to move slowly. Careful. Have to be very careful today. The sheriff's back was still to him as he approached.

"Hey, Kevin," Peltzer said over his shoulder, his hand touching the basement door's knob and turning—

"Huh?" Gavel kept his voice soft, so that the sheriff wouldn't be able to determine how close he was. The weapon came up. It was heavy. The muscles in his arm shook. But there was power there.

"This the door to the garage?"

Gavel hesitated. "No. It goes to the basement."

"Oh." Peltzer let go of the knob, turned a little, and reached for the next door. "This one?"

"Yes," Gavel lowered the weapon behind his back. "Why do you want to go in the garage?" The clothes were hidden behind the washer. The pieces in the trunk. Did they stink? Did he slop any blood on the car?

The sheriff made a move to face him. Gavel set the trophy on the table nearest him.

"I thought I heard a car starting up when I got here," Peltzer said, "You know anything about that?"

"Well . . . well, yeah, 'Course, I was thinking about

going out and getting a little more something to drink." He pointed to the bottle he had laid on the stand near the chair. "That's my last one."

"You were going in your robe?" Peltzer studied him.

Gavel licked his lips. Boy, they were dry. "No. It's just been a while since I started the old Chevy. I wasn't sure it would turn over."

"You know you had the garage door down?"

Gavel stopped himself from bouncing on his heels. He smiled crookedly. "Geez, Martin, I didn't even think. My head's not the clearest thing in the world right now."

Peltzer smiled back with understanding. He stepped away from the garage door. "I understand. Look, Kevin, you gotta take it easy. You had me worried."

Relief washed over him. For the first time, he realized he was damp with sweat. Gavel wiped at it, nodding like a jerk. "Yeah, I know, I know. I'm really sorry, Martin. I'll be more careful. I just had a little too much at Murphy's last night. You know."

"Are there any problems, Kev? Anything I can—"

"No, no. Just, you know . . ." His mind worked fast, throwing a thousand stories up at once. "This girl there, you know, and I bought her some drinks and she just shined me on and I got a little depressed so I overdid it." He looked into Peltzer's eyes. "I'll be more careful next time, Martin. I promise."

Peltzer patted his shoulder, "All right, Kev."

"Believe me," Gavel said, knowing he was explaining too much, but letting the relief pull him along. He rubbed his temples, to show how sore they were. "Believe me, Martin, there's no *way* I'll do that again."

He laughed, and Peltzer laughed with him.

"You take care of yourself, Kevin," the sheriff said, moving to the front door. Gavel stayed right behind him. "You have a patrol later tonight, don't you?"

"Eleven o'clock."

"You want me to call in someone to cover—"

"No, no,"

"—you sure, I can just give Carmetti—"

"No, it's all right. I'll be there. I just need a couple

hours' sleep and I'll be fine. Okay?"

Peltzer nodded, smiled. "All right. I didn't mean to worry you by stopping by. You're a good officer. I just don't want to see you screw that up."

"Thanks, Martin."

"Anytime." They shook hands and Peltzer left.

Gavel shut the door. Every muscle in his body gave out then, and he had to lean against the door until his strength returned. He breathed deeply. Good . . . good . . . his heart beat was returning to normal.

There was really nothing to worry about, he reminded himself. It had been close, but the sheriff was gone. He had fooled him. Everything was safe. The gods still protected him.

He would clean up his mess, now. Then he would rest. Get something to eat. Gather his strength.

As far as Kevin Gavel was concerned, tonight was still on.

Peltzer wasn't fooled — not completely. He left Gavel's house feeling distinctly uneasy. He'd known Gavel for a few years now. He'd shared a drink with him on a couple of occasions. He'd even seen him strike out with a lady or two at Murphy's Bar, the favorite hangout for the Winsome Sheriff's Department. But he had *never* seen Gavel abuse the alcohol; in fact, most of the officers knew Kevin as a two-or-three-beer-a-night guy.

So what in the hell would send him onto a drinking binge? More than just a rejection from a pretty girl, that's for sure,

Peltzer walked back to his car and sat behind the steering wheel, thinking. When he got some things straight in his mind, he picked up the radio mike he'd had installed in his personal vehicle several years ago for emergencies, and called the station. He asked Connors to check if there were any accidents or anything out of the ordinary last night, particularly near Benson Road and the new neighborhoods. Connors wasn't gone for more than a minute before he reported back that there was nothing.

No grisly accidents. No killings. Nothing out of the ordinary. So some horrible scene hadn't sent Gavel into blind drunkenness.

Still, something about that nagged at him. He thought a bit more, then put a call through to Carmetti, who had ended her shift on the east side the same time as Gavel last night. She was at home, fortunately: it had been her day off and she'd just gotten back from her mother's. She said that she had gone to Murphy's after work, to have a few and socialize a bit, and, no, she hadn't seen any sign of Kevin Gavel all night long.

So there it was. Gavel put it all together: drinking alone, probably at home, the haggard look, lack of sleep, the confusion, and trying to start his car in a closed garage. It added up to something serious—and Peltzer had no idea what that might be.

He thought back to that scene in the garage. Attempted suicide? There were easier ways. Then again, maybe Gavel didn't feel like he could cut his own wrists or hang himself. Maybe he wanted to do it indirectly: just start a car engine inside the garage and relax, let the exhaust do all the work.

Or maybe it was just as Gavel had said. Maybe he was worrying himself sick over nothing.

But Peltzer scowled at that. Instinct told him something *was* wrong, and Peltzer was a man who listened to his inner voice.

So he didn't move, didn't pull out and go home. He just sat there and stared up the road at that strange house on the corner. After a few minutes, he called through the radio to the station again. Connors answered, sounding a little bothered. *Probably thinks I'm checking up on him with these lame requests,* Peltzer thought.

"Connors," he said into the mike, "I want you to check something for me."

"Go ahead."

Peltzer's eyes wouldn't leave that house on the corner. "See if one of the squad cars is still checked out."

"You mean, other than on patrol?"

"Right."

There was a wait of about a minute. Then Connors came back on and said, "Yeah, two. Carmetti still has hers. I think she said something about using it to go to her mom's."

"Check. The other?"

"Kevin Gavel."

Peltzer listened to the crack of the radio for a long time.

"Sir?" Connors asked. "Did you get that?"

Why would Gavel be trying to start his old clinker of a car if the police cruiser was right next to it in the garage?

"Sir?"

"Thanks, Bill. Out."

He hung the mike back, stepped out of his car and walked back to Gavel's house. There, he sat on the side of the house, on a little brick fence that bordered the lawn.

He stared at the garage.

Watching.

Listening.

Gavel waited half an hour before trying the Chevy again. Three times he went through the act: twisting the ignition and repeatedly stamping on the gas as if he could squeeze life into the machine. Nothing worked. Its age was showing. It had been quiet for too long. The poor thing just wouldn't roll over.

Gavel cursed the luck. He'd felt very strongly about taking his own unmarked car, but now it looked like he would be forced to use the police cruiser. Not a good omen. Still, he had enough confidence in his protectors now to recognize there must be a reason for this last minute change.

As he transferred the wrapped pieces from one trunk to the other, he thought the risks through. Carmetti, he knew, would have the route around the junkyard tonight. She'd get on at eight, and still be there when Gavel reached the corner of Barker and King. It always took about thirty minutes to make one go-around, so he'd have to be sure to park once she had passed and get the job done quickly. Keeping her from seeing the patrol car would be tricky, but not impossible. He would have to leave a little earlier than previously planned, however, so that he'd have time to wash out the cruiser's trunk before starting his shift. Also, he'd have to dig up some dark clothes from the hamper, for most of his stuff hadn't been washed yet. The uniform could wait until after he'd cleaned the car.

And speaking of cleaning . . .

He closed the cruiser's trunk and peered into the Chevy's rear. A few tiny pools of blood, nothing too bad. He could wash it out in half an hour. Then he'd have to start the big job in the basement.

The scale of the mess downstairs made it necessary to throw his robe off and redress in his bloody T-shirt and jeans. No use dirtying up clean clothes. He was always very careful of waste.

Peltzer listened to the crappy car try to start. Three times it coughed into life, revved its cylinders, only to die in the echo of its own rumble. It seemed a pretty stupid way to commit suicide, when the car won't even cooperate.

But there was that police cruiser right next to it. If Gavel was out to hurt himself, why not use the car that would start right up and run for hours?

Peltzer shook his head. The pieces didn't fit yet, and he just hated an incomplete puzzle — especially when he was afraid of what the final picture would look like.

The glowing dial of his watch read 7:10. He had nowhere to go tonight. No one was waiting at home for him. No one would call the station asking his whereabouts. He was used to that, had lived with it for five years now, since his divorce, but a flash of cold, the kind that hollows a body, still took the wind out of him. He breathed deeply of the winter air. It took a little longer than usual to become his alert self again.

All right. He'd keep his mind off his own life by examining Gavel's. Think it through.

Gavel wasn't dressed to go out, so he was probably just seeing if his old clunker would start—but he didn't want anyone to *know* he was starting it. Next, there were those slamming sounds, metallic, that he'd placed as either the trunks of the two cars or the hoods. Now there was no sound at all. He was somewhere else. Getting dressed?

Peltzer waited fifteen minutes. Still no sound, no movement inside. Maybe Gavel took his advice and was now slumbering peacefully. Good enough. *That'll give me enough time to get a sandwich at Harley's Subs and, hopefully, return before anything interesting happens.*

If anything interesting is going to happen.

He looked at his watch again as he stood. Seven thirty-five. With a sandwich and drink in him, he figured he could stand a few hours of surveillance. This was his most promising deputy, after all. He wanted to help if he could, whether Gavel accepted it or not. At the very least, this night would give Peltzer some experience in field work.

At 7:45 Nick and Pauline entered the theater just as it was going dark. The dinner was good, but Nick hadn't realized the restaurant would be so crowded. They had discussed skipping the movie, unsure that they'd make it in time, but neither was prepared to go on to the rest of the night yet. They rode by the theater—"Just in case," they told each other—and found that there was no line for tickets. They parked, hurried in, passed the popcorn counter without temptation as their stomachs were still full of seafood, and spied some good seats just as the movie began.

Nick paid little attention to the flick. He was thinking ahead, to how he would introduce his plans for the rest of the evening. He tried to judge their date so far, whether she seemed open to a suggestion, but things were too normal for that. It was turning out like any other date they'd had. Now was the snuggle portion, where Pauline laid her head on his shoulder and he put his arms around her. He was glad for that, for they had been holding hands for the last hour and his palms had become uncharacteristically sweaty.

So, Pauline, he imagined himself saying, *let's take a little drive out to the junkyard.* He winced. Pauline stirred next to him. Their eyes met. She smiled. The explosion on screen made her eyes twinkle.

Jesus, can I really do this? Does she suspect? If I don't go through with it, will she be disappointed?

The emotions surging inside him were worse than the first time he'd asked out a woman on a date.

But when Pauline put her head back on his shoulder and let her hand rest on his stomach a little lower than usual, he knew he *would* go through with it, come what may.

Eight o'clock came, and Ed Kelton, sole owner of Winsome Junk, arrived at his place of business. He waited in his car for ten minutes before he saw the flash of headlights come around the corner. He ducked down as the police cruiser passed. When it was out of sight again, he got out and went around to his trunk.

He removed three bulky objects, specially modified for his mission: a metal shield to push in front of him while he was in the hole, a sawed-off shotgun that he could strap around his shoulder, and a flame thrower, courtesy of his old war friend, that he had fiddled with until it provided a shorter range with maximum focus. In addition, he had a hunting knife strapped to his belt, several fluorescent flares that would provide light in the lair, and *two* flashlights — no way he was going to be caught down there without light.

He closed the trunk and checked for one more bit of equipment. It wasn't a weapon, but a form of defense: something to give him courage and determination and maybe a little luck, Beau's tooth, the only token he had from his children, hung from a string around his neck. Its smooth hardness was comforting against his chest. He patted it twice, took a deep breath, and set out.

The street was deserted, as always. He ducked beneath the iron gate and followed the memorized route through the labyrinth of TVs and stereos and lamps and shadows and every bric-a-brac imaginable. As he went deeper, something began to itch at him. Not fear, really, though he was on the edge of that now, but something closer to reason: Why not do this during the day, when the creatures were probably sleeping?

It made sense. He figured it would have made sense even if he was not stumbling through the dark amidst towers of sharp corners with his heart pounding a million times a minute. He might have stopped and thought it through and actually turned around to wait until dawn, might even have sought some safety and peace that night, if he hadn't come upon the hole by the crates and been gripped by a rage that drove all reason away.

He nearly missed it. The crates had been disturbed, some of them moved so that they covered the rest of the junk filling the hole. When he realized what had been done, anger made his face go red.

Someone had just screwed up his careful plans!

Not only did it ruin his time schedule, but it told him that *maybe* someone else knew about the beasts. Who? Not the police or any of the state boys. They wouldn't just cover it up and hope for the best. Who, then? Was there anyone who really believed this pile of junk would hold those things for long? Perhaps some bum, some trespasser, some idiot who just wanted some temporary peace. Actually "who" didn't really matter. The important fact was that word would spread.

Unless Ed got rid of these things *immediately*, his junkyard, his town, would be known as the home of monsters.

"Shit!" His emotions were tearing at him now, coming from every direction: anger, desperation, terror, hopelessness, despair. Muscles twitched. Blood shot through him so fast he felt like jumping. His temples hurt from the insistent pounding against his veins. He remembered that he once had alcohol to blunt these effects, but now there was nothing to stop them. They came coursing back in full raging bloom.

He had to do something, take some action. More than just stand there, dancing and cursing. Fortunately, he was still thinking clearly enough to use the energy to his advantage. There was no time to look for another hole, if there was one, and, anyway, he'd probably find the same half-assed cover job there, too. So this one would have to do. He laid his weapons aside—always within reach—and wrapped his hands around the first wooden crate atop the pile.

The work was slow, but steady. His adrenaline prevented his muscles from tiring. His mind alternated between creative curses that occasionally made it past his lips, and how best to move the next object blocking his way.

In an hour, he figured, the hole would be uncovered again. Not once did the idea of going home until daylight return.

Nearly half an hour after Ed Kelton started his work, Deputy Kevin Gavel emerged from his home with a shaved face and clean clothes. Peltzer nearly fell over the waist-high fence in his hurry to keep out of sight. Gavel passed by without a glance and continued down the street on foot, unaware that he was being followed.

They went a couple blocks, turning three corners, before Peltzer realized his deputy's destination. He waited outside the fast food place that Gavel had entered and tried to figure this all out. Why didn't Gavel take the police cruiser here? What was wrong with it? Did Gavel bash it up? Maybe that's why he was so upset that he had to get drunk last night. Kevin was that kind of guy. Probably felt suicidal if he got B's instead of A's in high school.

So what was he going to use for patrol tonight? Was he going to put it off until the last minute? That *wasn't* like Kevin. He always owned up to his mistakes; mistakes were rare in his case anyway.

Peltzer stepped back into the shadows. Gavel was coming back. He'd eaten inside rather than take out. The food would have been cold by the time he had walked home.

By nine o'clock, they were both back: Gavel inside doing whatever, Peltzer outside sitting on the fence, still wondering what the hell this was all about.

A little before nine, Ed finished lifting the final few metal beams from the hole. He was sweating and breathing hard, but the exertion felt good. His anger had been spent. His arms ached, but that was passing and they felt much looser now, ready for anything. He was pumped for the harrowing journey ahead.

He put his gear back on and moved to the edge of the tunnel. He bent to peer down into its depths. Impenetrable darkness. The unknown. Again, fear struck him, a lone feeling that sucked cold sweat beneath his skin and rubbed it against his nerves.

Do I really want to do this?

The answer didn't surprise him. The fear could not supplant his determination. He knew that the flashing memories of his children that horrible night, the blood, the *screams*—none of it would end unless he did this.

He reached around his belt and removed one of the fluorescent flares. It looked like a white piece of plastic until he snapped it in half; then a blue glow ignited inside, a controlled chemical reaction that would light his way into hell.

He dropped to his knees and tossed the tiny tube into the hole. Without even hesitating for a last breath, Ed raised the metal shield in front of him like some Roman warrior, and he descended into darkness.

If Ed Kelton had waited a few more minutes above ground, he might have heard the noise of other people in the junkyard. He might have investigated the sounds. He might actually have given up the night due to complications, and gone home to a warm bed.

But he was burrowed deep underground and couldn't hear anything but his own heartbeat.

The source of the noise was two good friends who were finally in the spirit of things—due mainly to the three beers they'd had half an hour previously. They tried hard to be quiet, but their giggly condition made that impossible.

Even with hazy heads, they moved through the dark maze with little concentration. Larry felt some inkling of dread, some distant memory of monsters trying to intrude on his fun, but he battled it away with a few half-whispered jokes.

For his part, Mark was laughing unrestrained. He followed every outburst with a bowed head, finger to his lips, and a loud *"Shhhh!"*—which would only cause them to laugh harder. The strain that had pulled at them the previous few days was completely forgotten, as were many things. They weren't exactly drunk, just light-headed and uninhibited, comfortable with each other's company like the old days. For now, there was only the present, where two old friends would make sure *their* plan came off with great success.

As they approached the Pontiac, Larry waved for Mark to shut up: they weren't sure whether Nick and Pauline had arrived yet. However, their efforts at silence in their condition were small: Larry held the six-pack in both hands so he would stop losing his balance and Mark clamped his jaw shut in an attempt to keep the laughter in. Both boys crept up to the Pit on tiptoe, trying desperately not to break up at how ridiculous they felt. Naturally, they were not aware of the noise they did make, or they would have made a run for it right then to escape Nick's vengeance.

At the wall, they peered into the darkness between the tires. The light was out, but that didn't mean anything: Nick might not want to do it with the light on, a variable that worried Larry a little. They turned their heads to listen next. No heavy breathing or cries of passion. It was quiet. They listened a full minute, just to make certain.

"All right! They're not here yet!" Nonetheless, Larry spoke in a whisper.

"To the roof?"

Larry squinted—his way of concentrating through the haze in his head. "Wait," he said. "I wanted to check something."

"What?"

His eyes bounced open again. "Oh, yeah! I remember now. I want you to go inside the—"

"Go inside? Are you nuts? They could arrive at any second!"

"—go inside," Larry continued calmly, "and I'll open the vent on the roof, and you tell me if you can see me from the mattress. Don't worry. We got time."

But Mark wasn't moving yet. "If we have so much time, why don't *you* go inside?"

"Aw, shit, don't start this, Marky—"

"I'm not starting anything. I just don't want to be the one who gets the shit beat out of him if Nick should show up all of a sudden."

"All right, dammit I'll go." From his jacket, he pulled out a nail with a string tied around its head. He handed it to Mark. "Use your shoe or something to pound this into the vent door. Then pull the string to open it." He expected some more whining, but the enthusiasm with which Mark sped off on his mission stifled Larry's wariness. *The guy just doesn't want to get his ass kicked for something that's my idea,* he told himself, *I can understand that.* Then he remembered that, if he didn't hurry, *he* would be the one to get his ass kicked. He found the key to the Pontiac and scurried inside.

Mark should have been on the roof by then, but the beers in him made the climb more difficult. Larry stared up at the ceiling. He stamped his foot impatiently. There was a long wait as he listened to the soft thumps against the vent door and an occasional curse echo from the roof.

Then, finally, the nail was in, the string was pulled, the vent opened, and Mark plugged his face in.

Larry stood at the end of the mattress and sat. His knees gave out so easily that he wondered if they would lift his weight again. He looked up at Mark.

"All right," he called. "Pull your head back a bit. We don't want to stick our faces right into the hole."

Mark did so. He let the stick-catch hold the vent door open. "Can you see me?" he whispered.

"Nope. Too dark."

"We must be lucky," Mark said, "There're a lot more clouds now than there were. Blots out the stars."

Larry grunted and started to get up—until Mark said, "Hey, Lare, stay there a second."

"Why?"

"I want to see if I can see you."

Larry fell back on his butt again and waited. There was nothing for many seconds. He felt itchy, certain that he'd hear Nick and Pauline approaching any time now. "Well?" he whispered urgently up to the vent.

"I'm not sure," Mark answered. "Wiggle around a little."

"Oh, stop that! Can you see me or not? Hurry up!"

"No, I can't see you."

"Shit!" He hadn't counted on this. His mind began to work, struggling with the laziness the beer forced on him, searching desperately for some solution . . .

"I got it," he said, and stood with some difficulty. When he had his balance, he waved his hand around until it hit the bulb nearby. Three twists and the orange glow filled the room. Larry sat back on the mattress. "What about now?"

"Yeah, you're clear. Can you see me with the light on?"

Larry looked up. "Nope. You're in shadows."

"Good. But how are you going to get Nick to turn on the light?"

It was a good question—the plan hinged on it. Larry didn't want to deal with it now, though. He just wanted to get out of there and onto the roof. They could worry about the details once they were safe.

To pacify Mark, he said, "If you were going to bop a

woman with Pauline's body, wouldn't *you* have the lights on so you could see it?"

"Guess so," Mark answered. Actually, he figured the only way he'd have a woman with Pauline's body was if the room was pitch black so that *she* couldn't see *him*. "Hurry up," he added.

Larry twisted the light out and stumbled out of the Pit. He made sure to replace the key behind the back tire before climbing to the roof. He could understand Mark's previous difficulties; ascending the Pit was a hell of a lot more difficult when you had a few beers in you.

But he made it, as he knew he would, and there he waited with his best friend, together again, waiting to play a dirty trick on one of the gang.

Just like old times.

Larry and Mark were not the only ones to enter the Pit around then. Ray Holscomb arrived a few minutes after them and paused outside the iron gate to read the sign. Actually, he knew what the sign said, he'd seen it so many times, but he wanted time to think.

Do I really want to do this?

The question wasn't met with fear or bravery, only indifference. He could go home now and his life would not change. He'd be picked on by friends and enemies and probably remain without a girlfriend far into his twenties, if ever. Or he could charge blindly into the *real* pit, fight *real* dragons, and come out a hero.

Both choices offered death as an outcome, one way or another.

Quite a range there. He felt no pull toward any of them right then, standing outside the junkyard in the cloudy night. His internal voices were silent. No *Go for it!* or *Run away!* The choice would be his completely.

The indifference disturbed him. He thought he would need some sort of passion to do the job. In fact, he'd had that passion earlier, when the taunts of his friends were still fresh in his mind. That pain seemed years away now. At this moment, he was just a lonely kid standing

211

outside a spooky junkyard, and no matter what decision he made, no one would hear of it unless he told them.

The laughter decided him. Distant, familiar giggles, echoing from the past like ghosts. They were the same voices that had humiliated him; people who had misrepresented themselves as his friends; people he thought he could trust. And they were laughing again.

He thought it must be a powerful memory. Something in his subconscious was bringing back this pain to show him what life would be like if he didn't go forward. The laughter would come to him even in lonely places like this. He would never be able to escape it. Never.

Unless he went forward.

So he went forward, beneath the unlit sign, past the concrete shelter, across the small clearing and into the dark maze of garbage. He didn't let the shadows affect him. He had no impression of being swallowed, as the other boys had. He was inside himself, trying to push away the laughter that still came from the night.

The struggle ended when he reached the hole — the hole that should have been covered over. The junk they'd used to plug it yesterday was strewn about. The crates, too, rested a distance from the hole. And there, in the center of the mess, the black tunnel yawned open completely unobstructed.

Ray gasped. The exposure should have made the hole less mysterious, but just the opposite was true. Now Ray could see it all: the disturbed gravel spiralling away, the hard ground's gradual decline, and the tangible darkness that rose to the very lip of the earth's wound.

He stared at it for a long time. No matter where he moved, it still took on the same disturbing image of a black eye peering out at him, prepared to suck him in when he approached. And as his own eyes searched the cyclopian depths, he grew more certain there was a dark mind hidden down there somewhere — a warm, wet, living, *thinking* thing buried deep beneath the surface.

And he was going to crawl into that on his own. For the first time that night, Ray shivered.

He tried to clear his head; he had to think again. *The*

212

junk, he reminded himself. *How was it moved? Did the rats do it?* His hands gripped the helmet he had brought. *Are they out here now? Are they watching me? Waiting for me to crawl into their lair?*

He scanned the shadows around him. He couldn't catch any movement or glint of black pupils. He didn't hear anything, either. Of course, that didn't mean they weren't there. After some thought, however, he decided it didn't matter. He was there to destroy their home as well as them. If they had nowhere to hide, then they would be exposed and become easy prey. That simple.

And it all depended on him crawling into that black eye.

He took a deep breath—the air wasn't freezing, but it provided a sting that invigorated—and placed the helmet over his head. It was his brother's motorcycle helmet. A band had been attached to it so that a flashlight could be held right over his forehead, much like a miner's hat. He switched on the light now and swung the beam around the yard. It was fairly powerful, and provided Ray with a certain degree of comfort.

He stepped down the decline, toward the hole. The top of the hole came up to his knees. If something were hidden right at the edge there, it could reach out and pull him down. Ray waited for it. When a minute had passed without incident and his nerves were under control again, he went to his hands and knees and shone his light into the pit.

He was surprised that the darkness wasn't impenetrable. The flashlight illuminated lumpy gray walls sprinkled with the ends of roots from some long buried weeds and other plants. The floor was as curved as the top and sides; the tunnel would have been cylindrical if not for the primitive excavation by its builders. Ray looked farther on. The hollow remained level for a few feet, then dipped severely, curving and falling to a depth Ray could not see. His light touched the farthest curve of the wall, and he thought he could make out, against the rock, a faint blue glow. Reflection from water? He couldn't hear any splashing. Must be something else.

He made sure his belt was on tight and let the plastic bubble fall around his stomach, then went feet first down into the hole. It was tough going initially. He couldn't get his head positioned so that the light on his helmet would do any good. When he could look down, he saw nothing but darkness . . . and that mysterious blue glow. In a way, he was grateful for that blue light; if not for that, he wouldn't have been able to see his feet at all.

The walls were tight, feeding the rising claustrophobia in his mind. His body sweat provided some lubrication, but the going was tough over that dip. Fortunately, during the descent the tunnel walls opened wider to allow him more elbow room. His back and the plastic bubble hanging over his stomach still rubbed up against the rock—scraping dirt into the air which hurt Ray's throat—but he carried on.

Not once did he imagine himself returning to the surface with its fresh air and wide open spaces. For Ray, there was only what lay below.

It took ten minutes to reach the end of the descent. There, he dropped into a roomier chamber. Beneath his feet he found the origin of the blue glow: a plastic strip with something inside it that looked like glow paint he used to use on Halloween. He thought he remembered seeing these kinds of things in war movies. They were used for light. He looked around. Looked like the thing worked fairly well.

The question was: Who the hell put it there?

Ray scanned the chamber. The flashlight's ray followed his motion, detailing that which the phosphorescent tube weakly gave form. The chamber wasn't very large, only about a third the size of the clubhouse. There was barely enough room to stand up in. He followed the walls around. The chamber continued to the right, narrowing into another tunnel—a tunnel that was, fortunately, larger than the one he'd just come down. He would be able to walk through it if he bent over, and there would be room to turn around should he need to make a hasty retreat. The drawback was that the walls bent to the right in a smooth arc, so he couldn't see where the tunnel ended.

Not that he had much choice. It was the only way to go besides back up.

He moved ahead and bent over to keep his head from contacting the ceiling. Against the tunnel's distant wall, he could make out another blue glow. Someone else was definitely down here, clearing the way for him. It made him feel a little braver knowing he wasn't alone—until he realized that this person might be dead by now, and could very well have created a feeding frenzy amongst the creatures down here.

Ray considered retreating. For a reason not even he could put into words, he continued forward.

The glow against the wall became more distinct. Ray wondered how long the flares lasted. They could have been down here for months, for all he knew.

Then who moved all that junk off the hole? The creatures? No, he didn't buy that. No matter how big, they wouldn't have the balance and grip necessary to move all that garbage. It had to be a man, maybe several.

Despite that fact, he continued with caution. The flashlight wiped back and forth across the tunnel's width, examining the tiniest crevices for movement or the glitter of a tooth. When he reached the flare, he looked down the tunnel and saw another glow waiting for him.

Follow the tubes: that seemed like the best plan right now, since the tunnel was only going one way. But what should he do if the tunnel branched into two or three directions? Follow the man before him or use his own reason?

It was too much to consider right now. He'd let his instincts decide when the time came. For now, he kept moving toward the only destination open to him. He focused his concentration on the path ahead and behind, his senses heightened for any trace of company, while attempting to ignore the panic that closed in on him like the dirt walls.

He breathed deeply, took in a lungful of warm, stinking air. It would only get worse, he knew, as would his fear. It was frustrating. After just ten minutes of this subterranean world, he realized that he'd better meet and destroy the enemy soon, *real* soon, or he would fall to the floor, roll into a ball, and enter his own little world of darkness and madness.

At 9:30, Nick and Pauline came out of the theater. They'd both enjoyed the movie, but not enough to push away thoughts of what would—might—come next.

When they got in the car, Nick found himself searching for words.

"Good show," he said.

"Mm-hmm."

"Well." He was behind the wheel now, Pauline snuggled up next to him, and he started the engine. "You hungry or anything?" *Come on, dammit! Ask her!*

"Nope."

"Thirsty? We could probably find a coffee shop—"

"Not thirsty, either."

She had her head turned so that she stared at him. Her eyes had a shimmering, glazed look that he couldn't read at all. Her mouth, too, was expressionless, as if she wanted to say something but couldn't do anything but breathe through it.

He was about to ask if there was anything wrong when she said: "Do you want to go somewhere quiet?"

The way she said it, a little nervous and coy, and the way her hands wrapped around his arm—all of it pulled the air out of Nick's lungs. He felt a splash of cold, then warmth, squirt through his body.

Jesus! Say something, idiot!

"Yeah," he said. She hesitated, waiting for more. Her lips formed around something—but he beat her to it. "I think . . . I think I know a place we could go. It's quiet. And comfortable. I've spent a lot of time there with friends."

"With Ray and those guys?"

"Yeah. But they won't be there now," he added hurriedly.

Something passed between them, then, some under-

216

standing. Despite that, Nick felt uncertain. She leaned over and kissed him gently on the lips, nothing hot or passionate—but when she pulled away a few inches, their noses barely touching so that it tickled, and her eyes dove right into his, wide and glimmering and completely open to him, she whispered, "Let's go," and he knew that his fantasies would become reality tonight.

It scared the hell out of him.

They arrived at the junkyard fifteen minutes later. Nick had driven carefully, not wanting to appear too eager. It was difficult, what with Pauline's head on his shoulder, occasionally nipping at his earlobe and giggling at his flinch, and his imagination flashing erotic pictures in his mind. Amidst the wonderful jumble of emotions, though, there was something disturbing about the whole scene. It was what he wanted, sure, but he seemed to be bouncing against the disparity of wanting something and actually having it.

Of course, he had no intention of backing out, for he really did want to be with this woman. The problem, if you could call it that, was that this woman happened to be Pauline Martinez. They'd spent a lot of time together. He knew what made her laugh, what made her cry, what foods and music she liked, how she'd react in certain situations, how she needed a hug whenever she had that certain look on her face—he *knew* this woman like he'd known no other. She was not just one of the well-built centerfolds he'd always fantasized about. And suddenly there was a lot of responsibility stapled on to his wish to be intimate with her. He had fears, now, fears that he might somehow hurt her emotionally, or disappoint her own needs tonight—stuff he'd never even given a first thought to in the past.

So what the hell was all this about? A great night ahead of him, and something inside him was going to fuck it up. Why?

For just a second, he wished he could talk it over with someone close, who wouldn't kid him about it. Ray's pudgy face flashed before his eyes—and was gone.

He was alone with his girl again.

They parked and sat in the quiet, their arms around each other. Nick felt Pauline's warm breath against his neck. It was nice. There was something lazy about the moment, more comfortable than the nervous stimulation he'd felt on the way over.

Then they broke away and looked out the front window. At the junkyard.

Pauline sounded doubtful again. "This is it?"

Nick put his best face on. "Yup."

"A junkyard."

"Not the junkyard, but the place that's inside the junkyard."

She looked again. "You mean that concrete place there? It looks—"

He interrupted quickly. "No, no. We built a clubhouse in the middle of the junkyard." He told her about the Pit. "It's really comfortable," he assured her.

She gave him a lopsided grin. "It sounds kind of neat. Do you have furniture, too?"

"Well . . . it has a mattress."

She was silent, biting her lower lip.

Oh, Christ! I knew this wouldn't work out! Why couldn't you have just gone to some cheap hotel—

—Because I don't have the money, asshole.

His hand reached for the ignition key. He was about to apologize and say he'd take her home when she put an arm around him again and said, "All right. Show me."

"You're sure?" he said before he could stop himself. She already had her door open and was stepping out. "Yup!" And she gave him one of those great smiles.

He mumbled, "Thank you, God," jumped out of the car, and came around to take her hand. They walked into the darkness together.

There was some hesitation before they moved beneath the iron gate, a feeling of trespassing that held them back. Nick assured her as best he could, and gradually

218

they moved into the labyrinth. Pauline made faces the entire way, as if she were about to tread in something gooey or twist an ankle. Occasionally she called his name, alternating between a frightened and warning tone. His only response was to hold her closer and mutter, "It's okay. Really. There's nothing here but shadows."

"That's more than enough!" she pointed out.

Still, they continued forward, stumbling down the corridors and sharp corners like a pair of drunks. No matter how awkward, Nick always kept one arm around her waist, keeping her near so that he could shield her from the shadows, comfort her—and prevent her from running away.

They made it to the Pontiac entrance, jogging the last few yards. Pauline squealed—then laughed. The clearing left the junk piles a comfortable distance behind. It felt safe here. She wrapped her arms around his neck and he joined her laughter.

Neither saw the shadows that scurried across the Pit's roof to hunker down and watch them.

"We made it!" Pauline said, dazzling him with another smile. Her voice was throaty from exhaustion, but Nick thought it sounded sexy.

"See, I told you we would. And no one will bother us here."

"They wouldn't dare! Who would be stupid enough to go through that scary maze at this time of night? It would be bad enough during the day!"

"Well, you're a very brave woman."

"No, just stupid." She laughed at his mock reaction of hurt. "Don't worry." She kissed him, short but sweet. "Some things I'm pretty smart about."

He didn't want to take even one arm from around her waist, but he forced himself to gesture at the Pontiac. "Allow me to show you my estate, Madam."

"Said the spider to the fly," she murmured.

"What?"

She giggled. "Nothing." She walked with him to the Pit. They moved leisurely, in no hurry at all. "So—" she

219

started, and suddenly Nick was rushing ahead, falling to his hands and knees next to the old wreck of a car. "Nick?"

"Found it." He stood and showed her the key. He inserted it in the Pontiac's door, unlocked and opened it, and stood by like a proud limousine driver, waiting for her to enter.

Then he noticed her expression. "What's wrong?"

"Nicky . . . a car?"

He realized she wasn't getting the whole picture. "All the way through," he explained. "I told you, we built up a wall of tires—right here." He patted the wall resting on the car's roof. "This is just the grand entrance."

She was smiling again—actually beaming at him. "Hey, that's clever. You should go into engineering."

She bent down and accepted his helping hand into the car. He didn't think it necessary to mention that the Pit had been Larry and Mark's creation, or that he could tell that some of her enthusiasm was an act. It was enough that she liked him sufficiently to enter such a dark, primitive place at night. He noted how she stepped very carefully into the car, as if any contact might bring down a barrage of dust and dirt. That was okay. She'd get used to it.

Once inside and Nick had the light bulb screwed on, her impressions *were* changed. The place was fairly roomy, as Nick had told her; it still wasn't the cleanest place in the world, but she thought it must be better than a lot of places boys would hang out. Certainly better that what she had expected from a junkyard. Even the mattress looked clean.

"So. What do you think?"

Nick didn't expect her to jump up and down about it. Still, she was genuinely charmed by the place. "I like it. It's clean. Looks like it's in good shape. Oh, look, you even have a TV." She twirled around. "Of course, it could use a woman's touch. Not enough decoration. Those bumpy walls look horrible."

"We've been thinking of curtains," Nick offered, grinning.

"Oh, have you?" She laughed again. The echo off the concrete wall sounded like softly bursting bubbles, he thought. "Yes, I could just see you and your friends putting up curtains in here."

"Big black ones. With yellow lightning going through them."

"Yuck!"

"It would be cool." They laughed once more, and Nick moved toward her. She stepped aside a bit; something shifted on her face. Her toe bumped into the mattress. They both looked down at it.

"A mattress," said Pauline. "Just like you said."

"Mm-hmm. I wouldn't lie to you." Their eyes met again. His fingers barely touched her arms. He leaned forward to kiss her—

And she was moving again, toward the concrete wall. "What's this?" she asked.

"Part of an underground sewer. The roof, I think."

"Why would they take it out of the ground? It looks in good shape."

"Maybe they're using different material these days." He stepped toward her once more. Slowly. Trying to look calm. "I don't even know what the other side looks like. It's pressed up against some other junk. There might be cracks all through it."

"Oh. Could use some curtains here too, I guess. Maybe some—"

"Pauline."

She turned to him. She looked like a child expecting a tongue-lashing from her parents. He stopped an arm's-length from her. He was tired of all this dodging, and he didn't like that expression on her—it made him feel like he was doing something wrong.

"Pauline," he said, "I care about you a lot. I wouldn't hurt you for the world. And I wouldn't say these things just to make love to you."

She stared back at him with that same expectant face.

Nick stayed where he was. "This whole thing is new to me, but I'm glad it's with you. I don't know what will come . . . after . . ." He faltered for words, trying to

221

find the right ones, the *true* ones, that would bring her to him.

Before he could find those words, however, she was in his arms, looking up at him with a new face, one with new expectations.

"We can talk about that later, Nick," she said. "It's just that . . ." She shook her head, looked away. "I don't know."

He ran his hand through her hair. Her head eased back with the motion, her eyes half-closed. "Do you want to stay?" he whispered.

In answer, she kissed him. Hard and passionate, an exquisite world of warm, wet tingles. They slowly worked their way to the mattress.

Above, the two friends alternating the best position from which to look through the vent, Larry nudged Mark in the ribs and grinned. Mark returned the smirk without a twinge of guilt.

Below them all, Ray thought he heard some movement in the tunnel ahead, and froze.

Friend or foe? Man or monster?

He couldn't take a chance, either way. He opened the stopper on the tube of his weapon and tore a firecracker from his belt. The lighter clicked on in his right hand. He was ready, goddamn it, *ready!* In under a second, just the blink of an eye, he could squeeze the bubble under his right arm, spray the monster with gas, and light the firecracker.

But that certainty didn't bolster his spirits. Even if he'd had a submachine gun and an army in front of him, the last thing he wanted to see in this cramped, dark place was a ravenous monster.

Another sound ahead.

Ray gulped. The gurgle sounded incredibly loud in the confines. He shifted his position, and groaned. His back was getting sore. He bent his knees to relieve some of the strain in his back, and considered duck-walking the rest of the way.

Why couldn't the damned ceiling be a little higher—

Another sound. Like the wind blowing leaves across a yard. Or sharp claws sparking against the rocks.

Ray moved onward, his nerve slowly fading. The flashlight picked out the farthest bend in the tunnel, but the source of the noise was beyond that, maybe just inches beyond. He scooted forward just a little more, searching, searching.

Man or beast? Man or beast?

If it was a man, they could join together against the beasts. He wouldn't be alone down here in the grip of these closing walls—

Dammit! Another rustle. Fainter, less distant. The thing must see the light on the wall and it's backing away.

A human wouldn't do that.

He had to be sure. Ray shuffled a few more steps, his stubby legs bending under his weight like some Russian dancer. Just a little farther and he would pass the next flare left by the stranger. Maybe then, if it was a man ahead, he would be able to see Ray in the blue glow and they could—

Christ!

The air exploded with sound and action. The smaller male rat—though it appeared huge in this tight tunnel, at least as wide as Ray and half his standing height—the *monster,* roared with a sound that grated through Ray, and charged around the turn. It was everything Larry had described: thick, matted hair standing up on it like the bristles of a brush; solid muscles straining to push the black mass forward; claws sharp enough to grip the tough floor of the tunnel; red, flaring eyes; and a snout already dripping saliva, peeling back to reveal teeth that could tear flesh away with a single shake of the head. An honest-to-God, fucking *monster!*

And it was heading right for Ray.

Ray screamed, his high-pitched cry barely breaking above the creature's wail. The combination threatened to bring the tunnel down around them. Ray stumbled back, his hands scrambling to cover his ears against the jarring noise. He realized an instant later that he should be squeezing the bubble, vomiting gas all over this thing, *destroying* it. His hands clenched—and terror punched a hole through him. In his initial scramble to cover his ears, the lighter, his dad's perfect-working, never-let-you-down gold lighter, had flown from his grip to land somewhere in the darkness behind him.

He *had* to take his eyes from the charging beast, just *had* to turn away from it and search for the lighter. It was the hardest thing he ever had to do. As soon as he turned, the creature repeated its deafening roar, as if in protest of being ignored.

Ray desperately followed the ray of light from his helmet as it bounced around the tunnel. Gray rock, layers forming rings, ribs, encasing him, roots still poking through at this depth like worms trying to get at him—it all came at him in a blur.

Everything but the gold lighter.

Ray screamed, most of the sound breathy, bubbling with snot. He was at a bad angle, on his back and his legs twisted under him; he couldn't get the damned light to touch the floor. He grasped wildly into the darkness. His fingers dug into dirt and rock, kicking up dust that began to choke him.

The roar again. *Shit, it was loud!* The beast was closing. He didn't have to see it to know that. He wasn't conscious of it, but he could pick up the sound of the digging claws now, the strong, hot breath, and could even feel those powerful jaws opening wide so as to snap around his head—

He touched the lighter. He pulled it into his palm and twisted forward. Terror hit him again, nearly taking his life this time. The beast was much closer than he thought. If this had been a nightmare, he would have woken up by now—but the goddamn thing kept coming.

Hurry, hurry—

Ray fought the paralysis in his limbs. He reached down to the bubble's tube, found it, pulled. It didn't budge. A quick glance showed him that he had fallen

224

over on it. He wouldn't be able to aim the damned thing without changing his position, and he didn't have time for that, he was almost all out of time.

HURRY—

The beast's head was lowered, the eyes clearly blazing with ferocious triumph. It was putting everything it had into this final push.

Ray screamed again, a long desperate scream that he prayed would bring the world down on them and stop the charge. His eyes bulged, searched for escape. His fingers curled in frustration, felt something rough in his palms . . .

His attention centered on his hands. He had the lighter in one, a firecracker in the other. There was nothing more he could do but bring them together. The fuse sizzled. He threw it. Then he laid back and waited for the great weight to hit him.

The throw was not a particularly good one, but the beast was so close that it didn't really matter—its open mouth filled most of the lower half of the tunnel, anyway. The sizzling stick dropped in around its tongue. The creature swallowed hurriedly so as to clear the way for the meat—and the firecracker exploded. The right side of the thing's neck burgeoned outward, like a popped balloon. Gray-mottled flesh flapped and sprinkled the tunnel walls with red organs.

The roar stopped. The creature's front legs gave out, plunging its head into the ground. Its momentum carried it forward, skidding against the floor so as to tear more flesh from its underside. It slammed against Ray, rolling him a little way, until they both came to rest with Ray's feet pinned beneath the carcass's chin.

Dust filled the tunnel, Ray coughed, gasped for each breath, while struggling to remove his penknife from his back pocket. Once free, he plunged it repeatedly into the dead creature's head.

When the dust settled, everything was calm again. Ray still spit dirt from his mouth, but he could breathe with only intermittent coughs. His throat burned from his last scream. After a quick look around, he listened for more enemies. He heard something horribly loud, pounding and jarring, and he curled into a ball behind the dead creature's body so as to stay hidden. A minute passed before he realized the noise was his own heartbeat erupting against his eardrums.

Exhaustion hit him then. It took great effort to kick the beast's head off his feet, and he had to rest for ten minutes after. But he kept up a constant surveillance, twisting the flashlight on his helmet in the direction still unexplored, then back behind him, just in case.

Once he brought the light low to study the thing that had attacked him. It looked a little like a rat, like Larry said. A hell of a big rat. But there was something different about it. The head was misshapen, covered with thick lumps that were part of the skull. Ray wondered what kind of shape their brains must be in. The body was different, too. Obviously muscular and strong, yet it appeared sickly with its mottled skin color and missing patches of hair.

Disgusting. Definitely worthy of the title monster. And he, Ray Holscomb, had killed one. Just barely. It came back to him just how close he had come to being killed himself, actually being *eaten,* and he had to rest some more to let the sickness pass.

When he felt he could move again, he was indecisive as to which direction he should crawl. Forward or home? He looked at the dead monster. Ordinarily, it would have scared him and he would have left without a second thought. But he had seen this thing when it was *alive* and *charging.* Now it was a lifeless lump, dead at his feet. He had done that. He had killed it. He had succeeded in doing just what he had planned.

And he didn't doubt he could do the rest. His weapon hadn't worked too well this time, but he was confident that his mistakes would not be repeated. This one creature he would leave to drag out and show the world. The other creatures he would burn to the bone.

Confidence renewed, Ray checked his weapon — it worked fine — capped the tube again, and carefully crawled over the carcass of his first kill. He continued down the tunnel, then, to a destination he could not possibly imagine.

Ten o'clock came. Sheriff Peltzer was thinking seriously of giving up; except for that brief time when Gavel wandered out to get a hamburger and fries, the deputy hadn't shown his face outside all night. It was only an hour until he was to go on patrol. Peltzer was still curious whether the patrol car was in good shape, but he had to get up early for work tomorrow himself. He decided to give this shift another fifteen minutes.

Fortunately, the night wasn't too cold. There was a slight wind, and black clouds had been gathering for the last hour or so, but Peltzer was confident that his bum knee would warn him of any storm.

He stood up off the fence to brush his pants, and wondered if he should bother sitting down again. Why waste another fifteen minutes? Just get in the car and leave.

He yawned. That decided it.

He got two steps before he heard Gavel's garage door rumbling open. An automatic, thank God; he would have seen Peltzer otherwise. The sheriff jumped back into the shadows of the side of the house and peered around the corner.

Another engine—this one much stronger than the first, not as congested. The police cruiser. The black-and-white pulled out of the garage. Not a dent or scrape on it, as far as Peltzer could see. But there *was* something here that puzzled him: Gavel was driving the car out of uniform.

Now, ordinarily that would not have raised an eyebrow on Peltzer's experienced brow. He hadn't expected Carmetti to wear a uniform today when she took a cruiser to see her mom. The absence of a uniform was as good as a cab's OFF DUTY sign to most of the people of Winsome.

However, Gavel had a patrol in an hour. He hadn't used the police car to get his food. He'd tried to start his old clunker instead—*with the garage door closed*. What were the missing pieces here?

Peltzer forgot about home. Just watching this strange scene made his curiosity come to a boil; the obsession had returned.

The cruiser's front wheels touched the street and stopped. There was an electric hum as the garage door closed again, then Gavel drove out into the street.

Gavel wasn't at the corner before Peltzer was rushing for his own car and gunning the engine to life. He thanked his lucky stars that he hadn't driven one of the patrol cars home tonight. Gavel knew his personal car, but the dark of night and the glare of headlights would take care of any detection.

The only worry Peltzer had was where his deputy was going.

Gavel arrived at the junkyard fifteen minutes later and parked three yards from the iron gate. Peltzer turned his headlights off and slowed. He was nearly to the intersection of Barker and King when he spied the cruiser stopped just around the corner.

Quickly, with the grace of a man who has dealt with panic before, he backed up and parked around the corner and across the street from the front gate. From where he sat, he could just see the rear of the cruiser. Its exhaust was still spitting smoke; Gavel must be messing with something that prevented him from shutting off the engine immediately. Peltzer was grateful that the engine noise had probably covered his own jerky halt.

He looked at his watch. Carmetti should be driving by soon on her patrol route, if she hadn't already. It would look suspicious to have a cruiser sitting out in front of the junkyard, so Peltzer guessed that she had passed by minutes ago. Gavel knew the route, so it wouldn't be hard to figure the driving time. Peltzer knew it fairly well himself, and he figured she would be driving by again within the next half hour. What was Gavel planning to do here that would only take a half hour?

The cruiser's engine turned off just as the sheriff got out of his car. He let the door drop back without clicking, then went as quietly as possible to the corner fence, where he crouched and listened.

The cruiser's door opened, closed. Soft padding on the concrete: Gavel must be wearing tennis shoes, or something soft like that—certainly not the hard shoes of his uniform. Peltzer put him somewhere in front of the iron gate. Gavel must be standing there, looking around for any witnesses or trespassers.

After half a minute, the padding came back. It approached the corner. Peltzer crouched lower. He checked his waist. Thank God he was still in uniform; his gun was there, in his hand, ready for trouble. In his nervousness, he nearly forgot to unbutton the holster flap.

The padding came closer. Gavel was definitely heading toward him. If he decided to check around the corner for witnesses, he would find one real quick. What he would do then was up in the air. Maybe nothing.

Then why am I all jittery? Why do I have my hand wrapped around my gun?

Fortunately, Peltzer didn't have to deal with such a situation. Gavel stopped, just a few feet away from the corner.

Did he hear me? Peltzer wondered. He listened intently. His hand stayed on his gun.

There was a prolonged silence, followed by the groan of metal, a slight creak, then some thumps and crackling paper . . .

The trunk. He's in the trunk. What's in the trunk? A gun?

Peltzer bent lower, though his legs were already screaming under the strain. He inched his face to the corner's edge. He had to take a look. Now would be the best time, with Gavel's back to him. *Do it quick!* he told himself, but his muscles were unresponsive, numb from his crouch and the drug of fear.

Hurry, goddamn it!

His eyes passed the edge. He turned his head a bit to get a better look, and nearly knocked himself off balance,

229

into the gutter. He steadied himself—then nearly fell again when he saw what Gavel was retrieving from the cruiser's rear.

What the hell . . . ?

Gavel twisted away from the trunk with his arms full of newspaper balls. Actually, they were larger than just newspaper crushed together, maybe about the size of a small hardback book. There must be something inside the balls, Peltzer figured. The newspaper was merely wrapped *around* the object—lots of objects, by the look of it.

Peltzer brought his head back just as Gavel turned to take another quick look around.

What the hell are you doing, Kevin? What's in those newspapers?

He looked at his watch, then glanced around the corner as the padding softened. Gavel was gone, somewhere in the junkyard. When he returned, Peltzer checked his watch again.

Forty seconds. Peltzer prayed it would be enough.

Gavel was at the trunk. He gathered another armful— not so much, Peltzer noted, that he might accidentally drop one and slipped back into the junkyard.

Peltzer moved—and nearly met disaster right there. His knees were still weak after the strain of crouching, and they had a hard time holding him up now that he wanted to run. His balance slipped all over the place, but he made it to the trunk and held on until he felt he could return without incident.

His watch told him he had fifteen seconds left. There were about a dozen pieces left in the trunk, a few covered in plastic garbage bags instead of newspaper. He grabbed one and scurried around the corner—just as Gavel came padding back.

Peltzer moved away from the corner so Gavel would not hear his heavy breathing. He wondered fleetingly if his exhaustion was due to being out of shape or the fear that had hit him when he'd nearly stumbled into the gutter. Didn't matter now; he had what he wanted. To business.

He waited a few moments to give Gavel time to duck into the junkyard again, then set about carefully opening the package in his hands. It was slightly damp at two ends, splotched dark with something sticky. Peltzer's first thought was: barbecue sauce. But why would Gavel be hiding beef inside the junkyard? Planning a party there later? Maybe another drinking binge?

He peeled back the layers of paper, twisted and folded, until he reached what he thought was the center. There was nothing there. It *was* just a ball of newspaper—

—until he caught some dark form slip out from two folds down and hit the pavement at his feet with a soft *plop*.

Peltzer stared at the shape. He couldn't place it for the longest time. He knew what it looked like, but his mind repeatedly denied the image and searched for some other explanation. But there was only one thing it could be, and it slammed so hard into the sheriff's guts that he nearly retched right there.

It was a joint, a knee or an elbow, bent like a boomerang with tattered flesh at either end. Its paleness was nearly luminescent, except for the splashes of blood and the stringy ligaments at the ends.

The fine hair and scattered freckles upon the flesh told him that it belonged to a human being.

He backed away. Foul air, carrying a scream, bulged in his throat, but he kept it down. *Jesus Christ, Jesus Christ, oh Jesus Christ*—his mind worked, over and over, unable to reach beyond, like a needle caressing the scratch in a record. Outside his daze, he felt himself fall against something, a wall, and suddenly he needed its support. He curled up against the coarse surface, pressing, *pressing*, wanting desperately to sap its strength.

It didn't work. His world went numb.

He might have sat there all night, a pale, shaking lump couched in shadows, if not for the sound that disturbed the night, a shrill burst that nudged his mind onto a single track again.

Kevin Gavel was whistling a tune. *Whistling* as he went about his work.

231

The shock disappeared, replaced by outrage. Peltzer rose to his feet again. The human joint was forgotten, left to lie on the sidewalk until neighborhood kids found it the next morning. Peltzer's intent was solely on that whistling maniac who was gathering his last armful of goodies.

He approached the corner. There was no attempt at stealth this time. He just didn't give a damn. His legs moved with purpose, though they were still weak and caused him to stumble a little. His arms and hands were still wiry too, but his fingers fit snugly around his gun butt, and his muscles pulled the weapon from the holster, and that was all that mattered right now.

He reached the corner and still had enough presence of mind to pause and peek around — after all, Peltzer never did get a good look at Gavel's front; his deputy could have a weapon tucked into his pants.

Unfortunately, the question could not be answered. Gavel was just disappearing between the iron gates with another armful of newspapers.

Peltzer remained still, his muscles rooted, as he let his mind collect the facts that had battered him for the last few minute. Logically, those bundles Gavel carried must hold the rest of the butchered victim or victims. Why Gavel was leaving the pieces in the junkyard he didn't know, but it appeared to be a procedure Gavel had followed before. And that meant previous victims. Not far from Maclean's Grocery. Inside the ten block area where the Winsome kids disappeared — and where Gavel had many a patrol route.

"Christ," he breathed, and then he let the curse go before it could wrap around his thoughts again. This was it. The very confrontation he'd been waiting for. The fact that it involved a man that he had once considered a friend meant very little to him now. The horror overshadowed any other emotion.

Sheriff Peltzer brought his gun level and followed his suspect into the darkness of the junkyard.

Only one would return alive.

The Pit was getting warmer inside. It wasn't due to the weather.

Nick and Pauline were deep into each other's arms, each other's eyes, each other's lips and mouths. They had begun by making out, and for a long time it had seemed it would not progress beyond that—to the deep disappointment of two hidden pairs of eyes above. However, the inhibitions melted under the rising heat, and it was all the two inebriated voyeurs could do to keep themselves from cheering when Nick pulled off Pauline's top.

He was now trying to kiss her neck and look over her shoulder at the same time. His fingers struggled with the bra. Since he had never seen one up close, there was some difficulty in opening it.

"The front, stupid," Larry whispered.

Mark, next to him on the roof, looked at him. "What?"

"The front. It opens from the front."

Mark leaned over, blocking Larry's view just for a second to get a better look down the vent. Larry pushed him back when he heard Pauline groan.

"Shit," Larry commented. Nothing new was happening.

"You sure it opens from the front?" Mark asked.

"They all do these days. I'm just surprised she's wearing one in the first place."

Mark gave him a scowl. "She's a nice girl, you know."

"Yeah, yeah . . ."

"I mean, I know her." The wind brushed through his hair. He looked around at the night sky, the black clouds. "Maybe we shouldn't be up here."

"Oh, God, not *that* again. Why can't you—"

They both shut up and stared through the vent as another groan came from Pauline. The bra had been momentarily forgotten. She now had Nick's shirt off.

"I'll be asleep before they even slip off their pants," commented Mark.

"You would be," whispered Larry. "Just, for God's sake, have some patience. A good plan needs time. You'll see." He took a sip of beer to warm his guts. "Eventually, this place will be exploding with action."

233

Ed Kelton could tell he was getting close to something important by the strong stench that hit him. The bad news was, he was running out of flares.

He hadn't expected the tunnel to go on for so long. He figured it must twist and turn under most of his property, maybe even slip under some of the streets and shops. He'd been planting his flares farther and farther apart the longer he'd gone on, but now the supply grew short. It worried him. He had two flashlights if he needed more illumination, but the flares' primary use was to act as bread crumbs, so that he wouldn't get lost should he need to make a hasty retreat. The path had branched off only once during his hunt. He'd chosen the tunnel to the right because he thought he heard some sound from there; he decided he could return to take care of the left tunnel later, but if the corridors decided to split into tributaries further on, he wouldn't have enough flares left to explore even one direction.

He stopped. Took a whiff of air. Something ahead soon, he was sure of it. He set out toward it.

The smell was getting pretty bad, so much so that he wondered if he should have bought a gas mask from his war buddy. Well, he told himself, if these creatures could live with the odor, so could he. He would just breathe through his mouth from here on out.

That wasn't the only handicap, however. His legs screamed to be stretched. Unlike Ray, he couldn't stand in the tunnel with only his back bent; he was a big man, and correspondingly the tunnel walls were that much more claustrophobic. Occasionally he would step a little higher than usual, an unconscious attempt to give his legs a little more room, and catch himself just in time to prepare for a sharp bump on the head against the ceiling.

He did that now, and flinched at the retort destined for his noggin. Nothing happened. He shone his flashlight up and was surprised to find that, without any change in temperature or atmosphere that he could feel, the ceiling had risen an additional two feet: enough to stretch his legs.

Someone's watching over you, Ed.

He took a moment to rest. He peered into the tunnel behind him, to make sure nothing was sneaking up on him, then shone the flashlight up front again. He discovered that, not only had the ceiling expanded, but so had the walls; he had wandered into a chamber, thankfully much larger than that one near the entrance. It looked about the length of an apartment he'd once lived in New York decades ago, about twenty feet across, fifteen wide. As much as he had hated that room, at least he had been able to stand straight in it. Unfortunately, this place had been carved for those beasts. He guessed that, to them, it would be considered roomy.

He moved deeper into the chamber and tried a small sniff of air. The stench that he had been following was powerful here. It took some effort not to gag on it. He couldn't imagine it getting any worse.

And if it can't get any worse, then this must be . . .

His thought was interrupted by a rustling motion—and a soft, inquisitive growl. Ed whirled, aiming the light across the chamber, his flame thrower's nozzle right behind it. There, in the opposite wall, was another tunnel. It appeared less polished than the one behind him. Sharp rock thrust from the walls and ceiling, like ancient teeth, and the shadows they created in his light stretched back forever into the stone gullet.

Foreboding—and dangerous. Those projections nearly obscured the slight glimmer of eyes that crouched low in that tunnel.

Ed stumbled back. He tried desperately to keep the light steady on those eyes. He didn't want them to disappear in the dark.

The eyes rose. The flashlight's beam now reflected their deep red. Behind them, the soft growl grew to a rumble.

Ed had to fight to keep his place. The urge to run and scream, to give in to the panic that squeezed his heart, was nearly overwhelming. But he concentrated on that face that rose before him, studied every detail of that snout, those teeth, those eyes. They had definition now. He would keep his imagination at bay, the facts were in front of him, in this real living thing, and if he accepted them, it would be easier to meet the challenge without flinching.

Finally, one of the bastards that murdered my children!

Bloody, familiar scenes flashed behind his eyes.

And his anger grew.

Ed pushed himself to his feet again, then realized he would have a better aim if he sat on his knees. He moved with great caution, so as not to send the beast charging. It wouldn't wait too long, though. The thing was snarling so loud now that saliva spilled over its lips.

On his knees, flame thrower pointed ahead, Ed stared across the chamber into those eyes.

His look had power. What had before been a snarling beast now snapped its mouth shut and became silent. Ruby eyes stared back, as if its mind was only now comprehending that Ed might be something more than meat.

The moment was long. The only sound was that of their ragged breaths. It echoed through the chamber, wrapping them in a windstorm they could not feel.

Seconds later it died, and there was silence. For a moment, Ed thought there might not be a fight, that they would both just turn and walk away from each other.

Then, in a lightning flash, the creature was charging. Its roar hit him, so loud that his ears buzzed, so close that he could smell the thing's rancid breath over the chamber's odor.

Ed didn't have time to aim. He squeezed the flame thrower's trigger and screamed.

The beast slammed into the needle of fire. Orange and red waves washed over its head, alighting the rest of the body.

Yet it kept coming. Ed kicked himself backward. Something tugged at his shoulder, but he couldn't turn to look. The warmth of the weapon's burst and the creature's blaze burned at his own skin. He raised one arm to cover his face. His eyes squinted beyond his fingers. He could see through the sharp light, to the dark form engulfed within. The initial blast had burned its face to the bone. The snout was a black stump. The eyes were black holes now, seeping a dark liquid before that, too, was boiled away.

The beast fell hard. Air locked in its lungs was pushed out; the oxygen briefly fed two small tentacles of flames from its nostrils. The limbs struggled, clawed fingers digging furrows into the ground around it, then the next instant lay helpless as the fire burned the skin and fat away.

The creature had landed close, so close that Ed's right boot caught on fire. He kicked at it, pushed dirt on it, but the heat, like a fist slowing closing, continued to envelop his toes. He stumbled up and stamped his foot repeatedly against the ground.

The flames finally died—in time for him to realize he had a new problem.

He was standing, bent at the waist, so that his head barely touched the ceiling—and from this new height he discovered that he could not breathe. The top of the chamber was stuffed with moving smoke, its black mass slowly emptying into the tunnel ahead. The flames, now dying on the beast, had sucked a lot of the oxygen from the room. Ed ducked low again; the air was better down here. But it was still uncomfortably hot in the chamber, and he knew it would only get worse.

Retreat came to mind. He couldn't stay here with the fire going, and he couldn't go forward where the poisonous smoke was flowing. He *could* go back and check that tunnel that had branched away, then come back once the fire had burned itself out. It was, really, the only option.

He was about to retrace his steps when he realized there was something else wrong: his burden was missing. He looked around and found the flame thrower resting against the far right wall. He remembered the tug on his shoulder when he'd jumped away from the creature. The strap must have snapped. He cursed and reached for the weapon, his mind clicking over what he might use to secure it to his body again—

—and watched in dull horror as a black shape the size of a German shepherd appeared from the tunnel behind him and bit savagely into his forearm.

Blood exploded around the creature's muzzle. His blood.

Pain clawed his nerves, no longer dulled by surprise. He pulled back and tried to rip his arm from the vicelike jaws, but that only doubled the agony. His free hand reached for the nozzle of his weapon at his side—and another surge of horror brought the fact that the flame thrower was still against the wall, on the other side of the thing rending his arm away.

Ed screamed, in frustration as much as pain. His world was going black, but he didn't know if it was unconsciousness or the fire's black clouds descending. He didn't have much time, either way. He had to keep his mind working, moving around the pain, until he could find some escape . . .

His fingers touched something metallic. He pulled, and through the tears he saw it was a knife. He didn't have time to reposition his body for a prime strike. The knife came down, crooked, uncertain, yet with enough power to slice through the monster's leg.

The beast reacted in a flash. Its opened its mouth. The neck muscles contracted, pulling the head around to scream at its wound, at the offending weapon, and finally to lunge at Ed's throat.

But Ed had his torn arm back and was already moving away. He twisted on his butt, to kick the giant rat in the face. The blow stunned it, long enough for Ed to scurry back, back toward the tunnel, to escape.

He would have made it had he not, in his panic, tried to use his injured arm to support himself. It crumbled beneath him. Blinding, unmerciful pain raked through him. His left side was completely helpless. Desperate, he turned onto his other side and used his feet to kick at the rock floor while the fingers of his right hand dug in, as unfeeling as metal claws, to pull him forward, *forward*—

And the rat was on him again. It grabbed his right foot and laid into it. In seconds, the creature had his boot peeled away. Ed struggled, but his strength was tapped. Its entire body weight was behind the two front paws that held his leg against the ground. He could do nothing but thrash wildly as those rows of razors gnawed away the flesh around his ankle, cut into the ligaments and muscles, finally to scrape at the bone.

The chamber vibrated with his screams.

He wouldn't give up. *Couldn't.* If he died down here, it would be the same as dying in the heat and flames of hell — and he would never see his dead wife again, not down here.

His free leg pummeled the creature's head. His eyes, though weakening, searched desperately for *some*thing he could use as a weapon. The flame thrower was well out of reach. The knife was gone, maybe flattened beneath the beast. All he had were his fists.

He glanced lower, knowing he didn't want to see what was there. He'd already lost his foot. Now the snout was chewing its way up the length of his leg, pulling and tearing and crunching, sickening sounds few humans have heard. It made Ed fight that much harder — but the creature stood it all, never once letting up on the grip its hands had around his knee.

Ed grunted again with the effort of sitting up. He tried to punch his fist through one of those burning irises, but the attack lasted only seconds. He fell back again — what he thought would be his last time. He was left with a final, sickening image still strong in his mind: he was slowly, inexorably being eaten alive.

God, dear God, please!

But as he fell back, he was assailed by a new sensation, something less than pain that managed to break through his agony. It came from a place untouched by this horror, the middle of his back. His good hand touched the offending object, grasped it, held it in front of his eyes. It took nightmarish seconds for him to recognize the glint of metal.

Shotgun.

He didn't think about it. Just placed the metal stalk against the monster's forehead, right between those fucking rosy eyes that went dark as they looked up at him. The bloody jaws opened just a bit, as if to scream, *"Oh, fuck!"*

Ed didn't want to hear it. His finger found the trigger and kissed it.

The metal pellets incased in the shell slammed through the rat's skull, tearing the brain into fragments. The dark eyes went wide, the body limp. Black, syrupy blood mingled with Ed's own rich crimson.

Two down, he thought, as relief pushed at the pain and numbed his nerves. *Two down, only two fucking monsters down, and I'm already dead. How many more?*

It was no use. He had to retreat. He'd be lucky to reach the surface alive now.

He laid the gun aside so he could better position himself with his good hand. Once ready, he pulled back, biting off a painful cry, until his leg was free of the dead monster's mouth. When he finally rested, he dared a glance at the injured limb. What he saw made his world grow darker.

Everything below the knee was gone. Strips of flesh, bathed in red, covered the gore like tattered clothing. A white bone, still shiny with saliva, stuck out a few inches beyond that. The bone had whittled furrows around the end: a result of the rat's gnawing.

Ed lay back and forced his eyes to the smoke above. He sucked at the room's short supply of oxygen. Nausea pushed beneath his belly. The chamber spun. Every few seconds, a random muscle would jump uncontrollably, torturing his nerves with the movement.

Oh, God, I'm going into shock.

Panic surged. He couldn't take it, not another jolt. Yet they kept coming. He fought for control. Failed.

I'm a dead man . . . a dead man . . .

He tried to move toward the tunnel, to escape. Disoriented, he bumped into a wall where he thought the tunnel should be. The mistake might have taken him over the edge if he hadn't seen the flash of metal lying a few feet away. He fell flat on his stomach and reached for it. The touch of the warm casing took some of the edge off. He pulled the flame thrower close and bent his body around it, like a child holding a teddy bear at night. He couldn't rest long or he'd die, but the short respite helped him to think a little more clearly.

Okay. I can see the tunnel. Not far. I can make it. Gotta get out quick before—

Something, he didn't know what, pushed through his haze. A presence, something massive and very dark that overshadowed the room. At first Ed thought it had to be Death, come to carry him away. But then he heard the rumble, the claws gripping the rough floor . . . and the chewing sounds.

He stayed very still. He couldn't reach the tunnel before one of those things would attack, he was sure of that. No matter how hopeless, though, he should have tried for it, should have made that desperate rush for escape.

But an overpowering urge held him back.

He felt it. His senses were alive with its presence. There was more than just another beast in here with him. Maybe more than Death itself.

He remembered his reserve flashlight, unclipped it, and shone it at the wall. The light exposed rock turned black by the smoke, ragged bumps and claw marks and whiskers of roots.

And then it touched a gap.

About six feet ahead there was another tunnel that connected with the chamber. Ed had not noticed it before because the walls and ceiling did not narrow, merely slid away into the dark gulf.

The presence was coming from there. Ed stared at it, at the escape tunnel behind him, back again.

What the hell's in there?

Maybe the very thing that had started all this. Maybe what would end this nightmare if it was destroyed.

Ed's tortured mind grasped at the salvation. He moved toward the gap. The presence fed him as he neared. It kept him alive, prevented the comforting darkness that pressed at his consciousness from seducing him. He soon found he could drag himself with less pain than before as long as he kept his eyes on the gap.

Fortunately his curiosity did not dissipate all of his caution. The flame thrower's nozzle led him the whole way, his fingers maintained around the trigger. The fuel tank dragged behind, clanking against the uneven floor as recklessly as his own body.

He stopped ten feet from the gap, now centered on its entrance. It was as far away as the charred remains of his previous victim would allow. He rested his back against the crusted ribs for support. When he was ready, he brought the weapon's nozzle up along with the flashlight.

The gap was really only an addition to the chamber, a neighboring room that was more narrow and went back about twelve feet. The flashlight circled the walls, then zeroed in on the center.

Ed flinched back, a hoarse scream ripping at his throat.

Secreted within the hollow was a giant creature, a massive black shape that filled the width between the walls and rose up six feet. It was another of the creatures, Ed could make that out, but so large that its presence had forced him across the chamber to meet it. He had no doubt the monster was the mother of these other beasts, the reason Death, Terror, and Beau had been killed and *dragged* down to these depths. She must do nothing but sleep and eat and place demands on her own children. A demon queen. Even a sort of throne had been built for her: belts and human bones and ligaments and long pink strands Ed thought must be muscles wrapped around the mother rat's middle, beneath her haunches, and under her chin. They splayed out from where they were connected to the walls and ceiling, supporting the monster's weight like some giant web.

The beam remained on the black shape. She looked back at Ed—or so he thought. Her eyes were as large as his hand, milky-white from near-blindness. Ed wanted to turn the flashlight off, to back away and just get out

242

now — but the presence kept him there, that horrible image in the dark hollow pulling at him like a black hole pulls at light. He lay there, his life bleeding out his leg and arm, and swept his light around her form with the skill and intricacy of a lover's hand.

It was natural she would resemble the others. Her skin, gray and mottled, though it was obvious a ferocious power lay beneath. Her hair, long and matted with grease and sweat and dried blood. Strange bumps, like cancerous boils, bubbled around her face and stomach. Ed lowered the beam, sickened.

The light caught strange shapes that carpeted the floor. Around her lay the reasons for the odor that had drawn Ed to this chamber: months of killing had created a storehouse of human and animal meat. The children brought it down here for their mother. All to keep this dark god satiated.

Ed lifted the light again. The monster stirred, apparently aware of the beam; when he removed it from her face, she relaxed. Her back haunches supported some of her weight, the rest suspended by the web. She continued to gnaw on what was left of a human head, held now between two clawed hands. She twirled it slowly, so that her teeth could tear the flesh from the skull in one strip, like the rind of an apple. The tail of a spinal cord still hung limply from the food; it wagged as the skull spun.

"Christ," Ed said. He couldn't move, couldn't even think beyond the image that slapped at his sanity, yet still that curse, so often used in the past, came naturally to his lips. "Christ, oh, Jesus Christ . . ."

The mother rat stopped eating. She sniffed the air, twitching her head as though to pick out the single new odor amongst the miasma that engulfed her.

Didn't she hear her children dying? he thought. *Didn't she hear the fire and the gunblast and the screams.* But then he remembered he was the only one that had screamed, and only when the beasts were growling and ripping. *They've probably brought other victims down here, animals and humans, to tear at them while they were still alive. She thought they'd killed me. She knew she'd get her share later. But now . . .*

243

But now there were no sounds of her children eating. Now there was Ed cursing like a fool and the tendrils of charred rat-flesh just beginning to reach her . . .

A cold hand squeezed Ed's heart. He started to move away, then curled and hissed as every nerve in his leg exploded.

The mother rat, already alerted, listened. She aimed her snout and sniffed loudly. Ed shone the light on her face, hoping to blind her. But the eyes were already gone, for the most part. So were the ears. What was important was the smell, the stench of living food. And she had him pegged.

Ed watched those milky eyes zero in on him and narrow—and then her lips rose to reveal a mouth deformed by the size and number of teeth. Yellow goo dripped out around the gums, frothing with excitement.

Ed's body shook. He thought he was going into shock again before he realized the entire chamber was shaking. The growl had started so low that it had been below his range, but now the rumble filled his ears. He struggled. The pain was so wearying that he knew he would never make it. But he still had his weapon. He could still do what he'd set out to· do. He would willingly die to succeed.

He aimed the nozzle at the creature's head. She may have sensed the threat—Ed was still living, and was therefore more than just another tender morsel—but she wasn't afraid; she strained at her supports, wanting only to get her muzzle around his warm body.

Ed took a breath.

"This is for my children, damn you!"

He pulled the trigger.

A foot-long flame shot from the nozzle, lasted two seconds, then died back to a small flare that might have been enough to light a cigarette.

The cold hand returned. Ed pulled the trigger again and again, but the fire never grew from the small bud that surrounded the nozzle. Either the pressure was gone, somehow damaged during the fall, or he had nothing but fumes left in the fuel casing. He didn't have the strength

244

to turn around and examine the hose. Nor did he have the time. The place was rattling with the mother rat's roar. And above that, an even scarier sound: the web holding back the creature was groaning.

Oh, Christ, gotta get out NOW—

He wasn't about to wait for the final snap that would send the darkness washing over him. Despite this suicide run, Ed Kelton was a survivor. He was also aware that, if he didn't kill *this* monster, his life and the life of his children would be wasted for nothing more than rat food.

He used his good arm and leg to push himself up. Behind, he could hear the brutal cracks as the ties that bound the monster fell away. It spurred him on. He struggled toward the tunnel, the only exit back to the real world.

As he moved, something grabbed him.

Ray heard the screaming and the crash that sounded like waves hitting the beach, but not once did he think of retreating. He continued forward, doubly wary now. The screams were those of a human being—but who? Who would be down here at this time of night besides some stupid kid who wanted to be a hero?

He passed the fork, where the tunnel diverged into two, and did not hesitate to follow the next blue flare. He reached the sharp corner at the end of the tunnel, turned it—and ran face first into a cloud of black smoke. Ray gagged, fell to his knees in search of air.

He knew in the back of his mind that it must be a fire, but for now, locked inside the tight rock walls, he conjured up evil magic and dragons. He would have turned around and gone back right then if there had not been additional screams—in fact, human *words*.

The hose of his weapon led him down the corridor. The smoke had cleared to a mere tendril by the time he reached the end of the tunnel, so that when he stepped into the chamber, the horror awaiting him was very clear.

There was a monster nearby, but it just laid there, unmoving, its head seemingly more deformed than the one he'd killed. He assumed it was dead, but remained wary of it. Across the chamber, he made out a charred ruin. He could discern a rib cage; the rest was covered with black goo that still dripped to the dirt.

Then he saw the man. In his fifties, fairly muscular, his skin black from the fire, Sweat stood out on him in large droplets, shiny in the dying fire. He was alive, and struggling to get away from—

"Holy *shit!*" Ray screamed. The roar of the mother rat covered it.

Larry never mentioned anything about that!

He stood stunned for ages, until the need for urgency hit him. He knew he'd better move fast if he were going to get out of here alive. He turned to go . . . and his eyes touched on the man fighting to get to his hands and knees. He was missing part of his leg. One arm was mangled. Ray felt sick, wanted to turn away—but the sight shifted a burden onto his conscience: if he left now, this man would die.

Ray faltered until the man cried out. The pure anguish stung Ray's soul, and without another thought he rushed to give aid.

The man screamed when Ray touched his shoulder. His eyes jerked up to the boy, bulging with madness, every muscle in his face strained against a blow he felt certain would come. Ray backed up a step, repeating, "No, no! It's okay!" Ed heard him; relief relaxed his expression—until the roar of the mother rat struck them both and returned the deadly urgency of their escape.

"Take my arm!" Ed screamed at him. He slapped his good hand against Ray's foot. Ray grabbed it and pulled. After much straining, they moved about eight inches.

"Keep pulling!" the man demanded, but Ray's attention kept going back to the monster. The strength in those claws that pushed at the ground and furrowed it, the glowing eyes that beaded in on him, sent Ray reeling. His balance slipped. He would fall soon, unable to rise. He *had* to get out of here, with or without this man.

But the man had hold of his arm. Every ounce of his reserve was in that grip; Ray could not shake him.

"Pull!" the man kept screaming. *"Pull!"* Ray pulled. They moved another ten inches before Ray had to take a breath.

The roar was maddening now. *How can anything go on screaming that long?* Ray wondered. The numerous straps that held the creature back were snapping all over; dirt and chunks of rock fell from the ceiling and walls as the web pulled apart. Giant paws reached for him. Jaws snapped spikelike teeth together, throwing spittle high into the air.

Ray panicked. He clawed at Ed's arm, slashing lines in the skin that quickly filled with blood and spilled down his shoulder. The man didn't even feel it; he had more than enough pain to deal with. And he did not let go.

"Stop it, stop it, *stop it!*" Ray cried. Every muscle strained to get away. "Let me *go!* Goddamn it, I gotta get *out of here!*"

Ed heard the words and looked into the face of his savior. His eyes squinted, as if he were looking through murky water. Something looked wrong. Ed didn't loosen his grip or insist that Ray pull, but merely stared at the boy's shattered form and asked, "What's that hanging next to you?"

Ray paused in his fight long enough to look at his side. Yes, there was something there, something heavy. He felt it on his back, too.

Dammit! Why didn't I—

The panic subsided just enough to let Ray think. He grabbed the hose and looked at the man as though he had the answer. The man was silent, but his changing face gave him away. He must have realized that hanging on would be useless with the progress they were making; he must have seen now that Ray was just a scared boy. The expression of disappointment that passed over his wrinkled features shook Ray deep inside, and returned to him his determination.

Ed let go of Ray's arm just as the boy moved toward the mother rat. There was still a part of him that wanted to run, but he stood his ground, pointed the hose, and squeezed. It went exactly as he'd practiced; even the aim

247

was right on. Gas rained out, drenching the monster's face. She tried to turn away, but her surviving straps prevented it. Her eyes closed, as did her mouth, and her front hands came up to block the spray. Her arms were too short, though. The gas covered her and pressed the hair of her head and neck to her flesh.

Ray squeezed again, feeling a giddiness coming on. He'd stopped the monster from charging. His weapon was working. This time he aimed at the monster's belly, exposed as its upper half was still held by the web. The pungent odor of gas mixed with that of the rotting meat. Ray sucked it into his lungs, basking in its triumphant reek.

When he was done, he'd exhausted three-fourths of the gas in his bubble. The hose inside wouldn't reach the last bit without some readjusting, and Ray didn't have time for that. He backed away. What he'd used was enough.

A rush of putrid air smacked against his face. The newly enraged monster strained to get at him, screaming. Ray forced himself to look beyond those jaws that begged to rip him apart, to those white eyes. He met them, held them. His own jaw set. His left hand reached around and drew a firecracker. His other hand produced the golden lighter.

The mother rat sensed what was coming. She froze, her haunches in the midst of a surge forward, her forward claws gripping two straps that hung from the ceiling. Those eyes, though nearly blind, stared back at him. Expectant.

"Fuck you," Ray growled, and flicked the lighter.

Nothing. Not even a spark.

"Oh, Jesus, not again," Ed slurred from behind.

Ray flicked the lighter again. Nothing but a click. Again. And again. Click-click. It was gone. Empty.

The mother rat seemed to smile. The lips continued curling back and the maw opened wide once more to allow enough room for the roar's passage.

Ray stumbled back at the mixture of sound and wind. He felt certain his ears were bleeding once the initial blast passed, but there was no time to check; the man he had tripped over was pulling at him now, urging him towards the middle of the room.

"What? *What?*" Ray demanded.

"Over there!" Ed pointed.

Ray couldn't see anything, just shadows. A rock fell from above and hit him on the shoulder. He held the bruised area, his eyes scanning the ceiling through the black smoke for more bombs. The rock face seemed to shift as he watched, vibrating with the scream of the monster.

The desperate need for escape returned to him. He pushed at Ed's hand and cried, "No! I *can't!* I have to get out of here!" Emotion welled in his throat when he saw Ed's terror. This burly man was as frightened as him, but much more helpless. "I'm sorry," Ray stammered. He turned then, trying to wipe the image of the man from his mind. He started forward, toward the tunnel that promised escape. And stopped.

The tunnel was blocked by the final child beast, the larger male who had wisely stayed away until the weapons were exhausted. The howls from behind paused for a moment. Ray twisted his head, saw the mother rat sniffing the air, aware of her child's presence. The child rat growled. The sound sent its mother into a frightening tantrum. Ray put his back to her again, to blot her away for now, but he couldn't help hearing the snaps of the web and the creak of the walls and the hungry cry from a mother who no longer feared death.

Ray concentrated on the child rat. It was difficult to think of it as a child because of its size, more than half his own height. It moved slowly. Its eyes held him. Its nostrils sucked hungrily at the odor of panic in its prey.

Ray was dead. The certainty touched him, and he was angry that it didn't provide the relief he had always thought it would. Instead, there was a rising beat inside him — the force of survival that would keep him screaming and fighting until the rat bled him to unconsciousness.

The child rat snarled. Its pace remained the same; there was no hurry; accuracy and success of the kill had

249

to be maintained.

A scream rose in Ray's throat, one laced with hysterical laughter. He fought the building pressure, afraid the explosion would startle the beast into charging. He thought he was succeeding—

Then something grabbed his foot. He opened his mouth. A mere squeak came out. He would have laughed if his knees hadn't weakened and nearly pulled him to the ground. The image of the mother rat gnawing at his leg filled his mind, tipping him toward insanity. He looked down, prepared to give the scream another try . . . and saw that it was only Ed Kelton, the man who shared this nightmare with him, who held his leg.

Ed pointed toward the center of the chamber.

"What?" Ray screamed. *"What? WHAT?"* The man's lips moved. Ray had to lean close to hear him over the cacophony of the mother rat.

"One . . . more . . . shot," Ed spat. Blood rose behind the words and spilled over his lips.

Ray straightened and searched the room with his eyes. There was nothing! What was the old man talking about—

The glint of metal reached out from the shadow of the unburned dead rat. Ray could see the carcass better from this position and he recognized the fatal wound in the creature's skull. The metal tube just below it suddenly took on great meaning.

One shot left.

The warm air behind him reminded Ray of the monster still fighting to reach him. He looked for the child rat. It was still blocking the escape tunnel, still advancing, maybe just a pounce away. It stopped, reading the hope in its prey's face. Ray risked a glance at the shotgun again to judge its distance. The child rat followed his gaze, also caught the glint of metal. Its molten eyes burned.

They rushed it at the same time. Both exploded with a ferocious cry. Out of the corner of his eye, Ray saw the black mass coming at him, dust erupting behind it, and knew that if he didn't pick up that weapon, aim it, and

250

fire before the beast reached the same point, he was in for a horrible end.

He leaped—

—and grabbed the shotgun in time to twist it into the oncoming beast. The rat's maw fell around the short barrel. Its muzzle hair and cold-running nose brushed against Ray's hand. There then followed an explosion and a spout of brains that covered the far wall. The rat groaned and relaxed into death.

Ray dropped the gun and scuttled away, crablike, his eyes unwilling to blink or otherwise tear his sight from the monster that had come so close to devouring him. In his shock, he did not notice the silence that descended in the chamber, as dark as the smoke above, until it came to a shattering end.

The mother rat knew her last child was dead. The rage engulfed her, and with a final push whose strength was reflected in her rising wail, her remaining bonds snapped away. She hit the ground hard and lay there while dirt clouds floated around her. All movement stopped. Ray wondered if her massive weight had not killed her, as when whales beach themselves.

But those white eyes did not close. The nose did not stop twitching. The quiet was slowly filled by a deep rumble which grew louder as the mother rat's head lifted. Her maw pulled open with a sickly wet sound. Her shoulder hunched, pulling away the last vestiges of any support.

The mother rat was free. And she was furious.

There was movement next to him. Ray managed to pull his eyes away from the monster to look. It was Ed. His head was pulled back, to face Ray upside down, and he spoke only one word: *"Go!"*

The chamber shook. He looked up to see the mother rat's legs straining to push her forward. Her wide middle slashed against the walls of the gap, carving out the rock that dared hold her back. She moved faster, still glaring at Ray.

Ray took off. He stumbled, his knees still weak, but he made it to the escape tunnel. As he ducked through, the plastic bubble still strapped around his shoulders hit the narrow wall, spun him around, and he fell facing the chamber.

He should have gotten up then, run like hell, never looking back. But he couldn't help staring at the scene before him.

The mother rat rushed out of her hollow and headed straight for Ray. She had to pass over Ed to do so, however, and when she tried, he landed a solid fist in her throat. She flinched. Her pained cry was slightly frayed due to the blow. But it wasn't enough to sway her from her intent. Ray watched in catatonic horror as the monster slammed her muzzle into Ed's chest. The beast shook her head as the teeth chewed deeper, the claws tearing back each layer so that the maw could eat into the next. Ray heard the man's ribs snap apart, like rifle bursts in a valley. Finally, the beast grabbed hold of something between those crooked teeth, and pulled back with effort. The organ came away . . . and the mother rat faced Ray again with Ed Kelton's heart swinging from her bloody mouth.

"Fuck!" Ray screamed. The rush of adrenaline electrified him; he turned and began the longest run of his life.

His journey was a blur. His eyes never focused on anything. Occasionally he would catch the blue haze of a flare and know he was going the right way. But right way or wrong way, he had to keep moving. He bumped his head several times in his haste, ignored it. He used the aches in his muscles like whips against a horse's flank. His bubble weapon bounced against the wall several times, knocking him off balance, and he tried to unstrap the damned thing, but there was no room and no time for such action. He had to keep *moving*.

He made the first sharp turn and was halfway down the second before he heard the frightening thunder behind him. A twisting arm of dust caught up with him. Despite the burn it brought to his eyes, he could see, in the distance and fast approaching, the dark form of the mother rat. She had become so large over the months that she didn't fit in these narrow tunnels. But that didn't stop her: as her powerful muscles pushed forward, the walls exploded outward, to eventually cave in behind her bulk. *Like a fucking groundhog!* Her progress should have been slow with the amount of earth she had to lift, but she had witnessed the death of her child: there was nothing that would slow her now.

Ice lanced up Ray's spine. *I'm not going to make it.*

Amidst that giant black form, the white eyes, almost blazing with the monster's fury, narrowed on him. She roared again, pushing a whirlwind through the tunnel, and strained harder against the walls. Her strength was untiring; she bore down on Ray like a wild locomotive.

In seconds, the distance between them was halved.

Ray ran harder.

They were deep into the labyrinth of junk, which allowed Sheriff Peltzer many places to hide and watch his deputy. Gavel stopped in a small clearing surrounded by dark, foreboding shapes, a few that reached taller than a man. He laid the last armful of his lover on the pile he'd already made, then kneeled and opened one of the packages. Peltzer peered through the twists of metal near his face to see what the newspaper held.

Again, it was unmistakable, even from this distance: a human hand. Gavel waved his own hand above it, to help the odor drift.

"Come and get it," Peltzer heard him say.

That was enough for the sheriff. He stood and made his way around the garbage. When Gavel stood again and began to walk away, he walked right into Peltzer's gun.

The sheriff just let him stand there for a moment, so that he could study the man's face. It was, naturally, shocked to see the gun, even more shocked to see who held it. Gavel struggled to regain some composure, but every posture looked and felt forced. Of course, it didn't matter *how* Gavel appeared outside; Peltzer could see the guilt in his eyes.

"What's going on here, Kev?" he asked. The gun

remained level

"What do you—"

"Don't play games. Just glance behind you and tell me what that is."

Gavel actually went through the act of looking at the pile of wrapped meat and shrugging. "I just saw it myself, Martin. I don't know where—"

"I saw you put them there." The words hissed out through Peltzer's clamped jaw. "And I can tell you you're missing a piece. I opened it outside."

Gavel didn't say anything to that. A gust of wind came by and blew hair in his eyes. He brushed it away with great care; he was trying to buy time.

So Peltzer cocked his gun.

Gavel started. "Hey, wait . . ."

"Tell me about it, Kevin. Tell me how a human being got cut up and wrapped and brought out here for God knows what reason. I want to hear the explanation." He brought the gun up. "And it sure as shit better be a good story."

Gavel's reserve was cracking. He'd been found out. His gods had betrayed him. He should have listened to the omen that had been jumping on his back all this time. The car had been wrong, the night had been wrong—

"Who is it?" Peltzer demanded. He gestured to the pile.

"Just some runaway," Gavel answered simply.

"And . . ." He choked back something that made his throat sore. In the distance, he heard a scuffling sound, probably cats. "And all those other kids?"

Gavel thought of lying, of just saying he didn't know what the sheriff was talking about, but there was a certain calculating desperation that settled over him. He shrugged instead and stated, "Well, there's no evidence, Marty."

Peltzer pointed at the pile. "I've got all I need right there."

Not if we stand here long enough, Gavel thought. And, really, wasn't it better to let his own personal angels take him out of this world than some impersonal state-sanctioned law?

But he had underestimated his sheriff yet again. The same thoughts flashed across Peltzer's mind, and he knew what the justice system was *really* like. Even with the evidence he now had, there was a good chance Kevin Gavel would only get life. And that wasn't good enough, not by a long shot. Not for the torture and mutilation he'd committed against those innocent children; not for the families who would be changed forever; not for this town who had trusted the police to protect them rather than taking them out one by one; and not for the personal betrayal against Peltzer himself. No, life in a cushy prison was not justice.

He raised his gun and aimed the sights squarely between Gavel's eyes.

Gavel was so surprised by the move that he froze, his final offering to a world that hated him, that of a perfect target.

Both men held their breaths.

And suddenly Ray, screaming for his life, rushed out of the darkness, passed between them and away. Startled, Peltzer watched him go. Gavel was just as surprised, but he knew when to take advantage of an opportunity. He rushed the sheriff and they fell to the ground, each struggling for possession of the gun. They rolled around the clearing, biting and clawing and managing a solid punch now and then, yet neither could get the other to let go of the weapon.

Then, abruptly, their fight was frozen, Gavel atop Peltzer, both with one hand around the prize. The ground beneath them shook. The towers that surrounded them rattled, spilling small pieces of metal and wood, threatening to topple completely. A rumble approached from somewhere in the darkness. Neither man knew quite where to look until the thunder stopped and was replaced by the *thump-thump* of heavy feet and a wail that could not have come from anything but a demon — all of it heading right at them.

The mother rat exploded on the scene, as surprised by the two men on the ground as they were by her. The men held the gun so that it pointed in the sky, but they shared a similar instinct and leveled the weapon at the monster. Peltzer alone squeezed the trigger. The angle was wrong, the man's fear too intense. The bullet went high, missing. But the shattering report brought the beast to a halt. She skidded a short way in the loose gravel, one forepaw still raised for her next step. Stunned white orbs blinked at her attackers.

Peltzer was still stunned by the sight; he could only stare back. Gavel, too, was paralyzed; however, he had the advantage of suspecting such monsters existed in the world. And though he knew this must be one of the angels that had helped him so often in the past, who was probably here to take away the evidence that Peltzer wanted so badly, that didn't mean she recognized her servant. She would treat him as just another piece of meat; in fact, he had planned on it just seconds ago. Now, lying helpless beneath the beast, it didn't seem like such a good idea.

Quickly then, he slammed a fist into Peltzer's stomach and wrenched the gun from his grasp. He stood, faced the mother rat. She stared back, puzzled.

"I'm sorry," Gavel said; he brought the gun up and fired.

She flinched at the hole pushed through her shoulder. Dark goo shot out on the junk behind her, following the momentum of the bullet. A solid shot, but without any stopping power. All Gavel accomplished was to tell her exactly that these forms around her were the same that had killed her children: dangerous food.

She pushed her head forward. Gavel saw nothing but rows of teeth and glowing white eyes coming at him out of the night. The growl she issued nearly kicked his legs out from under him. He lifted the gun as best he could and fired twice more: the first too high, the second into a thick, furry arm.

Still not enough. The mother rat charged, releasing a howl that shook even Peltzer into motion. Gavel forgot about the weapon in his hand; some primal terror had control of his mind and body now; he turned and ran for all he was worth. The mother rat followed.

Peltzer rolled out of the way a split second before being crushed by the weight above the scurrying claws. The monster limped slightly, he noticed, but there was still a lot of speed left in those legs. He watched, stunned, until the giant faded into the darkness.

Then a single thought broke through his disbelief: *Kevin's gonna be rat food.* It didn't startle him in any way. He got up slowly, even took the time to wipe off his pants. A smile began to grow on his lips as he heard another roar in the distance — followed by Gavel's plea.

Then he remembered the boy who'd run by. He went rigid. No gun, no weapon of any kind. He'd be a fool to rush deeper into this dark maze without protection.

He went anyway. He'd be damned if he was going to let one more child die in Winsome.

Nick had Pauline's bra off and felt slightly embarrassed at the way he was staring at her breasts. She only smiled at his attention. Her arms wrapped around his neck and pulled him down to a wonderfully warm embrace. His finger touched her nipples; he knew enough not to knead hard. She groaned in response, then whispered in his ear: "All yours."

He thrilled and became worried at the same time; he didn't even have his pants off and already he felt like he wasn't going to last much longer. And he knew that thinking of some goddamn baseball players wasn't going to help.

He lost himself in the warmth and the soft sensations . . . so he was confused when Pauline pushed him away.

"What was that?" she said.

"What?" He looked down at himself, wondering if he'd somehow offended.

"That noise," she clarified. "It sounded like a shot."

"A shot? I didn't hear anything." Before he was done saying it, two more shots reached them. Their eyes met, uncertain. Then Nick's attention dropped to her bare front. "It's okay," he said, and pulled her closer.

"But Nicky—"

"It was only thunder. You saw the clouds outside."

"Yeah," she breathed, unconvinced. But Nick's touches and kisses eventually took the worry away. She floated wherever he would take her.

Nick thought he'd better hurry. Things were getting a little uncomfortable. He unzipped his pants and Pauline helped him out of them. They embraced again, long and delicious.

And then she whispered in his ear, "Better put it on now, lover."

"Huh?" He lightly bit the side of her neck, but she pulled away again.

"Put it on now. It'll just take a second."

He looked at her, completely at a loss. "What?"

"Condom," she said, a little irritated now at the prolonged pause. "Rubber." He looked at her blankly. *"Birth control,"* she added.

It was the one thing he hadn't thought of. He was always under the impression that the woman took care of that. At least, that's what his dad had always grumbled. Well, they'd just have to be careful . . .

"I, uh, forgot them."

"What? You *forgot?*" She was genuinely hurt. Suddenly she felt exposed; she crossed her arms across her front. "I thought this was special for you."

"It is! Don't get mad. I can pull out—"

"Nick," she said, giving him a hard look, "that does *not* work. You should know that." She sighed. "There is no way I'm going to do *any*thing without some kind of protection." Her fingers danced through his hair. "I . . . love you, Nick. A lot. But I'm not going to get pregnant or some disease from you or anyone else."

And then she was standing and pulling her clothes back on. Nick watched her dully. Things were happening too fast here. The touching and kissing and heat were *gone*, and now he was left with a deep dissatisfaction and slightly damp underwear. He rose to his knees and grabbed her hand.

"Wait, wait, wait a minute, Pauline, please. Don't

leave. Things were going nice—"

"Things were going great, Nick, but I told you, I—" She stopped and tilted her head. Nick thought, *What now?*, but he, too, listened.

They heard a scream, riding the crest of a growing rumble. It was coming closer. Nick's first thought was that it must be a prank; he'd halfway been expecting one all night, despite his warnings. But . . . that scream was too convincing. It sent chills through both teenagers, the kind of cold uncertainty that must hit rustlers when they hear the thunder of a stampede somewhere in the darkness around them, or riot police when they hear the calls of the discontented and stand before the first wave holding pipes above their heads.

Pure, helpless terror.

When the pounding began on the outside Pontiac door, Pauline screamed. She pulled her clothes on quickly, fighting off Nick's attempts to get hold of her. He wanted to keep her still and quiet, so that he could try to understand what the person outside was saying. It shouldn't have been very difficult; he was repeating it enough times.

"Let me in, let me in, goddammit, LET ME IN!"

Nick stood, still only in his underwear. The doubt was gone. Anger bunched his fists together. As far as he was concerned, someone out there had just scared his girlfriend half to death and cost him a wonderful evening. Pauline tried to call him back, but he stomped forward, toward the Pontiac entrance, prepared to beat the living hell out of whoever was on the other side.

Ray had dashed by the two figures without thinking of stopping or even calling a warning. The mother rat wasn't after them, it wanted him. When he was in the darkness of the maze, his heart was seized with terror again. He didn't recognize his surroundings. He was lost.

He kept running, forcing his legs to carry him on, all the while prepared for an attack from every strange corner he passed. He heard the shots behind him, but they did not slow him. His panic was justified when he heard the roar of the monster and a new scream from her latest victim.

Not even bullets can stop her! Christ!

He ran on, ripping his clothing and, occasionally, his flesh against metal spokes or slivers of wood that tried to hold him back. He took one corner too sharply, caught his shoulder bad on the frame to a microwave. He tugged until the coat tore away and turned to continue his mad run.

Then stopped. He *knew* this area. It was *familiar.* Just around this next bend and he'd be at the Pit.

Sanctuary! — as far as Ray was concerned.

He took off, reached the car in half a minute. The roar of the beast was still behind him, as was, surprisingly, the scream of the stranger. But he had to forget that, wipe it away just long enough to open the car door and dive into the Pit.

He wasted valuable seconds trying to do so without a key. It wouldn't give. He couldn't figure out what was wrong, why it held back. He slapped it repeatedly, calling out for someone, *any*one to let him in. He could see the light between the cracks of the tires, so someone *had* to be in there, just had to be —

The image of the key arrived. He scrambled for it. Long moments were devoured trying to stick it in the door's slot, moments that brought the monster closer. His fingers kept shaking. His eyes blurred from the intense concentration. The key would dig in a little, just kiss the tiny groove, then slide away. Ray wanted to scream.

Metal, wood, and other junk sang out around him; the mother rat's fierce storm was already beginning to shake the hodgepodge columns circling the clearing.

Then, at last, the key slipped into the slot — and Ray was hit hard from the side, knocked down. Fingers clutched at him. Something big and dark grunted as it pulled its weight over him.

Amidst his screams and weak flailing, Ray came up against an unfamiliar face. It was Kevin Gavel. His free hand struck out and held Ray by the neck; his other brought the gun to the boy's head.

"*What the fuck's in there?*" Gavel demanded.

"It's a, a"—Gavel's hand clutched tighter; in the distance, the monster's cry was closing in—"a clubhouse!"

"*Get it open!*"

Ray nodded; it sounded like a hell of a good idea to him.

Gavel lifted him to his feet by the collar, pushing him against the car door. The gun remained aimed at Ray's head, but Gavel risked a look back at the maze.

"*Hurry it up!*"

The key was already in; Ray only had to twist it and the door was open.

He swung it wide just as two nearby columns of junk toppled to make way for the mother rat. She charged them, ravenous for blood.

Larry and Mark had heard the shots and the screams. The only reason they didn't move was because they were afraid their footsteps would be heard by the lovers in the Pit. Their eyes did move, however, so they never really got a good look at Pauline's breasts—a fact Larry would always regret and Mark would be moderately grateful for.

When the screams reached the Pit's entrance, demanding to be let in, Mark looked at his companion. "I know that voice."

Larry's face scrunched in puzzlement; it was difficult to concentrate with four beers in him. Mark had to provide the answer:

"*Ray! It's Ray!*"

He stood. Larry tried to grab him, but Mark was already rushing with an inebriated gait toward the edge of the roof. When the yelling below would not end, Larry finally shrugged and joined his friend.

"It *is* Ray!" Mark said. He was about to call out when another shape appeared, a man, who raced across the clearing and slammed into their friend.

Then they saw the gun.

"Jesus!" Larry said. Their heads ducked back away

261

from the edge, but not enough that they couldn't see what was going on down there. "Who is that guy?"

Mark shrugged. He looked up. The rumble he had thought was thunder was getting closer—and now it had an unmistakable animal quality to it: a gravelly wind that threatened to crack, similar to Godzilla's roar.

The monster crashed into the clearing. Two towers of junk on either side of it toppled over, spilling sharp metal across the clearing. The creature didn't seem to notice. It turned its pasty eyes on Ray and the stranger and charged.

"Jesus!" Mark screamed over the torrent.

"Christ!" Larry finished.

They retreated from the edge completely. Neither had the courage to record Ray's fate. Instead, they returned to the vent and gathered close to each other as if for warmth.

"That's what you saw?" Mark asked.

Larry nodded. "But they sure as hell weren't *that* big."

They took some time to catch their breaths. Eventually their eyes drifted to the open vent.

"We gotta," Mark said.

Larry debated with himself. It didn't take too long to decide that saving Nick and Pauline's lives might be worth a beating. "All right," he said, and they pulled the vent door out of its niche.

Larry stuck his head down the hole before Mark even had time to volunteer. He was gripped by terror when he saw the empty mattress. "Hey!" he called.

Pauline appeared and twisted her head around the Pit walls.

"Up here!"

She looked up and gasped. "What are you—"

Nick came forward and took her in his arms. He had his pants on again, his shirt still unbuttoned, and his eyes wouldn't leave the Pit's entrance. "Pauline, I think there's something more out there than—"

"Nick, look!" She pointed up at Larry. Larry smiled, conscious of how ridiculous this must look.

"Hi, Nick!" he said.

Nick stalked over until he was beneath the vent. His expression was feral; Larry already felt the beating coming on.

"What the *fuck* are you doing up there?" Nick demanded.

"Just hold on, Nick, I—"

"I warned you, Larry! You're a dead man! How long have you been up there?"

"Nick, please, just—"

"Goddamn it, if you saw anything . . . I . . ." His rage tripped the words. He pointed a finger at the voyeur; Larry only saw the fist behind it. "I'm going to kill you! When they carry you into the hospital, you're just going to be one mound of bruises—"

"Nick, just shut the fuck up!" Larry screamed. His face had gone red, mostly from his upside down position. Nick was about to shout back, but the screams and inhuman sounds outside suddenly reached a new level. There was a loud bang, the sound of tearing metal and broken glass, and the Pontiac rocked toward them.

Before Pauline and Nick could react, Larry pushed his arm through the vent. "Come on! Take my hand! We gotta pull you up!"

There was no more arguing. They had no idea what was going on out there, but by the sound of it, they didn't want to be trapped in the Pit when it came through.

Nick grabbed Pauline and held her beneath the vent. Larry strained his arm to reach them.

"We can't," Pauline screamed. "The hole's too small!"

Before she was done, a weight fell hard against the roof and the crack that had not been tarred yet opened wider. The weight dropped again and again—it was Mark jumping on the break. The board slowly bent inward at the crack. One side of the vent fell away, scraping Larry's ear. He cursed Mark, since he hadn't been warned, but remained in place with his arm hanging down as his friends' sole lifeline.

It took very little time, but to the four teenagers it felt like the minutes counting down to Armageddon. The board finally gave under Mark's weight, and hung limp like a trap door. The new hole joined with one side of the vent; it still wasn't very large, but it was enough for Pauline.

She jumped and, with Nick pushing from below, managed to grab Larry's hand. Mark reached down to help. In the interval of a breath, she was up: bruised and cut by slivers, but safe.

Nick knew he wouldn't be able to make it up just by jumping; even with his height, he wouldn't be able to reach Larry's arm, plus he weighed a lot more than Pauline. He had to have some base. Quickly, the sounds around the Pontiac nearly deafening now, he rolled the TV beneath the vent, climbed it, and jumped. He missed. His landing was not graceful: his feet slipped from the surface of the TV and he landed hard on his back. Larry and Mark called his name. Pauline, peeking between them, screamed.

The mattress was there to break his fall. He heard their screams, the insistence that he hurry . . . and then the words that made him *move:*

"Nick! Something's coming through!"

He didn't wait to see what it was. He vaulted atop the TV and lunged at the hands that reached for him through that little hole. He strained toward one, missed, felt his finger rub against flesh, grabbed for that, missed, falling, he was *falling*—and felt flesh wrap around his arm and pull him out.

The cold night air pushed at him just as something exploded into the Pit. He didn't care. Pauline was hugging him and he fell into that warmth, forever grateful.

The four teenagers fell across the roof, away from the vent, each gasping for their share of fresh air. Even with all the unnatural noises in the Pit, it wasn't until the roof bucked beneath them and they heard Ray's screams that their panic reawakened.

Sheriff Peltzer reached the clearing around the Pit in time to see Gavel fire at the monster. It was a wild shot, far short of the mark. *One bullet left,* he thought. The near miss didn't slow the mother rat a bit. She was either invincible or willing to die to sink her teeth into Kevin Gavel.

I know that feeling.

But it was the boy he was concerned about. He didn't know what the kid was doing here, but it was clear Gavel had him now. The deputy pushed the gun against the boy's temple and the two disappeared into the open car just in time.

The mother rat didn't pause. She hit the car hard. Glass exploded out of its frame. The car tilted off its outside wheels. Metal groaned and cracked. The monster pulled away, apparently unstunned. She pushed her bulk up to the broken window and forced her head inside. Peltzer thought that the glass left in the frame must be tearing into her flesh, but she seemed unaffected by it. With a speed that belied her size, she soon had her head and shoulders completely inside the car. Her back feet gripped the ground, then the window ledges, pushing and squeezing forward toward her prey.

Peltzer felt stunned again. He had seen the beast up close, but had not gotten a true sense of her size until she was next to the Pontiac. It was certainly as tall as the car, and half as long. He knew, then, that it would take a hell of a lot more than a few bullets to kill that thing. It might just take an unheavenly act from God Himself.

He looked away from the grunting figure slipping deeper into the car, and let his eyes graze the night sky. Instead, he locked on to the four figures atop the Pit's roof.

"Holy—Hey!" he screamed at them. He scrambled over the mess of junk scattered across the clearing. His hand grazed his holster, came away empty. He felt completely helpless as he ran toward the monster . . . but those were *kids* up there, and he would not let them go.

"Hey! Get down from there!"

The figures turned toward him. He ordered them down again and they seemed about to do so until one stood and screamed back, "Our friend's in there!" The figure pointed down at the Pit. As he did so, the car shook again, and the wall of tires wobbled, spilling some of the boards from its top. The kids on the roof cried out; one was a girl, Peltzer heard.

He ran harder.

Ray sprang into the car, heedless of the gun at his head. Gavel stayed right behind him. They slammed against the inside passenger door, Gavel's body pressing so hard that Ray felt his breath squeezed from his body.

"Get it open, get it open, get the *goddamn door open!*"

Ray tried. His hands could barely move because of the pressure on them. They roamed the surface of the door, searching for any piece of metal he could pull that would relieve the crush.

With a deafening crash, his world spun. The car shook and rolled toward the Pit. The ground came up to Ray's window. He closed his eyes, believing it would come right through, but the car jerked and they were upright again. Behind him, Gavel was screaming in his ear.

Ray's hands searched faster. They rubbed so hard against the interior they became red and raw. He wanted to call out to Gavel to let up on him, just give him enough room to look down and see the damned handle, but he couldn't get any air into his lungs. His eyes grew wide with the thought of suffocation. His search grew more panicked. Around him, he felt the car's frame rattle and occasionally rock toward the Pit again.

"It's coming, it's coming inside, hurry, HURRY!"

Ray caught some movement outside the window. He spared a quick glance and could have sworn he saw Nick jumping on top of the TV. It only fueled his panic, for he believed the lack of air was making him hallucinate. Next would be unconsciousness. And then death.

His fingers brushed by something cold. He grabbed it and pulled up. The crush from behind pushed him into the Pit as the door yawed wide. He hit the ground with his face. Gravel cut his chin and gathered on the inside of his lip. He spit at it as he was yanked to his feet again and nearly carried to the end of the Pit. He noticed that the TV was sitting in the middle of the room, but there was no sign of Nick.

They hit the wall hard, causing the tire column to rock a bit. Gavel twisted them around so that they faced the entrance. Ray was in front with Gavel's arm circling his neck, fingers groping his shirt front, and the gun alternating between Ray's head and the black form pushing its way through the Pontiac entrance.

Ray had his breath back. He tasted blood inside his mouth, ignored it. His eyes were so intensely concentrated on the bucking car that they hurt. As he watched, the monster's face pressed against the passenger window, where he and Gavel had been only seconds ago. Huge milky eyes slapped against the glass, splaying a gray-white film, like pus, across the window's length as they stared straight at him. The mother rat screamed.

"Shoot it!" Ray screamed back. *"Shoot it!"*

Gavel wanted to shoot it—God, he wanted to *bazooka* the goddamn thing—but he knew that he only had one shot left, and he was far from convinced that even a bullet through the head would do any good. He kept the barrel pressed against Ray's temple, praying that, with this hostage, he'd be able to make some sort of deal with the monster as well as the sheriff.

The mother rat roared again. The car rocked with her struggles. Around them, the walls began to sway. A few of the tires near the roof slipped, threatening to topple their respective columns. Above, people were screaming.

Neither Gavel nor Ray heard the sounds from the roof. Their entire world was focused on the monster trying to get at them . . . until Gavel heard the sheriff's voice outside. He strengthened his hold around Ray's neck and pushed them both to the side wall. Ray took most of the blow. Gavel whipped them around again to face the car. The tires swayed. Ray glanced up and was startled to see the end of the roof board and the dark, moving clouds between the crack. This place was coming down.

His eyes returned to the car just in time to see a powerful paw slam against the window. A spiral crack appeared.

"Sheriff!" Gavel called. His head was twisted toward the wall so that his voice would carry better outside; still, his attention never left the car and the black shape within. "Martin! I know you're out there! Answer me!"

The cold metal of the gun pressed against Ray's head, just above his ear. He squinted at the pain it was already causing.

"Martin!" Gavel yelled, his voice reaching the edge of control. "You better kill that goddamn thing in the car or the next bullet goes right through this kid's brain!"

Sheriff Peltzer felt somewhat safer once the mother rat's entire body was in the car. Even the scaled tail had slipped in after her. He made it past the litter of metal and raced to the side of the Pit. He stopped where he could still keep a wary eye on the back of the Pontiac.

Four figures stared down at him from the roof.

"Get down!" he ordered, "Now!"

"We can't," the taller boy called down. "Our friend's in there. We have to help get him out. The hole up top here may be the only way."

"All of you don't have to be—"

He was interrupted as the nearby wall suddenly bunched toward him. The boards above creaked. The teenagers stumbled to catch their balance. Peltzer backed away, certain that the place was coming down. It didn't happen, but the voice he heard and the threat it made just as effectively seized his stomach.

"Kill that monster Martin!" Gavel repeated through the gap in the tires. "Kill it or I'll blow the boy's head off! Do you hear me?"

Peltzer knew, from the fear in Gavel's voice, that he would do it; he would put a bullet right through that boy's brain, regardless if it was his last shot or not, and Peltzer would have to live with that failure the rest of his life.

He stood before the wall again and called out, "You've got my gun, Kevin. What the hell am I supposed to kill

268

it *with?*"

"Just *find* something! You're the sheriff. You're good at *finding* things. You found me, didn't you?"

"Better save that last shot for yourself, Kevin. It might be better than being eaten alive."

"It's going into the boy, Martin, unless you kill that goddamn—"

And then the mother rat broke through the window.

Glass shattered across the Pit. Metal buckled with deafening screeches as the mother rat's weight rolled over it. She wasn't all the way through, but it was only a matter of time. Her front feet slid through the loose gravel on the ground, trying to find some purchase, while the toes of her right hind leg gripped the window frame and pushed.

Slowly, painfully, she was emerging.

Ray was mesmerized by the creature. He had gone swimming in the ocean once, during a vacation years ago, and seen a shark glide by beneath him. The cold terror that filled his veins now was comparable to that— except this monster would not swim out of sight, and there was no beach where Ray could find safety.

Gavel continued screaming at the sheriff, until his voice began to lose all control, his words unintelligible. Ray stood frozen in position, the gun scratching at his head, the monster across the Pit straining to pull him into its gullet. Very little could have broken such total concentration—except the sound of a familiar voice.

It was Nick, from somewhere high. Ray tried to turn his head, but Gavel drove the barrel into his cheek and forced it back. He could still move his eyes, though, and he searched the Pit desperately for his friend.

A hand fell from the ceiling and waved. Nick called his name again. Gavel wasn't aware of any of it, with his head still twisted to the wall and his ears echoing with the monster's hungry cry and his own hoarse demands. When Nick's head ducked down from the hole. Ray nodded just enough to acknowledge his presence.

Nick motioned for him to grab his hand. Ray's eyes went from that impossible hope to the TV standing below. It would help, but . . . He looked back at Nick and shook his head. Nick thrust his hand out again, obvious anger behind it.

A hot stench hit Ray in the face, pulling his attention forward again. The mother rat was nearly in. Only her fat haunches had to squeeze through the metal window frame, then she would be free. Her tail thumped against the car's roof in anticipation. The blanched eyes locked on him again. The maw opened wide, an impossibly large pit, and erupted with a rage that promised the most horrible death imaginable: to be eaten alive.

A final surge, and the creature's weight burst the frame.

At the same moment, Ray turned and screamed into Gavel's face: *"It's coming through!"*

Gavel jumped. His face widened, as if it were exploding outward, and full-on panic possessed him. He threw Ray to the side, crouched carefully like they taught him in training school, and fired his last bullet. Be it luck or a flinch at the sound of the shot, or even Gavel's gods working against him, the mother rat turned her head at just the right moment; the bullet plunged through her cheek, snapped off several teeth, and drove harmlessly out the back of her jaw.

A lot of blood. A lot of agony. But nothing that came near to being deadly. In fact, Gavel could see as he crumpled against the wall that he had done nothing but create absolute, berserk *anger*. In his teary vision, the nightmarish image dissolved into a massive dark bulk. Her triumphant roar mixed with his own helpless scream, filling his world with the sounds of hell.

Darkness descended like the vengeful hand of God, and the ripping began. In the span of a heartbeat, he was unrecognizable as a human being.

Ray watched him die.

When Gavel pushed him away, he ran toward Nick's hand. He reached the TV and jumped on top of it, only to fall over again. The bubble, his weapon, was knocking him off balance, so he pulled it off along with his coat. He climbed again and jumped high.

Nick just barely caught him. Ray wasn't as tall as Pauline and himself; he had needed more than the TV to stand on. But it was too late to try again. This hold had to do, or Ray was dead.

Nick pulled, but the weight and the slim hold worked against him. Already their hands were slick with sweat and someone's blood. He grunted again and again, strained the muscles in his back until they cried out for rest, but all he could manage was to hold Ray precariously over the feeding monster.

Ray watched the death of Kevin Gavel from this position. There was an instant of great pleasure in seeing the man with the gun fall, but then he awoke to the hellish creature that had caused the death, and he realized the thing might not stop with just Gavel's flesh.

As if on cue, the mother rat looked up from her mess. Blood smeared her snout like child-applied lipstick. Her eyes narrowed on his suspended body. She smiled, and a long blotched tongue fell out and wiped at her stained teeth.

The better to tear your fucking heart out, my dear.

Ray nearly lost hold on his bladder. He looked up at Nick and kicked his legs as if they were wings.

"Jesus Christ, Nick, pull me UP!"

Nick strained again — and Ray's slick hand slipped from his grasp. If Nick had not been on his stomach so that his other arm was free to grab out, Ray would have dropped to a horrible end. As it was, they connected again, this time Nick's hand solidly around the other boy's forearm, and the desperate struggle to raise him began again.

"Mark!" Nick screamed. "Larry!" Ray thought he was yelling the words at him — but then new arms appeared out of the enlarged hole. They were little help. They stretched from every possible position, but they couldn't reach Ray; Nick's own long arms kept him out of grasp. They continued to try, however, screaming amongst themselves and at Ray. Unfortunately, no number of words would raise him closer.

271

Below, the mother rat ignored the commotion. She scattered Gavel's remains with one swipe of her claws. Her attention was now riveted to the bait dangled before her.

"Hurry!" Ray screamed, and his friends struggled harder. In the background, they heard Pauline's hysteria. Ray stared up at Nick and, between clenched jaws, said simply: "She's tall."

Nick blinked. He screamed for her.

The monster approached. She seemed in no particular hurry. She stepped atop the mattress and hunkered down, her eyes squinting now, the fog within appearing to ignite with an expanding fire. The beast growled.

Ray saw the TV still below him, a perfect stepping stone for the monster. He kicked furiously at it, but he was too high, barely able to even hit the antennae.

"Hurryyyyyyyy!"

To an outside observer, it may have looked like the mother rat was making herself comfortable on the mattress, perhaps preparing for a good night's sleep. But Ray knew as well as her that her muscles were drawing back, taut and tingling, to build the energy she would need to propel her mass into an attack.

The growl grew louder. And louder. Building to a wail that set off vibrations throughout the Pit. The clubhouse shook with a rage that threatened to reduce it to rubble.

The monster's howl had sole possession of the night, cutting away voices, screeching cats and metal, even the wind, every ear in the junkyard its victim . . . until Ray knew for certain his time was up, and his final, fearful cry coalesced with that of his hunter.

The monster pounced.

She did use the TV as a leg up, but it couldn't hold her weight. If it had, Ray's lower half would have come away in her teeth. But the wooden frame of the television shattered. Sparks exploded and glistened off the disintegrating screen. The structure collapsed, as did the rolling carriage holding it, and the mother rat's forepaws pinwheeled in front of her as she began to fall back. Her jaws lashed out—

272

—and caught hold of Ray's foot. *She had him!* And there was nothing that would make her let go. Nothing.

She fell fast, back to the Pit's floor. The weight that descended would have ripped Ray apart had she been left suspended above the ground with her snout curled around his foot. But the distance to the floor was less than six feet, and the mother rat ended with her back feet on the ground, supporting her upright bulk, toes splayed with the pressure, like some ridiculous ballerina. Her head strained upward so as to maintain her hold. Blood seeped into her mouth, human blood, *food*, and her feet began to twist in circles to an internal music.

Before Ray fully realized he was still alive, he looked down and saw the snout draped over his foot, the black, disfigured nose pushing messily against his shin. Beyond that were the eyes, burning now, and just below the head the short front paws reached desperately for the rest of his leg so that she could loosen her jaws and begin gnawing.

His first and only clear thought was: *That's going to be a hell of a needle they'll need for my tetanus shot.*

And then some of the worst pain that life could offer struck and pulled him into agony.

He screeched, high and stinging. His eyes squeezed tight; red flashing lights burst on his lids. Something jerked his shoulder—either Nick pulling again or the mother rat attempting to shake his hold away.

He forced his eyes open and kept looking up, up to where his friends waited. Looking down would be deadly. It would be like staring into the eyes of Satan himself. He couldn't afford that; he couldn't lose his nerve now. Just please, he wanted to say, please God and Nick, *don't let go*.

He gasped for breath, praying it would drag some molecules of strength with it, and gagged. A stench from below burned his sinuses. It must be Gavel's remains, his mind flashed, the odor of dying flesh: just how he, Ray, would smell if the monster kept shaking his leg like a shark.

—But something was wrong with that. This smell was

different. It was familiar. Urine? Shit? Body odor?

What am I doing gotta pull pull dammit pull—

And then he recognized it.

It took every bit of courage to pull his eyes down again, to look past his own blood streaming around the mother rat's muzzle, past those fiery white circles, past the strained muscles working to rip him apart—down, down, to where the offending liquid leaked across the floor.

The mother rat could not see where her feet landed. She only kept them dancing so as to keep her balance. She wasn't smart enough to know that by bringing her full weight down she could rip Ray from his friends' grasps and do what she wished. To her, lowering herself meant letting up on the food, and she would lose it. So she kept up her dance, moving in circles, her excitement mounting each time the living flesh cracked and squirmed in her mouth and a bit more of the warm sugary life trickled down her gullet. But it was because of this crazy dance that she could not see where she was stepping; it was only a series of distant sensations: soft yields from the mattress; solid grips from the dirt ground; sharp pinches from pieces of the shattered TV; and a brittle, sliding uncertainty from Ray's abandoned plastic bubble, from which her weight now forced gasoline onto the Pit's floor.

Gasoline! Ray's mind screamed at him. *Gasoline* burrrrns!

The thread of hope gave him enough strength to raise his face to Nick again. He saw that his friend was near panic himself. His face was pinched with strain, pale, awash in sweat. Ray had to spit his name twice before he could tear his attention from the monster below. When their eyes met, Ray tried to keep his voice matter-of-fact, so as not to push further on that fear.

"Got a match?"

Nick looked at him with concern. A bead of sweat dropped into his left eye; he ignored it, both hands otherwise occupied. "What?" he asked.

"Got a match?"

He looked to Larry and Mark. Pauline had the arm length necessary but not the strength to lift Ray, so Larry was bent into the hole nearly to his waist while Mark held his legs. Their concentration went solely to their task, so they did not notice Nick.

He looked at Ray again, still uncertain. "A what?"

"Have you got a fucking match?" Ray screamed.

Nick nearly lost his grip; Larry was in position and grabbed Ray, in time to compensate. "I haven't," Nick yelled at him. He didn't have to be so loud; there was no other sound in the Pit than the beast's soft grunts and the occasional creak of Ray's footbones. Nick turned away from the sounds, raising his head as far as he could to talk to those outside.

"Has anyone got a match? We need a match!"

No one had one. Only Nick smoked, and he didn't bring stuff like that when he was on a date. The others had no need for matches. Nick turned to tell Ray the fatal news, but stopped when the sheriff's voice rang out.

"I've got some!"

Pauline moved to the edge of the roof. The boards shifted beneath her; for a moment she thought she would go over, so she fell to her knees and hung on. The sheriff, just below her, struggled with a book of matches until they were out of his pocket, then tossed them up to her. The night wind laughed. The matches changed course, not much, just enough. The book opened and took wing, fluttering farther and farther out of Pauline's reach. She saw what was happening and pushed her arm out as far as it would go, out over the steep drop, her other arm anchored to the roof boards for dear life.

The book tagged her fingers, jumped. She willed her hand out further. The book tickled her prints again, danced in the wind, and finally fell solidly into her palm. She closed around it, froze for an instant to recapture her balance, then pulled back and brought matches to Nick without stopping for a breath.

"I can't," Nick said when he saw them. He was holding onto Ray's arms now with both hands. "You do it. Just stick your hand through here"—he raised his head from the hole—"and set them in his hand."

She moved forward to do it, but Mark shouted at her. "No! You gotta light one. He can't light one down there. Just light one! Light it and hand it down to him!"

She pulled a match out, struck it once, twice, the third time rubbing its tip into a flame, and reached down through the small opening between Nick and Larry to hand it down.

Ray saw it coming. He felt the heat on his hands, saw the sweat on the various arms sparkle. He looked up at Nick. "Okay. Let go."

Nick didn't nod or acknowledge it in any way. He just jerked his hand off one of Ray's arms and clutched it around his other. Larry had hold of the same arm by the wrist. Ray's left shoulder flashed with fire, now that his entire weight and the mother rat's insistence were on it. But he held back the cry, afraid it might blow out the match.

His fingers scrambled around Pauline's hand, working their way up to the toothpick stub. She held it between two fingers, fingers that shook and made the match dance between their pressure.

Please, Pauline, I love you, but don't—drop—that—

Tendrils of pain shot up his leg. The mother rat grunted with relish. Hot, sticky air blew from her nose, up his tattered pants leg. She was working her way up now, ready to pull her entire body off the ground as she slowly swallowed the length of his body. The image sickened him. Even the match, now three-fourths burnt away, was losing its power to push away the murky blackness.

His hand met Pauline's again, and he had it. Pauline's arm disappeared back up the hole. Ray was terrified to find his fingers just as shaky as hers. Still, he was careful not to hurry its descent; he didn't want to frighten the orange nub away.

He glanced down and found the reflection of the spilled gas. He let the match reflect in the mother rat's eyes for a long second, just to let her know what he was up to. *This is for you, bitch, even if I go with you.*

276

And then he dropped it.

The colorless eyes followed it down. When it passed the monster's face, her jaws opened wide and she slid her teeth out of Ray's flesh. Cool air seared the wound. The mother rat rested on her back haunches as her gaze arced lower. To Ray, the match became a Christmas light, then a firefly, and finally popped into darkness.

Nothing moved for a long time.

Then Ray felt himself rise a little. But not enough. He still stared down at the mother rat. She was watching the area where the match had fallen. When nothing happened there, her gaze shifted. The brows rose; the teeth were born again. She roared, her throat now as hoarse as Kevin Gavel's before his was torn away. Ray thought it sounded like the most evil laugh he had ever heard. He closed his eyes and waited for the death in his gut.

The mother rat hunched down for the last leap—

—and her world exploded.

Blinding light engulfed the floor, the world's molten center finally touching the surface. It was followed by a *WUMP* that popped the mother rat's ear drums. Tendrils of flame leapt up from the primordial soup and clutched at the monster's flesh. The claws fought back, but they were quickly reduced to blackened stubs; the mouth snapped and screamed, but it was shortly melted shut; the eyes bulged with horror and rose to Ray's body, the food, as he was pulled away, into the heavens, out of her grasp forever—but they exploded like crushed grapes before the first frustrated tear could form.

In less than a minute, only blackened bones—its own and others that spilled from its stomach sack—remained. The flames licked at them indiscriminately. Their cracks of delight echoed throughout the Pit.

They pulled Ray through the hole just as the room below ignited. He collapsed into Nick's arms, and Larry and Mark hurried forward to share the burden. Pauline screamed something at them—they didn't hear—and bent to swat at the flames snaking around Ray's legs. When

277

Nick and the others realized what she was doing, they patted the burning denim until it was out.

A breath. Through their confusion and exhaustion, this much was clear: they had to get away from the Pit or they would burn along with it. Together then, they picked up Ray's unconscious form and hurried down the back of the clubhouse, coughing and gasping for fresh air amidst the stench of burning rubber. The sheriff followed their progress and met them at the bottom. He took Ray's body in his arms with seemingly little effort and led them all away from the Pit.

Peltzer continued on back to his car with Ray, where he would call the station and an ambulance. He didn't notice that the other four stayed behind. Once they were a safe distance, they huddled around each other and watched the Pit erupt. Orange and red flames spit black clouds into the sky. By tomorrow the city would be sweeping ash from their sidewalks, driveways and porches. The odor of burning rubber would not pass until the following night brought a wind to pull it out of Winsome. The additional smell just beneath the rubber, that of bubbling flesh and fat which none of the teenagers recognized, would only last a minute.

"All that beer," Larry lamented, watching the flames lick higher. No one heard him.

After

It made the papers, despite the state boys.

By dawn, the entire Winsome police force and fire department were sifting through the ashes. A paleontologist from up north arrived to examine the mother rat's bones, and those of her children dug up from the collapsed tunnels. The bones of Kevin Gavel—the skull several feet from the skeletal pieces found beneath the rat's pelvis—were of no immediate interest to anyone but Sheriff Peltzer; he breathed a sigh of relief while attempting to align *all* the facts that would have to be inserted in his report—a report that he was sure would shock most everyone who knew the man.

The state boys were the last to arrive. They spouted orders and tried to get some cooperation from the locals, but no one was in much of a mood to listen. Sheriff Peltzer gave them a private recital of most of the events, and added a few suspicious and accusatory glares behind it; he had no proof, but his instinct told him the government had *some*thing to do with this mess—perhaps an unfair assumption, but it sure kept the state boys quiet for a long while.

The five teens involved were taken home after some brief questions. The details could wait until later. Days went by, and when the whole story did start circulating, they all enjoyed some level of celebrity.

Ray got his wish . . . well, sort of. He *was* seen differently by his community: half thought him the bravest person they'd ever met, the rest thought him the stupidest.

His parents were decidedly in the latter category; they routinely chastised him and hugged him, with tears on their faces, for the first few weeks. If the subject were brought up in adult conversation, they would steer around it, certain it would reflect badly on their otherwise intelligent son. And if Ray ever used it against them in an argument, they would just roll their eyes and act as if it had no weight at all. Every offer to be interviewed, on local news or on national talk shows, was nixed; every request to make a speech at some group meeting or celebration was rejected; the single commercial solicitation, for the running shoes that Ray had worn when he was racing for his life in the tunnels, was just plain ignored.

The state boys, for all their "no comments," managed to haul the mother rat's remains and those of her children away before the media got to it. They then set about denying any knowledge of giant creatures in Winsome and quickly followed every statement with a "heartfelt gratitude for the bravery displayed by those teens and Sheriff Martin Peltzer, who managed to stop, once and for all, the horrible crimes of the crazed killer Kevin Gavel." Attention shifted. The "monsters" became legend, only half-believed. Most people in the country began considering it some sort of hype-metaphor for the human monster that had stalked the children of Winsome.

But the citizens of Winsome knew. They saw it in the faces of those teens, and in the eyes of their sheriff.

A year passed, and the nation provided easier news for the media to exploit. The Holscomb phone stopped ringing. Ray's parents breathed easier — as did their brave son.

Though he would have enjoyed being on TV, Ray understood their feelings. He never said out loud whether he thought he had been brave or stupid — he was modest when the first was mentioned, indignant when he heard the second — but he leaned privately toward stupid. If he had known all the pain he would have to go through *after* the adventure — the medical exams, the limp from his crushed foot, the tetanus shots (the needles *were* damned big, and they stuck them in his abdomen where they hurt like hell), the disbelief he met outside Winsome, the eventual psychological treatments, and the nightmares—he would probably have stayed home that Friday night.

But then, he reminded himself, Ed Kelton would be just as dead and the mother rat very much alive . . . and still hungry. After all, it was he, Ray Holscomb, who had killed the mother rat; he'd drawn her from her lair and his inventive weapon had blown her up. In fact, he was known throughout Winsome, throughout the nation even, for a short time, as The Monster Killer. It didn't disturb him too much that most considered the monster to be Kevin Gavel. Not after he'd heard what Deputy Gavel was responsible for.

In the end, though, Ray was most satisfied with his renewed friendship with Nick. Nick *wished* his father had taken all this as well as Ray's parents had, but the old man was furious beyond words, and when he was without words, he could only communicate with his fists. With Billy screaming the whole time and trying to jump on the old man's back, Nick received a beating like he hadn't had since his dad's semi-sober days. Nick got in a few good shots, but stopped when he realized that they only made his own suffering that much worse.

When the punches stopped, an ambulance was waiting at the door. Billy had called them. He never had before, never would have dared, but he had heard the story Nick told, believed it, and figured his brother had been through enough. The old man would have taken up on him too if not for the policemen who arrived right behind the ambulance and took the old man away in handcuffs.

And so little Billy Jurgen won his own fight against the monsters left in the world.

Nick relied on Ray's friendship and the help of Ray's family for the next year. It was a perilous time, for the chances of finding the right foster home was always uncertain. In the end, Nick made it to eighteen still a resident of the County Home for Minors, along with his brother, finished high school, got a job as a mechanic, and made a life for himself. Billy never left his side. They both wanted it that way.

Nick's relationship with Pauline soured quickly. It wasn't anything either of them could blame on the other. They were just unfortunate to have experienced a terrible event together—an invisible wall that no amount of effort could break down. They were heartsick about it. Pauline spent many nights crying and praying for some sort of solution—but nothing came. In the end, as the years passed, they came away from the romance with some foggy good memories and the realization that pain, even the pain deep in the heart, does indeed fade with time.

As for Larry, his life was turned upside down after that Friday night. He listened intently to Sheriff Peltzer's own story, how he had applied his instincts and improvisational skills to each situation that would have struck down a lesser man, and in the end had succeeded. It sounded like a great life to Larry. It didn't sound all that hot to his mom. He let her get her tears out of the way, though, and then explained to her exactly what Sheriff Peltzer had outlined for him: the school he would have to go to, what he could expect, what classes were most important, and which he could slack off in, and how he could come back to work right here in Winsome.

By the time he was done, his mother couldn't ignore the glint she saw in his eyes. She accepted it. What else could she do in the face of her son's infamous determination? But this renewed academic interest did have a drawback: the split between himself and Mark, a split that had only been marginally pressed back together with beer and a shared perversion, widened considerably. There was nothing either could do about it; what surprised them most was that neither boy felt he should do something about it. In retrospect, they realized that all they had really shared that last year was a common loneliness. When that fell away, as it eventually does, the Pit, their final link, just prolonged an inevitable parting of the ways.

Larry was saddened, but was too busy to worry about it. Mark was more affected. He had always thought friendships, really good friendships, lasted forever. Even when he was questioning Larry's Friday night plan, he still never considered that their parting could ever be on amicable grounds. So when Larry did stop dropping by, and they no longer had cause or opportunity to pass each other in the school hallways, Mark plunged into a funk.

He dived into self-pity for a few weeks, then decided on a rash action to pull himself from the murk: he asked Pauline out on a date. She politely turned him down. He was surprised that the rejection didn't crush him — well, at least it didn't hurt after a week. He tried again, with a different girl. She politely accepted, though he could tell she wasn't very enthusiastic about it. Didn't matter, though; he had discovered the secret that Ray found before diving down the monsters' hole: that every little dare opens a little door of courage in its wake. No guarantees, but . . .

By the following year, he had a girlfriend and a new group of friends he had met through the Science Fiction Club at school. By his senior year, new doors seemed to be opening up all over the place.

But he never forgot his first real friend, Larry Santino, nor the last great adventure they shared — the one that Larry had guaranteed would be the best. *By God, it was that,* Mark would think — and then laugh to himself so no one would ask.

Though they separated and formed new relationships over the years, and though they even moved on to other parts of the country, the five friends always maintained a single powerful link. For nothing could wipe away those images that surfaced when they sank into the pit of sleep; there, where their souls were caressed open to allow the hidden doubts to penetrate.

By morning, the unthinkable would be locked away again, forgotten or ignored.

But there were those nights, usually in early spring, right around the time of their great adventure of years past, when their minds, coldly logical in unconsciousness, would return to those doubts: doubts that circled facts in a whirlwind of images; doubts that no one in Winsome would ever put into words . . .

Rats that grew beyond normal size. Deformed, crazed. Mother rat affected, and thus her four children at birth.

283

But . . .

Where is the father who sired those children?

And on those nights, even with thousands of miles between them, the five would wake up, together, and scream into the night — and then, once awake, wonder why.